Treason doth never prosper; what's the reason?
Why, if it prosper, none dare call it treason.
— SIR JOHN HARRINGTON, 1561-1612

Call It Treason

a novel by George Howe

To

Happy

1925-1945

Call It Treason

Look Backward

The war is over, and for all one can see in the streets or newspapers, or hear around the cracker barrel or campus or bartop, it is forgotten. Forgotten so well that it is ready for a repeat, as old tunes like "Baby Face" have to be forgotten before they can be revived; or long skirts on women. There are places and days where it is remembered: May Thirtieth, and behind some drawn curtains, and in congressmen's speeches at election time and in the memoirs of generals and in Mason jars of everlastings in country cemeteries; in the country a man has more time to remember. In Europe they think we have forgotten, as we did before. It is not forgotten there. In the European Theater the stars trip in, left wing or right, to a fortissimo of brass, and pack up at the finale till the managers call a réturn. The chorus stays on the job between times, and the battered scenery remains in place.

Some of the numbers are soon forgotten all around. Thus, in Combat Intelligence, after the target is reached, after the platoon or gun is located by G-2 and destroyed by G-3, there is no need to record how it was found, or by what agent; or by

3

what trick of uniform or intonation or marksmanship he got his report through the line on time. No need to remember, for the circumstances never repeat exactly, and the lesson of one mission is not much use on the next. And none in another war.

Some of the acts you forget on purpose, and some you never forget.

For all the erasures of time, one question stays with me, unanswered but unforgotten: why does the Spy risk his life? For what compulsion, and after what torment in himself? The gunpoint never forced a man to loyalty, and still less to Treason, whose rewards at best are slim and distant. If the Spy wins, he is ignored; if he loses, he is hanged.

Not long ago the postman dropped on my drafting board a letter with a German stamp; when I translated it the puzzle of two years before returned to tease me, and by writing out my memory I may have found a key to the Meanings of Treason. I say Meanings, because it has more than one. Here is the letter:

Berlin, 10 January 1947

Honored Sir:

From this letterhead you see that I am a physician. We are lucky enough to live in the American sector (if there is luck in living at all) where there is still a memory and hope of freedom. Since it is your sector too, let it serve to introduce me. Its ruins are no different from those of the Soviets across the Brandenburg Gate. But the plane which broke our roof in 1945 was a Liberator; so in Berlin I have a queer distinction over friends who were bombed out by Stormoviks.

With me live my wife and my younger son Klaus, who is seventeen now. My older son Karl is a corporal in the German Air Force. I still say "is" from habit; though the last word his mother and I have from him was written in February 1945 from an American prisoner-of-war camp, somewhere on the Western Front.

That is two years ago, but we have still hoped for his return. Many German soldiers are still prisoners in Russia, and a few even in France and England. Sometimes they straggle home to Berlin, like Hermann Bechthold in the next block, who walked in to supper

4

one night after two years in Siberia, still in his ragged Feldgrau. Either they did not let him write home, or he forgot. But Karl would never forget, and yet he does not write.

The trickle is drying up now. It is six months since Hermann returned.

In spite of my persistence over these two years, and a few tears of my wife's, neither American military authorities, nor what is left of German, nor even the International Red Cross, which cares for all prisoners, could ever give us word of Karl, till yesterday. Yesterday the colonel who commands your Denazification Branch called me to his office. I supposed he was ill, so I ran over from my clinic. But he was well; he even smiled. He offered me in Karl's name a medal of bronze, which he calls the Medal of Freedom. He says it is a prized decoration among Americans. The citation, kindly translated into German by one of his staff, reads that our son is "presumed lost by enemy action on a hazardous mission voluntarily undertaken in the cause of Freedom." These are long words. The "enemy" in the citation can refer only to the Nazis, who were my enemies for twelve years. They were yours for only four. The citation itself must mean that Karl spied against them for their enemies, who were the Americans. I should not be ashamed of him, provided only he risked his life for his own free conviction, and your army did not force him to it as the Nazis did.

This colonel does not know you and did not know Karl. He was not even in Europe for the war. But his records show you know our boy and might tell us something about his "hazardous mission."

The colonel found your address across the ocean, and I venture to ask you to write me about our son's last days, if you remember them still. This letter will be my last attempt to learn. You may understand that the uncertainty which shrouds them lies like a heavy shadow on our own, and that hope can be as bitter as despair. Tell me as much as your own country's security will allow, but do not let your own mercy spare me.

Respectfully,

Gunther Maurer, M.D.

A man is alive as long as he is remembered, and killed only by forgetfulness. Let Karl Maurer remain a corporal in the Luftwaffe. I wish I could approach that all-embracing memory

5

of him which is History, if you look backward, but Resurrection itself, if you look ahead. One man has not the power, nor even all men together. Here is as much of the story as I could remake after the two years, from my memory and from the fading memory of the others. I could not watch it all, but one man swam an icy minefield in the Rhine with part of it, and another stammered out some more in a cellar. The American captain who recruited the corporal remembers some, and so does the sergeant who strapped his chute. The German colonel whose life he saved sells papers now; and the Fräulein who knit the socks he never wore has married a GI, but her memory is not dim.

I telescope time, I usurp omniscience in the telling; not to invent but to resurrect. Let Frau Maurer ask that divination which is motherhood if those parts of her son's story which none could watch are not as true to him as the rest. Such sympathy is truer than record, and I trust it more than the word of the Tiger, who stood on the bank with him that February night in 1945. *Credo quia absurdum.*

I must start further back, before we knew the corporal, so that the doctor will understand that his son was not recklessly sent into danger, but joined a service which had had a long career—and an honorable one, if espionage deserves the adjective. Where the colonel uses the word enemy he means it, not personally, but professionally, as colonels have always used it. The doctor should accept the medal as a token of—or a release from—a debt which this republic cannot acknowledge that it owes, nor he in Berlin dare admit his son has earned. And though the colonel says only that he is "presumed lost," I do not think his father will see him again.

One

Seventh United States Army, "born at sea and baptized in blood," came a long way before it met the son of the Berlin doctor. In 1943 its embryo, First Armored Corps, struggled across the thirsty rim of Africa, slugging it out with Marshal Rommel and his Afrika Korps. It chased the enemy into the sea at Cap Bon. "The enemy" is always singular, never plural. Seventh stopped up the bung of Sicily and cut across his escape by bridging the Mediterranean from Africa to France, from Algiers to Cavalaire and Saint-Raphaël, while the Fifth holed up the alleys of Italy.

The jump to Southern France was Operation Dragoon. Dragoon was one of the great invasions of history. Just because it did succeed so neatly, history forgets that the southern defenses of the Wehrmacht were as strong and as secret as the northern, and that as much knowledge—and at longer range than across the Channel—was needed to bare them. Only three divisions landed on the Riviera that 15 August 1944, but they went through the minefields, after Eighth Fleet had cracked the artillery, like you-know-what through a goose. If some veterans of Dragoon have a grudge against history's ingratitude, it is not because the profession has ceased to court obscurity, but because they sweated out the preparation, and proved it was accurate.

From the field at Blida, outside Algiers, they launched some thirty agents, with chutes on their backs and short-wave sets on their chests, into metropolitan France, then occupied by the enemy in the north, and by Pétain, the almost-enemy, in the south. Off paper they called them "Joes." On paper (when they had to write) they called them "agents." The British called theirs "bodies." Those who did not know them would call them spies. Of the four titles, "Joe" is surely the kindliest.

Most of the pre-invasion Joes were French, for finesse, with a sprinkling of Corsicans, for ruthlessness. From inside the Métropole they radioed back to Africa the location of every enemy detachment south of Lyon: group, army, corps, division, regiment, battalion (that was the last strategic unit of the Wehrmacht) right down to the single battery and machine-gun nest. Just before D-day someone at SHAEF in London wanted to know about the anti-tank wall on the Saint-Raphaël target beach. From the reports of the Joes the Team made him up a structural drawing complete to the size and spacing of the steel reinforcement: half an inch thick and eight inches apart each way. (The Joes were right, too, for you can touch your finger to the twisted steel of that wall today.)

By any code except the laws of war, which are no more than sounding brass, or brass sounding off, these French men and girls were not traitors, but patriots. Even by the German code. They risked their lives among their own people, and for them, and with their help. When the German police hunted them, they had only to knock at a farmhouse door to be safe. Even the Vichy police sometimes hid them from Laval's Milice, who were the real traitors to France. Only a few French Joes were ever denounced. The Milice shot one of them after the

8

routine racking in the prison of the Rue du Paradis at Marseille, but still he did not blow.

Once dropped inside the Métropole, the Joes lurked in the furtive half-world of the underground. They slept in the huts of the Maquis, hiding their radios in abandoned cellars or in the empty caves along the banks of the German retreat. The impetus of Dragoon heartened the Maquis, and even brought them some deserters from the Wehrmacht. With directions and dynamite from the Joes they blew the bridges ahead of the German retreat. At Montélimar on Route 7, the home town of nougat, there is still a two-mile row of gutted rusting trucks and guns flung at the side of the highway like dirty snow, where the troops of the German Nineteenth Army were caught one summer afternoon between the light tanks of Task Force Butler and a river without a bridge. Keeping just far enough ahead of the retreat for accuracy, the Joes paced Seventh Army along the coast to Marseille, up the Rhône to Lyon, northeasterly to Dijon (where it joined Third), and across Burgundy to the outposts of the Reich. That is no farther than from Washington to Boston. It is hard for an American to measure the narrow scale of Europe, and to learn how the centuries have forced it to its hatreds, and above all to forgive that even among the terrors and urgency of that short action some Frenchmen and Germans aspired from their own expected victories to no more than a short time of revenge first, and then of rest. In Europe the state can be the enemy of its citizens, and everyone must take a side.

East of the Burgundian plain the valleys narrow to defiles among the Vosges, guarded by ancient cities which for centuries have been the bastions of the Rhine: Besançon, Vesoul, Lunéville. In this terrain the Germans had time to cross a bridge before it was blown, and then blow it themselves. Their retreat grew slower. They posted machine-gun nests of half a dozen men, sometimes just burrowed into a foxhole (they called it a wolf-burrow) with orders to stay until relieved. And they did stay, as prisoners packed neck-deep with snow, or as corpses in the pit, while the garrison itself had time to forage the country and cut trees to block the roads behind them.

The sleety winter of 1944 came down. No matter how stubbornly the German Nineteenth resisted, American Seventh more stubbornly still crept forward, through and around the fortresses, from Épinal to Lunéville, and even to Saverne, which looks down on Strasbourg and the Rhine. In December, far to the north as continental distances go, von Rundstedt launched the Battle of the Bulge. The threat spread out from Belgium in both directions along the Rhine, from Switzerland to the North Sea, and neither communiqué dared make a claim, and the world held its breath. Elements of Seventh had moved into Strasbourg itself, on the very bank of the Rhine, but had to get out in a hurry New Year's Day because Bastogne, far to the north, way out of their theater, had been encircled. It was the time of the Great Scare. Command Post withdrew to Lunéville again, leaving the old palace at Saverne to the more expendable staff of VI Corps. But 101st Airborne held at Bastogne, and the threat was lifted. Seventh still clung to their wedge of Alsace, with the Germans south of them at Colmar, and north of them in the forest of Hagenau. It was a minor campaign if you weren't there.

With the enemy backed against his own frontier, the French Joes were no more use to the Team. Its information had to come out of the Reich itself, and it needed German Joes to get it, or Joes who could pass for German. A few Alsatians might have the right accent to get by the Gestapo, but Alsatian loyalty was always a riddle—to both sides. Any Joe might have been dropped across the Rhine disguised as a foreign worker, for hundreds of thousands of aliens, from every country in Europe, were being shunted across Germany from one work camp to another. But in their boxcars and underground factories the labor slaves would have no access to the military news that G-2 needed, and no way of bringing it out if they did.

Besides, the French Joes had liberated their own country already, and had little ambition to liberate another. They deserved to rest. But the Team could not let them go loose; they knew too much. Hiring a spy is like compounding with a blackmailer. His knowledge is never erased, except in the one way the Team did not care to try. It kept the French Joes on, with pay and life insurance the same as Uncle Sam's GIs, even when their usefulness was over. As Army advanced, the Team went a little ahead of HQ, requisitioning a convent or a château off to the side of the main convoy route, in a village or among the woods, for its jeeps and the big radio truck, its field-safes and disguises and code-pads. Near by, it would set up a hideout for the French Joes, who must be watched—for any agent might be tempted to double—and yet not watch. The French Joes got up in the morning whenever they felt like it; took turns at cooking, on whatever stove the dispossessed owner had left behind, the good rations of the American Quartermaster Corps; read all day and boasted all night—idle, valiant, immoral, and untouchable. The Team called the hideout the French Joehouse because all the Joes had worked the Rhône campaign; not only the six Frenchmen but the Pole and the Russian and the Belgian girl. The Russian was Paluka. The Belgian girl was Giovanna. From talking or dancing with tiny honey-haired peaches-and-cream Giovanna you would never guess that she had jumped solo from a B-24 one winter night, landing upright in a snowbank of the Vosges, or that her chastity had been the price of the report she brought back.

The enemy had his spies too. You hear whispers of Admiral Canaris at the Abwehr, but Hitler had fired him in '43. Less often you hear of Kaltenbrunner, who followed him. But it was Skorzeny who built the Brandenburg Division of saboteurs and committed them—a team for each sector—against the

11

Fremdenheer—the foreign armies—of the West. He kidnaped Mussolini from his rock. His agents could be anywhere. He flew a grounded Liberator back across the lines of Seventh with eight of them inside. By luck she was challenged, and justice was done. After that the Team's operation planes flashed recognition signals, with the colors and the code changed each eight hours. The Team even saw one of Skorzeny's parachutes unfold over the pine woods west of Strasbourg, one night that was dark enough to hide the plane but light enough to show the brown-and-green camouflage of the chute.

"The way I feel about that," said Captain Pete, "it's no wonder our own Joes are in danger on the other side."

"It makes your throat tight," Fred agreed, as he ran in to phone the alert.

But they knew he was too late, for the chute was low already and the forest was thick.

There was a week near the front when the MPs checked every GI who passed—on baseball scores, or the names of movie stars, or any questions which Skorzeny's agents might not know how to answer. One Joe, captured at Dachau a week before the war ended, was confronted by the Gestapo with a letter he had posted to an American officer in the mailbox of the Red Cross canteen way back in Épinal. It was lucky for him that Seventh overran Dachau the next day. In the Battle of the Bulge Skorzeny dressed *his* Joes in American uniform to penetrate the American positions. Once he landed seven by F-boat* on Long Island. Some Americans may remember the scare even now. The FBI caught them, and six lie in potter's field in Washington. The seventh turned evidence and is back in Germany again. Another agent was caught at the Canadian border, just because his dollar bills were the old-fashioned outsize; even Skorzeny could not learn all about his enemy. Now that it is all over, Fred and Pete have grown a

* Faltboot—the folding rubber boat used by agents on both sides.

sort of sporting admiration for Colonel Otto, and are even glad he was acquitted of the same crime they tried on him. The court hangs Keitel, a professional soldier, and lets spymaster Skorzeny go free. Had his false-uniform trick worked, as it almost did, and as Fred's and Pete's usually did, they wonder what he would have done with 109, who was his opposite number on their side.

They hoped—they knew—that Skorzeny would find no Americans to spy for him. It would be hard to find a German to spy for them. Between a French Joe and a German would be all the difference between patriot and traitor. But as the winter ground along, they learned that in the Wehrmacht itself, besides many Nazi fanatics, there were helpless rebels too. It may surprise some people now to learn that democracy even used communism to help win the war. Among the German troops a few others looked beyond frontiers, and even beyond life itself, to the last brotherhood of man. They betrayed their country, and some died doing it, because they were above country. Some were traitors for self-love, and more for adventure, and a few for the love of others. On the "hazardous mission" in the doctor's citation there was one of each. Riches and risk and faith: they are the three decoys of Treason.

The likeliest place for the Team to recruit German Joes was the prisoner-of-war cage at Sarrebourg in Lorraine: 455th P/W cage, Continental Advance Section. This building was an old brick and stone barracks built way back before the First War, when Alsace and Lorraine had been German. It was a kennel of war which had sheltered many armies. No one knew how old it was; perhaps it dated from Bismarck's time. From 1918 to 1939 it had been French. Till Seventh captured it in 1944 it had been German again, and now is French once more. Its three stories of casements are barred with iron. Rows of small chimneys carry the smoke from the pot-stoves which punctuate the dormitories. The stone corridors have rung to generations of hobnail boots. Surrounded by a high wall with barbed wire

13

on top, it lay, ominous and hideous, waiting for other wars, in the center of the plain. A moat of mud encircled it. The bombed and shuttered houses of the town stretched along the pitted road. Every tree had been cut for stovewood or road-blocks, till it seemed that the town itself, like the Kaserne, existed only for war.

Every afternoon a truckload or two of prisoners was driven in from the front to be "processed" for the labor camps farther back. The cage MPs all spoke German; some could hardly speak English. Over the gate they had built a big white arched sign with black Gothic letters. It read WILLKOMMEN—the German for "Welcome." Some prisoners would laugh, and others cry, when the driver rounded the bend under that grisly joke, swaying on their feet like cattle loaded for market, as the crowded truck turned and ground to a stop on the cinders. Why not cry? It was the time when they had lost most of France and half of Italy, and the Russians had broken to the walls of Breslau.

The old drill ground in the middle of the barracks had been turned into a compound for them. Sniffling in the long gray-green coats of the German Army, or the dull blue of the Luft-waffe, stamping their frozen boots in the slush, they waited a few days in the cage through the formalities of delousing and interrogation, till they were shipped westward to make room for more.

At the interrogation it was surprising how little they knew. By the Geneva Convention they need tell no more than their names, ranks, and numbers. Often, it seemed, they knew no more anyway. But since they all carried their service records, the little brown or blue Soldbuch which lists a soldier's or air-man's past and present units, the Team could get a fair knowledge of German battle order from their papers, without crack-ing the prisoners' ignorance or rectitude. They did not seem to care, provided they could keep the identity books when they moved on. They were not different from battle-tired Ameri-

14

can troops—just, on the average, a little shorter and a little blonder. Most of them were sullen, and some defiant, and some bolder ones happy to be caught. But none showed fear except the SS men, who more than once tried to scrape the blue-circle tattoo of their blood-type from the crooks of their arms because they had been told the Americans shot the SS without trial.

The Wehrmacht was a unified command long before our own. That is one reason it won for as long as it did. It was divided into three branches: Heer, Kriegsmarine, and Luftwaffe, like our Army, Navy, and Air Force, with the SS to stiffen the combat troops. The letters mean Security Squad, but the SS were an army by themselves. There ought to be a German word to cover the whole, like "serviceman," but the best the Germans could think up was "Wehrmachtsangehörige," which is steep even for a German. Hitler was head of the whole Wehrmacht as well as of the Army. Under him the mild-eyed Himmler commanded the SS and the police—all kinds of police. The two main branches of police were Security and Criminal. The Germans write long but talk short. They abbreviate these titles to Sipo and Kripo. Kripo had many subdivisions like Schupo and Orpo and Hipo. The colonel used to say it sounded as if the Marx Brothers had quintuplets (and the rest of the Team laughed each time, to please him). Sipo had only one baby, which was Gestapo. That is only an abbreviation for Geheime Staatspolizei, or Secret State Police, but you could never tell a man was in it unless you got a look at his square dogtag, which he would seldom gracefully allow.

In the compound the services kept apart from each other. Army grouped in knots separate from Air Force. Both avoided SS. They all shuffled around the compound in an endless column of the different arms, whispering to one another in the chilly fog which is Rhineland for winter.

Out of these whispers word somehow spread that a soldier could, if he were ignoble enough, volunteer in a well-paid service for his captors. No one admitted to planting the rumor, for the Convention forbids a belligerent to draft its prisoners. But if they volunteer, what then? The Team did not ask the Swiss inspectors. The word must have passed along the dark stone floors of the dormitories, from sleeping bag to blanket roll, when the guard's boots pounded low at the far end. Between two German soldiers it could be uttered only with scorn and heard with surprise and contempt. But the gossiper who passed it on with such loud indignation might be the first recruit next morning, or it might be his neighbor on the cold floor, scratching his lice, blinking in the dark, turning his ear in the shoddy to hear better, and snoring to pretend he was asleep.

The recruits never came in pairs, or in the open compound, but singly; perhaps by whispering to the doctor at sick-call or plucking furtively at the sergeant's arm while lingering over the garbage cans after mess, with a "Please, Herr Sergeant" in broken English, and a hitch of the shoulder or a smile. The sergeant had been alerted. Not then, but later, he would call out his prospect for a detail, with a bunch of other prisoners so there would be no suspicion that he favored one. He would lead him to the snug little office in a corner of the barracks and turn him over to the recruiting officers who waited there. They spoke German too, as well as he; were German, in fact, by every standard but a paper and an oath. They had studied the prisoner's Soldbuch before the sergeant brought him in. They knew whether it had been faked, as Skorzeny had tried more than once in order to plant his spies among their own. The officers may have known the prisoner's home town or even his family. What temptations, what eloquence they used to buy his treason only they could tell. Perhaps it was nothing but a cigarette and the pride of sitting beside an officer in a soft armchair at the stove; perhaps the lure of danger or the promise of wealth; perhaps the hope of a better

16

world. Or most likely, since there are even fewer villains than heroes, a little of all together.

Before he was established for espionage he had to be checked by Security. Security cabled the German dossiers in Washington. Simultaneously, certain black-cassocked agents who traveled between Germany and Switzerland—the arm of 109 was long—called on the recruit's family or friends in the Homeland, perhaps with a little package of coffee or even a note from the boy, tucked in a briefcase. It cannot have been hard for a priest, to whom all hearts are open even when he is bogus, to learn whether the Team should trust the boy. But such trips were dangerous for the Swiss agents, because Switzerland was jealous of her neutrality, and so is the Church. Washington was more cautious still, so it might be a week or two before word came back from America and Germany—and the two had to agree—that it was safe to hire him. Meanwhile he could not go back to the prisoner barracks to those who had not seen the little office, who did not know Treason, nor forward to the Joehouse to those who had given themselves to it already. He knew too much—and, so far, too little—to be trusted. He spent the days of his probation alone in the old steel cells of the barracks guardhouse.

To house the German recruits the team took over an inn nestled in a clearing among aromatic firs, a mile above their own château—half the service called it the Schloss, which is German for the same—and far enough from the French Joehouse so the two groups could not meet on their short strolls. There were not more than half a dozen houses in the hamlet of Birkenwald, each with its orchard and garden. The villagers were woodsmen. By a law which was older than war, they could cut only ten per cent of the timber stand each year, and had to plant two trees for every one they cut, for the forests were worth more than the cropland. In the valley below, the convoy highway twined and rumbled twenty miles eastward to the

17

Rhine under the load of halftracks and armored cars, but the creaking of the great trunks and the friction of the snow-bent needles drowned out the noise of war. The inn was called the Goldene Brunnen—the Golden Well—in black Gothic letters on the peach-colored stucco. On a clear day you could see the lopsided spire of Strasbourg cathedral beyond the river plain, and hear the German guns roll from Kehl across the Rhine.

Monsieur Apfel, who owned the Golden Well, ran it as a Joehouse exactly as he had run it as an inn, except that the Team chose his guests. When he grumbled that they would not let him entertain the forester of the Département (who only two months before had been the forester of the Gau) they pointed out that this official came only in the lull of the battle, and that if there were no battle he could not expect their twenty full-time boarders, with American rations enough for his own table as well. What better could he expect in wartime, in sight of the battle line? One forester? He chose the twenty liberators.

His wife and daughter transformed the rations into fare much better than the American mess at the Schloss. He himself presided at the zinc bar. He had no beer, for the hopfields in the Rhine plain had all been burned, but there was plenty of tart greenish wine, and schnapps made of potatoes, and sometimes kirsch or framboise, which looked the same but tasted a little better, being distilled from cherries and raspberries. The innkeeper must have wondered why so many men in khaki chattered German in accents all the way from Austrian to East Prussian. But like most Alsatians he was neutral, and like a good innkeeper asked no questions, even though he may have guessed the answer. The blackboard in the classroom was always carefully erased. The conversation of the Joes was impersonal; it was their training, as it is a diplomat's, to keep it so. Like harlots in the parlor, they never spoke of business.

You will understand that the Joes had to be spared self-reproach. To this end, no one in the German Joehouse spoke anything but German, not even the Americans. It was an unspoken (and unspeakable) pretense that the Joes were really a crack task force of the Wehrmacht itself, specially picked— no one could have said by whom—for a mission which the high command should have assigned them, and perhaps soon would, when it rid itself of Hitler, Keitel, Jodl, and a few such others. A mission which would bring victory to the Reich, an echt-deutsch mission. One was not to forget that the Joes were working for the real Germany and against the false. Each had chosen his course among the caverns of his soul, had signed the deed and sworn the oath to Treason, free and alone; and alone, a man does what cannot bear the eyes of others. There was always the danger that he might repent the covenant if another German learned his name—or an American either—or if he met one of the French Joes, the ex-enemy, or, later, at his first flash of a Gestapo dogtag. If he repented, the whole service might be blown. That is why the Team compartmented the Joes, and itself too, like so many bulkheads in a ship.

To his comrades each Joe was known by a nickname. His real name, signed on his contract with the United States of America, lay in the locked and guarded field safe. When he had seen his oath deposited there, his blindfold was replaced, and he could never come back to the Schloss till his mission was completed, lest he might somehow give away the location to Skorzeny and the Luftwaffe. The Team took nicknames too, for self-protection, and wore the same green coveralls as the German Joes, without insignia. It was an honor when the Joes took an American for one of themselves.

Most of the Joes were privates in the Army, but other ranks volunteered too: a sailor, two aviators, and a converted trooper of the SS. In civil life they had been butcher and priest, engineer, gardener, chemist, and truckdriver. There were three Communists. One Joe was a baron, one was the son of a general. There were no Jews, because there were none in the Wehrmacht. They were all soldiers of discontent, and they had nothing in common but having worn the uniform of the same

19

country and conspired, for whatever reason, to betray it. The Americans, culled by 109 out of the whole United States armed forces, were as various as the Germans. They had a chemist and a butcher in the detail too (there was always a gleam in the eyes of Gustaf, the German butcher, when Angelo, the American, carved the goose), besides an architect, a banker, a bartender, a locksmith, an actor, and two lawyers.

Stripped of identity in the little office at the cage, dressed in American fatigues and combat boots, tagged only with a nickname, the recruit would be brought up to the Golden Well at suppertime. They primed his first meal with a schnapps at Monsieur Apfel's zinc bar. The Joe-handler introduced him to the comrades around the table in the day room.

This handler was an American infantry sergeant, a second-generation German from Milwaukee. The Joes called him "Vati," which is an endearment something like "Pops."

"Boys," Vati would call from the door, "this is Hans"—or whatever cover-name the recruit had drawn.

He took him the rounds man by man. "This is Harry, Jojo, Toto, Red, Théo, Ludwig the Second."

The new Joe's eyes always widened when he saw how many others were ahead of him. Some of them he must have recognized from the cage—perhaps the patriot who had just denounced traitors, perhaps a tentmate from before the capture. The Americans watched for a flicker in his eyes as he went round, but watched in vain and never asked, for he would never tell.

Sometimes the shifty-shabby spy of legend slipped by Security, but Vati had learned to judge men, and shipped him west to the work details. The Joes who made the grade were neither furtive nor boastful. They looked like a score of troops who might have been gathered in any army, perhaps a little over the average for discipline and balance and cleanliness. They belonged to no army now.

According to their natures, they would stand up and grasp

the recruit's hand, or turn in their chairs and smile, or merely mumble and reach for the heaping platter. The silent meal went on, with the new Joe next to Vati his first time.

They slept two or three together in the guest rooms of the Golden Well. Some psychologists claimed it would be better to give each Joe his own billet, or at least each mission, so they could not talk together at all. Others held that Treason, like misery, loves company, and there was more chance of a Joe sticking if he had the others near him. But it was impossible to keep them apart, for they had to take their training and their meals together.

Vati's schoolroom had been Monsieur Apfel's own dining room. He and his family had to eat in their kitchen now. The floor of the schoolroom was red tile. In the center stood an oak dining table, bleached with years of scrubbing and surrounded by a dozen uncomfortable Alsatian chairs. The door was always locked, whether class was on or not. At class time the wood shutters were closed too, and the room was lighted only by a fluorescent ceiling lamp. Even Monsieur Apfel was not allowed in this room. The Joes themselves took turns cleaning it.

Vati had got hold of a big blackboard and some pink chalk. At ten each morning he opened the session with a lesson in English. First he wrote the German word in script, then the English in capitals, as:

"Fahndungsblatt—BLACKLIST."

He held up a copy of the booklet which the Gestapo issued every Tuesday, listing deserters and suspected spies.

"They change the color of each issue, adding the new names and omitting those who have been caught. Keep out of it." Vati laughed, but the new Joe would be apt to shiver.

Sometimes he drew a picture between the words, as:

"Panzer   TANK."

This may seem elementary, since some of the Joes knew a fair amount of English, but it was about as much as Vati could

21

teach. Later in the morning the officers and the other noncoms took over with the important instruction. That was the identification of enemy weapons and insignia. It was astonishing how little most of the Joes knew about their army outside the routine of their own company weapons and drill. They had to learn the groundwork: that a striped triangle on a signpost meant division headquarters while a square meant regiment; that a Panther tank had eight bogies and a Tiger six.

Just above the Golden Well, before the back road from Sarrebourg to Strasbourg turns sharp from the forest into the clearing of the little village, the carcass of a German anti-tank gun lay on its shattered emplacement. The gun had been hidden there to ambush American tanks at the turn, like a brown-green snake alert in the grass. A lucky shot had smashed its muzzle brake and splintered the barrel lengthwise like a reed. Its trail tilted crazily against the trunk of a fir. Near by, someone from the village had planted crosses over two turfless mounds on the slope, nailed half a dogtag to the bars, and hung the two straight-rimmed German helmets of the crew, camouflaged just the color of the gun itself. The colonel offered to stand a round of schnapps to the first Joe who identified the piece, but the only man who knew it was a 5 cm. Pak 38* was an artilleryman who had served the same model on the Russian front.

A Joe needs head as much as heart. It is not enough to dare the jump behind the lines; he is worse than useless if he cannot bring out a clear account of what he sees. The difference between reporting a battalion and a regiment, or between a 5 and an 8.8, might mean the success or failure of a divisional attack —or even, Pete foolishly thought, could win or lose the whole war.

Down the hill the Team set up a training jump in a clear-

---

* The Wehrmacht calibrated guns in centimeters instead of millimeters. This is the 50 mm. gun of 1938. "Pak" is short for "Panzerabwehrkanone" or anti-tank gun. "Flak" is short for "Flugzeugabwehrkanone" or anti-aircraft gun.

ing among the firs. It was guarded from the curious by two GIs, night and day. Dropping a man ten feet into a sandpile through a hole in the platform was not like the real thing, even with all equipment strapped on. But it was better than jumping blind for the majority of Joes, who had never even been up. Buck and Merle, the two dispatchers (in uniform they were sergeants of the Marine Corps), had so many jumps behind them that they could tell the Joe every second of his mission from emplanement till he landed, buried his gear, and started on his watch. Yet who but Treason could tell what it would be to leap on his country's back out of the black night, and sidle past her spires, her sleeping kinsmen and wakeful geese, to betray her to the enemy beyond?

One Joe who returned—he was going to be a priest after the war—had seen two bodies swinging from a tree near Stuttgart, and tacked to the trunk a crude sign: SO STERBEN DIE VERRÄTER DES VATERLANDES. Thus perish traitors to the Fatherland.

It was harder to get out of Germany than to get in. The danger of the drop was small compared to the hazard of getting back through both the front lines. As he crossed, a Joe might be shot by the Americans for a German patrol, if he had not been hung by the Germans for an American spy. The colonel punished the tattler who had seen the bodies and the sign by exile to the French Joehouse, for talking shop was forbidden—especially that kind of shop. But everyone knew the Joe had done it from a kind of pride, as if to show that his own target area was more dangerous than the others, and he therefore braver or cleverer to have returned alive.

"Don't you see, Père Nod," Fred reasoned (it had seemed an amusing pun to give a theology student the alias of absinthe), "not only might you frighten your comrades so they could not do their work, but among them there may be a Judas who can betray you after the war if he so much as knows you have been in Stuttgart?"

"Mea culpa, Lieutenant," Père Nod answered humbly. He

23

was a learned and merciful young man, but weak on weapons and battle order, so it was little loss when he was banished to the inaction of the French Joehouse.

At the same time, the Team knew it could not expect that twenty Joes, in the comradeship of the dormitory at the Golden Well, under the danger that awaited detection, could perfectly maintain the fear, the silence, the distrust, the loneliness which are an agent's first protection.

Every few days Army G-2, back in headquarters at Lunéville, sent down demands for information. They came from the guarded war room, where a great map of the theater from Switzerland north to Mainz and back into the heart of the Reich stretched across one whole wall, hidden by a sliding black curtain. It required permission from General Patch himself to pass the armed MPs and draw back the curtain. Sheets of plastic overlay were tacked on the map. On the plastic the operations officer marked every day the symbols the Team was teaching in the Joehouse twenty miles nearer the front: a series of crosses, of circles, of triangles in different crayons, tracing the long retreat of the German Army from the broken Siegfried Line back to the Rhine. And though no one could acknowledge the German Joes, it was they who had reported most of the history on that plastic.

Is there a message center at Osterzell, G-2 would ask, as the direction finders indicate? What artillery can be expected at Mannheim? Will the Danube line be manned at Ulm?

The Danube seemed a long way off for troops who did not yet command the Rhine, and the question was a hard one to answer even if they got there. To come nearer home, where was the big gun that had the bead on corps command post at Saverne itself? It had not hit the old palace yet, but a shell landed on the motor pool and killed a dozen GIs at once.

A Joe named Antonius—he was a sergeant in the Heer—found it for them: a six-inch Bumblebee howitzer on a flatcar,

24

beautifully camouflaged with boughs and netting, on a spur track just beyond the Hagenau tunnel. Antonius slipped through the lines in his own Feldwebel uniform. It was astonishing how many people passed through the lines where there was no natural barrier like a river—farmers driving cows to market, or a midwife going to deliver a baby in the next village. It was not hard for Antonius to enter the German lines. Operations had only to alert the American outposts not to pot him, going through the hole in the mines.

He swapped rations and Raulino tobacco with the crew of the Bumblebee. They rolled the flatcar out to show him how they had cut a hole in the planking to take the steep recoil, and how fast they could run it back into the tunnel as soon as the round was fired. The barrel could be elevated thirty-nine degrees to lob shells over the hill. No wonder they boasted that the Yankee planes could not see it, "Though they're hunting hard enough, God knows," laughed the Kanonier.

"Das war prima!" * Antonius chuckled when he told the Team next day.

He ran his long schoolteacher fingers through his black hair. The gun crew had invited him back to watch the firing at six in the morning, but at five he was spotting the emplacement on a 1:20,000 map for a major of Eighth Air Force. At 0550 two of the major's planes smashed it up, though they still could not see it even as they dropped the sticks.

Whenever such a call came through, the Team in conclave picked one Joe, or at most two, for the mission. Two were more risky than one, in case they were spot-checked by the Gestapo. But two had greater life expectancy than one. For missions deep in the Reich it chose a pinpoint for the drop, from captured German field maps. An open field or a clearing in the woods was best, not too near a town. It was often many miles beyond the Joe's real target, to avoid the charted Flak or to

* "That was tops!"

25

assure solitude long enough for him to bury his chute. Then the Air Force major had to approve the pinpoint, for he had a risk as well as the Joe.

To fit the time and place of his mission it created his cover —his false identity and a plausible reason for his trip. It set up a shop to forge Soldbücher, travel orders, train tickets, and ration stamps; to press out the zinc dogtags every German soldier wore at his neck; and to fake the eagle-and-swastika rubber seals without which no military paper was valid. The Wehrmacht called this symbol the Hoheitszeichen—the Seal of Supremacy. The Team called it the bird.

A Joe's dogtag and uniform and trip ticket had to agree with the entries in his Soldbuch. The Team had a storeroom of captured uniforms to fit every size and rank, and an old-fashioned hooded camera for taking the pictures to paste inside the front cover of the booklet, and a chemical to age them. It had two volunteer penmen, once company clerks in the Heer, to forge signatures, and Mike, once adjutant in an Austrian mountain regiment, to make sure that the Joe's travel rations of food and soap were entered correctly. A soldier could be thrown in jail for having too much soap in his knapsack, and shot for claiming too much on his travel orders. Like any German soldier, the Joe had to have a good reason for being on the road. Sometimes he was shipping from the hospital back to the front, and then he needed a scar and a wound-ribbon, and the code number of his illness or wound, on the medical page of his book, had to match the symptoms which the Gestapo might order him to describe.

The question he would have to answer oftenest was "Where did you spend last night?" To that he must give either the address of his Safe House (if the "priests" had found one) where someone would still dare to lie for America if the Gestapo checked back, or the name of a town which had just been bombed, so they could not check back.

All this briefing and preparation took three days, after the

Team got going. Documents thought that was fast. G-2 complained it was too long. They said the intelligence might be stale if the Joe could not even start after it for three days. But they did not know how complex and delicate the cover had to be, if the Joe was to return alive. They had no mercy on a Joe, maybe because they never saw one; they never understood, as even Vati did, that, far from being a machine, he was twice as complex as a man, because he was two men.

On the night of a mission, Vati would slide him out to the waiting car, to start for the front if he were passing through a hole, or for the field if he were dropping. A wink after supper, or a treat at the bar, was the signal, but there was no farewell. Yet the Joe could not always keep his eyes from staring or his voice from breaking, no matter how careful he was; and the others sometimes caught the tension in spite of orders. They might clasp his hand under the table, or whisper "Hals- und Beinbruch," which is a queer way to wish a friend luck, for it means break your neck and leg. The Joe was "du" to the others by now. English has no word for the "thou" of Europe, which means affection or contempt—or both at once—but never means respect, except in prayer.

The life behind was erased, and the life ahead was hidden. He went to a secret as he had come from one. But it was no wonder if sometimes at the Golden Well he had overheard the briefing of another Joe—was it not his business to spy?—or if in that taut interval just before his mission he confided to one —to one alone, sworn to silence—perhaps along the road, perhaps at night when the Kehl guns crackled, perhaps from bunk to bunk, what his real name was. Or where his wife lived. Or, most dangerous of all, where the Americans were sending him.

If only to leave in some German memory the trace of his existence.

Two

One morning early in January three of the Team sat in the office at the cage, waiting for volunteers. Since the Battle of the Bulge began, not a single new recruit had joined.

"They're scared," said Captain Pete gloomily, "and so am I. We've only got three so far. Unless someone breaks through to Bastogne we may never get another. This ought to be a lesson anyway. If First Army had planted a few Joes they wouldn't be in the soup now. Maybe if Washington lets us raise the pay—"

There was a knock at the office door: three shorts and a long, the Morse for V.

Before he had time to answer it, the door opened just far enough to let a slim figure in Feldgrau slip through. His body stood across the crack, but Fred, from his corner, had time to see a group of prisoners in the corridor, kneeling with brushes to scrub the stone floor. The newcomer turned the knob softly, pushing lightly with his hand behind him till the click showed the door had latched. He stood his mop against the wall, then saluted Pete gravely in the old Wehrmacht way, with fingers to cap like the American salute. It had almost gone out since the Nazis brought in the straightarm, which they called the "German greeting." He was a full six feet, but lithe; he looked handsome and urbane as Satan. There was no jauntiness left in the cage, even among the Americans, and the prisoners shuffling through the slush outside the window, beyond the wire stockade, wore sacking around their feet and newspapers over their ears. But his Schiffchen (his boat, as they called their service cap) was cocked at just the right angle to show the wave in his glossy black hair, and his Feldgrau, though darned, was creased and clean. Fred even noticed that there were no spots on the knees of his pants, proving that he had goldbricked out of kneeling with the rest of the cleaning detail. He could see that this Kraut was an old campaigner.

Pete was not a majestic specimen of the conqueror. For all his beetling eyebrows he was too short and too sloppy. Even so, the first three German Joes had shaken and stammered a little when they came through his door. The newcomer did not seem impressed by him, nor by the sight of the stove and the armchair and the open carton of Camels. He began respectfully enough, standing at attention with his feet at right angles as the Wehrmacht taught. Maybe he was too respectful, Pete thought uneasily. Pete always doubted; that is why he was the best man in the Team.

"I have heard, Herr Captain," he began in German, "that you offer good pay for certain services to those who have qualifications like my own. If one might ask what the pay would be?"

He pronounced Pete's rank in the German way: Kapitän.

"Who told you that?" Pete countered, raking him up and down, or rather up, with his black eyes. "Take off your coat or you'll get pneumonia, and sit down."

The newcomer waggled his forefinger. "One never reveals the source. And I am glad to get warm."

With a sigh he sat down in the armchair, placed to face the light. Pete smiled, not without admiration. He offered the Camels.

"Well, suppose we did. If we did, what are your qualifications? And further, who are you?"

"I am the Tiger," the visitor began. "Are you sure they cannot see or hear out there?"

He bent his head toward the stockade. Pete nodded.

"From you I have nothing to hide. Indeed, I have come far for this moment."

He appraised the cigarette, then took a deep drag and began his history.

His name was Rudolf Barth. He had been born in Duisburg in 1917, which made him twenty-eight, if it was true. His mother had died in childbirth. His father, to forget, moved to the dockyards of Mannheim, where the Neckar meets the Rhine. It cannot have been easy for Herr Barth to bring up the boy.

"All the same, I was his son, so he owed me a little sacrifice. It was the hard life after the First War which made him a Communist. I am a Communist, too, but not for such a cowardly reason. I have reached my faith by long thought, since I was young. To prove how weak he was, let me tell you that at the time of the Putsch he switched to the new party. My father was not a brave man."

"Was? Is he dead now?"

The Tiger shrugged. "Weiss nicht. They did give him a better job when he was converted. They set him to organizing the dockworkers for the party. National Socialist German Workers' party, indeed!" He rolled the Nazi title off his tongue with scorn, the whole of it.

"Arbeiter! Why, after that he never worked again, as far as I could see. And he seemed to hate me all the more. I was the fastest runner and the highest jumper in the Rotsport. That was the Communist sport club in the city schools before the

30

party put us out of business. I won the thousand-meter when the new Mannheim stadium opened."

"You wouldn't do any high jumping if you worked for us," Pete laughed, "except downward. But you might have to run. You look as if you could run fast. How about swimming? You must know how to swim if you live between the Rhine and the Neckar."

The Tiger shook his head. "I never took up swimming, but it would be easy for me to learn. I hold the sharpshooter's medal. Intelligence work—that's what I like best. My first job was to deliver a letter to a girl in Munich. The track coach gave me the fare—third class, the cheap Halunke!* She was waiting to the right of the station door, as he promised, reading the *Münchner Illustrierte*. She did not look up when I slipped the envelope between the paper and her fingers, invisibly, without looking at her, like a well-trained agent. I still do not know what was in that letter. It may even have been blank, to initiate me without any risk to themselves. It shows I am loyal that I did not steam the flap open to find out. Later we were married, when I was just eighteen. I wonder if we didn't get married for the sake of our own party. I confess that I ran away from her a year later to join a circus, and I haven't seen her since. I trained the animals; that's why I choose the name Tiger. A harmless vanity. There was good money in circuses before the war. We traveled all over Europe in boxcars with strong iron bars. There were many women who came to the show because they loved animals. I taught them to love Communism. It was a pleasant way to help. One of them taught me French. Vous voyez, je suis débrouillard." †

He rattled on in his machine-gun Baden accent, throwing in a little French slang now and then to prove he knew that language too.

"Just before the war they called the circus in from France.

* Bum.
† You see, I make out all right.

By that time I had worked ten years under the canvas. I was chief trainer and head of the whole animal convoy, with a good salary and two dress suits. None of us wanted to go back to Germany, not even my beasts. That was a sad day when we had to roll home across the Rhine bridge, with the animals all roaring with hunger inside the red and yellow cages. They have probably been eaten themselves by now. I was sure He planned to start war that summer, and had ordered us back for the Wehrmacht."

The Tiger smiled pleasantly. You never heard German soldiers use the word Nazi; it was always "the regime" or "the Party." You never heard them say the name of Hitler, not even the title of Reichskanzler or Führer or Mehrer.* It was always "He," as the Tiger used it now, but you knew whom they meant, for you could almost hear the capital H.

"To keep out of it I got a job in Daimler-Benz: work essential for the defense of the Reich. On the side I started a new cell. We called it the Kaiserblume, so they would think we were no worse than royalists. We carried the patch under the collar to show each other when we dared, like this"—he flipped the tab of his tunic—"a neat blue cornflower. We called the group a cell because it started out small, and when it grew too big we split it in half, like cancer. I bet that's what He thinks we are. Sabotage is what we loved, because we could not often shoot. I taught the other workers in my section how to slow down. Drink some mustard soaked in flour and vinegar. You will swell up at the joints so you can't work for a week. Have you ever smoked a cigarette dipped in hair oil?"—he reached for another Camel— "It gives you a beautiful rash which the doctors never diagnosed. Believe me, the tanks which Daimler-Benz turned out have done your troops no harm. But it was no use; the Army got me in forty-one."

Pete had heard some tall boasting from recruits, but his

* Chancellor, leader, expander.

jaw hung open as the Tiger went on. The Tiger had jumped into Crete four times with the airborne engineers of General Philipp's Festungsbrigade Kreta—the Team pricked up its ears at that. When the island was secured, they shipped him to the Russian front, for the campaign was not going too well at Stalingrad. In Budweis, on the way, he was wounded. He showed Pete his left hand, with the first two fingers gone.

"I did not want to fight the Russians," he explained, "so I used an old Czech pistol I had kept from before the war. It was easy to make it look as if a sniper had done it. They were shooting men for losing fingers then, even if it was only by carelessness. But will you believe me? They gave me the Cold Storage Medal, as we call it, for service on the Russian front, though I never got east of Bohemia. Then my wound got infected; I hadn't counted on that. But things usually work out. They sent me to the reserve hospital at Bregenz across the lake from Switzerland. When the stumps healed I was released from active service.

"I was a corporal by then, with a wound chevron and a sharpshooter's badge and the Iron Cross Second Class and of course, the parachute badge—you know it, the eagle swooping down with furled wings. They put me in a company of old-timers to guard the Antwerp supply line from the Belgian guerrillas. One day we had a skirmish near Bastogne . . ."

(That very day Bastogne was under siege in the snow, and Skorzeny's men were inside the lines in white parkas just like Quartermaster issue.)

". . . and I skipped out when the firing stopped. Worked westward to join the guerrillas. At the Luxembourg frontier a customs guard asked for my Soldbuch. I shot him through the head and took his badge. That convinced the guerrillas, in spite of my Feldgrau. They found him lying where I said. Naturally, I had taken his money. There was quite a lot of it, too; he must have taken bribes for contraband in both directions. More than a thousand marks, and even one American dollar. I have kept the dollar for sentiment's sake; also because it is hard money."

He rubbed his thumb and forefinger together in the Continental gesture which means avarice. From his breast pocket he drew an old-style outsized dollar bill, the kind that had trapped Skorzeny's man at the Canadian border.

"I have heard that the capitalists in your country frame their first dollar on their office walls in the skyscrapers. I bet their dollars are no more honest than this one. Anyway, the guerrillas found me a civilian suit and let me marry one of their girls. She called me Panther instead of Tiger—her black panther. But soon we fell out of love. In the war of the heart disguise is useless. It was time for me to move again.

"I burned my Feldgrau in the stove of our dugout, and even my Soldbuch. The comrades wished me farewell when I explained that I had a higher mission. I only kept the little snapshot from the front cover to show you that I really am a corporal. With civilian clothes, it was not hard to work my way down to you."

He held out the square photo, with his signature and a scrap of the swastika seal across the corner, as they should be, and pointed out the double bar on the collar tab, with a black band and a capital F for corporal of Fortress Engineers. Pete raised his eyebrows incredulously.

"You think it is impossible to do such things in Germany, Herr Kapitän? It is hard, but not impossible if one is nimble and has the will. I was listed in the Blacklist so long ago that by now I am given up for dead. I am safer now than ever. For the Gestapo, I am what they call in Haiti a zombie. I know that a soldier who travels is supposed to have his papers stamped each day by the transport office or the mayor, but one can forge the stamp. It is hardest near the front to do such things, but deep in Germany where the people do not fight, but weep for their fighters instead, and in the occupied countries, which hate the regime anyway, one can manage to be free even in wartime. I can speak like an Alsatian, you see." And he drawled "Straws-s-burh" for them in mimicry of the local accent.

The first time he met an American patrol he threw his arms in the air and told them in gestures, for English was the one language he never claimed, that he was a German deserter. They turned him in at the Sarrebourg cage. Since the commandant could not let the Swiss Red Cross who inspected the cage think that he imprisoned civilians, the Tiger was given an old German uniform from the stockpile.

He sidled forward and spat into the stove. "One should not praise one's wares too highly, lest the purchaser suspect them," he grinned, "but you can see you will be well repaid by sending me behind the lines. I suggest Mannheim, for I know it. If you give me a radio operator too, I can supply you with all information from that important city, and shall have means of wiring you for supplies as I need them. Why, if you gave me enough money I could start a revolution against Him from there, as the sailors did in the last war from Hamburg. Hamburg is no more important than Mannheim. If I convert Mannheim I shall have cut Germany in half. You will see, I shall prey on Him."

"You sound something like Him yourself," said Captain Pete. "I think He is more likely to prey on you."

"Not bad, Herr Kapitän," cried the Tiger, beating his knee. "A Communist Führer. I thank you for the compliment. But do not think I am all dreamer. I know a cave in the Bensheim quarries against the cliffs of the eastern side of the river, where the direction finders will never believe a radio could hide, no matter what their beams tell them. At Number 27 Wharf Street in Mannheim is a bunker where we can shelter whenever we need to. If any of your agents—do not deny again that you have them—needs help, let him go to that house, rear room right on the first floor, knock four times like the V-signal, and say to whoever opens it 'Greetings from the Tiger.' Schönen Gruss vom Herrn Tiger. It is my father-in-law's apartment, my first father-in-law. He is a good comrade too. He knows that you will come. But don't tell him about the circus.

"I should need at least ten thousand Reichsmarks, but in bills no larger than one hundred, please, since they trace the larger bills. Better have planes available later to send in more pistols and cigarettes, together with sulfa drugs in case of certain diseases which slow up the mobility of a team. I shall recruit many more when I get in. Not so much from the Wehrmacht, for the German soldier is a slave, and I do not concern myself with such details as machine guns and drills, but from the richer field of politics, like those pioneers at Hamburg. We shall be your forward army across the Rhine. I shall call it the Tiger Brigade. Wait, it will be a Communist Bürgermeister who welcomes the Seventh Army to Mannheim. I can stay out the war there, no matter how long it may be, undermining Him more each day. It may be I shall even join the SS for appearance's sake; who can tell? Perhaps I shall be the last guard on the Rhine bridge. It is I who shall capture Mannheim for you, and all the time I shall be safe, safer than among the Soldaten in this prison."

"I don't doubt you are in danger from them," Pete interrupted drily.

"And only two requests do I make, except to ask again what salary you pay. One, that I have twice the usual life insurance, because I have two wives. Second, that I go home as a sergeant. I have earned the promotion. But there, I have given you all my secrets and my dreams, and you tell me nothing of yours."

Pontifically the colonel boomed from the corner. "You have told us all your hatreds, Corporal Barth, and they are many. Tell us, what do you believe?"

The Tiger's exaltation flagged. His eyes roamed the ceiling, then he stood up in deference to the eagle. He smiled urbanely.

"If I seem theatrical, Herr Colonel, I tell no more than the facts. If I mock others, it may be that I mock myself also. I believe that every man should have his chance. I offer you my courage so that injustice may be destroyed."

There was a silence. Pete pressed the bell on his desk. The Tiger understood his interview was over. He grasped his mop as if it were a rifle at ground and waited at attention beside the door. An MP came in.

"Take this prisoner to the probation cell," ordered the colonel, but only after a pause, as if he were coming out of a trance.

The colonel kept a notebook in his foot locker. That night he wrote in it: "No. 4 OK for subversive. Physical courage for ops A-plus. Understanding of issue—nil, hence doubt moral strength for followup."

In the jargon of the Team "followup" meant putting your finger on a target for the bombers, even if the target was your own home town. Herbert had shot two lieutenants when they caught him deactivating a bridge mine, but that was not followup; it was just self-defense. Jojo had slipped a stinger and a dime-sized compass to an American PW. That was not even so much; it was just comradeship. Antonius had spotted the Bumblebee, but that was classed more as revenge for the twelve GIs. These missions were all tactical; followup was strategic. So far, no Joe had had to give the word which would knock out a division or a city in his homeland.

Three

A dozen Americans of Seventh Army Combat Intelligence sat around the table in the field office at the Schloss that evening after supper, debating whether to hire the Tiger. The Schloss was called Station S, as the German Joehouse was G and the French F. A big map of Western Germany at 1:250,000 covered one wall, with the sofa below it. Against another stood the dark green field safe which contained the contracts of the Joes. Next was a Bechstein grand which someone had liberated from a Nazi official during their short stay in Strasbourg, and the fourth was a single casement, bolted and shuttered for the night, with a big old-fashioned Cremone bolt running its full height.

Operations was playing the piano softly; he claimed it made him think better. Documents was studying the map, standing on the sofa with his spectacles almost scraping the wall.

Pete, who was Recruiting, opposed hiring the Tiger. "He is the biggest liar I have seen in all Europe or America. If he lies to his own people he will lie to us. I don't think we ought to touch him. I'd really like to sweat him out and see if he isn't a super-Skorzeny boy."

The colonel smiled. He fancied himself not only as a commanding officer who knew that deserters were slippery, but as a psychologist who had found the reason why. He wedged a new candle in the empty schnapps bottle. Station S had no electricity.

"Pete doesn't realize it," he told them, "but that's exactly the reason we should hire him. Just because he is such a tall liar, I mean. The minute a man passes those lines he becomes a liar automatically, and it's better to have a big one, with some international experience, than a petty first-time liar. The Tiger is clearly the Olympic champion, both for speed and endurance; Pete is right there. But the two Joes who got theirs in the café at Munich last month got it because their lying wasn't big enough, or fast enough, or both. Anyway, they are no use to us now, poor kids. In this racket you have to distrust an honest man, though I don't deny the possibility there might be a Joe so transparently and ridiculously noble as to make the best agent of all. I haven't come across one yet. Till we do, I want to stick to the good old-fashioned double-crossers. It isn't a question of ethics at all, for which our wives and Sunday school teachers should be glad. Look at it another way: you might not want to risk an honest man, but this Munchausen would be no loss to anyone. The only question is, will he help us or hurt us? All this on the assumption that Security okays him."

Pete said, "I bet he'd give away the location of his own Joe-house for a thousand marks—that is, after he'd taken our money first and got across the line with it."

"Yes," the colonel answered, "I think he would, though he might hold out for ten. However, we'll be moving it soon anyway, as soon as the push starts. Besides, he's not in a very strong position to bargain with Skorzeny, if there's any truth at all in his story. I don't think he can hurt us much; he doesn't know a thing yet except where Pete's office is at the cage. If they bombed Pete they'd hit a thousand Krauts at the same time. Not a bad exchange. All I ask is, can he help us?"

"He certainly has a high disdain for those technicalities G-2 pesters us for." Pete smiled. "You know, Colonel, things like guns and divisions."

"No sarcasm, please, Captain."

But the colonel really liked Pete. They used to work in the same law firm. It was the colonel who had got Pete his commission.

"No, I wouldn't put him in any spot intelligence. This is what Washington calls a morale operation. I don't see why we shouldn't try one. Mannheim must be about ripe now. The Eighth has done a little bombing around the edges already; not much, but enough to get on the nerves. Docks and gas tanks, and objectives like that. The flames have probably spread. They'd do a little more for the asking, I guess. Does anyone here know the town?"

Everyone shook his head; but Documents, who took down the Joes' life histories when they joined, remembered that Antonius had an uncle there.

"Good," said the colonel. "Send one of the Swiss in to check that address of the father-in-law. He will be sure to turn up something. Meanwhile let the Tiger stew. If he has lied to Pete I will ship him west where he can't do any harm. If he has told the truth, I am going to drop him in on the chance he can do a little damage to the Herrenvolk. Not that I expect his revolution quite yet. The only thing that worries me"—he glanced almost shyly at the captain—"is using a Communist. I don't think it has ever been done, but he should be all the better for the job."

"Who's teaching Sunday school now?" Pete crowed. "If you are set on hiring him, give him double pay and he will become honest, if that will ease your mind. Who wouldn't? Injustice, he says! Everyone gripes about injustice. For instance, that gold leaf I deserve . . ."

So the Tiger stayed in the probation cell at the cage. In a week the report came out of Switzerland that as far as Mannheim went everything he had said was true. The cave was in Bensheim all right, a fine place for the radio. The bunker was underneath 27 Wharf Street, and the father-in-law was upstairs. Not only that, but he would do what he could to help the Tiger or any of his friends, within the limits of his own safety. They could not ask for more, and wondered in what confidence, where the walls and the very river had ears, the old Communist had dared give that promise to a stranger in a black cassock.

The colonel was so elated by this proof of his good judgment that he did give the Tiger double pay—and it was plenty —and extra insurance and his "promotion" too. Documents made him a Soldbuch in the name of Ludwig Kett, staff sergeant of Festungspionier Bataillon 6, on mission to inspect steel reinforcement in the Rhine and Neckar defenses. The Tiger grinned like a child, though it was rare for him to smile, when his picture was taken with the silver pip on his shoulder strap. Pete still grumbled.

"He'll bitch us sure as fate, and I'll get a chewing out from you for having followed your own advice in recruiting him."

But Finance would give him only fifty thousand marks expense money instead of the hundred thousand he wanted. Even the colonel had to agree it was enough. "If it takes us a year to reach the river, he couldn't spend that much on subsistence. I know he'll have to do some bribery that may run up, and these are unvouchered funds, so nobody will know even if they are wasted. But there is a limit to everything. Why, he couldn't carry more than five hundred bills in his money belt. But don't stint his other equipment. Drop a separate tube if you have to."

There was a good deal of feeling that the Tiger had hoodwinked the colonel. Finance was the only dissenter who got anywhere; the rest had to obey. The Tiger shrugged eloquently when the fifty thousand in rainbow bills was handed to him at the dress rehearsal, as if to say you couldn't stint a revolution, and an unsuccessful one was worse than none at all. But he folded the bills deftly, disposing them evenly around his belt so there were no lumps, and smoothing his hips like a woman with a new girdle. Supply packed a big aluminum cylinder with a set of grid maps of Baden, a tommy cooker with a canteen of recharging gas, a box of dog drag, five cakes of soap, two lighters, two fountain pens, a three-color hooded flashlight to guide the relief planes, and two sets of civilian clothes. A long-term mission like the Tiger's might need to wear uniform one day and civilians the next, but it was fatal to be caught with both. Down to the soap, this equipment had to be German, and it was not easy to assemble so much even by combing the cage and trading American materiel with the prisoners.

The Tiger moved into the Joehouse to wait till his operation was laid on. He took training with the other Joes. Vati and the battle-order captain reported he was a poor student. Not that he couldn't learn if he tried, but he just didn't listen, as if military reporting was of no importance. Perhaps, for a morale operation, it wasn't. But he knew all about the Gestapo. Vati even had him lecture the others.

"You cannot tell them by their clothes." He laughed wryly. "Sometimes they come right out with MP uniform, wearing light blue facings to their collars and shoulder tabs. Sometimes they wear the straight police uniform with the flat-topped black helmet. But most often they disguise themselves as soldiers like us. No, you cannot tell them by their clothes. Only by the plaque around their throats, like a soldier's dogtag, but oblong instead of oval. And who gets a chance at a Gestapo throat? For big offenders, like Giraud when he escaped, or the assassins of Heydrich, they paste up a Steckbrief on every lamppost. For smaller fry like us," he winked, "they pool the names and descriptions in the weekly Blacklist, alphabetically, and send them to all provost offices in the Reich. Lucky they change the color each time; you can see at a glance whether they're up to date. Sometimes that gives you time to break trail. If you want to keep off the Blacklist you need at least two identities, for if once they link you to a description in it . . ."

He tightened his hands around his neck.

The Tiger never became friends with the other Joes, perhaps because he was older. They never called him "thou," in spite of the shows he would put on in the day room. He would make a cone out of a newspaper, balance the point on his chin, set fire to the top, and carry it around the room, face tilted, till it burned right down to the end without toppling or even singeing him, while the other Joes cheered. He soon became an expert in the jump training, darting over the bars like a monkey or an acrobat, and turning his somersault on the sand without ever a bruise or a turned ankle.

"That guy must have *been* in a circus," said Buck, though he knew nothing about the Tiger's past. "He lands as soft as a cat."

The colonel decided to give him Paluka as radio operator, and to have him carry the crystal walkie-talkie right in his pack instead of dropping it in the tube.

"I am sending Paluka," he explained, "partly because he's our best and most seasoned operator—and I'm beginning to have hopes for this unorthodox operation—and partly because he's Russian."

"Besides," said Finance, "he's on the payroll already at the French Joehouse. That will help make up for the extras the Tiger talked you into."

The colonel went on, "I don't know whether he is a Communist like the Tiger. I doubt whether he himself knows. He can't speak German, which is all to the good; he'd be sure to make some blunder if he did. He and the Tiger can get along in French. If the Gestapo catches him, it might save his life to be Russian. They would expect him to be anti-Nazi, if you see what I mean."

"Poor penetration of enemy psychology, sir," Pete broke in. "They would string him up all the faster for being Russian. But throw him to the slaughter, too."

The colonel paid no heed. "His friends would expect the same; to them he might be sort of an advance guard of the revolution. Hands across the continent, so to speak. Besides, he is getting stale at the French Joehouse, and he is too good to be wasted. Your tourist missions don't give us a chance to use the radio the way we did in France. It can't be any fun for him to cook for those Frenchmen and Poles and Italians; not that he has to, naturally, but you know Paluka. He loves excitement. He can't sit still. Also, he is getting too fond of Giovanna, have you noticed? She is a nice girl and did her stuff for us in France, but we've got to get rid of one of them."

"David and Uriah," intoned Documents, turning back from the wall map.

But the colonel went on; he had no interest in Giovanna. "The corkscrew Harvard mind." He smiled to the others. "Love always makes trouble in a Joehouse. Immorality I don't mind—"

"Who does?" Pete snickered.

"In fact, come to think of it, that might be a good reason to hold on to Giovanna, aside from the difficulty of releasing her. It keeps the Joes satisfied. But I'm afraid Paluka's falling for her in the soulful Slavic way. That's bad. There will be an explosion if we leave them in that cottage together. It's like an ammo box already. Anyway, he's the only first-class operator we have left, and he will get a kick out of dropping in again. He's begged for it many times. He's the only French Joe I dare send in, with the big push coming up. Ask him what he needs for himself."

As the Tiger was greedy, Paluka was modest. All he wanted

was a set of woman's underwear, besides the standard thousand marks pocket money.

"Cela pour mes propres affaires." He laughed. "Ce n'est pas trop, il faut convenir." *

"Salaud," Pete growled. "Stinker."

Paluka cuffed him playfully on the ear. Old Paluka, with his square flat Slavic face, his iron-gray hair, his wide smile of gold, his booming laughter, his quick-footed strength! He was like a clumsy nurse. When he winked, he winked with both eyes. He was no taller than the Tiger, but he weighed fifty pounds more. Many times he had risked his life for the Team, but no one ever heard him say why. He had probably long since forgotten the reason himself. He never asked for extra pay. He never spoke against the Germans, or against the Communists in his own country.

He risked his life for fun, if such a thing seems possible. Yet not fun exactly, because the radio operator had the dull job of sitting bowed in his shelter all day and all night. He had fixed hours to transmit and receive. Between then he dared not leave his little square suitcase set, his crystals and code pad, for fear of missing some unscheduled call, or of being delayed by an air raid or a police check or any of the breakdowns that beset Europe at war. If the Gestapo caught him, they asked no questions; the radio was a death sentence in itself. They killed him then and there, or, if they were subtle, made him transmit false messages in his own code, with a pistol at his head, and waited till his usefulness was over. The Team had tried ways around that, by using a warning acrostic in the code, but Skorzeny was not so dumb that he couldn't break it.

The only explanation is that Paluka risked his neck simply for the love of danger. The other Joes wanted the war to end for one reason or another—revenge or reunion or just the aching for quiet—but Paluka hoped it would last forever, as long as there was a mission for him.

* "That's for my private business. You must admit it isn't too much."

45

He had been born forty-five years before at Taganrog in the Ukraine. That made him even older than the Tiger. His father, Sergei, had been inspector in the iron mines named after the October Revolution. His mother, Galina, still lived there, he supposed. Once he showed Fred a faded picture of her— a wide, shrewd, wrinkled, earthy face just like his own, hair parted in the middle the same way. Paluka had been just too young to fight for the Czar. In the letdown after the armistice he had got two years at the new Soviet technical school in Alexandrovsk, studying electricity. He served two more in the new Red Army; it was all the same to him. Then he went to work in the mines himself, hacking out iron ore for the rearmament. When his father died in 1922 the new inspector fired him.

"It was a question of something he called solidarity. The miners had loved my father; perhaps the inspector was afraid they would vote to make me inspector myself. He got me a job as radio operator on an ore ship to ease me out of Russia, and now me voici. I must always be underground," and he roared at his own joke.

The first time the ore ship touched Marseille he jumped her. Marseille is a tough city, but Paluka was tough too. He picked up a job at the Potin electric shop, repairing motors. In two years he was section chief. On the side he repaired radios and gave night classes at a gym off the Canebière.

"Swimming and acrobatics I myself taught," he would say proudly, stretching the muscles of his enormous arms, "and boxing. That's how I got my gold teeth."

Though he was Russian, the French Army tried to draft him. He stalled them off with arguments about his age and nationality till after Pétain's armistice, when there was no more French Army. In the few days of 1942 between our African invasion and the German occupation of South France all the boats that could do so slipped out of Marseille and headed across the Mediterranean. Paluka got aboard one of them as ship's electrician. When she reached Algiers he jumped ship again, this time to enlist for the Fifis.* He was always one leap ahead of the excitement. But there was no fun serving in an exiled army and drilling on the warm beaches of Algeria waiting for the reconquest that might never come. He watched the American Eighth Fleet grow in the harbor, and made a bet with himself that it would be in action first.

"It was really exciting," he explained, "especially since they had come from so far away."

About that time the Team opened shop in Algiers itself and put in to AFHQ for French-speaking radio operators. General Giraud, who was building up the Free French Army while De Gaulle was building up the government, released Paluka with the grade of "infantry reservist." Perhaps he was glad to get rid of so unorthodox a soldier. Paluka became the first French Joe.

He made three jumps from Algiers into France with his radio on his chest. On one of them he got himself a job with his old electric shop in Marseille, no questions asked, which entitled him to a German passport as a foreign worker. The night the Kommandantur issued it to him he pushed out a folding rubber boat, sculled to an American submarine waiting offshore, and steamed back to Algiers with the little gray passport in his waterproof money belt and a couple of gun emplacements remembered in his thick head.

"Just in case I need a passport when we get into Germany," he explained. He still had it with him. It was the only valid German identity paper in either Joehouse. The rest were all forged by Documents, but it would have taken an expert to detect them.

On his next trip, in-June, he spotted the Second SS Panzer Division, which the Germans called Das Reich, starting north at night, a few days after the Normandy landings, to help con-

---

* Slang for "Forces Françaises de l'Intérieur," the title by which De Gaulle promoted the Maquis (which means brush-heath) from guerrillas to belligerents.

tain the beachheads. It was the flash from Paluka's little six-volt walkie-talkie that let the Team alert the Air Force and the Fifis and SHAEF in London, so that between them they stopped the heavy armor dead in its tracks. If that crack division had reached the Normandy battleground it is possible the Wehrmacht could have flung the whole of Operation Overlord back into the English Channel.

Paluka was the only French Joe who had jumped into Germany. When Seventh Army was halfway up the Rhône Valley—where you would have thought there was action enough—he had begged for a mission into the Reich itself. He took off alone from the Marseille airfield and holed up for a week in the deserted guardhouse of the cemetery at Kaiserslautern in the Pfalz. Jumping into Germany, he reported, was worse (or, as he looked at it, better) than jumping into France, where an agent had only the Milice to fear. In Germany it was the whole frightened populace. On that mission his ignorance of German prevented his learning much, but he slipped back all right. Perhaps the Gestapo thought him too stupid to be a spy, but Pete knew that just walking along the road he might have been picked up and shipped to a labor camp where he would be silenced for the rest of the war. If he had been caught with his radio, he would have been silenced too, more permanently. Paluka did not mind the risk, but the others did not want to lose him for nothing. Here in Alsace was his chance again, with a German-speaking teammate; and it might be his last, for anyone could see the enemy was beginning to crack.

It would be risky to have the same operation drop Paluka as a civilian foreign worker and the Tiger as a soldier, for sergeants in Germany did not travel with Russian laborers. So Documents fitted him out with papers as Paul Rosoff, private in Infantry Battalion 836 of the East Legion, which Battle Order knew was built of Ukrainian "volunteers." Documents had to set up the presses for a special Cossack Soldbuch blank, copied from a captured one, with the entries in both

48

Russian and German. For good measure he printed "in the name of the Führer" an Award for Valor, second class, in silver, "as granted to members of the Eastern Peoples" and Mike, the Austrian lieutenant, forged the signature of General-Major von Henning, commander of the basic division of the legion.

Rosoff, Paluka's cover surname, was not so different from his own. It had to be a little different, not only for his own safety but for his family's, in case the Gestapo got it in the Blacklist. The Paul was his own, and they left it, for he might have been too slow-witted to answer to another, if someone called him in the street. Every Joe had three names: his own, locked in the field safe, his nickname at the Joehouse, and his cover name for the operation. Paluka was a good nickname. He was dumb and husky, just like Joe Palooka in the comics. He was a Joe, and his name was Paul, and the "uka" sounded vaguely Russian.

"Like 'Babushka,'" explained Documents, who had thought up the laborious pun. "Etymologically it may not be fully correct, but it is near enough to be a masterpiece of nomenclature."

At the French Joehouse Pete had to lure Paluka from Giovanna's arms, which hardly went around him in the feather bed. They both cried, even when Pete told him he had a new mission and promised them one more night together before Paluka took off.

At the storeroom Supply squeezed him into the biggest Feldgrau on the rack, and sewed on his left sleeve an eagle insignia taken from the same Cossack who had yielded the sample Soldbuch, and a silver "Ostlegion" on the black armlet. Big as the Cossack had been, the uniform was still too tight for Paluka. He looked down at it and broke into one of his rumbles. He took up a boxing stance, the seams creaking at his arms.

"Come on," he shouted in French, "whoever I'm meant to fight, Americans, Russians, Germans; Nazis or Cocos—Das spielt keine Rolle."

49

It was the one German phrase he had learned: "It makes no difference." Coco is the slang for Communist.

Pete and the colonel took him up to the German Joehouse to "marry" the Tiger. The mating of a team was important, for one and one do not always make two. There had been narrow escapes where one Joe had disobeyed the other, or where, from either malice or discontent or stupidity, the Joes had told different stories to the Gestapo. The colonel, a little sheepishly, had warned the Tiger not to speak of his communism; Pete warned Paluka that the Tiger was captain of the team. Vati ordered schnapps for both of them at a corner table in the bar of the Golden Well. The innkeeper knew enough to leave the room after he had brought the glasses over, and the Joes knew enough to pretend they were old friends, even with no one listening in. The introduction had to be in French, the only language they both knew.

"Thou art going to Mannheim with the Tiger, Paluka, to transmit for him. Okay?"

He nodded. "Das spielt keine Rolle. When do we start? Soon?"

"Soon, after the signal plan is worked out."

"He understands I am the boss?" the Tiger asked.

Paluka repeated his indifference, and pointed to the empty schnapps glass. He rubbed his cauliflower ear.

"Our host is not generous with his liqueurs," the Tiger agreed. "The glass is like a thimble, and the bottom very thick."

But he nodded, so they knew he agreed to his teammate, and the colonel ordered them another round. The Tiger was so sure of his own agility, and Paluka so indifferent to danger, that the mating went off as well as could be hoped, for two such different Joes. The Tiger would rather have had Paluka follow him in later, claiming there was no use risking two lives, and even the whole Tiger Brigade, by a double drop, but he was overruled. As the colonel pointed out, there was no use risking two planes either. It soon became clear that the Tiger planned to use Paluka's radio not so much to send out information from Mannheim as to demand arms for his revolution, as he called it. This worried Supply, who was convinced his Colt 45s and cigarettes and clothing were simply going to be funneled into Skorzeny's hands, to be used against Seventh later on.

"Or else they will wind up in the black market," he prophesied. "In any case, the money will go right into the Tiger's pocket. Remember, this isn't like France, where we could drop to reception committees, with flashlights and all, and trust the Joe and his tubes would be safe, and even pick him up with a Lysander if he got lost. In Germany the controls are really tight."

But he couldn't budge the colonel. "You don't realize that the Tiger is like a kid in a candy store. He wants all he can get, whether he can eat it or not. That doesn't make him a crook. Didn't some of our French reception committees eat up revolvers and grenades? You never asked them for an accounting."

"That is because they were honest men," put in Pete.

"Listen, the Tiger may not be a savory character, but no one puts his head in a noose for a carton of cigarettes. He must have *some* kind of ideal to take the risk, even if we don't understand what it is. Maybe it's Stalin. Maybe Paluka's is the Czar. You don't argue about a pair of rayon panties with Paluka, do you? Even if this one operation fails, there isn't much lost. But if it succeeds it will make a big hit back home, and may even crack the Rhine frontier right in the middle. Like a blow in the center of a man's spine."

He leaned back, dreaming of glory.

So it was agreed that if the Tiger, via Paluka's radio, called for more supplies, Communications would alert the Brigade they were on the way not only by the scheduled call code, but by British Broadcasting messages too. They could be picked up on any short-wave set inside Germany, in case Paluka and his TR-1 were out of touch with the Tiger himself. To be safe, Paluka would have to stay in his cave. To be useful, the Tiger would have to move about. It was good for the mission to have two ways of communication, as it was good for them to have two sets of identity. The BBC signal would be DREI SCHWARZE KATZEN WERDEN BALD DEN HUND FRESSEN—three black cats will soon devour the dog. Anyone who monitored BBC during the war remembers scores of such inane messages. They were addressed to espionage teams inside the Reich, American as well as British. BBC had the only wave length that covered the whole country, and when the Germans dared to listen outside they listened to BBC. The penalty for tuning in was death, but they still listened, in attics or caves or under a haystack in the open field, and the messages got through.

"The marriage of Paluka and the Tiger didn't go off so badly," the colonel pronounced after the rite. He looked at the almanac. "Lay the operation on for the sixteenth. That will be quarter moon. Lay it on in the A-26."

Over the rustle of the firs he listened to the German guns in Kehl and the American in Strasbourg, dueling across the Rhine. Seventh American was not yet ready to jump the river, and Nineteenth German would never be. "Mannheim seems a long way off from that, but they tell me we're really going to move in a few days. Good old Paluka; I hope he'll be all right. The master race is getting jumpy about all Russians, inside the Reich as well as out."

"That gorilla is a better American than lots who wear the uniform," Pete growled, "even if he can't speak our language."

Four

This is the way the doctor's son joined.

One night, a week after the Tiger had been signed, two MPs were making the rounds outside the brick wall of the Sarrebourg cage. High up on the wall at each corner was fastened a big reflector to throw light on the gravel path in both directions. The bulb was powerful enough—maybe five hundred watts—so that usually no part of any path was dark. On the tiresome fifteen minute beat, pacing with their pumpguns cocked, patrols could see their way to the next corner without danger of being ambushed by an escaped PW or a native sniper.

But this night there was no moon. A cotton-wool mist, spongy with the chilling drizzle, swallowed the light only twenty yards each side of the big corner lamps, and the centers of the paths were as dark as if there had been no lamps at all. That is why they heard him before they saw him, as they neared the southeast corner. A voice, a persistent voice but not very loud, was singing ahead of them, in English. It was a few minutes before midnight of 15 January, 1945.

Un - der - neath the lamp post, By the bar - rack gate

sang the voice.

"Probably a drunk," one of the MPs whispered, tightening his grip just the same.

"Who could get drunk around here?" the other whispered back. "Besides, he doesn't sound drunk, and no one is supposed to sing anyway—and that's a German song, even if he's singing it in English. 'Lili Marlene'; I used to hear them broadcast it from the monastery at Cassino. You go ahead."

The first MP sidled warily along the damp brick wall till he could see the corner through the mist, and the other followed a few paces behind.

"Hände hoch!" roared the first.

That is German for "Hands up!" In Lorraine it would be understood by a civilian as well as a PW.

"Hey, Bill, come here."

For the boy's hands were already up. He was standing under the lamp with his face to it, so anyone could see him from either of the paths. He wore the long blue-gray coat of the German Air Force, with the medical brassard on his left sleeve, a red cross on a white ground. The coat was too long for him, the sodden skirt of it was ripped and heavy with mud. Water dripped on his face from the rim of his steel helmet. His fists were bare and red, stretched way out of the cuffs. They were clenched to fight the ache of his arms, held over his head in the gesture of surrender, but sagging from the weight of his soaking sleeves. When the MP shouted he stiffened them again with an effort and kept on singing:

Fare thee well, Li - li Mar - lene

till the second MP came up and slapped his pockets, under the cover of the other's gun, to see what the trick might be. They were empty.

"I speak English," said the boy. "In the Medical Corps we are not armed."

"Okay, Kraut, hands behind the neck and march ahead. Bill, you better walk backwards. He might have friends out there."

They walked him silently, with one gun at his back and the other facing him, the hundred yards to the big welcome sign at the gate, and into the gatehouse where the duty officer sat in front of the stove. This was not the first German prisoner who had been brought in to the duty officer singly like this and in the middle of the night. Before he asked any questions the officer told him in German to lean with his forehead against the wall and his toes back of the white line chalked on the floor. In this position a prisoner was helpless. He could not draw a gun, or even a stinger, without losing his balance.

The MPs frisked him more thoroughly, but he had nothing on him except the Soldbuch in his left pouch pocket. According to page one, his name was Karl Maurer, which means Charles Mason. In the flap at the back of the book were snapshots of a man of fifty with a microscope beside him, of a woman slightly younger, and of a boy about fourteen. Also an identity pass of the Luftwaffe Medical Corps and a student card from the medical school of Friedrich-Wilhelm University in Berlin. That was all. He had no money. The dogtag around his neck was the regular German oval of zinc with three slots punched in the middle, so that if a man were killed one half could be broken off and sent home, while the other was buried with him. It seems to make more sense than carrying two separate tags, as GIs did.

His dogtag looked like this:

That meant he was recruited as muster number 225 in the twelfth anti-aircraft replacement battalion of the Luftwaffe, and that his blood type was A.

"He speaks English, sir," the MPs said.

"Then maybe he's a spy. Where did you catch him?"

They told him how he had waited for them under the corner lamp, singing "Lili Marlene." The deputy officer looked at the boy, who stood before him at attention. More likely a deserter than a spy, he thought, though he could be both.

"A smart boy to sing in English," he said.

The lieutenant hummed the first line of the song:

Vor der Ka - ser - ne,   .   vor dem gross - en Tor

"But say, didn't we draw a phony war, when they sing it in English and we come back at them in German? He was smart to take the weather into account too, if he wanted to be captured alive. You might have shot him, mightn't you, if you had come on him suddenly out of the dark without hearing his voice first? A smart cookie."

"Yes, sir, we would have. And, sir—"

"Yes?"

"Do you think it would be a good idea to detail a couple of extra guards for the rest of the night, in case he has friends out there?"

The duty officer looked from the guards to the boy. "I think not. The others need their sleep too; but use your whistles if you want to. Guns likewise. On your way, soldiers."

The MPs saluted and went out to finish their watch.

"At ease, Maurer," the duty officer said.

The boy relaxed, first clicking his heels and bowing to the lieutenant, who pointed to a wooden bench in the corner of the orderly room where the details sat while they were waiting for relief. The boy sat down. His coat began to steam on the side nearest the stove.

"Perhaps it's easier for you if we speak German," suggested the duty officer.

The boy nodded.

"You're hungry, I expect."

He nodded again. "Very, sir."

"Reveille is at five, and you'll get breakfast then. Why must people walk in on me in the middle of the night? Now I'll have to rout somebody out of the barracks to find you a blanket roll."

But when he looked at the boy again he changed his mind. He was a married man, with two sons in junior high back in St. Louis.

There were some sandwiches wrapped in waxed paper on the foot locker against the wall, for the guard detail to eat when they felt like it, and a pot of coffee on the stove. The tin cup hung on a hook in the plaster wall.

"Help yourself."

"Bitte."

"Bitte sehr."

He did not look while the boy ate the sandwiches. He turned his swivel chair around to the desk and riffled through the Soldbuch. Air Force books were blue, not brown like the Army and, he noticed the eagle holding the hooked cross was different too—flying, not roosting. He had never seen one from the Medical Corps before. He pulled the lamp closer to make out the different entries, most of them in script. The regime discouraged script, for it was a barrier to the use of German abroad. But it takes time to reform a nation's handwriting. The lieutenant liked trying to read script. It was harder than speaking the language, which anyone could do. This was G-2's job, not his; he was just fooling around to kill time till the morning. He would turn the book in to them in the morning, along with the boy.

At last the boy stopped eating. The lieutenant turned around. He could count that six of the big sandwiches were gone.

"Where did you come from?" he asked.

The boy started to stand, but the lieutenant motioned him back to the bench.

"Out of a cellar, sir."

"Here in Sarrebourg?"

The boy nodded.

"Whose?"

"I do not know the name, Herr Leutnant."

"Where, then? I mean if you don't know his name, at least tell me what house he lives in. We'll have him up for harboring. There's a stiff penalty for that, and it will be a good example to this Godforsaken town. Never trust Lorrainers. Even your people can't. There's no way of telling whether they're German or French at heart."

"Most are both, sir. If you pardon, I will not tell where the man lives who sheltered me, and I repeat I do not know his name. I did not want to learn it."

The duty officer shrugged his shoulders and yawned. If the boy wanted to be stubborn, it was still not his job. In the morning, let G-2 find out where he had hidden.

"You might as well sleep here on the floor, if you want to, till reveille."

"Thank you, sir."

The duty officer straightened in his chair, wondering whether he was getting too soft for a tough job.

"Don't thank me, Kraut," he growled. "This isn't for your comfort, but so someone from God's country can get a little rest. They say the Russians don't even take prisoners alive, still less feed and billet them."

The boy took off his coat. It was drier now. He rolled it

into a pillow and lay down in a corner of the room. In two minutes he was asleep. The MPs came back to be relieved, but did not waken him, or even grouse when they saw their sandwiches were gone. They tiptoed out to change the guard.

When the bugle blew at five the duty officer shook him and turned him over to the reception center. The guard there sent him out with a German trusty to wash up and eat. At nine he was back to face the officer of the day, who cursed the boy for making him start interrogation so early and the trusty for letting the boy into the mess hall without the interrogation.

At this first screening of PWs one man of the Team always sat in with the officer of the day, to save time later on. This day was Fred's rotation. Corporal Maurer gave them his name again; the lieutenant wrote in on the muster. At "name of parents," the corporal began to talk. He told them about the doctor, but the officer of the day could not follow fast enough to write it all down.

The doctor had practiced in Trebbin for many years, until in 1939 someone remembered that five years before he had spoken against the Party. So he was forced to move his practice to Berlin, hoping that memories there were shorter than in the country. Even though he was against the regime, and refused to join the Deutsche Arztebund,* and was over military age too, he volunteered as a field surgeon when the war came and operated on the Russian front till a shell fragment tore into his right knee. And even after he was discharged, lamed for life, to take up private practice again, he never hid his opposition. It was only his value to the sick of the city that kept him out of a concentration camp. The boy told them about his mother, who spoke excellent English and had taught some of it to him; and about his kid brother Klaus.

The G-2 lieutenant interrupted, with his Waterman poised over the questionnaire. "I don't care at all about your father's life history, Corporal, or much about your own. I do want to

* League of German (Nazi) Surgeons.

know what your unit is and where, and what division it belongs to, and where the division command post is. Answer me that."

But the boy shook his head. He had torn out the second leaf of his Soldbuch (the duty officer had not even missed it) as soldiers were ordered to do in case of capture, but seldom did. That was the leaf which listed their combat and replacement history.

"I can't say more than is written in my Soldbuch, Herr Leutnant."

And the lieutenant had to let it go at that, because of the Geneva Convention.

"You're deep," was all he said.

It was only later, when he came to trust Americans, that the corporal told the rest.

He was only nineteen now. At seventeen, like all German boys, he had been given a draft number and called to serve his year in the Labor Corps. But because of the training he had picked up in his father's clinic, they let him volunteer in Air Force Replacement, instead of digging ditches. Each branch of the Wehrmacht had two equal forces, replacement and combat. Replacement inducted and trained the recruits. It issued Corporal Maurer his dogtag and sent him to a six-month cadet school at the university to learn first aid and pharmacy. Before he got through he was eighteen, and old enough for active service. He went to combat; first to anti-aircraft at Tempelhof Field in Berlin. But the big attacks had not started, so they assigned him to the 88th Flak Battalion at Cassino as medical supply corporal. From the monastery on the mountaintop his battalion fought off the American raiders, no doubt singing "Lili Marlene" as the MP had heard them, while they swiveled with the Vierling* and gave Kesselring's artillery freedom to sweep the defile below. And no GI forgot that German fire had held up Fifth Army for months at Cassino. Even when

---

* 20 mm. four-barreled anti-aircraft gun.

Eaker's planes pulverized the ancient abbey in March, it was not till May that the tide of Fifth poured through to Rome.

With the loss of Cassino what remained of the unit merged with Flak Battalion 852, of the 9th Flak Division. The corporal was shipped to Pfalzburg in Lorraine—only twenty kilometers from the Sarrebourg cage where he was telling his story.

They had not been there a week before Seventh Army tanks surrounded the position and cut them off. He was frightened that day, he admitted. His battery was set up on top of the gateway in the old city wall. Three Shermans churned around behind the wall and stood between him and Germany, slowly depressing their sights to blast the strongpoint into dust. The crumbled pink stone would not have withstood one round, let alone three, and their pom-poms were no more use against the Shermans than peashooters against a rhinoceros.

Most of the crew threw up their hands and surrendered to the tanks. Neither the corporal nor the Team knew it, but the rest of them had passed through this very cage and were already mending roads in France before he was walked under the welcome sign. The old gateway at Pfalzburg still stands.

Corporal Maurer did not surrender. He took a high jump from the top of the wall, into the town square, and then he had to run. He couldn't run east into the muzzles, so he ran west, around the statue of Erckmann-Chatrian. It was almost dark, and easy to hide in the woods. There did not seem to be any fixed line such as his father had described from the First War. Without knowing how, he found himself at the edge of Sarrebourg next sunrise. American signs and vehicles and troops grew thicker with each kilometer. He scuttled into the barnyard of the first undamaged house he saw. He was not deserting, he was trying to escape capture.

For three weeks he hid in the friendly cellar, living on the iron ration* in his knapsack and the little his protectors could

* Eiserne Portion, an emergency ration of coffee, rusk, salt, and meat concentrate.

spare him. He still refused to tell which house it was, and G-2 did not press him.

"They even gave me one of your good rations called K," he said, "but I could hardly expect it would repeat. I cannot think how they got hold of such good American food."

"I can," muttered the lieutenant.

"Finally there was no more to eat, so last night I was forced to surrender. That was not cowardly. Please to inscribe me as a prisoner of war."

He still stood at attention, gazing defiantly around the shed to prove his bravery. "Many more would surrender," he blurted out, "except for the stories of cruelty we are taught in the Wehrmacht. But the lieutenant and the guards were kind to me last night. Besides, my father has always been against the regime. Yet do not think he is anything but true German, as I am. We have suffered from the regime. Since they came in we have not spoken English at home as we used to when I was a child; therefore I have forgotten much, and you must excuse me."

"Take him away," the lieutenant commanded.

Corporal Maurer was hardly more than a child now. He had high cheekbones, the skin over them pink and taut as a crab apple, and small white teeth like the kernels of bantam corn, and white knuckles too small for his roughened hands, and freckles on his crinkly snub nose. He had taken the delousing bath before being brought in for the interrogation, and the prisoners' barber had given him a close haircut. His pointed ears stood away from his wirebrush-cropped skull. The promise of a sandy mustache struggled on his upper lip, but he hardly seemed old enough to shave.

He spoke English carefully, with a good schoolboy accent. He bowed like a schoolboy reciting a lesson he is proud to have learned. He frowned when he thought and he smiled all the time he talked, as if he worked things out the hard way first. After the G-2 lieutenant had listed him in the roster, the trusty, a huge German artillery sergeant, took him to the equipment shed for his blanket roll and mess kit. The lieutenant looked after him.

"Let him send a Red Cross postcard home first, if he wants to," he called. Then he turned to Fred. "That kid can't be a spy; he's too young. Not only that, he's too—" he struggled for the word—"too happy. I know I'm supposed to be a ferret, but a sharp nose ought to smell out the good as well as the bad. That lieutenant on duty last night has got spies on the brain. He sees one under every stone. Well, that's my job to judge, not his. If the kid knows his stuff, why don't they put him to work in the dispensary? The T/5 has been transferred, and Doc Brophy needs a man. He could interpret for the sick ones, and show up the ones who pretend to be sick."

So Corporal Maurer was assigned to the cadre, which meant he got PX rations like the trusties. Like all the prisoners, he received the same pay from Uncle Sam as he had got in the Wehrmacht—in his case, corporal's pay of seven dollars and thirty cents a month at ten Reichsmarks to the dollar. Besides that, he earned eighty cents a day for working. He worked silently and quickly, even sternly. The Germans had left the Sarrebourg barracks in such a hurry three months before that their drugs were still stacked on the shelves of the high-ceilinged dispensary. It seemed foolish not to use them up.

A unit from the Black Forest had been stationed in the barracks before Third Infantry took Sarrebourg, and the white walls of the clinic were stenciled with homesick mottoes like "Black Forest, my homeland!" and "We are the sons of the mountains." For punctuation marks they used little colored decalcomanias of an edelweiss.

The boy climbed around the shelves like a monkey. He could read the German labels better than Doc Brophy, the medical silver-bar, and translate them into English for him. He was almost as deft as the doctor himself at wrapping bandages and he did it with a technique the prisoners seemed to know. Not that the cage got many serious cases from the field, for they were shipped to the big hospitals, but there were often accidents and quarrels and even self-mutilation in the cage itself.

The doctors were afraid of an epidemic of dysentery, or typhoid, or even typhus. The Swiss inspectors had a right to close the cage down if they saw fit. The commandant didn't want that to happen, with such a good stream of prisoners flowing through. The prisoners were frightened too; they had been educated to fear Americans. The shock of capture itself was enough to terrify them, and how could they know that the outgoing truckloads passing the incoming at the welcome sign were not headed for the mass extermination they had all heard described by veterans from Russia? The whole German Army believed that Roosevelt—their propaganda sheets called him "Jewboy Rosenfeld"—had ordered the castration of any SS men captured alive, and some penalty, only maybe lighter, for the ordinary soldiers and aviators.

The cage was dirty and cold and it stank, but they were safe as long as they stayed in it. Anything was better than what might lie outside. The PWs often invented illnesses and aches for an excuse to visit the sick bay and so put off the day when they would be shipped out. Malingering in German fooled the American doctors, but the corporal had seen it before and was not fooled.

"Some are truly sick, Herr Leutnant, but many pretend. Do not be severe, for it is only that they are a little afraid. In the Luftwaffe the penalty was a day without food, besides the shame of being caught. I have been afraid myself so I cannot accuse them. But when I was fighting against you I used to take down all names and complaints in the outer tent and put a small circle on the paper of those who seemed to be pretending. They did not see my circle, but the doctor inside, when he saw it, treated them or discharged them as he thought best. It was simple and nobody was shamed. In the field he did not have time to investigate all, or to treat everyone who came, or even to be angry with the pretenders. When he saw a circle, he just prescribed a day without food as the first part of their treatment. Soon there were no pretenders."

He kept the stockroom cleaner than the American T/5 who had preceded him. Instruments and bottles were always ready on their shelves, and there were no more empty or corkless jars, misplaced needles, or dirty dressings. The T/5 had seen no reason why the prisoners rated American medical treatment at all, since they had been killing Americans only a few days before.

But First Lieutenant Brophy, MC, did not think of that side at all. He was glad to have a German weed out the fakes and stand by at the real cases—almost as good as an interne, besides being an interpreter for him. And if he did not know the English name of a drug, First Lieutenant Brophy gave the corporal the Latin name from the pharmacopoeia, and next day the boy had memorized it in all three languages. When First Lieutenant Brophy left his struggling practice in Hartford to do his part in the war he had not expected to draw a PW cage in Lorraine. It was not his idea of men in white, or in khaki either. He wanted action or home. Teaching his new aide pharmacy, and learning German from him, gave him a new interest in the war.

One afternoon at the end of the clinic, when the corporal had been working a fortnight, he saluted First Lieutenant Brophy as usual before locking up and said, "If I can help end the war by going back into Germany, Herr Leutnant," he bent his head to the east, "I should not be afraid. If only to tell them how foolish to fight against such equipment as you have. He would never have started this if He had seen what I have. Penicillin, for instance, as much as you want. And spare parts for vehicles which can be interchanged. Also, I could tell them that some of you are friends. Please do not take this lightly. I have thought about it hard, ever since I came to your dispensary. You are the only one I know how to approach."

"I know nothing of such things, Corporal," Brophy answered stiffly, "but I should not like to lose you. And, Corporal, the British pronounce my grade 'Leftenant,' and the Germans 'Loitnant' as you have just done, but the Americans pronounce it 'Lewtenant.' Not that it matters much between us medical men, but you might just like to know to perfect your English. And we are not friends."

The corporal leaned forward on an impulse. "Do you know, sir, that the German slang for Americans is Amis? In French that means friends, thought not pronounced the same."

Brophy needed him in the dispensary and could not imagine how a boy of nineteen could help "end the war." But any chance to end it was better than none, for he was homesick. The next day he walked into the Team's office in the corner of the Kaserne.

"The rest of us don't know what monkey business you fellows do, Captain," he told Pete. "Except to be sure it *is* monkey business when you pick up our smartest prisoners instead of sending them to the work details."

"Why does it surprise you? That's the way Uncle Sam picked us, you know—choice of the smartest."

First Lieutenant Brophy swiped at him with a stethoscope. "I have the smartest kid working for me, smarter than you or anyone else I've seen since I left Hartford, and he wants to end the war. I don't want to lose him, but if he's in your line maybe I'd better give him up and find another orderly."

Pete nodded. The recruits always wanted to end the war—who didn't?—whatever their real motives might be, greed or fun or faith. He pushed the Camels toward Brophy. "What's his name?"

"Karl Maurer."

"Oh, yeah, the Luftwaffe corporal who serenaded the MPs. I thought he must be smart. The one the OD called Happy."

"It's a good word for him." Brophy nodded.

"Fred told me about him. I should have got around to him

before. If you think you can spare him, we might have a job for him. But don't ask what kind of job, and if you send him in he can't go back even if we don't take him."

"You'll take him all right, and a little appreciation to me, please, for being willing to give up my prize assistant."

"Gee, thanks. Now you won't have so much time to write V-mail to your girl in Hartford. Such self-sacrifice deserves at least a Silver Star. I'll mention it to the general next time he comes to call. Greater love than this hath no man."

Brophy brought him into Pete's office the next afternoon at closing time, so as to make the visit seem casual, then tactfully disappeared, leaving the corporal standing awkwardly among the half-dozen who had heard the rumor there might be a new German Joe. He looked around the room shyly, like a school-boy, but proudly, like a soldier of the Wehrmacht in the propaganda books.

"Sit down, Corporal," Pete said. "You needn't be bashful with us. I want you to feel you are among friends."

He spoke in German. The corporal sat down, not to make himself comfortable but to obey an order. He sat upright, with his hands on his knees. He looked respectful and attentive and alert, wary even. They could tell he was nervous, for his knuckles were whiter than they should have been. Who wouldn't be nervous? He declined Pete's offer of a cigarette. He wanted it, for even the cadre didn't get much tobacco, and ordinary PWs got none. But he wasn't ready yet to accept a favor. He looked from one to the other of them like a kid waiting for the hard question in an exam. Pete blew smoke rings from his own cigarette.

"Now don't tell me why you want to work for us, Corporal, if you don't choose to. I have no right to ask"—and indeed this was the first time he had ever even wondered—"but you can tell me if you feel like it."

Corporal Maurer shut his eyes and frowned. "I want to work for freedom, sir," he said, "that's all. Für die Freiheit."

There was an awkward pause. Freedom was a word used in orders of the day, and sometimes in the editorials of *Stars and Stripes*. There is a soldier's vocabulary at each extreme: the monosyllables he speaks but never writes, and the long words he reads but never utters. "Freedom," dropped into that barred prison room, was as shocking as smut in a parlor, and it was an American who blushed.

The boy opened his eyes and ended the pause himself. "I don't want to pull a gun, though I suppose it might be necessary for my own safety sometimes."

Pete smiled. "It might, but we wouldn't ask you to go out of your way for sabotage or assassination. We're not gunmen ourselves. Just information."

"It sounds worse, Captain," he smiled back, "when you word it that way than when Fritz Gruber sits at the controls of our Vierling. Before I was captured I kept thinking how little he understood what he shot at. Since I was captured I have been thinking that most of your troops, if you will excuse me, know too little about us. Only what you hear from Doctor Goebbels. He is not a medical doctor."

"You see," someone whispered from the shadows, "he wants to educate us. That's always the way with amateurs."

"You know, I suppose," Pete suggested, "that you would be a traitor to your own country?"

"Excuse me, Herr Kapitän," he broke out, "I do not agree. My father would not agree. I should be more loyal to Germany than Doctor Goebbels has been."

"Perhaps not," Pete said drily, "but the Gestapo would certainly agree, and they are the ones that might count."

"Do you Germans really think you have a chance to win?" boomed the colonel from his dark observant corner of the room. "Psychologically it is an interesting delusion, and a tenacious one."

The boy flushed. He wheeled toward the voice. "I don't know, sir. I don't think so myself, but that has nothing to do with my being here. If He deserved to win, I should still fight for Him, no matter what the chances. As to that, the boys in the battalion think what the officers tell us."

"And the officers?"

"They have to sound confident, sir; it's their business. I have never heard the true opinion of any officer."

"Touché, Colonel," croaked Documents.

"How much pay would you expect, Corporal?" asked Finance.

"I don't expect any, sir. I could not accept it."

"Oh, yes, you have to take some money. The United States government won't hire anyone without pay. Our usual salary is —— dollars a month. That is —— Reichsmarks." *

The boy stared. His corporal's pay was seventy-three Reichsmarks.

"We can keep it for you till the end of the war, Corporal," Pete said awkwardly. "It will help you when you get back to medical school."

"He can't have insurance, though," muttered Finance. "It isn't regulation unless they have dependents, and he's too young to be married."

"Pipe down, Shylock," Security whispered to him. "Do you want to make sure of losing a good man?"

After a moment Pete spoke up. "How do we know we can trust you, Corporal? Maybe our colleague Colonel Skorzeny sends you to us."

The corporal spread his hands. It was clear he did not recognize Skorzeny's name, just as few GIs would have recognized the name of 109.

"I don't suppose you can know," he answered, "but you could find out something about my father from the doctors of France and maybe of America. He is known everywhere. He even has a friend who lives in your capital. At least, he was a friend before the war."

* Deleted by request.

They pricked up their ears. All of them had taken their training in Washington and in the woods around it, the same training they were passing on to the Joes.

"I don't know him myself, but I have heard my father speak of him. His name is Doctor Schober. He is not a physician but an economist. I think he works in your State Department."

"And you would be willing to jump into Germany in your own uniform to find out what information we might ask of you?" the colonel badgered him.

"Yes, sir. That is what I came to say."

"And you know you would be shot or hanged if you were caught?"

He nodded.

"And you would give away to us the location of your own 852nd Battalion? If we didn't know it already, I mean," he added hastily.

"Yes, sir."

"Knowing that it would be bombed?"

The corporal did not answer, but he nodded, with his eyes on the ground.

"And without pay?"

"I decline to be paid for it," he said harshly. "If you must allot money, keep it for my father so that he can buy equipment for our clinic after the war."

At a nod from the colonel, Pete stood up. "Well, Corporal, write down your father's and Doctor Schober's names and addresses for us here. We will think for a while. Meanwhile, I am afraid we cannot send you back to the dispensary or out into the barracks with the other prisoners. You will have a room of your own for a week, till we decide. And above all, don't speak of this conversation to anyone, understand? I mean not to any American. You won't see any Germans for a while."

"Zu Befehl," which means "At your orders."

He stood at the door, ready to be guided out. Pete punched

the desk bell for the guardhouse. A sergeant of the guard came in.

"Take this prisoner to the cell on the third floor."

"Yes, sir."

As the door closed on the khaki and the blue-gray, Pete smiled. "There you are at last, Colonel. The Christlike Joe you spoke about the other day. The pure-hearted traitor."

"You needn't laugh," the colonel answered. "I don't expect you know much about music, but Wagner has a phrase that seems to describe this kid. The pure in heart made wise by love."

He hummed the theme from *Parsifal:* "Durch Mitleid wissend, der reine Thor."

"I don't understand you young cynics." He sighed. "There *are* people who take risks for their beliefs, you know, without thinking of reward or excitement. It isn't stylish, but I hope my own son may have enough honesty—"

"To spy on F. D. R.?"

"Watch your step, Captain!"

"Well," shrugged Pete, "we have certainly picked up the whole range lately, what with a crook like the Tiger and a Tarzan like Paluka, and now this innocent."

Corporal Maurer walked up the three flights of worn granite steps ahead of the American sergeant. Through the window on the landing he could see a thousand compatriots shuffling in the line to the mess shack, tinkling their zinc kits. Supper would probably be not much different from the supper thousands of American PWs were getting at the same time beyond the Rhine, except for real coffee.

The cell itself was built of wattled steel; the two dormers were barred with iron rods. But it had its own stove, with a binful of wood beside it, and a real two-by-six cot covered with United States Army blankets, instead of a roll laid on the stone floor.

"Das ist prima!" The corporal laughed to the sergeant.

The sergeant closed the steel door and threw the bolt from outside, then opened the wicket and leaned on the little shelf.

"Don't worry, buddy. Nobody ever stays in this cell very long. You can use the bucket in the corner, but put the lid back. Sorry to speak of it to a guest, but some of your pals in barracks aren't too careful. I'll send you up some chow. But don't expect sympathy from an American KP like you get from me. A new set of Uncle Sam's fatigues, too, so you can get rid of that old fleasack you've been wearing the last few years."

He clanged the wicket shut. His prisoner nodded absently; he was gazing down at the crowd in the compound.

That night the colonel made an entry in his notebook: "No. 7. Subversion NG. Admits fear. Too honest for job? If so, reliable for followup. Query: mental courage vs. physical?"

Corporal Maurer stayed on ice only four days. Security had a German Who's Who which told about the doctor and even named his two sons. Someone in Washington got hold of Schober, who had a title something like Special Assistant in the Division of Economic Coordination, and a Canadian wife. The combination sounded reliable. Switzerland confirmed by code cable that the doctor was as anti-Nazi as a German could be and still survive. So his son was in.

Fred spirited him out of the cell the night his clearance came through, with the Luftwaffe uniform in a barracks bag over his shoulder. At night, so there would be no prisoners around to recognize him, and so he could not remember the way from the cage down to the Schloss and the Golden Well. All traffic on the ten-mile convoy route was blacked out. The jeep showed nothing but the little cat's eyes. Even if there had been a moon the firs would have hidden it. The road was full of potholes tailored to remind the spine that the truck, quarter ton, has no springs. Sometimes Fred had to get out and make sure he was really on the road, wondering whether a few lampposts would not have been worth in time and materiel what

72

they might have given away to snipers and the Luftwaffe. A kilometer ahead of the Schloss he tied a handkerchief over the boy's eyes. He had to guide him like a blind man up the spiral stone stairs to the field office. The Schloss was three hundred years old, but no one had got around to putting a rail on those stairs; they were a hazard in the dark, even with your eyes open and a flashlight in your hand.

He took off the handkerchief and sat the boy on the sofa. The contract was waiting, a contract between Karl Maurer and the Government of the United States of America which WITNESSETH:

that employer shall pay employe the sum of —— dollars* each month while said contract is in force;

that employe shall faithfully perform all duties which may be assigned to him by the employer;

that employe further agrees a) to subscribe freely and without reservation to any oath of office prescribed by employer and b) to keep forever secret this employment and all information which he may obtain by reason thereof; and FURTHER that this contract is a voluntary act of employe, undertaken without duress.

"Voluntary." The corporal put his finger on the word, smiling up at Fred over the schnapps-candle, as if he had scored a point in a close deal. He affixed his fingerprints to the bottom of the sheet, and they both signed it. "In the Reich," he laughed, "criminals are fingerprinted, not soldiers. I guess I am a criminal now."

"Maybe so," said Fred, "but we're calling you Happy from now on, so that no one need ever know your real name."

He reflected that the officer of the day had chosen the perfect adjective, for "happy," like the French "exalté," carries just that note of vision which adds gaiety to faith.

The storekeeper, without curiosity, carried his barracks bag to the raftered attic where the GIs slept, to hang with the

* Deleted by request.

bags of the other Joes who had joined before. Six of them hung from the collarbeams, swaying a little when a gust hit the roof. Like Bluebeard's closet. Next morning he would stencil on the bag the single name "Happy."

Fred locked the contract and the snapshots in the field safe, under a new manila file headed with the same name. Happy had passed from the service of the Third Reich to the service of the United States. From now on, till he was repatriated at the end of the war, nobody who did not know the combination of that safe would know his name was Karl Maurer. From now on he was anonymous.

"You will take care of my pictures, please?" He smiled as Fred tied the handkerchief again. "I shall want them when I come back from my mission. If I should not come back, tell my father that I volunteered. You did not force me, as the regime does by threatening one's family."

"Don't worry, kid." Fred patted him on the back. "You'll come back all right. They always do."

But they didn't, not always.

He followed Fred down the stairs again, blindfolded, his hand on Fred's shoulder, hugging the wall, and into the jeep. They started the winding two miles up to the German Joe-house. When they were out of sight of the Schloss Fred let him take off the blindfold.

"I am *not* ashamed of signing," he blurted suddenly.

So Fred knew he was, a little. "We couldn't exchange you back to the Luftwaffe now anyway; you'd have to return to the cell and wait a couple of weeks for a labor detail, after all the prisoners now in the cage have been processed. If you want to do that, let me know before we reach the next house. After that it will be too late to change your mind. No more dispensary detail, however you decide. They would not be too easy on you in the road gang either, if they knew you had run out on us."

Happy began counting the alternatives on his fingers, keep-

74

ing his eyes open for a house. "But it is plenty tough. If He should win, it would be—the way it is, forever, in Germany. He can't win anyway, as the officer in the dark said. Without Him the end will be easier for us. He has done much for Germany, I don't deny, like building the Autobahns, but it is slavery. I can't have anyone think, even in the regime, that I am afraid. You know, don't you, Herr Leutnant, that I am not afraid?"

"Everyone knows you're not afraid; you're braver than I am."

Fred knew he sounded pompous. He knew Happy was not afraid of the Gestapo and still less of the road gang. He was afraid of something in his own mind. He was afraid of the word spy.

"Well," Happy sighed, "after the war things will be better, even if you win. My father says that since there are good Germans and good Amis there may be a real Reich of the world, as he had hoped to see after the other war."

He had convinced himself all over again. This time Fred was sure he would stick.

"Ja," the boy murmured, "für die Freiheit."

The jeep pulled up in front of the Golden Well. The other Joes were waiting in the day room to start their supper. They ate late like civilians, not at five like the GIs or the prisoners. Fred called Vati and introduced the recruit to him.

"Vati, this is Happy. Let's have a schnapps together."

They drank a toast to what they could not utter. Vati himself was never to know Happy's real name. Fred left them together from then on and went back to the Schloss.

The Team all liked to sneak up to eat at the Golden Well once in a while, for Monsieur Apfel's cooking was much better than their own, even though it started with the same ingredients. It was a week before Fred had the chance. They day he did get up, the Joes were playing baseball. That was part of Vati's instruction. As Fred drove past the orchard Happy hit a double—a smart crack of the bat and a fast sprint to second. The others cheered him, except the Tiger, who never cheered.

In one week the good food had filled Happy out. He looked taller and huskier; his sleeves, anyway, seemed shorter and too tight for his muscles. His mustache was almost a real mustache. He was growing into a man.

He winked at Fred from second base, balancing on his toes, squatting with his hands on his knees, getting ready to steal third. He did not wave. It was part of Security's rules that outdoors the Joes should not recognize any Americans.

Monsieur Apfel rang his handbell from the door of the inn. The game broke up at once. The Joes trooped in to lunch, Happy and two others walking together, their arms about one another's shoulders. Until you heard them speak German, you would think they were a bunch of GIs off duty.

Each Joe was in special charge of one American, as campers are in charge of a counselor. Happy was on Fred's list and Paluka on Pete's. The Tiger, as far as he accepted counsel, was on the colonel's.

Vati said Happy was the smartest Joe in the classroom, even though he was the youngest. "You ought to see the act that the Tiger puts on with him, pretending to be a hard-boiled top sergeant chewing out a rookie: 'Achtung! Get up! Sit down! Roll over!' And Happy makes out he's scared to death, stammering 'Ja*wohl*, Herr Stabsfeldwebel,' and trying to salute straightarm every time he rolls. It's a riot. He's smart, so smart that I put him in the same room with Père Nod, who is smart too, but in some different way."

Père Nod had come back from his week's exile in the French Joehouse. Paluka's love affair with Giovanna drove him out. He offered to jump into Germany, or go back to his parish under a priest's oath of secrecy, or wait at the German Joehouse for assignment. Anything but stay under the same roof with Giovanna and Paluka.

None of them ever discovered the name of the battle-order

instructor; he wasn't really one of them, but came down every other day from some higher echelon in G-2 and drove back without waiting for mess. They just called him "Captain." He could chalk down on Vati's blackboard any German table of organization from army group to machine-gun squad. He told Fred that one day Happy approached him after class.

"It seems that you know more about our army than we do ourselves, Herr Kapitän."

"I don't know about that," the captain answered morosely, carefully erasing the blackboard, "but I certainly know more about your army than I do about my own. Anyway, let's not call it your army any more. We are both part of Uncle Sam's army now, my boy, whether you like it or not."

"I will like it better when I get my mission, sir. Now I just listen to the guns. But I know one must study before he is trusted alone."

"I don't know anything about that; it is not my field," the captain answered stiffly. He raised his harsh voice. "Don't try to pump me. I don't know that you or any of the others are going on missions. Remember you are not to talk shop at the station—or anywhere else. Watch your tongue, soldier."

"Zu Befehl, Herr Kapitän."

"But you were right about the crew of the Würzburg radar this morning." The captain softened. "I should have known there were three."

"It is only that I happened to take the right wheel and earphones once, when the regular signalman was killed," said Happy respectfully.

It was the twelfth of February, three days after Third Infantry had wiped out the Colmar pocket and four days before the Tiger and Paluka were to drop. They were all documented and equipped. The only thing left was to enter the last-minute dates on their forged travel papers, so there would be no time lag on them the morning they landed behind the lines.

Once an operation had been laid on, the Joes who were to

drop grew strained and nervous up till the moment itself. You could tell when they were going to drop by their silence and by the greed with which they ate, as if behind the lines they might never eat again. The tension spread to the others too, without their knowing why. The Tiger was no exception. He had stopped boasting. He did not open his mouth except to shovel food into it, and just as soon as the chairs were pushed back he went to stand by himself, frowning out the big picture-window that faced eastward toward the Rhine and Germany.

Only Paluka did not seem to have a care. Pete had literally dragged him from Giovanna's bed at the French Joehouse and laughed when he described the weight. Paluka felt fine now that he had left her. He had found that the Saxon artillery-man who had served on the Russian front—the one who had identified the 5 cm.—had picked up a little of his own language. Against the rules, the two of them were chattering and joking in Russian. Nobody else understood them, but it was easy to see that adventure suited Paluka better than love.

That very evening Pete came down from the cage with a top secret request from G-2. The colonel opened it in the field office at the Schloss. It asked where the command posts of 9th Flak and 25th Infantry Divisions were. Probably somewhere southeast of Mannheim, G-2 thought. Elements of 9th Flak had been found supporting rear-guard action west of the Rhine, but 25th Infantry was only a rumor brought in by a talkative PW. Neither division had been committed as a unit. 25th Infantry had not even been reported since it was destroyed at Stalingrad; it sounded like a new formation with an old name, built up in reserve to contain any bridgeheads that Seventh Army might establish on the Rhine. Perhaps they were both from the Wehrmacht pool, assigned to combat where needed. PW interrogation was inconclusive. Observation requested, wrote G-2, as to location, strength, and armor in area Ammersee-Mannheim, with report on or before 22 February.

Happy's battalion had been part of 9th Flak, which at least proved that it existed. But he did not know where the division headquarters was, just as many GIs at the front would not know Seventh Army headquarters was at Lunéville. At that time the Germans still held all the Rhine bridges except far north in the swamps of the British zone, and a foothold on the west bank up to a few kilometers below Strasbourg. The Joe who went in to find this information would have to parachute and find his own hole through the line to get back by the deadline. He would drop in by plane, but would have to get out by himself. The Army was moving fast now. Nobody knew where the line would be by the twenty-second. The colonel hoped it would not be the river itself, for the Germans would surely blow the bridges if they had to retreat that far; and then the Joe would have to swim, and air recce had reported the Rhine was mined. No Joe had ever had to swim the Rhine.

"It's definitely a tourist mission," he observed. "I couldn't trust the Tiger for that kind of information, even if we didn't have his morale operation so carefully set up already. Whoever goes in will have to travel solo, and light, and fast. He can't take a radio because covering so much ground he'd never have time to set up in a safe place. He'll have to get back on his own and bring his report verbally. There isn't time to lay on another flight before the sixteenth, yet I don't want to scrub the Tiger and Paluka. The only thing I see is to send a third Joe with them."

"The A-26 is too small for three," Operations objected, "especially if it has to haul the Tiger's tube."

The colonel stroked his chin. "Let's cut him down then; maybe his operation doesn't need quite as much as he thought. Cram his pack tight. You were right, anyway, a tube drop isn't safe any more, the way the Krauts are on the watch now.

Pick your Joe and get his cover fixed up in time to drop with the others the night of the sixteenth. So long as he doesn't take up too much room I can fix it with the Air Force to carry three. They shouldn't need their rear gunner if they move as fast as they claim. Find a pinpoint. I suggest this side of the Ammersee, then route your man to Kempten and Ulm and Mannheim."

He laid his centimeter scale on the wall map. "That's about four hundred kilometers in five days; not too fast for a simple objective."

It took most of the evening to find a good pinpoint on the 1:20,000 captured German staff maps. The best place that showed up was an open field nineteen kilometers southwest of the lake called the Ammersee, deep in Bavaria, way beyond the Rhine. The plane could drop off the Tiger and Paluka at their pinpoints, only a little east of the river, and carry the third Joe on to his.

The Team picked Happy for the third Joe, partly because he weighed only a hundred and thirty, and partly because medical cover was the safest and quickest. The route was chosen so he could zigzag from the pinpoint back northwestward toward the river and cross it on the big railroad bridge connecting Mannheim on the east bank to Ludwigshafen on the west. Seventh Army might even get to Ludwigshafen by the twenty-second. Or maybe, if the Third to the left and First French to the right had a bridgehead by then, he could cross at Mainz or Speyer or Strasbourg. At the worst, he would have to try swimming. It was dangerous to gamble a couple of German divisions against the chance of one man getting across, but the A-26 couldn't carry another. It was too crowded even with three.

Fred went up to break the news to Happy on the morning of the fourteenth. They walked out into the apple orchard behind the Golden Well.

"Your chance has come, kid."

Happy shook himself a little and gasped, but he looked Fred in the eye with his crinkly smile. "I'm glad it has. You Amis have trusted me. After the war, please think of us as I have thought of you. Above all, don't worry about me, and for myself I have only one request. Take care of my pictures."

He said it in German—"Bitte, verwahren Sie meine Lichtbilder gut," as though he didn't trust his English to tell how precious his family's photographs were.

"Don't worry about yourself, either. We don't often send a soldier in so soon after he enlists, but you've learned more in a week than the others in a month. We don't worry, so why should you? We know you can swim if you have to, and keep your eyes open and mouth shut when you're on the road. We'll have a briefing on that road tomorrow morning. Maybe you *will* end this war a little ahead of schedule."

It was easy to equip Happy. They simply got down his own uniform from the bag in the attic—it had been cleaned a little, but not too much—and put his own long overcoat on him with the red and white brassard. They even let him keep his own dogtag. Usually they stamped out a new one with a fake serial number, but there was no time to set up the press. Anyway, if the Gestapo got as far as checking a Joe's dogtag back to his induction center, he was as good as lost already. Besides, Happy wanted to keep it, and Fred knew why without his telling: so that if he were killed his family could find him.

For his family's sake they did have to give him a new name and hence a new Soldbuch. They chose Karl Steinberg for his cover name, with an address on Cecilienstrasse in Magdeburg. Air Force photos showed the street had been bombed so the Gestapo could not check. And Happy knew Magdeburg well enough to sound plausible if they questioned him.

Documents and his two forgers copied the entries and signatures from Happy's own Soldbuch. He remembered all the entries from the two pages he had destroyed. German procedure was to cross out the units when a man transferred, but leave them legible. That far there would be no inconsistency. Then they forged an entry for HQ Company of Third Flak Training Regiment in the barracks at Munich, and a separate transfer, to be hidden till needed, detaching him to combat assignment with Mountain Regiment 136. One beauty of the German Einheits-Prinzip, or unity of command, was that they switched men around, Army to Air Force and vice versa, so there was nothing strange about this transfer. The Luftwaffe started the war as the elite service of the three; it had always been overmanned. Now that it had been knocked out of the air the ground forces drew steadily on its useless manpower, not without a grim pleasure.

The choice of Mountain Regiment 136 is where battle-order scholarship came in. On the eighth that regiment had slipped out of the Colmar pocket west of the Rhine, and moved north to Trier. This retreat was so recent and so ignominious that Flak Training in Munich could not be expected to know it; yet Happy would not be in danger of running into the regiment he was supposed to join. That was the second worst luck a Joe could have.

The false Soldbuch was so plausible that Happy thought it was his own till he came to sign the cover name across the snapshot stapled inside the blue paper of the front cover. It was artificially dog-eared and dirty and stained. It even had a few errors, for it was suspicious to forge too perfectly. In the back flap Documents stuck an identity card of the Medical Corps, made out in Happy's cover name.

"Just remember you're still a medical corporal," Fred told him, "but that your name from now on is not Maurer but Steinberg."

"Am I likely to forget my own name?" He laughed. "Don't worry. I'll bring the two divisions back under my cap. Once you make up your mind, the rest is easy." And he actually patted Fred on the shoulder to reassure him.

"I just want to be certain that you would let my father know if anything should happen to me—not that it will. He would not be ashamed of me, but he would want to know."

"Don't you worry about that, kid. You're keeping your old tag, the one you wore in combat, and we're keeping your old book for proof. Only remember the Wehrmacht has your number too, so don't show it."

They were worried for him just the same. He was too young to waste, and some of them, without saying so, even to themselves, shared something of the same dream for after the war. Paluka could take care of himself anywhere, and Fred did not care what happened to the Tiger, so long as he didn't blow the others. He could not tell Happy that since he had been in Germany a month before, the whole country for a hundred miles beyond the Rhine was on the watch for American chutes. As Seventh Army plugged closer to the river, the panic beyond it grew. Every village had an all-night watch. Each forest guard had a brace of police dogs trained to bark at the hum of a plane and at nothing else, and to jump for the throat at their master's nod. That was why Supply issued dog-drag powder. It was kind of a reverse catnip. One Joe had had to kill a dog with a plank because he had no powder and did not dare to shoot.

That panic was why the Joes had to drop well east of their target and work back. With good documents and ordinary luck a man could average a hundred kilometers a day—more, if he worked the Autobahn—and still keep his eyes open. The colonel had given Happy four hundred for five days.

It was dangerous to fly in full moon because the dogs barked more in moonlight and the ground watchers could see the chutes better. It was dangerous in dark moon too, because the pilot could not see the pinpoint. Even the A-26, though it was guided by beams from Belfort and Metz, liked to see the terrain. The sixteenth would be quarter moon, which was best. A Joe had to jump at exactly the right instant. Word had got round the Joehouse, in spite of Vati, how Red had missed his pinpoint because he did not jump at the signal. Was it carelessness? Excitement? Terror? And the dispatcher had to push him through the hole. He landed a dozen kilometers off pinpoint—not bad at three hundred miles an hour—with his shrouds tangled in a tree outside an SS movie house, just as the show let out. Red had not come back.

ive

ghth Air Force put up the Liberators, and sometimes the
26 for the jump operations, complete with pilot and navi-
or. They based on Harrington in England. Being so small
1 fast—a rooftop hopper—the A-26 was safer than a Lib-
tor for a fast climb after the drop. But they only had one to
ure, and the Team could not always get it when they wanted
It was the C model, with the transparent bombardier nose
1 four swiveled fifties in the tail. There wasn't a field any-
ere near the Rhine undamaged enough for the take-off. The
d at Strasbourg was so pockmarked it looked like the man
the moon. The field at Lunéville, laid down for Army CP,
s too small for anything but the Cubs and other light planes
d by generals and couriers. So they used the field at Dijon,
e hundred and twenty miles back westward in France.
Jn the morning of the fourteenth two cars started from the
1loss to the Golden Well to pick up the three Joes. Fred
ive the little Simca with Happy's operation funds and docu-
nts in his own belt and the uniform rolled into a barracks
g in the rumble. Pete drove the command car behind, with

room for the Tiger and Paluka. They parked by the practice jump, out of sight of the inn. The three Joes, still in fatigues, waited in the bar with Vati over untasted bowls of coffee, while the others finished their noisy breakfast in the day room beyond. When the door opened they scrambled to their feet. Vati shook their hands.

"Hals- und Beinbruch," he whispered, so the others wouldn't hear. But as they tiptoed out the tumult in the day room dropped, as they say quiet comes over Death Row when a man heads for the little door.

"They won't pay much attention in class this morning," Vati told Fred on the stoop. "It's always this way the day of an operation."

The five men piled into the two cars. The Simca led, because it was more likely to break down than the command car. It had been taken from a collaborator at Marseille back at the invasion. It had given good service since then, carrying the Joes to places where there was no Army motor pool, or where the Team dared not enter one. In every French village there was a mechanic who could service a Simca, just as you find Ford mechanics at home. But the Germans had bombed the factory long since, and now the little car was held together by makeshift parts devised by the GIs in the Team's own pool. It was standard operation procedure to drive two cars to the take-off, in case of a breakdown. There would be trouble from MPs and real danger from civilians if a German Joe should be caught on the road in France.

The little French car, painted olive drab with a white USA number on the hood, panted up the side of the hill.

"Just remember two things," Fred warned Happy. "From now on you are Steinberg, and I'm going to call you Maurer sometimes, too, hoping you won't answer. The other thing is, as long as you're in France don't speak a word of German. You and I will speak English; or if you want to practice a little French, that will be okay too."

86

Happy nodded. They were already halfway up the side of the Vosges when they started from the Golden Well. Fred reflected that mountains are better barriers between nations than rivers. When you come to think of it, rivers are not barriers at all, he decided; they are avenues. Certainly the Alps around Switzerland and the Pyrenees between France and Spain had stood off invasion more than the Rhine or the St. Lawrence or the Rio Grande. But then they had stood off friendship too. Alsace had been French as often as German, yet the names of the towns and the language of the people and the look of the houses in the villages were as German as they were across the Rhine.

Then, once over the summit of the Vosges, red tile gave way to slate roofs, and stuccoed walls to stone. They were in France again, rolling down into the Burgundian plain. It took four hours to drive back what it had taken Army four months to fight for in the opposite direction. They passed through the little towns of Luxeuil and Remiremont. At every stream there would be a splintered German roadblock on each side, with stacks of rubble around it and maybe the skeleton of a spire beyond. MPs signed them through the obstructions and over the one-way Bailey bridge. The rest of the town would be empty but intact, with miles of untended farmland till the next contact point. They came to Gérardmer, the whole town empty and the buildings unroofed and gutted. They threaded their way toward the lake through the crazy rubble in the streets. The wreckage was as bad as anything in Normandy. It must have been the first destruction Happy had seen since Cassino, and Cassino had been only a single monastery.

"Who did this?" he asked Fred in an awed whisper.

The only man in sight was a hunchback raking leaves in the empty park beside the lake.

"Maybe you, and maybe we. Let's ask the old man. Only, remember, if we did it, it is still your fault for starting the war."

They avoided each other's eyes. The old man straightened on his rake when they stopped beside him. He took a Camel from the pack Fred held forward; then Fred offered him the whole pack.

"It's the Boches who did it," he said. "General Haeckel himself gave the order." He pronounced it "Ékel" as a Frenchman would.

"He gave the people one day to move out. That was the twelfth of October. Then he set fire bombs. To make sure the town was ruined, he fired back into it after you came. Two of your men are still here, for he left delayed-action bombs as well."

He gestured toward the end of the park. "Ah, you should have seen Gérardmer in the old days: opera in the casino, baccarat, roulette, everything; and a hundred boats on our beautiful lake. You may think I am crazy to rake the leaves, but it has always been my job. I am the first man back, because I have no family, so I need no house. The stones in the street are too heavy for me, and there are too many. But I can still rake the leaves. It was not necessary for Monsieur le Général to give such an order. We had done no harm."

At the end of the park to which the old man pointed, two American helmets, with the front-line netting camouflage still on them, hung on crosses like the two German ones above the Golden Well. Fred drove no closer, for the park might be mined. Graves Registration would pick them up soon enough.

The road grew flatter. They passed no more ruins. It was three when they got to Station D, in a village halfway between Langres and Dijon. Station D was a château three hundred years old and three hundred feet long, a staging area where the Joes got their last briefing before the take-off and waited overnight if the operation itself was scrubbed. Many sorties had to be scrubbed even after the take-off, because of Flak or weather, or because the pilot could not pick up the pinpoint.

One Joe had actually taken eight dry runs before he finally jumped.

Station D stands about fifteen miles east of Dijon, in the hamlet of Lux. The little river Tille runs through the meadow back of the huge stone building. A high wall surrounds the forty acres, with an iron gate on the village side. There were never more than two or three Joes in the station at a time, but even for so few the Team had to maintain secrecy, in spite of wasting a whole castle on a couple of Joes and a dozen mechanics. In a French village where all the able-bodied men were still either prisoners in Germany or fighting with Delattre's First French Army, it must not be known that the innocent-looking soldiers in American fatigues were German soldiers themselves.

General Haeckel had used Station D for a signal command post too, four months before. Two Joes had infiltrated it then and knew all about the layout even before Third Infantry captured the town.

"Except in the matter of plumbing," they reported, "Goering himself could not ask for more." So the colonel put in a requisition for it himself, as soon as Haeckel got out.

The Joes were forbidden to pass out through the iron gates, but it was hard to contain them when they had nothing to do before the drop but play checkers and pitch horseshoes. They were ordered, if a Frenchman got inside, to say they were Americans—and say it in English or French. Or, better, to say nothing. The village never suspected they were Germans, because no one in it understood anything but French. It was as fatal to speak German in France as it would have been to speak English in Germany.

Pete's command car rolled in the gate just behind the Simca. It wasn't often that the two cars on this trip could stick together so well. The Tiger and Paluka piled out of the big car and Happy out of the little one. Paluka turned a cartwheel on the grass. Happy stretched out his arms and touched his toes to get rid of the cramp from the long trip.

"The American cars," observed the Tiger, "are worse than an oxcart with square wheels. Now how about something to eat?"

The American mechanics and radiomen and dressers who manned Station D piled out of the row of French doors with Lieutenant Jack, who ran the place, when they heard the cars. Two Joes were there already from Station G, Antonius and Toto, waiting for good flight weather. The Germans shook hands all around, greeting each other in French or English. There was no use now in hiding what they were there for.

"Thou makest France seem less new to me." Happy smiled at Antonius.

Lieutenant Jack heard the Tiger grumbling. He had no use for grumblers. "Nobody eats in my château until he washes," he decreed. "There is no water in the place except what you bring up in a bucket yourselves, but we have a perfectly good river. Toto, get some soap and towels from the PX. Then the bodies can wander down and take off some of the dirt before they come inside."

By "bodies" he meant the three Joes; he affected British phrases.

The five of them walked around the tower and across the courtyard to a tiny dock jutting into the Tille. Tall horse chestnuts leaned over the bank to dip their buttons into the water. There was a dam only a hundred yards downstream, where two housewives of the village were scrubbing their laundry. You could sit on the stones of the dock and wash up. By dipping into a narrow slip, made to berth some long-forgotten canoe, you could soap and rinse your face and arms and hands without getting your feet wet. The river was near the freezing point. Only the sluggish current, bearing down toward the dam, held off the skimming of ice. The Tiger slithered a hand into the cold water, drew it out with a grimace, passed it over his face as a cat washes himself, rubbed off the mud with a towel, and spat eloquently between his teeth at a leaf floating downstream. Happy stripped off his OD undershirt, knelt over the slip, washed, and rubbed himself dry. Pete and Fred followed. But Paluka took off everything.

"Mes amis, we should get used to swimming wider and colder rivers than this."

He dove flat into the Tille, circled, and climbed out on the dock with a grin of his gold teeth. He rubbed himself with the little OD towel, no bigger than his own chest. He lowered his voice. "I mean the Rhine. You notice that the blanchisseuses do not so much as turn their eyes at my nakedness, toward it or away. Hélas! to be ignored at forty-five."

Everyone laughed.

"Thou, mon ami," purred the Tiger, "art the triumph of matter over mind."

They walked back to the château. Lieutenant Jack had the table set, with red and white Burgundy in GI enamel pitchers. Fred told him he had no right to such a racket, when all they got near the front was raw Elbing.

"Why not?" Jack said. "Unvouchered funds, and we're in the heart of the vineyards. Would you refuse milk at a dairy farm?"

"Don't joke," Pete growled. "I'd give all the wine in Burgundy for a pitcher of cowjuice."

The barracks bags were already upstairs on the three new cots set out by Toto and Antonius. Fred expected that the five Joes, on the eve of jumping, would not be able to help show some excitement, if not about their own missions, at least about the war. But the talk was as impersonal as in a boarding house. Happy hardly spoke at all, for he did not know French well enough to keep up. They chattered about wine and cars and women and Happy's two-bagger, but where such talk in a boarding house would have been emptiness, among the dozen foreigners in an alien country, with a French cook passing the Spam, it was plain discretion. The Joes had been well trained.

After supper the Tiger played solitaire at the table, glower-

91

ing and muttering at the cards. Paluka threw darts into the cork board on the wall. The rest lounged in front of the fireplace, which had a double-deck marble mantel with a relief of a naked Diana and her stag. The Americans caught up on old numbers of *Yank* and *Stars and Stripes*. Toto brought in an armful of sticks for the fire. Antonius tuned in the radio to BBC news. That day, BBC broadcast, the Russians had surrounded Breslau and three thousand bombers had attacked Berlin. When he heard that, Happy jumped up from his armchair.

"Can we go outside for a little while?" he whispered.

The Team had got in the habit of whispering. Fred nudged Pete to come along. It seldom snows in Burgundy, but the dampness bites into the bones. Through the drizzle, daylight had sunk imperceptibly into dark. They made Happy put on an OD knitted cap, the kind GIs wear with their helmet liners.

"You treat us as carefully as race horses, don't you?" he mumbled through the wool, and his face came out with a grin.

The Tiger seemed to understand. Pete sometimes wondered whether he didn't know more English than he let on.

"Up till the day of the race," he muttered in French, turning over a card. "After that it is every man for himself. I have heard that the American parachutes are made of paper."

We knew the Tiger didn't mean it; that was his way of showing fear. But Paluka whirled, threatening his teammate with a dart poised in his hairy hand. "Shut up, type of a camel," he ordered hoarsely. "You know it is a lie."

"Pardon, messieurs," the Tiger purred. "I am only teasing the boy." He put the queen of spades over the king of hearts.

Pete opened the glass door, as big as a shop window at home, and the drizzle swept right into the room. The three of them walked out on the broad stone stylobate of the château, to keep off the slushy grass. Fred closed the door behind them.

"I couldn't listen to the radio," Happy blurted. "I cannot

bear to think that German cities are bombed and that I shall guide the planes. My own family lives in Berlin."

Pete patted his shoulder. "They'll be all right, kid. The bombs aren't aimed at civilians. Berlin has the best warning signals and the best shelters in Europe. Just the same, we know how you feel."

"Do you mind, sirs," asked Happy shyly, "if I call you 'thou,' as you call me when we speak in German, and do you mind if we speak a little German now? It will make me feel better."

"Why, sure, kid, go ahead. There's nobody around."

But Fred paused just the same to make sure the kitchen window was closed and nobody was listening from the shadows outdoors.

"I hope you won't forget," Happy started in German, "that I am a German soldier still. When the colonel asked me at the barracks whether we would win the war I tried not to answer. I know we won't. The high command must know it too, but I could not bring myself to say it. There are many German soldiers who think as I do; they tried twice to get rid of Him. Though they failed, there are others who will try again. They hoped that our freedom would come from inside the country before the destruction spread too far. Three thousand bombers over Berlin! It is getting late, while He still sits safe in His bunker. The peace will come for us all only when He is destroyed. If we cannot do it by ourselves inside the Reich, we should help you do it from outside, as German soldiers. But it is hard to be so lonely. That is why I ask to call you both 'thou.' After the war, when the Reich of the world comes— after the horse race, as Herr Tiger says—do not leave Germany alone as I expect to be alone till then. America must be in that Reich too, not like the First War. My father says that is how He got power, because you went away. Wenn man viel ist, dann kann man viel tun." *

* We can do a lot if we stick together.

"The man who left the bomb at His feet on the twentieth of July," Pete pointed out, "was a good German soldier, a regular. I remember he was a colonel. Thou hast no cause to fear, it will not be as hard as it seems. Within a week thou wilt be back with us."

"I know about that bomb," Happy said slowly. "Two of the patriots who made it were my friends. They were caught because they failed. In the cadet school they made us watch movies of their execution. It was in the Plotzensee prison. They were garroted by means of a leather collar tightened around the neck, while flashlights from the guard tower played on the two chairs, and the cameras turned. The briefcase in which the bomb was left at His feet belonged to another friend of mine, who luckily was killed in the explosion. My three friends are three reasons why He must go, even if we lose the war, even if many lose their lives. But do not think a German soldier likes to lose either."

Pete and Fred were worried just the same, for that kind of compunction is what they dreaded most. Nobody could blame a Joe for being afraid of the jump, or even for holing up when he reached the other side, to keep himself safe, and giving no information, or false, when he was overrun; but a conscience like Happy's, stalking his treason, could, if it overtook the quarry, ruin their whole racket. It was not unthinkable that it might take him right to Skorzeny himself.

They walked back through the door; Fred ran ahead to switch off the BBC. They sat down together on the sofa. Pete threw another log on the dying fire. The room was empty; the Tiger and Paluka had gone up to bed already. They poured Happy some whisky for a bracer and looked across him, hoping to read in each other's eyes that his outburst was just the normal funk before a Joe's first jump.

"It's funny," Pete mused, "that you should have to start so far back in order to land so far inside the Reich."

"Ja, like taking a long run before the big hurdle. I only wish

94

I had time to see more of France. It is very like our own country, but different somehow. I don't see so many animals, and certainly there aren't so many men. You will say because they are all in Germany. That old man in Gérardmer might have been raking leaves in the park in Berlin outside our front door. I used to pass such a hunchback there when I was a kid, on the way to school. I hope that when the Amis take Berlin they will try to spare our street. You know the name and number, for it is in my old book, but I will not speak it now. If they at home do not kill that madman first and put an end to the trouble He has given the world! Then you would not need to take it."

He sipped the whisky in silence, staring at the burning twigs.

"Well," Pete yawned, getting to his feet, "let's turn in and think of something else. We're all getting stale. We'll go over it all in the morning just to make sure nothing is forgotten, but let's rest now. Take thyself a little luminal from the bottle on the shelf, there at the stag's feet, to get some real sleep."

Happy shook his head. "Do you think I need to be drugged to keep my word?"

He meant it pleasantly enough, but the answer would have been, "Yes, maybe." He had put his finger on a lesson they had to learn fresh each time, that the dispatching of a Joe had to be built up to a crescendo. He must be keyed up more and more for the moment of the jump, like tightening a string to raise its pitch. If he faltered the pitch was lost, and the riskiest spot was that wakefulness the night before his drop.

They dragged their feet up the stone staircase and left Happy at the door of the room where the other Joes were sleeping. He shook hands with his schoolboy bow.

"Gute Nacht," he said, and they answered, "Gute Nacht."

The others lay on Army cots under the lighted bulb set in the lofty ceiling, asleep in their GI shorts beneath GI blankets. Paluka grinned in his slumber; the Tiger snored softly, his self-mutilated left hand twitching on the outside of the olive drab.

Pete and Fred went back to make sure the doors were all locked. It was an excuse for another drink.

"Do you think the kid seems all right?" Pete asked. "He's your baby, you know."

"Yes, I do. That kind of talk gets you worried, but you have to weigh the human factor, as the colonel says. In fact, I don't think he would be as smart an agent unless he *did* have a touch of doubt, and I'd rather have him get it out of his system before the jump than after. Don't worry about him. If the Tiger came out with any talk like that I'd scrub him on my own, regardless of the colonel, but Happy will be all right. He's *got* to be all right. We'll be up the creek if he doesn't bring back those two divisions on schedule. Anyway," Fred yawned, "I'm going to bed now. Yes, I'm convinced he'll stick."

"I'm convinced so too, I guess, but it always seems to be my job to do the worrying."

"Listen, Pete, that kid's crossroads is *now*, before the jump. If he is sure tonight, he is going to be plenty surer when he comes down in that potato field. He'd better be sure then."

"Well, if it makes him happier to think he's doing it for Germany rather than for America, it's all the same by me."

"But he thinks he's doing it for both; don't be so dumb."

"Oh, I'm not as noble as you and Happy," Pete yawned, "but I'm not as crooked as the Tiger either. Frankly, Paluka is the kind of Joe for me."

They fell asleep, hoping for clear flying weather, because it took a well-seasoned jumper to withstand the letdown of having his operation scrubbed, or flying a dry run. Toto, the Joe who had had eight, was so unnerved when he did drop that the dispatcher had to push him through the bomb bay. Besides, when a jump was laid over, they had to remake the Joe's travel orders for the new date. There was a locker at D full of blanks and birds for just this purpose, but no American could forge the simplest script signature as plausibly as Mike could do it at G.

It dawned clear and cold. If the weather held the operation would take off as scheduled that night. They spent the morning checking the boys' cover stories. It wasn't a hard job, for they had been well rehearsed at G. They entered the final dates with the movable German date stamp. Paluka was returning to Mannheim—he was supposed to be stevedoring for the 776th Landesschutz Battalion—after leaving the breechblock of an 8.8 at the Kramag underground repair shop in Würzburg. The Tiger was headed for the same outfit, to check the steel in a new pillbox. They were traveling together, the Tiger to see Paluka didn't skip, and Paluka to orderly the Tiger. Since both were in the Army, that was plausible. In both cases their destination was marked on the trip ticket only by a field post office number, a letter, and five digits around the bird. There had been plenty of research to get that number right. In the old days of the war German company clerks spelled out the name of a man's unit on his travel orders and Soldbuch, but since the landings Wehrmacht standard operation procedure was just to stamp his postal number, so that if he were captured the enemy could not tell where he belonged—unless he chose to tell, which sometimes happened. But Documents had got around making a separate stamp for each entry on a man's papers by designing a brass seal with movable pins for the numbers, and if Battle Order didn't know the right numbers they would press five at random and smudge one or two, so the Gestapo couldn't check. Still, it was safer to know.

The Tiger and Paluka were dropping at N060945, nord de guerre grid. That is a clearing fifty miles northeast of Mannheim, near the highway from Würzburg. It was a small clearing, but they were lucky to find any so near the target. There would have to be a couple of seconds between the two drops, to avoid fouling, and at the speed of the A-26 that might land them a kilometer apart. The Tiger agreed to meet Paluka at the crossroads in Oppingen, in case they missed each other in the woods, for either of them might be delayed in burying his parachute and striptease. Since Paluka was really, as well as ostensibly, a Russian, he could pass for being stupid enough to stand at a crossroads for hours and wait there till his boss arrived. Then they would travel westward together.

Happy's pinpoint was much farther east. He was carrying a sample of blood for test from the field hospital at Munich to the base hospital at Bregenz, near the Swiss border, the same hospital where the Tiger had convalesced. The Tiger had briefed Fred on this hospital, and Fred had passed the description on to Happy. From the shelves of the dispensary at the cage Happy himself took an empty glass tube encased in aluminum, and enclosed in turn inside a wooden case stamped HEERESGUT—army property. It was part of the stock the retreating medical unit had left behind. Without knowing what it was for, First Lieutenant Brophy had got a sample of blood from a GI leukemia patient in the base hospital at Lunéville, so that in the unlikely event that a guard was so careful as to check by microscope, he would find something wrong with it, to justify the trip. Mike had forged a letter of transmittal from Munich to Bregenz, sealed and stamped with the field hospital seal; Documents had printed the letterhead and seal from captured samples. Sentries seldom dared open official mail, but if one of them did he would find the trip in order.

So that he could break trail, Happy carried another travel order detaching him to his new regiment, the 136th Mountain, crossing the Rhine westward at Mannheim. Happy's cover was one of the simplest they had ever had. Except for his name, he was traveling as himself. Yet it was impossible to foresee every detail. The best they could expect was to give the Joe a plausible story for the first day after his drop. It was usually enough. After that, any Joe with wit and courage bluffed his own cover story as he went along.

The take-off was laid on for 2330 hours that night. The Joes would have to be at the field, dressed and ready for strapping on the chutes, at 2200. As the day wore on the Tiger grew more irritable. He objected to meeting Paluka at any place so public as the Oppingen crossroads.

"It would have been better," he claimed, "if he jumped a few days after me, as I told the colonel, and came to my bunker. Thus I could prepare the way for him."

They tried to shut him up, for any last-minute friction in a team might break a Joe's nerve. But it could not break Paluka's.

"Don't bother about me, young man," he answered loftily. "This will not be the first parachute I have buried. You forget that I have taken these risks before."

They made the Tiger repeat the address of his father-in-law in Mannheim, so that if they failed to meet at all, or if the Tiger should desert, which Fred and Pete both thought possible, Paluka would know where to run him down.

"Right hand door, first floor rear, 27 Wharf Street. Knock four times like the Victory signal. That will be the password of the Tiger Brigade. Then say 'Greetings from the Tiger.' You must say it in German: 'Schönen Gruss vom Herrn Tiger,' for my father-in-law is an ignorant man who understands no language but his own. Mannheim? I know it like that"—he held out the mutilated hand—"and it is waiting for me."

Paluka rehearsed the familiar signal, tapping on the table the three dots and a dash of the Morse code for V, and repeated the German words in his fuzzy Russian accent.

"This begins to be like the old days." He grinned happily. "Though I do not speak perfectly, I shall be understood by those who wish to hear."

"The signal is a secret between us, hein?" said the Tiger anxiously. "And the address. No one else is to know, not even other comrades like the young Happy in the next room. Such might betray us to the Gestapo, from fear of torture perhaps, or even from what is called conscience. I should then have the right, should I not, mon capitaine?" he appealed to Pete, "to . . ."

He drew a finger across Paluka's throat. Pete nodded. It was

99

true that the leader might eliminate a teammate who endangered the mission.

"Provided when you return you prove to us that it was needful. Otherwise . . ."

Pete drew his own finger across the Tiger's throat, and they all laughed.

"You do not trust me," Paluka tipsily accused the Tiger. "Do you think if the Gestapo should arrest me for a stupid Russian that I would denounce you to save my own skin? Before that I should swallow my tablet. My loyalty has been proved before yours."

He made a motion as if he were biting into the cyanide—tablet L—which a Joe could carry in his cheek in case of capture. Tablet L was cased in rubber, so he could swallow it and remain unharmed if, at the final moment, he chose to talk. Paluka smacked his lips with a grin. The Tiger shrugged, packing money into his belt. "That would be less pleasant for you than for me."

Station D put on a special dinner for drop nights, chickens which the cook had swapped for Spam with a farmer, and three bottles of Montrachet, the finest white Burgundy. They ate early, to allow plenty of time for dressing the Joes. Paluka was half drunk already. He kept the others laughing with stories about his health club in Marseille, how the weaklings would totter in from the Canebière for a buildup, and the incredible feats they could perform after a single hour on his mats.

"Migraine, weak back, l'alcoölisme, impotence," he roared, "all are cured by le système Paluka."

Even those GIs who couldn't speak French had to laugh, till Jack looked at his watch and signaled to start the dressing. He closed the shutters and switched on the lights in the two equipment rooms, closing one door on Paluka and the Tiger, and the other on Happy. Paluka squeezed into his borrowed uniform with hardly a glance at it. The Tiger studied his in the mirror. He made Corporal Chuck, the six-foot-three boss

100

dresser, tighten the red, white, and black ribbon for the Iron Cross, which he had really won, and straighten his marksman's badge and the wound chevron which was to justify his mutilated hand. He adjusted the Schiffchen to the right angle, patting the cockade and the eagle to be sure they were tight.

Happy's uniform was his own; Chuck made no change in it, just checking that the red-piped shoulder straps and the caduceus patch and the silver eagle on the collar tab were firm. It was complete down to the special Medical Corps first-aid kit at his belt. He filled each canteen with German brandy which had been captured at the 169th Volksgrenadier officers' mess in Kaiserslautern. It was lucky any was left. In the flap of each Soldbuch he clipped a few extra ration stamps, the brown and white squares issued to traveling German troops. In each knapsack he stuffed a cake of unmarked chocolate and four sandwiches, two sausage and two cheese, made with the darkest French bread he could find. He had crossed France to Carcassonne for some captured Wehrmacht hardtack, and could have split a can between the Joes, but it was more apt to crumble at the drop. Gray bread was bootlegged so widely in the Fatherland that there had never been danger in carrying it.

There was no room for more, for the knapsacks were already loaded with the Tiger's extra requisition, which the colonel had decided not to drop by tube. Chuck strapped a mess kit and a corrugated gasmask tin on all the belts. On Happy's he clipped the leather first-aid case, and on Paluka's and the Tiger's the sheathed infantry bayonet. Into one compartment of each he tucked the square German issue compass with luminous dial; into another half a dozen Benzedrine tablets, alternated with aspirin, for Benzedrine was American; and into a third, at the opposite side, the single L tablet, in an envelope marked GIFT, the German word for poison.

Happy winked at Fred to show he saw the irony of it. "I fear the Amis bearing gifts." He smiled.

Their steel helmets were strapped outside their knapsacks,

101

and they wore on their heads only the peaked cloth Schiffchen, like the GI overseas cap, over which the jump helmet would fit. Paluka and the Tiger carried regulation Walther .38s at their sides. Since medical personnel do not carry sidearms, Supply had found Happy a little Walther 7.65, the police model they call the Olympia, to fit in a shoulder holster under his tunic. It fired seven .22 cartridges.

Over the uniforms Chuck zipped the heavy eggplant-colored coverall, called variously a zoot suit or a Mae West or a striptease. The legs were bulky enough to fit over the black three-quarter field boots and heavy enough to anchor a man once he landed. He folded a jointed shovel, wrapped in the issue overcoat, inside the seat pocket of each Mae West. This was safer than strapping it to the front shrouds of the chute where it might come loose in the drop. This shovel was the most useful equipment a Joe carried, because unless he could bury his chute and striptease he might alert the whole countryside before he had time to get away, and in that case no cover was strong enough to withstand the questioning of the Gestapo. Chuck tucked a Colt .45 in each right leg pocket, ready to draw in the air, for a Joe could never be sure where he might land. He was supposed to bury it with his chute, for every German knew it was an American weapon—and coveted one. For this very reason the Joes seldom did bury it. Antonius had had the nerve to sell his to a Luftwaffe sergeant, boasting he had captured it from an Ami in Lyon. He got five hundred marks, so it was sure the Tiger would not bury his.

They were crowned with padded rubber jump helmets, which would have to be buried with the rest of the gear. Paluka's head was too big even for the larger of the two sizes; Chuck slit it up the front. The small size was a little too big for Happy, so he fastened German adhesive tape inside the band. The helmets were strapped to the chin and anchored to the webbing on both sides of the Mae West. It was essential that a Joe should not lose his helmet on the drop, for he could crack his skull without it if he landed, or was dragged, against a tree or stone wall at the tumble. Chuck tied a parachute-model American knife to the striptease and tucked it in the outer sleeve pocket so it would be on hand to cut away the chute on landing. In addition to the German compass, each Joe carried under his glove a dime-size American one for quick reference if he needed it in a hurry at the getaway.

It was so cold that each Joe wore two pairs of German Army mittens, and a wool helmet under his cap. Paluka disdained the use of ankle wraps, knee guards, heel pads, or any other protection against the tumble. They were just in the way, he said; you had only to flex your knees ahead of time, then roll. Besides, they left marks on the skin that might give you away if you were searched.

"When I jumped in Crete," boasted the Tiger, "I feared neither search nor anything else."

"Then tonight you will need twice the courage of a German soldier," Paluka told him grimly.

It was lucky that Happy was dressing next door.

Paluka was the only one to carry a radio. He insisted that the little box, the discovery of which would hang him, be fastened openly to his chest instead of on his back, so he could protect it with his hands at the tumble. On one operation a Joe's radio pack had loosened at the drop; the dispatcher had had to slash it clear, and the radio fell to earth, wasting the whole operation and warning the Flak to open up on the plane when it had turned back.

Paluka held the radio against his chest, to show how he wanted it fastened. "This way I can hold it clear and repack it in my knapsack before I start marching. Without my radio I do not exist. La radio, c'est moi. The crystals and code pad you may hang in their felt bag about my neck."

Each of the Joes got a wristwatch with a luminous dial. Happy's and the Tiger's had come in the same shipment from Switzerland, but Paluka's was French. It might alert the Gestapo to find the German sergeant and the Russian private with the same make of watch. Chuck was careful to scratch the backs of the cases, and the crystals, to make them look long-used, using two different knives and one of the cook's hairpins, and to trade some of the Team's own sweated leather straps for the new ones.

When the Mae Wests were finally adjusted the Joes looked like the rubber man in the Michelin tire advertisement, and the chutes were still to come.

"Thou must gain flesh, little one," the Tiger said to Happy. "The frozen earth will be hard to thy bare bones."

"Then I shall not land as heavily as you or the Cossack."

At least, Fred thought, he had not lost his nerve yet, to speak up like that. But Fred was beginning to lose his own. The pinpoint was as safe as any pinpoint could be. Happy had been briefed at G on the terrain for five miles, in case he landed off. He had rehearsed the cover of the blood sample and knew how to break his trail. He would neither cringe nor swagger, for the Gestapo knew that both showed fear. But Fred still worried. It was not in the rear or at the front that danger lay, but at the barrier between them: the Rhine. To cross it, with two divisions under his cap, Happy deserved every tip that Fred could give him, no matter what Security had ruled.

On the impulse, Fred called him back to the little room and shut the door behind them.

"If you meet difficulty at Mannheim, Corporal," he said, suddenly regulation and dropping the "du," "you may perhaps find the others at 27 Wharf Street, right rear first floor. Knock as in V. The password is 'Greetings from the Tiger,' and do not say I blew it."

Happy lifted the edge of his jump helmet to make sure he heard. He repeated the address. "The German first floor is the American second. Is that the one?" Fred nodded.

Jack knocked at the door. He beckoned with a glass of cognac in his hand. It was part of the buildup for the moment when the bomb bay would open. On the table in the big room lay three OD blankets and three GI overseas caps. Chuck wrapped the blankets around the Joes to hide the striptease, in case anyone looked through the windows of the cars. He perched the caps on their jump helmets. It was not much of a disguise, but the French were not critical of American military tailoring. They looked enough like three fat Indian chiefs to satisfy a quick glance from the Dijon connoisseurs, some of whom believed the Americans had whole Indian regiments equipped with feathers, tomahawks, and Navajo blankets.

Toto and Antonius had been scrubbed again, because of icing over their target. They shook hands dolefully and gave the Hals- und Beinbruch to the lucky three. The Simca and the command car were still parked in the forecourt. The moon was just beginning to shed a cold glimmer over the four peaked turrets of the château.

"We look like an escape from the Bastille." Happy grinned. "Good-by to France."

They piled into the cars in the same order as the day before, but Happy was so padded with his gear that he could hardly squeeze through the door of the midget Simca. Merle, who strapped chutes at the field, followed with Chuck in his own jeep. Benny, the communications corporal, locked the iron gates behind the three cars.

They wound through the single street of Lux and got on the main highway to Dijon. In half an hour they were threading through the Place Darcy, and a few minutes later filed up to the MP at the gate of the airfield on the west side of the city.

"Cigarette," prompted the MP, with his head inside the car.

"Machine," each driver whispered back.

That was the password for the day, up to midnight.

The A-26 was in the far corner, warming up. The propellers shone and the engines roared in the cold moonlight, squandering Mr. Ickes' gas. Chuck and Merle had got in

105

ahead. They were already pacing the steel mat beside the plane.

"I've checked the bomb-bay doors," Merle said. "They work all right. I wish there was room for me to go along. It wouldn't be a bad idea, you know, with a first-time jumper."

"They're crowded as it is; you'd better stick around."

The pilot and the navigator from Eighth Air Force were inside the operations shed studying the weather report.

"Well, Sergeant," said Pete, "while they're doing that you might as well strap on the chutes."

Merle nodded. He led the Joes into the little dressing room where he stored his gear. Dijon was a main transfer point on the north-south line for shipments to the front. The hangars had been destroyed by Seventh Army action while the Germans still held it. So the planes had to stand out all night. But the administration building was not too badly wrecked. Air Transport Command had an operations shed off the waiting room and had given the Team another to dress in.

It was Merle's special job to fit the chutes. They were the British type which open by themselves from a hook above the bay, without a ripcord, and they had less opening shock than the American. More than that, they distributed the weight so that the straps left no mark on a Joe's skin. The first thing the Gestapo did was to strip a suspect and look for strap marks on his chest and thighs. There was a theory that the British chutes spun in the air. No one knew where it started, but the Joes had never been troubled with spin on the way down, even though one or two had been unconscious when they dropped. It was the automatic opening that saved them.

Fred left the Joes with Pete and Merle and Chuck in the crowded shed. In a few minutes the pilot and navigator strolled out of their own. They were a major and a captain, both with silver parachute wings on their breasts and the winged figure eight on the sleeves of their Eisenhower battle jackets.

"How is England?" Fred asked. They had flown over that morning from Harrington.

"The same old pea soup." The major laughed. "I must say I like to get over to France, if only for some decent black-market food. There isn't much black market in England, you know; even when you find a good menu I guess the British just don't know how to cook. It's colder there too."

"Well," the captain put in, "I don't think we'll have much trouble tonight. Just routine. Last trip, icing forced us back thirty miles short of the checkpoint. Next time we broke out at a thousand feet but couldn't catch the checkpoint at all. Believe it or not, this is flight five hundred for the old 856th Command, and maybe there's luck in round numbers. Another squadron reported Flak over Stuttgart last night, and pretty heavy reaction at Munich, but we travel well north of Stuttgart and don't go as far east as Munich anyway. Do you want to check the pinpoints in the ops room? We've got a little Scotch there."

Outside of their planes these flying officers were the most casual people in the world, without any worries or even any caution. It wasn't always easy to correlate the Air Force charts, which were in degrees and minutes, with the Team's own ground maps laid off in coordinates; and 1:100,000 seemed a small scale when the Team had sweated out a landing point at 1:20,000. The Team would point out that the twenty-thousandth maps, being captured from the German staff, could not help being more up-to-date than anything printed in America or England, but Air Ops were not impressed. They were proud of the vaster scale of their own element.

With the help of the Scotch, and by spreading the two maps on the table, Fred could follow the course with his fingers: northeast and over the Rhine between Strasbourg and Colmar; over the Black Forest between Stuttgart and Frankfurt to the Spessart; then make their first drop. That was the Tiger and Paluka. There are not many towns in these mountain

107

forests, and by the same token not many flat landing fields. Fred always liked to pinpoint the drop right down to six digits, which means a square one hundred yards each way. The Air Force laughed at that.

"We can try to hit N060945 for you, if you insist," the major said, with his finger at the gap in the green, about the middle of sheet U3, "but you understand we're subject to conditions in the air. We may get icing of the wings over the Black Forest even tonight, though it isn't likely. When it comes to setting your man down in one particular back yard we just can't promise it. Even when we're right on the beam, even when we see the back yard perfectly from the air, which you boys seem to think is easy at three hundred miles an hour— even when we see it and gauge our speed to drop him at the right instant, we can't possibly foresee the drift his chute will carry him. I hope your bodies are prepared to land a little off that dot you're marking on the chart. By the way, rub it out. And repeat the color code, please."

"Red and blue."

"Roger. That goes for eight hours, and we'll be back by then. Don't forget to phone it on."

The wind was from the west, as usual that time of year. They would drop the first two off with the wind, then bear southeast toward Munich and drop Happy off at his pinpoint. The trip was close to the maximum range for the A-26.

Y488114, on sheet X5, Happy's pinpoint, was a bowl-shaped clearing among the hills, behind two farms. The two lakes to the east would make a checkpoint in the quarter moon. It was long enough for an easy run-in, even dropping from as high as four hundred yards, as they liked to do in the hilly Allgäu. But the Team had learned to doubt perfection. One building, besides the farms, overlooked the bowl. It was the old weather tower on the Peissenberg hill. Air Ops reassured them on that too; they knew there was no Flak in the tower, and if there was any radar the A-26 was too fast for reaction.

Then, having dropped Happy, their third piece of cargo, they would turn around and return to Dijon by the base of their triangle, hoping they had alerted no Flak on the way out.

The Joes came out of the dressing shed. The chute pack and harness made them even bulkier. To clear the pack, Chuck had restrapped the steel helmets—Happy's was Luftwaffe gray-blue and the others feldgrau—to the centers of their chests, like a huge single tit. Paluka had his radio strapped under his helmet, making his front still more grotesque. The bomb bay of the little plane hung open like the trap of a scaffold. A short stepladder waited below, as a concession to amateurs. The noise of the engines was so loud they could not hear each other speak, standing so close to it. Happy waddled toward them, fumbling into his belt for a cigarette.

"Don't waste them, Corporal," Fred advised him, drawing him away from the blast of the slipstream. "Those are German cigarettes, and you'll need them tomorrow morning. Take a Camel."

He thrust it into his mouth and lit it for him. Happy turned his back to the others, but still fumbled in his harness. At last he brought out the rubber-clad tablet of cyanide. He handed it to Fred, spitting out the cigarette so he could talk.

"Take this back, please," he said. "I shall not need it. If I did, I should never use it. Don't forget I am a corporal in the Luftwaffe, and please remember it when the war is over and you have gone home with the other Amis." His eyes wandered over the foreign field. "Tonight is like a Christmas card, isn't it?"

Fred noticed for the first time how much quieter the sky was than near the front; no rustling of the fir trees and no rumble of the guns. The stars danced and winked, the moon just threw its first glow over the horizon, and the snow was crisp and powdery under the hobnails of their boots. Where they stepped off the steel apron, the frost had just begun to harden the tarmac.

The aviators came out of their shed, elegantly casual. They wore scarves of orange ammo silk around their throats. There were no stiffeners in their caps. They did not look at the Joes, and of course they spoke English.

"Well," said the major, standing on the ladder, "it's H-hour, as *Stars and Stripes* would say. I suppose these characters know the commands. Right after Action Stations we give them the red light from the panel at the run-in and they move forward to the bay. My navigator here will pull the lever for the hole, and when the green light flashes he will shout 'Go!' on the intercom. And they go!"

Pete translated this into French and Fred into German, to be sure all three understood. They nodded. Buck had given them plenty of this instruction at G already.

As Happy was last out, he was first in, after the plane crew. Walking toward the hatch in the belly of the rear gunner's compartment, he passed under the wing. He lifted his flipper and traced the white and blue star on the underside, the new symbol of the American Air Force.

"Never been so close to one before," he shouted.

He walked directly between the leaves of the hatch. "Auf Wiederseh'n." He waved, and they called back, "Auf Wiederseh'n."

He ignored the stepladder. He hoisted himself on his padded hands up into the belly like a gymnast on parallel bars. It must have been the marrow in his will that hoisted such a heavy weight, for the others had to use the steps. The Tiger mounted without a glance backward. Paluka waved a fin and flashed his gold teeth. The three Joes were all aboard.

Merle climbed in after them to attach each pack-thong to a ceiling hook in the order of the drops, making sure there was not enough slack to tangle if one of the Joes should move out of series. He came out sweating.

"I hope it's okay, but it would be a lot better with a dispatcher aboard to hook them up separately," he grumbled.

No one took the hint. Merle pulled the stepladder away. Through the transparent nose they saw the pilot pull the lever which closed the hatch. The roar of the twin engines stepped up. The plane turned slowly on her rubber tires, shuddered under the unaccustomed load, and headed leeward down the mat, gaining speed. When they thought she must surely crash into the wall at the far end, she paused, roared for the take-off, and rose like a dappled bird. Her tricycle gear snapped into the nacelles and the fuselage. Lightless, and after a minute soundless, she vanished eastward toward the moon.

Pete ran into the shed to phone Benny at the château that she had gone. Benny would radio headquarters from his truck to confirm the color code, so the ack-ack would not open up when she returned. It was more businesslike than in September, when Skorzeny's Liberator got through.

She would not return for at least two hours. They had to wait till then. They hoped she would return empty; but in case the weather or the Flak interception forced her back still loaded, they had to be ready at the field with the blankets and cars to drive the Joes back to D after one more dry run like Toto's.

"Well," said Pete, "I don't see why we might not as well polish off the Air Force Scotch. It's sure hard to find in France, and they can get all they want in England."

They walked into the ops shed.

"Just one nightcap for me," said Merle, "then I'm going to take a little shuteye."

It was 0150 when she came back. Merle was snoring across two chairs. Pete and Fred and Chuck were half asleep. They did not hear the roar until she taxied almost past the windows of the hut. They stretched themselves and ran out into the snow. The blue and red recognition signals were still blinking from the belly of the plane. The aviators cut their switches. Through the top hatch they climbed out on the wing. They kicked out the ladder and climbed down methodically to the earth. When they hit it, they became as casual as when they had left. They looked around and under the plane to see that everything was in order, and left her on the mat as carelessly as a taxi driver would park his cab beside a curb, with the propeller still slowing itself down into separate yellow-tipped blades.

"How did you make out?" Pete asked.

"Oh, it was simple," said the major. "We had no trouble at all. No Flak, and we could see a big fire to the left that may have been Frankfurt."

"Did the boys jump all right?"

"Why, sure. The big husky one went first. Their pinpoint was only fifty miles over the river, but it took us an hour with the zigzag course we followed, and with slowing down for the run-in. Had to feint a little, so close to the Rhine. When he opened the compartment door I could see him in the mirror, taking a swig. I could have used it myself. That man has a gold mine in his face. He was flashing it at the others. He settled in over the bay. When my navigator here gave him the Go he jumped feet first like an old campaigner. The thin one was right behind. He slid to the hole, but he wasn't scared. Just careful. He went out sitting down. We could see them both swinging under the chutes, but the wind was twelve and I bet they drifted."

"How did the little one do?" Fred asked.

"Oh, he was all right," said the navigator. "We had to go a little farther for him, you know, and he must have sat alone after the others jumped. But when we gave him the light for the run-in he broke out the door. He lifted up a V to me in the mirror—you know, the way Churchill does, but with both his arms. Then he stood up and at the green light, when we gave him Go, he dove right through the hole as if it were a swimming pool. That kid has got nerve."

"I don't suppose you could see whether he landed or not?"

The captain looked at Fred with pity. "Why, if we hung

around long enough for that we would have the whole Ge
man Air Force on our tail. No, we just gained altitude as fa
as we could and hotfooted it home."

There was only a finger of their whisky left, but they did n
seem to notice.

"What do you think of that bunch, Major?" asked Pete.

The major yawned as he said, "To me they are just freigl
pal; I don't even look at them. A postman doesn't read yo
letters, you know."

And the captain put in, "Especially that kind of mail."

He did not want to admit they were spies, even though th
worked on the right side. It was the same pretense as in t
Joehouse itself. A German soldier had to be loyal to the Wel
macht. If he switched, the Germans paid him the tribute
terror and a savage revenge. The Americans, except the fe
who had reached into the secret of his treason, ignored
scorned him, whether he had switched for riches, or risk,
faith.

Six

There was no reason why Happy should have dived headfirst through the hole, instead of springing out with his hands clasped over his head, the way the Luftwaffe taught. It was not the way the sergeants had taught him on the practice rig either. Through the panel, with the slack from his own hook held in his glove, he watched the others jump. The cold night roared into the bay. Paluka had crouched briskly to the edge, turned back to smile, and simply walked out of sight into space. The Tiger had eased himself along the deck of the plane to the hole, sat on his hams for an instant, then cautiously let go. It seemed to make no difference either way. Both times the leather thong of the static line tautened from the hook, and the threads which held the chute flap unraveled in a twinkling. The man dropped with his chute, just as a berry falls when you pinch the hull. Buck had said the chute would open at twenty yards.

The jaws of the hatch closed after the Tiger. When they opened again Happy did not know why he stood as he did, bent over as close to double as the padding would let him, and

114

then tumbled like an inexperienced swimmer into a pond. Unconsciously, perhaps, he thought that to start headfirst would break him more cleanly from the speed of the plane to the immobility of the waiting earth, that by tumbling down head over heels he would somehow make the transition more complete between speed and station, between air and earth, even between America and Germany. It was strange that the Luftwaffe did not give jump training to all its recruits, even the ground force, but then there are many sailors who cannot swim.

He pressed his eyes shut. The chute opened without his knowing it. His first sensation was the sway. He might have been floating in the water. He felt a little swing as his heavy boots turned him around upright, and then a jerk, it could not even have been called a wrench, as the padded straps of his harness tautened under his thighs and armpits. He opened his eyes. The chute unfolded segment by segment, like a bud; he was swung in the air as its silk flower blossomed, swung a little westward with his feet and eastward with his head, for the wind was still from the west. It was as if he were the weight to the vast pendulum of his shrouds. Suddenly he remembered what the Tiger had said: the chutes were sometimes made of paper. He clutched at the forward lift web in panic, but the slow drift downward did not vary. He consciously shut out sight and sound as he had seen the wounded do on the operating table when he first poured the anesthetic into the cone. Through the padded helmet he no longer heard the roar of the plane. It was only when he felt warmth creeping up to his body from below, and heard the returning rustle of the earth, somehow more audible, more insistent just because it was less loud than the plane, that the gulf was crossed. He looked upward. The eggplant-colored silk bell of his chute, translucent like smoked glasses, blotted out the shape of the moon but filtered its light through. It seemed impossible that so vast a skymark would not be seen by the watchers. It was

Germany below him, watching from the ground. Try as he would to make himself heavier by pulling at the shrouds, to hasten the safety, or the danger, of the earth, he could do nothing but sway and drift at the mercy of the chute. It eclipsed most of the sky, and his chest padding blocked any sight of the earth.

Suddenly he felt the impact of a bough against one leg; he supposed it was a bough. He kicked at it angrily as a swimmer kicks against a snag. He raised his arms—they seemed like lead—and tugged at the leeward web to carry him over the obstruction. He cleared it and knew he was almost on ground. He spilled the chute, as Buck had taught him, loosening the windward edge to shorten wind and ease the shock of the tumble. He flexed his knees and pointed downward with his toes, to keep the impact off his heels. He let go the web to clasp his gloves above the helmet, getting ready for the roll. The earth reached up to stroke his soles, and at that moment he dove forward to the ground, rolling behind his chute, side-arm to shoulder to back and over. The frozen soil grated along his thick boots, ripping down the legbag of the Mae West. It was strange how much faster it was to drag on the ground than drop in the air.

He grabbed again at the webs below the painted cords, braking himself to a stop. He lunged forward with his torso, trying to hold the anchorage of his knees to the ground. Still dragging, he rolled to his back, gave a half-turn to the box on his chest, and tapped its lid. The four straps disengaged. The wind slipped the harness ahead of him and the silk collapsed on the frozen stubble as a sail collapses from a mast. He dared not rise, but he could feel with his elbows that he lay in the furrow of an open cropfield. Winter potatoes; a withered stalk pressed against his cheek. Turning his head without raising it, he could see over his shoulder the woods he had just managed to clear, the white birch trunks gleaming among the dark pines. Still nearer, and in front of him, was a woodpile, the man-long billets stacked together like a wigwam. Dragging the deflated chute under him, he twisted along the furrow toward the woodpile, then eased himself to the left over one potato-hill, to hide on the side where the moon cast its shadow. There was no snow on the ground as there had been in France. He could tell from the pressure of the earth against his thigh that it was frozen too hard for digging. He did not even try the shovel; the woodpile was easier anyway, a miracle of luck.

Like a dog burrowing in the sand he eased the base of two logs apart. He stuffed the chute, the rigging, and the straps into the harness and pressed down the flaps. The bundle was twice as big as an infantry pack, but he forced it between the logs into the hollow of the woodpile and wedged an armful of stalks across the opening. He unbuckled the jump helmet and unzipped the striptease, with the folded coat and shovel still in the tailflap and the Colt in the legflap. He slid the steel helmet over his shoulder from chest to back, to free his hands.

Holding the cap in his teeth, he ripped off the wool helmet altogether, for ears are meant to listen with. He wondered why the alarm did not break from a steeple or forester's tower, and the police dogs bark. Then he did hear the dogs, two of them, baying deep-throated and vengeful from higher ground somewhere back of him to the west, the direction he had to take. Then two shots from a gun, then silence. He could not tell how long the dogs had barked; the wool helmet would have muffled the sound.

He forced all his American equipment, except the Colt, into the cracks between the timbers, wedging it in place with some potato stalks and fist-sized stones which lay in the furrow. Without rising from his knees, he struggled into his overcoat. He could just buckle the Gott Mit Uns belt and fasten the two top buttons, but he did not dare to stand for the lower two. He slapped the pockets to make sure he had stowed

117

everything foreign. Nothing was left but the dime-sized compass, which nestled under his mitten, and the Colt .45, with the catch ready. Still kneeling, he ground his knees around to face the woods. He crept back to them on all fours, as a hunted animal creeps. At the edge of the pines he listened again, then dove into the underbrush and stood up.

He slid the little American compass from his palm, leaning against a trunk to steady the needle, for his hand shook. Then, as a landscape emerges at dawn, gradually but leaving no void, the briefing map took shape around him. He suddenly saw that he had landed exactly at pinpoint. He remembered this very field on the 1:20,000 Wehrmacht staff chart. He could tell without looking that a lane ran up the woods between two farmhouses, no more than five hundred yards, till it hit the road to Böbing, which could not now be more than five kilometers ahead of him.

Eastward a cotton mist floated in front of the woods; that would be over the farm pond which the map had shown. He was lucky to land between the pond and the woodpile. He had an odd feeling of being himself reduced to one twenty-thousandth. He felt that he could crawl like an insect over the black and white surface of the map, striding along the single black hairlines which meant "passable country road" or the double stroke of the engraver's pen which meant "metaled highways six meters broad," and climbing the gray hachures, each contour line rising ten meters.

Peering back at the plowed field from his lair among the pines, like a fox at a farmyard, he was tempted to dash back into the burrow he had made in the stack, curl up, and hide. His Benzedrine had begun to wear off; he gulped another tablet. Then he wondered if he might have left some telltale knife or cord unburied at the base of the stack, and whether he had dropped his Soldbuch where it could be found by the farmers in the morning. Yet he dared not go back the fifty yards, even if he had. It was his very existence to put as much

118

distance behind him by sunrise as he could. He dared not even take the lane, for fear the farms had heard the plane. He struck uphill to his left between the fir trunks, out of sight of the houses, following the N on his compass; then down a flat field to a snow-hedge of dwarf spruce, and found himself, sure enough, at the edge of the narrow clay roadway which he remembered on the map.

He looked carefully both ways before emerging. There was no one in sight on the road. He would have seen anybody if there had been, for the moon was only just beginning to override her height. He felt in his tunic; the money belt was still around his waist, the Soldbuch still lay in his left breast pocket with the false letter in its flap, the specimen case was in his hip pocket and the little Olympia still reassuringly solid in its holster under his arm. He threw the Colt and the tiny compass into the woods, for they were foreign. Now that he was oriented, he pretended to rebutton his fly, so that if anyone should be watching he could say he had stepped into the hedge for decency's sake. He jumped across the gutter and started trudging to his left.

He thought of the sandwiches and chocolate in his knapsack; he was not yet hungry, but there might be a sort of companionship in eating them. He did not know when he might find more food, even with the ration coupons in his pocket, and cigarettes were still harder to come by on the road. So he contented himself with swallowing half the brandy in his flask. The brandy was a hazard anyway, because noncoms, even medical, were not often lucky enough to pack it.

He looked at his watch. It was 0030 hours on Saturday, 17 February, 1945 that he had returned to his homeland from the sky. Y488114: he knew that sheet so thoroughly that he could dig a mark with his heel at the point on the road where the 48 grid crossed it.

Strengthened by the liquor, he strode boldly along the pebbles. The silence, the pines, the astringence in the subalpine air were not like his country, so far to the north, or Cassino, so far to the south, but once again he was treading the German earth he loved. To his left the snow-capped peaks of Bavaria paraded across the horizon, blue even in the moonlight.

Now, he thought, I have earned a parachutist's badge. Not many in Medical could boast it. He did remember one staff surgeon in the training battalion who was always boasting that he had jumped with the Sixth Airborne in Crete. And then he heard a voice so close behind him that he turned, so close the speaker might have been on his own shoulders. No one was behind him. The voice was his own thought, and he knew he would hear it again many times in his five days. It was a hollow otherworldly voice, like the Devil's stage whisper to Faust.

"Ja, but you jumped for the enemy. No wings for you, but only a placard on a tree."

He shook his shoulders to throw the gremlin off.

In half an hour he passed through the hamlet of Böbing. He knew, as if he had really been crawling on the map, that there was no way to avoid it, not even a footpath, but he had no tremors as he strode through the sleeping town. A cow lowed from a barn, and a gaggle of sleepy geese hissed at him as he passed. Otherwise the village was silent. Perhaps, after all, the dogs had not barked for him. To prove that he had no fear he stopped in front of the white plaster church with its onion dome to shift his knapsack and light his first cigarette and straighten his Medical Corps brassard. That band was good protection. The fraternity of medicine has no frontiers. He smiled wryly to himself, patting his own left arm.

I am exactly as I should have been if I really had picked up my specimen in Munich, he reminded himself. I am taking the shortest route to Bregenz. Then I am going back to my new regiment. I am crossing the Rhine at Mannheim, for after Bregenz that is the nearest bridge to German-held territory. No matter who combs through my Soldbuch, I can tell him when and where each entry was made, and whether the officer who made it is fat or thin.

He even recalled with a wave of comfort that a nurse from his father's clinic at Berlin worked in the Red Cross canteen in Munich. Her name was Irma Grimm. So if they asked him where he had eaten supper, he would say in her canteen; and if they should show her his picture in the Soldbuch, or take him to face her, she would lie for him, even under the name of Steinberg, for his father's sake. And even, he thought, if she knew why he wanted her to lie for him, she would do it just the same. There was nothing to change from the face of truth except that his name had become Steinberg instead of Maurer. He whistled as he strode along.

He would have his orders stamped each day at the transport office or the town hall. He would draw his rations like any casual of the Wehrmacht and sleep in the camps or bunkers wherever the officers directed him. He would find his two divisions as naturally as any traveling soldier might, by bumming rides in trucks and Volkswagen,* by sitting around the canteen between trips, by boasting to other soldiers about his own unit and letting them boast about theirs. He would find them and get back to the front with all the speed the Wehrmacht would expect from Steinberg and the Amis from Maurer. He would not pretend to glorify the regime, for only civilians and the SS did that. But he would not attack it either. If anyone gave him the Heil Hitler he would give it back.

He *was* Karl Steinberg, corporal in Third Flak Training, but soon to be assigned to 136th Mountain across the river via the big bridge at Mannheim. And he had only five days. It was stamped on his second set of orders by a mythical Leutnant Buhl, and in his mind by Captain Pete. Five days, and his feet had begun to hurt already.

But at five o'clock when the sun rose behind him he had covered eight kilometers without seeing a single traveler. He

* German equivalent of the jeep.

passed a three-story Hof, one of those patriarchal farmsteads where whole generations live together under the gable, and stock and crops fill the ell. The old men who faltered into the sunrise to chop faggots, and the women who scrubbed clothes with the soap made from the wood ash, looked up and waved to him but showed no curiosity.

"Grüss Gott!" they called, after the manner of South Germany. The Hof was more populous and wider awake at five than the stretch of France had been at noon. This was home, where people were used to hard work. If there were no more able-bodied men than in France, at least there were more animals. Not many horses, though; they had been taken for the field artillery—but every farmstead retained at least a cow and the inevitable troop of high-neck geese, tramping unanimously like a squad of infantry, and adding their green droppings to the mud.

Happy was really hungry now, but he could not lose time by unpacking his sandwiches. Over the next hill was the highway, where a soldier would not be suspected for resting and eating. The highway ran up to Schongau, and at Schongau there was sure to be some sort of a canteen, or a restaurant where he could cash his ration stamps. At worst he could eat his sandwiches where it was warm and get a cup of hot barley coffee. He might get a ride before then, from some convoy on the road.

Near the top of the slope, well beyond Böbing and before he hit the highway, he overtook his first traveler. It was an elderly man walking slowly up the path. He carried a cane in his right hand. With his left he puffed at a pipe; the blue smoke curled over his head. An old-fashioned shotgun was slung across the back of his prewar Army overcoat. On his head was a green cloth hunter's cap with a feather stuck in the left side of the band. Two black police dogs trotted tandem ahead of him. Happy did not like to overtake the man, who must be some sort of forest guard or Landwehr patrol to be out walking with a shotgun so early. But he could not afford to slow down to the same pace. He noticed that the old man's shoes had no heels at all; they were worn down flat to the soles. Well, Happy thought, if I have to face him, it may be good practice for later.

"Morgen," he panted as he came abreast.

The old man turned around with his whole body, not just his head. He switched the cane to his left hand and held out his right. The dogs squatted on their haunches, their yellow eyes darting up at Happy, their long tongues hanging between their sharp teeth.

"Good morning to you," he said. He spoke slowly as the aged do, not to reflect, but to spin time out. "Ah, an airman, a bird whose wings are clipped. A flying doctor, like Mercury on earth, with wings on his heels. Walk along with me for a while if you are going to Schongau. We don't often see aviators down our way."

He nodded his approval, puffing at the yellow pipe, which had stained his mustache yellow too. "Where do you come from, young man?"

"Why," Happy answered, taking a breath, "from Munich, from the Flak barracks, and now I am going to the big hospital at Bregenz, on the lake, with a blood sample for analysis. It is from a major who is ill."

The old man clucked sympathetically. "But you have a long trip to the Bodensee, and even if you must walk instead of fly you choose a roundabout road."

"Oh, I know it would have been shorter by the Buchloe train—"

"Seven hours via Kempten," cut in the old man sharply, "that is, to Lindau. Then only twenty minutes to Bregenz, if the trains run."

"There were bombers over Munich last night, and so many refugees crowding out of the city that I did not know when I could get away by rail."

The old man plunged his pointed stick in the ground and turned to shake his fist at the sky in the east, toward Munich. "Der feige Tommy; they are all cowards. God will punish them for bombing a city like Munich and dropping their death on women and children. It is said the Bürgermeister of Munich has killed himself because the regime will not make it an open city, but that is only Klatsch.* They don't even pretend to aim at military targets any more. They fly so high, to keep away from our Flak, that they can't really aim at all. But never mind, the papers say that London has got it back a hundred-fold; did you know London is three-quarters destroyed? They can't keep this up much longer."

He picked up his stick, still shaking with anger, and plodded along beside Happy. As with most Germans, his enemy was England; sometimes they hated Russia, but hardly ever America or France.

"We had Yankees against us in Italy, where I was stationed last year," Happy told him.

"Ah, the Americans! I have never seen one. Perhaps they are better."

Happy had thrown his coat back, it was so warm climbing the road. The old man peered at the red Flak piping on his collar tab and Schiffchen.

"Ah, you are like me; you are not a flier, but you destroy enemy fliers. Let me have the honor to present myself; I am Leopold Fidl, veteran of the Kaiser's war and now air-raid warden for the district from Böbing to Schongau. Thus I can claim to be of the Flak like yourself, and though I shall be seventy next month I walk my beat each day. And your name?"

"Karl Steinberg, at present of the Third Flak Training Regiment."

Herr Fidl stuck his stick in the ground and his pipe in his mouth, and pumped Happy's hand with both of his, in the middle of the road. He did not seem in any hurry to reach

* Gossip.

Schongau. Happy pulled his cigarettes from the canteen belt around his waist and offered one to Herr Fidl. The warden looked at the cigarette, then narrowly at Happy. It was not often that one was given a cigarette for nothing, especially a Neuerburg. He smelled it, muttered a thank you, and wrapped it carefully in his oilskin tobacco pouch.

"I will smoke it later, if you permit, in my pipe, so that I will not lose the tobacco at the tip. Only profiteers can afford to smoke cigarettes—and soldiers."

He smiled, and they walked on in silence.

"I live in Böbing, you know"—as if Happy could have known where he lived—"and it is my duty to climb the church tower at night to watch for raiders. Some say that the Tommies drop spies, and then last night"—he paused portentously—"last night I saw a small plane fly in from the west, though God knows all planes are big. It was not of the Luftwaffe! I know this because I have studied the chart which they issue to wardens. No one else would know it, for I keep the chart locked in the sacristy so spies cannot learn about our planes. There is also a chart of enemy planes, but this one came so fast I could not see its shape. It had a star. We do not have many planes here, thank God"—he crossed himself. They were passing a roadside crucifix—"of either the Reich or its enemies. That is a comfort of the Allgäu. But let me return to last night. When this plane approached the pine woods between Böbing and the Ammersee I saw it circle. A little later a parachute unfolded with a tiny dot of a man slung beneath it. In a few moments he was out of sight beyond the ridge. It is too bad we do not have an observation post on the Peissenberg likewise, though it would be too high for my strength to climb. Well, I think this occurrence so important that I am now proceeding to Schongau to report it to the Kommandantur, who will no doubt notify the competent authorities."

"Ah, Herr Fidl," Karl said, "if we should meet any spies from the Americans or the Tommies, you and I could take care of them. I see that you have a long shotgun which you doubtless aim straight, with your experience. Though we in the Medical Corps are not supposed to carry weapons, I have here under my left shoulder a toy with which I have practiced almost as much as you have. I can whip it from the holster in an instant—in less time than you could unsling your shotgun. I can shoot very straight with it, and if we should meet such a spy we could take him into Schongau together." He patted his shoulder holster.

The warden pulled on his pipe. "Yes, and my dogs would tear his throat if I nodded. Would you not, Gerda?" The bitch growled at her name.

"You were telling me," Herr Fidl went on, "how you came to be on this lonely road, so far from your destination."

"Yes. When I despaired of boarding the train, my cousin, Fräulein Grimm, said I had better get a ride with the first car which came through in my direction. She is chief helper in the Red Cross canteen at Munich, and consequently knows all of the truckdrivers. They come to her bar for coffee. It is always easier for a soldier to travel by truck than for civilians. So a few minutes later in came a sergeant who was taking a truckload of most important cargo to Garmisch. I believe that great things are brewing in your mountains of Bavaria."

The warden nodded his head without taking his pipe from between his teeth. "Ah, then, you do know somebody in Munich. One cannot be too careful. For a moment I suspected it might be you who had jumped from my plane."

Happy said reproachfully, "Do I look like a Yankee gangster? Do I talk like one?" They laughed together at the absurdity.

"It is true," Herr Fidl resumed, "all sorts of supplies for defense and even for luxury are being moved into our Bavarian Alps. One does not know exactly where, or for whom, but they say for the use of an important personage, a very exalted personage indeed. One sees the covered trucks heading south on all the highways." He stared stolidly ahead of him, but Happy thought he had winked.

"Anyway," Happy said after a pause, "since I have to leave the specimen at the Bregenz laboratory, I had the sergeant drop me off at what I thought was the shortest road to the west. But I must have made a mistake, for the road kept climbing and getting narrower until finally it went only to Böbing, which has the honor of claiming you as a resident. But do not worry. If the spy should unexpectedly jump out of these bushes, I will help you dispose of him with the little toy which I may not display." He patted the Olympia again.

The warden clucked his gratitude. "In a moment," he said, "we come on our right to the steep ravine known as the Krummengraben. At its foot is the paved highway which leads over the river Lech to Peiting and Schongau. For Bregenz you should turn left in Schongau; for Augsburg go straight ahead. My knees are so brittle that I cannot run down the valley as I used to; the path is indeed only for goats. I shall take the good road by Rottenbuch, though it is longer. So if my infirmity is delaying you, I beg you to go ahead without me. At the bottom you will be sure to find a ride. Even if you must walk a little, it is only six kilometers to Schongau. There is a canteen which is run by the ladies of Strength through Joy. My wife, who is one of those ladies," this time he winked openly, "works there two days a week and is awaiting me now. She tells me that they furnish all soldiers with a coffee which is not too bad. If you get there before me, tell her I shall be along soon. She did not see the parachute last night, as she was not in Böbing."

Happy shook hands solemnly with the disquieting old man and started ahead, eager to leave him but reluctant to offer a target for his blunderbuss. As he started down the crest, Herr Fidl called out to him, "Auf Wiederseh'n. Next time, make sure beforehand whether you are really in a hurry for Bregenz."

Happy turned down the brink of the eroded defile, so steep

and irregular, as the torrents had cut it, that he had rather to leap than to run. At each step he thought he might turn his ankle. His knapsack, his helmet, his gas mask slapped against his back. I should not have given him my name, he thought. I need not have given it; but I am glad I showed no fear, and the next time I shall not even be afraid inside.

When he reached the foot, he looked back. The warden was resting on his cane before attempting his own painful descent down the road, the shotgun still slung across his back. His dogs looked up at him hungrily, but he waggled his finger at them. Happy waved up from the foot of the ravine.

The old man shouted in a voice which echoed between the banks like a mountain horn, "The wicked flee where no man pursueth," and waved back. Then he disappeared down the steep road, one step at a time, as a cripple descends a staircase.

Happy stood on the highway, looking right and left. It was still early, even for military traffic. He started to the right, for the six kilometers to Schongau. The grass at the side of the roadbed was easier walking than the pebbly mountain path. He was so hungry now that he broke open the oiled paper package and devoured two of his sandwiches, one sausage and one cheese. He finished the brandy in his flask. He refilled the flask from the brook along the roadside, dashing cold water on his face afterward. He would have liked a cup of coffee, even from Frau Fidl, and an armchair in her canteen, for his shoulder blades were sore from the slapping of his Klamotten —all the equipment, like gas mask and helmet, that the Wehrmacht hung on a man. He had walked only a kilometer when an Army motorcycle with an empty sidecar drew up behind him. The driver was an Army courier. He lifted his goggles.

"To Augsburg?" he asked impatiently.

"Only to Schongau, if you can drop me there."

The courier grunted, easing his leather belt and resetting his goggles. Happy climbed into the sidecar. In five minutes they had passed through the village of Peiting, where the single-track railroad crosses the highway at grade. The track was rusted and the station boarded up, with a sign WINTERHILFE nailed over the door. It was a collection point for the Winter Aid, where people could bring any spare supplies to help the destitute. As if everyone were not destitute. The motorcycle bumped across the concrete bridge over the Lech, and Happy saw that it was not mined. The railroad bridge ran fifty yards to his left. The two debouched on a little square, facing a barber shop and a sawmill. The town of Schongau pyramided above, huddled around the monastery at the crest. In the square a sign pointed forward to Augsburg and left to Kaufbeuren. A steel signal tower protected the grade crossing, with a stone foundation at its base. On the stone sat a corporal of artillery and two privates of the Mountain troops, with the edelweiss embroidered on the left side of their peaked caps. The Mountain were the only troops whose caps had visors. Happy glanced, without seeming to, at the regimental number on their green-piped shoulderstraps. It was 96, out of Garmisch. One wore the silver medal of the Narvik campaign on his chest.

Their barracks bags stood beside them against the stone, and Happy saw part of a white Mountain snowsuit at the mouth of one, where the knot was loose. Mountain troops were as proud as motorcyclists; when the courier braked to a stop they whistled the chorus they knew would get under his skin:

If you drive a machine you'll make corporal,
But we are too dumb to understand one,
So we're content to be gunners.

Wer gut Krad fährt wird Unteroffizier,
Aber wir, die sowas nicht verstehen,
Sind viel glücklicher als Kanonier.

The cyclist frowned, his feet tapping the ground beside his machine. He pointed to the left. "Pickup point for the West," he told Happy pompously, pretending not to hear the troopers. Happy climbed out of the sidecar. The artillery corporal, seeing it empty, called out, "To Augsburg?"

The cyclist nodded, and the corporal took Happy's place. Couriers pretended to be important, but even they had to offer rides to soldiers on foot. The machine started again; it roared up the hill and out of sight through the village. Happy noted that it carried the striped fanion of a division staff on its license plate, with the number 367.

He strolled over to the empty place on the stone beside the Mountain troopers. One of them was reading a comic magazine; the other sucked idly on a straw, his cap tilted back and his coat open to the morning sun. They nodded lazily.

It would be comfortable to sit on the warm stone, more comfortable than in the sidecar, but Happy did not dare to wait at the crossroads for long. They had told him at G to keep moving, not fast enough to look eager, but fast enough to look busy. It was possible, he thought, that the warden had not suspected him at all; possibly he suspected him but was against the regime himself. Though when it came to spies everyone was a patriot. Most likely he had suspected him but not dared to make the arrest alone, and, knowing Happy could not escape, was even now telephoning from Peiting to alert the police in Schongau.

"Can a Landser* hope for a ride to Kempten from here?" he asked the Mountain troopers.

One of them looked at him, taking in the medical brassard on his blue coat. "Yes, you are just in time; that's what we're waiting for ourselves. The broken-down old bus should come limping around the corner any minute now."

Yes, but at any minute the warden and his dogs might come over the bridge. Happy forced himself to his feet.

"Well," he yawned, "I think I'll walk along the road. The bus will stop for me, won't it?"

* Wehrmacht slang for ground troops, like our "GI."

130

The others nodded.

"I'll get a little exercise." Happy smiled. "I slept too soundly in that sidecar."

"The yawn is plausible enough," whispered his gremlin, "but soldiers never walk when they can sit down."

The Mountain trooper laughed. "Exercise of the tail there, ja, but not of the legs. You'll find it's the same in our dear old bus. Look, Herbert," he nudged his comrade, "the ground force of the birdmen* must always travel so fast. Perhaps they think they are fliers that way."

The trooper knew where to hit, for the Flak were notoriously jealous of the fliers. Happy flushed. He almost let out that he was assigned to Mountain himself after the hospital errand.

"Né, né," the trooper laughed, "do not be angry. I am only kidding. If you develop leg muscles you can perhaps become a Mountain soldier like us, if you do not become a bird first. When we ski we fly as fast as a plane. But have no fear, Junge, the bus will stop for you when it comes along in God's time."

The road westward was paved too, but emptier than the north-south road he had left. He walked along as jauntily as his aching legs would let him till he had rounded the bend out of sight of the troopers. They could not see him, but from where he stopped he could watch the bridge. He sat down on the first kilometer-stone and thought of Monsieur Apfel's food.

"If they suspect an honest German cigarette," the voice whispered, "what will they think of gray sandwiches when they have nothing but black themselves? With all the victories of your friends, might they not have given you a can of Wehrmacht black?"

"A mistake of Chuck's," Happy admitted. "I'll warn him when I get back, for the sake of the others."

"The bus will come round the bend at any moment now," the voice reminded him.

* His slang for the Luftwaffe was "Fliegerei."

With his heel Happy dug a hole in the grass behind the stone. Since he might not have time to swallow the sandwiches, he dumped the cheese and sausage fillings on the round-topped stone and licked the margarine off the bread. He buried the treacherous gray slices in the hole and scuffed them over with his foot.

"You must be careful of everything," the voice commended him, "from parachutes to sandwiches."

He rewrapped the sausage and cheese in the waxed paper. They could not possibly be identified. He crumbled the cake of chocolate, though it was unmarked, so nobody could guess, even from the size of the tablets, that it was foreign. He slipped all the food back in his knapsack; he did not really have to eat quite yet.

He trudged along for five hundred yards more, to get away from the fresh-turned earth. The sputtering of a motor burning wood—the Holzgas that took the place of gasoline—came around the bend behind him. He turned to hail what looked like a mail bus. It was camouflaged green and brown, but still carried the curved horn of the Post Office painted on the sides. The bus drew up for him, and he climbed aboard. The driver was a woman in the uniform of the NSKK, the Nazi motor corps. She had a thin brown face, her hair was stringy under her field cap, and she gritted her teeth when she changed gear. Apparently this bus was a carryall for any soldiers who had travel orders, and a freight service too, for the back of the cab was piled with mail sacks and packages.

"Name and rank," snapped the woman, whipping a pad and pencil from the bag at her belt.

"Steinberg, Medical Corporal, Third Flak Training."

"Where to?"

"Bregenz."

"Well, I'm not going that far, but I'll take you as far as Kempten. An hour out at Kaufbeuren to eat, and several stops

132

on the way. From Kempten you won't have far to Bregenz. Where from?"

But before Happy had to answer she had chalked down Schongau on her pad. She did not ask for his Soldbuch or even for a ticket.

The two Mountain troopers were laughing at him from the back bench, in front of the cargo. They were the only passengers so far. They were always kidding; Happy knew the type. But they meant no harm.

"Physician, heal thy bunions," one of them called. And even the sourfaced woman laughed as Happy dropped down on the longest bench.

"Is it permitted to sleep?"

"No," said the driver.

"Yes," said the Mountain troopers. "Let the kid sleep, Fräulein."

"Scharführerin," * corrected the driver.

"You go to sleep, birdie. We will watch out and wake you up if any officers come aboard. Even if you are Saurpruss, we will look out for you." Saurpruss is what Bavarians call a Prussian. It sounds like "sourpuss" and means the same.

Happy took off his leather belt. He rolled up his overcoat to make a pillow. The gremlin whispered that he must not sleep till he was out of danger, but he shrugged his shoulders and stretched out, his legs hanging over the slatted bench. The Holzgas heated the bus like a stove. He fell asleep as his head touched the coat. Twice the bus stopped for refueling, but it was the Mountain troopers who volunteered to take out the ashes and shovel in the short chunks of lopwood. They did not wake him. While he slept the driver stopped to pick up more passengers or to leave off some of her packages. The trip took three hours instead of one, because of stoking up and ice under the worn tires and oxen on the road. Bavaria never hurries,

* Squad leader (female) in the NSKK.

133

even in wartime. It was noon when the bus drew up at the white railroad station in Kaufbeuren. The troopers shook him awake.

The benches had filled with soldiers by now—soldiers on leave, they were the ones who laughed, or returning from leave; soldiers like himself on military errands, soldiers singly or in pairs. Two were standing in order to leave him stretched out on the bench. Happy jumped to his feet. The two soldiers would remember him for lying on the bench while they stood, but would remember him more clearly still—and so would the other troops and the driver—if he apologized. An agent's safety, he had been taught, lay in being unnoticed, for being noticed led to questions; but luckily there were no officers aboard to ask them. He smoothed out his tunic without even thanking the two, rubbing his eyes to seem sleepier than he was. The others lifted their rifles from the luggage rack. He walked through the ticket room with the crowd and out to the platform.

In the buffet beside the near track a Strength through Joy canteen was set up—ersatz coffee brewed of barley and chicory. He had forgotten how bad it was after drinking American coffee so long. Some sort of beef stew. And a soggy cake for dessert, a kind of Strudel with synthetic frosting. He reached in his Soldbuch for the forged ration stamps, and changed a ten-mark note to pay for his lunch. A priest was handing out wooden rosaries, leaning against the wall in one corner of the room. He did not actually sell them, but he had a tin box into which everybody who took one dropped some kind of paper bill. Happy was not a Catholic, but he took a rosary just the same. He would give it to Père Nod, his roommate, when he got back to the Joehouse. He dropped all his change into the box. The priest gestured a blessing.

"Too much for a fifty-pfennig string of beads with a cross at the end," the voice told him. "Now the priest has noticed you too."

Kaufbeuren is the main stop on the railroad from Kempten to Augsburg. There were a hundred troops or so at the station, mostly infantry, but of many different regiments. On the platform a staff sergeant was rehearsing them in close order drill. Their uniforms were shabby; many had no rifles. One or two appeared to be still sick or wounded, with bandages and canes. Next to them another group, in civilian clothes, was being lined up in squads. They were mostly older men, but there were a few younger than Happy. Just kids, he noticed, with the Hitler Youth pin still on their jackets. He wished his father had let him join the Hitlerjugend in Berlin, so he could have gone on their hikes in the woods. Hiking would not have done him any harm, any more than baseball at the Golden Well. It would have been fun, even though the meetings were nonsense, with all the slogans that had turned Hermann Bechthold into a gangster.

Young or old, the recruits all wore the white brassard of the Volkssturm reserve. Most of them were armed, but with the obsolete Mauser or with old-fashioned fowling pieces like Herr Fidl's. On the center platform, beyond the underpass, a group of Russians lounged on their sacks, in feldgrau uniforms with the eagle of the Cossack Legion—like Paluka's own disguise—and with no weapons at all—square-faced, stringy-haired, slant-eyed, filling their mess kits from a pot of their own. The Germans paid no attention to them.

These three detachments were clearly all awaiting transport. Happy sensed the train-time expectation in the waiting room and on the platform. He was the only airman in the crowd. A pair of guards with fixed bayonets strode up and down the platform and through the station, but ignored him as if he were Russian too. The girl who drove the bus was still eating at the buffet.

Kempten, where he was headed, was on the way to Bregenz, where he pretended to be headed. The voice warned him that the Gestapo might suspect him if he did not take the fastest route. He wondered whether he could get to Kempten faster by the troop train than by the bus, but he didn't know when it was due nor which direction it would head. He didn't dare ask the guards, so he asked the girl.

"Oh," she told him indifferently over her Strudel, "these fellows are returning from the hospitals to the front. They go the opposite way from you, to the Reppo Depot at Augsburg, where they will be shipped to their own units again. Or to whatever unit needs them most. That's the way it is nowadays. You won't get a train to Kempten till some time tonight, if then. Better stick with me. Only I warn you, you'll have to stoke my furnace. The Mountain did it all morning; it's your turn now. And I can't have troops sleeping all over my bus. I'm starting as soon as I finish this delicious lunch. Even though I have to go out of the way to leave some packages at Aitrang, I'll get to Kempten long before a train will. Better go out and get a seat, because I may be filled up when I leave. Remember, don't go to sleep; I might have officers aboard this time."

He bought a copy of the *Allgäuer-Tageblatt* on the way, and got in the bus. Sure enough, there were only two or three empty seats left. In a few minutes the driver came out and started her car. Happy sat at the back, where he could look at the addresses on the packages. Without appearing to study the tags, he could read the names on several, like 36th Supply Battalion, Kempten, or HQ 375th Artillery Regt., Memmingen via Kempten. He read as many as he could see from his bench without exciting the attention of the engineer corporal sitting beside him. But he did not want to try to remember too many, lest he should forget them all; so he concentrated on the three or four addresses nearest Seventh Army sector on the Rhine, repeating them to himself with his eyes closed till he would be sure to remember without having to write them down.

He wondered why the bus was going out of its way to so small a town as Aitrang, till he noticed that half of the mail sacks bore the name of a prisoner-of-war cage, Stalag 206/B.

They were the regular civilian bags, the color of potato sacks, but made of strong hemp, and longer, with *Deutsche Reichspost* stenciled lengthwise, and a lead seal at the end. There were half a dozen, all bulging with packages. In the time he had been in the Ami cage at Sarrebourg, with all its thousand prisoners, there had never been more than one mail sack of packages a day.

The bus left the main highway and nosed southward along a narrow dirt road. After five or six kilometers this road ran parallel to a double-track railroad, the line from Kempten to Augsburg which he had just left at Kaufbeuren. The train which was to pick up the troops for the front passed them on an embankment, the half-dozen small boxcars, unpainted for far too long, swaying behind their wood-burning engine, grinding their flat bumpers together over the rough neglected roadbed. Then the bus turned left under a stone overpass and drew into the village of Aitrang. It stopped in front of a big two-story stucco building with a Turnverein sign across the front. It had been the regional sport club before the war. The playground beside it was surrounded by a double steel fence three yards high, with barbed wire stretched on top and rolls of barbed accordion between. At the far corner of this compound was a tower, in the window of which he could see the muzzle of an HMG, sited to sweep the packed cinders below. Across the front of the building itself was a big sign, just the same as the tags on the mail bags: Stalag 206/B.

An SS stormtrooper stood rigidly at the door. On his garrison cap, instead of a soldier's cockade, he wore the death's-head of the Totenkopfverbände, Himmler's special guards who ran the PW cages and concentration camps. The double-lightning sign of the SS was on his black collar tab. He did not relax nor change expression when the bus stopped, but inside the bus the driver called, "Someone help me throw the fodder to the swine, please."

The troops laughed; the two front men got out to help. They

opened the side door of the bus and carried all the sacks into the prison office, past the death's-head guard.

The prisoners had been playing baseball. Happy counted twenty of them. When they heard the bus drive up they threw down their bats and gloves and pressed in a row against the links of the inner chain fence. The muzzle of the machine gun in the tower moved a little to the left.

"It's the mail, boys," Happy heard one of them call in English.

When they saw the sacks being carried from the bus into the guard room, they turned from the fence and formed a line at the side door of the gym. This was a Dutch door, with a ledge on the lower half. The upper half was open.

But the voice of another guard inside the office grated in English, with an accent Happy thought was not as good as his own, "Prisoners will have to wait. We shall inspect for contraband."

The door slammed shut. One of the Amis flung his cap on the gravel. "Yeah, and then we may get a little bit of what's left over," he grumbled.

The trooper at the door heard him. He eased the Luger from his belt holster and moved toward the outer fence. It would be easy for him to shoot across the two, and the GI, seeing him, picked his cap up and followed the others to the diamond.

They were dressed in fatigues exactly like the ones Happy had worn at the Golden Well, but with USA stenciled on the back. He wondered whether the Wehrmacht had had them made that way, or whether Seventh Army had sent them in via Switzerland, as the mail must have come.

All the German troops had piled out of the bus to stare at the prisoners. They leaned against the outer fence with their fingers clawed between the links, watching the flight of the ball in the unfamiliar game, till the stormtrooper growled at them to keep away from the wire, as a keeper might warn against standing too close to the cage in a zoo. Happy lingered, tempted to whisper to the centerfielder, who was only three yards inside the fence. He had tossed his glove in the air, and now was passing the ball with the catcher as the others took their places on the bases. Happy could have whispered, "I am in the American Army too, and I can bat." The guard, at that instant, could not have heard. Happy wondered whether the fielder would miss his catch if he heard those words through the wire. He wondered who shagged the ball if a fly went over the fence. Certainly the death's-head guard would not, and the prisoners could not. The ball would probably be confiscated; then they could play no more till the bus brought a new one from Switzerland. At the Golden Well there was no fence around the diamond.

But the moment to whisper passed, for the driver came out of the office, tucking a receipt for the mail sacks in her belt bag. She picked him out where he stood lingering at the fence.

"Hey, Corporal, you have ridden free long enough. You've been dreaming for an hour. Come back and throw some wood in my boiler. We have to get places."

Happy obeyed. He shoveled out the ashes, stirred up the bed of fire, and threw a dozen chunks into the grate, closing the firedoor when they had kindled. Then he climbed aboard. Each soldier was sitting in the same seat as before the stop. His own seat was waiting for him, beside the engineer corporal. Looking backward, against his judgment, as the bus sputtered and lurched forward, he heard the crack of the bat. The prisoner who had thrown his cap down had hit a two-bagger; Happy saw him digging his toes into the cinders to round the bases. The gunner in the tower, who probably did not know the difference between a two-bagger and a riot, traversed his machine-gun barrel after the runner. The team whistled and cheered, as Happy himself had been cheered at the Golden Well. The two prisoners who were working on their knees against the far side of the compound looked around and whistled too. They were getting a garden ready for spring. Gaiety, that was what the Americans had, even in prison; and he remembered the dejected shamble of the German prisoners around the compound in Sarrebourg. Baseball was a good game, Happy thought. After the war he would teach Klaus how to play, and they might get two nines together in the Tiergarten at Berlin. The death's-head guard had resumed his stance at the door, not bothering to look at the game. Happy knew the guards were correct by the Geneva Convention, maybe more scrupulous than the Ami guards at Sarrebourg. But he felt all the same an odd sensation that the prisoners were freer than their captors, who must envy the liberty behind the wire fences, under the muzzle of the machine gun, as a housewife must sometimes envy the canary in her kitchen.

The cannoneer in the seat behind the driver muttered that it was a dirty trick for him, a sergeant in the German Army, to have to carry smokes and chocolate to American prisoners, who had probably been bombing German women and children only a few days before. The crowd grunted agreement. The troops sat silent and moody, swaying as the bus pushed on. From the crest of the first hill Happy, looking back, saw USA in huge white letters on the tiles of the Turnverein, to warn the enemy against bombing their own side, and maybe to protect the SS.

"The Wehrmacht pays every attention to the comfort and welfare of its guests," growled the engineer corporal in the seat beside Happy, with his eyes closed. "The best cuisine, hot and cold running water, beautiful waitresses, sports, gardens; nothing is too good. It makes one envious of the Schweinehunde."

"At least," Happy laughed, "they don't have to worry about our shellfire any more."

The engineer opened his eyes. He looked full at Happy. "Unless they are spies. I wish one of *them* was my guest; he would taste a little. Did you know they dropped a spy last night over by the Ammersee? See if it is in the paper yet. You have one right in your pocket."

Happy looked back at him. He knew the engineer must think it curious for him to have sat with the newspaper folded in his pocket, unread, for two hours. At the same time he could not appear to have read it already, because if it told about the spy he had not been indignant soon enough. He pulled the single sheet uncomfortably from his pocket and started to read, conscious that the engineer still looked at him sidewise. Luckily, the story was not yet in press, so the engineer related it himself as he had heard it on the radio, while Happy shook his head in indignation.

Herr Leopold Fidl, he said, the air-raid warden of Böbing, had seen a plane fly low over the woods east of his village. It had dropped a parachute. The warden's dogs had barked at the plane; he himself had fired, not with any hope of hitting the jumper (though this, the engineer explained at length, was clearly permitted by the laws of war), for he was too far away, but to arouse the village. A few farmers had waked up in time to see the chute drop out of sight. Rather than waste time on what seemed like a useless hunt, Herr Fidl, though infirm, had walked fifteen kilometers to announce the news to the Kommandantur at Schongau. He had recognized the plane as American and suspected that the spy might be headed southward toward certain installations near the Austrian border.

Southward, thought Happy; Herr Fidl is trying to protect me. And why Ami instead of Tommy? The unuttered friendship warmed his confidence for the first time since the jump, till the gremlin reminded him that the Gestapo was laying a trap for him by feinting the wrong direction.

Anyway, the Kommandantur had called for an alert in all directions and was sending a posse with dogs to comb the region where the plane had circled. Turn in all suspicious persons, it ordered, no matter how clear their identity might appear; the enemy forged the most impeccable German papers. Be on the lookout, it warned, for any stranger, whether soldier or civilian, who spoke with an American accent. Happy

141

listened, muttering his anger for the engineer corporal to see, but not too angrily to be a real soldier, and turned back to his newspaper.

The Wehrmacht communiqué in the paper spoke of heavy losses inflicted on the Russians in a successful effort to shorten the German lines west of Breslau. It announced that thirty-two Anglo-American terror-bombers had been shot down over the Westmark, but admitted a few local penetrations in that sector. Happy knew it was trying to gloss over more defeats. He wondered whether Seventh Army had launched the attack which everyone at the Golden Well expected. If so, it must have begun that very morning. At the Golden Well one never saw the German papers and it did not seem right to listen to the German radio. Vati did not forbid it, as the regime forbade BBC, but in some way it would have been disloyal to him.

The rest of the sheet was devoted to announcements of party meetings in Kempten and Kaufbeuren, to movie programs at the clubs for soldiers, to the latest speech by Dr. Goebbels, and to a quarter-page of death notices: deaths of heroes, with an Iron Cross printed beside the name; deaths for Fatherland and Führer; deaths for Fatherland alone; deaths by terror-bombs; and mere deaths—in descending order of importance.

In a box at the top, over the death notices, was a poem:

THE PEOPLE'S LEADER

The German saying has it,
When great the people's need,
When hostile armies threaten
Without the gate, and Death,
Lifting his lance on high,
Sweeps through the German land;
When from a thousand fires

The sudden horror springs;
Then the forest thunders,
Then the German earth

DES VOLKES FÜHRER

Es geht die deutsche Sage:
Wenn gross des Volkes Not,
Wenn dräuend Feindesplage
Vor'm Tor steht; wenn der Tod
Mit hoch geschwung'nem Speere
Durchs Land der Deutschen zieht,
Wenn rings aus tausend Flammen

Ein jäh Entsetzen sprüht,
Dann dröhnt es in den Waldern,
Dann gärt es tief im Schoss

142

Starts in her holy bosom,	Der heil'gen deutschen Erde,
And then, steel-hard and mighty,	Und eisenhart und gross
Stands forth the people's leader,	Ersteht des Volkes Führer,
The man whom God has sent,	Der Mann von Gott gesandt,
The hero of all power,	Der Held der grossen Stärke,
The savior of our land.	Der Retter unserm Land.

When Happy finished the paper he offered it to the engineer. "Your spy wouldn't learn much from reading this paper." He grinned. "And I don't believe he'd learn much from traveling this road. I wish we'd get to Kempten; I'm hungry again."

"No news is good news for the Allgäu," the engineer said solemnly. "But if he were riding this bus—and he might be, you know—he would have seen the Stalag. He may be reconnoitering to raid it, the way Skorzeny rescued Mussolini from the cliff in Italy. That was a real masterpiece, that little trick. He would have seen that regiment of White Russians that infest Kaufbeuren. I don't trust—"

Happy put his hand on the engineer's sleeve. He pointed to the cardboard sign tacked across the front of the cab, over the driver's head. It read DER FEIND HÖRT MIT.

"The enemy is listening, you know."

The engineer grimaced and smiled. "You're right. My wife tells me I talk too much anyhow."

He went back to sleep. The bus plodded along the snowy forest road, stopping each few kilometers to drop or pick up passengers. Now that the freight rack was nearly empty, they all stacked their rifles in it to make more elbow room on the benches. Each man who left had to stumble over Happy's feet to pick out his rifle.

The bus joined the main road again at Obergunzburg, where the driver stopped to refuel her woodbin from a locked shed behind the town hall. The engineer corporal helped Happy to carry the four-inch chocks for the Holzgas boiler. Then, with the sun still shining, a hailstorm descended, as happens in the Bavarian February. The driver braked at the head of the steep

143

slope down to the Iller. Happy shoveled sand from the road-side sandbox so that she wouldn't skid. That way they lost an hour.

It was five o'clock and almost dark before they crossed the steel bridge to Kempten. A cold rain was falling. The bus stopped in front of the post office on the Adolf-Hitler Platz, across from the railroad station. The soldiers picked out their rifles and slung them across their backs before stepping down to the curb. The driver checked each man off on her pad.

She looked up at Happy. "Corporal Steinberg, Schongau to Kempten?"

"Yes, Fräulein Scharführerin."

She checked him off and folded the list in her leather Beutel. He was the last man off.

"Corporal, give me a hand with these last two mail sacks, will you, since you aren't carrying a rifle?"

He shouldered the two together, following her into the Post-amt. As he dumped them on the floor of the corridor, he saw her hand the pad through a wicket to the civilian clerk in the office, and saw the clerk look meaningly at the clock. It was half-past now.

"Thanks," the driver called back to Happy. "Leave them there. Military transport is over at the station. Too late to get today's stamp* here; they'll do it over there and put you on a hospital train to Bregenz. Plenty of them these days."

He heard the wicket slam as he strode out the door of the Postamt. It was lucky her pickup was civilian; that gave him a little more time in case Herr Fidl changed his mind. Already there were five who remembered Corporal Steinberg and could identify him: the warden and the bus driver, the two standing soldiers, and the engineer. And maybe the priest. As soon as the door closed he ran across the square to the station, pulling his Schiffchen over his eyes.

In one day he had traversed the base of his Z. There was not

* Tagesstempel, the checkoff marked on all travel papers each day.

much to report from this stretch: the PW cage, a few troop locations from the mail sacks, which he could not verify, and the Russians at Kaufbeuren. But even negative information was useful. It would be news that there was little troop movement in the Allgäu, and no bombing damage. That would come when he headed north.

Kempten lies in a sort of weep hole for the Alps. To the southwest they climb steeply to Lake Constance, where a tiny bit of the Reich abuts Switzerland: Bregenz, where the big hospital was, and Lindau, and Friedrichshafen. From Kempten the railroad winds up through the mountains to reach these towns, but the main double track turns north toward the heart of Germany, with a good highway parallel to the railroad. It was up this highway, the bar of his Z, that Happy was to search for his two divisions. It passes through Memmingen and Ulm and Aalen. At Crailsheim it turns west, like the cap of the Z, hits the Neckar at Heilbronn, and descends it until the river flows into the Rhine at Mannheim.

Every Joe was briefed to break his trail, whether he believed himself suspected or not; for the Gestapo struck without warning their victims. The station at Kempten was none too soon for Happy, who on his first day had already been noticed. It was not practical for the Team to make two Soldbücher in different names, for the forging of a Soldbuch is a long process. So they would issue two sets of travel orders in the same name, but for opposite destinations.

Herr Fidl and the bus driver would remember he was Corporal Steinberg; they would also remember he was headed for Bregenz. Rolled up in Happy's spare socks was the other travel order, undated, because no one could foretell how long the first leg of his Z would take, detaching him *from* Bregenz on four days' convalescent leave, then to report to his new regiment via Mannheim. With it was a false seal of the Bregenz hospital and a revolving date stamp. The paper and the seal were hot; he would have to use them soon or throw them

145

away. Kempten was certainly not too soon. He decided to get out that night, so that when the hunt to the west began he would already be headed north.

The transport office, or Frontleitstelle, was usually in the station at important railroad towns. Happy pushed open the curtained glass door to the ticket room. On the landing of the double stairs a sergeant stood inside a circular desk, with a sign over his head.

The sergeant was stamping the travel papers of a long line of soldiers. Happy sauntered past and noticed through the open wicket of the desk that he had a wooden leg.

"Forwarded, forwarded!" growled the sergeant. "That's what I do all day long; just stamp 'weitergeleitet' on other men's papers. They go out of here convalescent and come back again sick or wounded all over again. Why doesn't someone forward me? I wish I could see a little more action myself instead of forwarding others into it or out."

Self-consciously he flicked an imaginary speck from his row of ribbons. He wore the bronze medal that meant twelve years' service.

"You Twenty-fifth Infantry are going to Aalen tonight," he called out through the loudspeaker. Happy heard the division number, but did not turn his head. "The train will be along in an hour. The 619th People's Regiment to Heilbronn. Same train but stay aboard longer." He switched off the speaker. "Now I'm not too old or too crippled to be in the Volkssturm myself and carry a rifle with you. Forwarded, forwarded! Ach, mein armer Kopf!" *

Happy pushed past, up the steps to the waiting room. Half the ceiling bulbs were out, to save electricity, and the smoke of many cigarettes made it still dimmer. A crowd of troops of all arms milled through the cold high-vaulted room or clustered around the tile stove against the far wall. Strength through Joy was selling a fragrant onion soup at the buffet.

* Oh, my poor head!

146

As at Kaufbeuren, the Volkssturm, or People's Reserve, were either too young or too old to serve in the regular Army. They were the last line of defense. In theory they were not sent to the front at all. They wore civilian clothes. Their only identification, to mark them as soldiers instead of snipers, was the white brassard on the left sleeve. But the Team did not forget that the year before the Wehrmacht had denied the same privilege to the Fifis. At Comblanchien, near Station D, where the Fifis attacked a convoy, the SS had herded the whole village into the church, set two HMGs at steady fire, and burned the church down on top of the dead.

Happy strolled over to the crowd around the bulletin board. There was an announcement issued that day and marked: "Only for the service: not to fall into enemy hands."

It warned all servicemen to watch for spies, and reported that one had been seen near Schongau. A description would be posted later. "The enemy is listening," the bulletin ended— "Der Feind hört mit."

Happy wondered whether Fidl was laughing to himself way back in his village, playing with him like a cat with a tethered mouse, knowing that since he had his name and destination in his mind, he could pounce on him at will, anywhere in the Reich, with the long arm of the Gestapo. Or whether the "other watchers" who had seen the A-26 had given the alarm, and Fidl, who alone had seen *him*, was suppressing his name for some reason he could not guess.

He went into the troop latrine. It was the kind they had in Italy, with two corrugated gray islands for your feet in a sea of porcelain. He locked the door, hanging his knapsack on the hook. Unbuttoning his tunic, he drew from his wallet the first trip ticket, from Munich to Bregenz. He had not needed to show it, but it had served its purpose by being ready to be shown. He chewed it to a ball, then spat it down between his feet. From his knapsack he unrolled the alternate, shipping him from Bregenz to the front. He dated it with the revolving

147

date stamp: 17 Feb. 45. Documents had already forged the staff surgeon's name, as supplied by the Tiger. He opened his Soldbuch to page eight, where an airman's hospitalization is recorded. Steadying the book against the panel of the door, he entered with his own pen the code number—seven—which he knew meant pneumonia, and dates for his entry and discharge: 3 Feb. and 17 Feb. It was just what he had often done legally for others. He attested them with the false bird of the hospital, and forged another name the Tiger had given to Documents: Assistant Surgeon Möller. He had practiced the slanting letters of that signature at G from the Tiger's model. Though it was third-hand, it should fool the sergeant in the half-light, in case he checked the order. His convalescent leave was already attested on the travel order; since it ran less than five days, it need not be entered in the Soldbuch. He poured the blood from the sample tube into the drain, and crushed the wood and metal cases on the corrugated island with his heel till they bent small enough to pass the trap. Someone was knocking impatiently at the door. He had to get rid of his fountain pen, so that nobody could discover it had the same ink as on his hospital entry. It might be too big for the drain, but he did not know how to empty it, and dared not crush it on the island for fear of leaving an inkstain, and he dared not flush more than once. He took a chance—at worst he could pretend to have dropped it—throwing it with the date stamp and seal into the drain, and pulled the heavy chain. Luckily they all passed the trap. He buttoned his tunic and opened the door with an apology to the soldier waiting outside. He strolled back into the waiting room. He had broken the trail.

The crowd was thicker and noisier now, their hobnails scraping over the tan tiles of the floor. All the benches were filled with tired soldiers, their rifles stacked against the wooden bench-ends. Many sat on the floor, leaning against the wall. He found a corner where his medical brassard would be hidden against the wall, for if Fidl should denounce him, that red

148

cross might blow his identity at once. Yet he dared not take it off till he was out of sight. He would rest a minute so they would not think he was hurrying. He sat down, his helmet and canister clanking against the wall. His head fell down between his shoulders and he was asleep.

When he awoke the waiting room was almost empty. A hand was shaking his shoulder. His terror was like waking out of a nightmare, but he was waking into one. It was the crippled transport sergeant who shook him.

"Where are you headed for, Junge?"

Happy tried to conceal the armband without betraying himself. He pretended to be sleepier than he was so he should not have to stand up and reveal it.

"On four days convalescent leave, Herr Feldwebel, then to my regiment via Mannheim. The 136th Mountain."

"Got your orders stamped for today?"

"Jawohl."

Happy nodded and reached cumbrously for the Soldbuch inside his tunic.

"That's all right, youngster." The sergeant smiled. "Don't bother getting them out. I don't suppose you want to hurry too fast. God knows when you could get a train to the north anyway. The last one out of here has gone. I can get you put up at the club across the street if you want. You look tired; I see so many like you here, released from the hospital too soon. That's why I let you sleep. But I'd change places with you just the same. Zurück zur Front!" he sighed. "Back to the front."

"No," said Happy, shaking himself, "I'm not tired. A little weak after the pneumonia, that's all. My leave is so short that I haven't time to get home to Magdeburg anyway, so I think I'll take it easy these four days. If there was an inn up the road, it would be a relief from canteens and Army food. Do you know a little inn somewhere, quiet, like peacetime? I don't know this country."

He sighed. The sergeant sighed again too. "Well, I envy that leave of yours. I don't blame you for wanting to spend it out of sight. To think my job is shipping sick kids like you to the front! Look, if you can pick up a ride outside—or if you'll wait a while I'll find one for you—get off at the next town. That is Dietmannsried, nine kilometers up. There is a nice Gasthaus there, just beyond the town, and the innkeeper will put you up if you give my name: Sergeant Hugel. Here, I'll give you a note to him. He knows my writing."

He scribbled on a scrap of paper. To Happy's relief, he did not ask his name. But the brassard would show when he stood up.

"I think I'll walk if it's only that far. They want me to get air and exercise after being in the hospital." He stumbled to his feet; useless to try hiding the brassard.

"Well," said Sergeant Hugel, "I see you're a medical man yourself. If you think it won't do you any harm, go ahead. The rain has stopped now. Good luck, and Heil Hitler!"

Happy pushed open the swinging door, trying not to drag his feet. The sergeant held it for him, switching out the lights first, and followed him down the stairs to the square.

"We're getting a vestibule built so the Tommies can't see the light when the door opens. This curtain on the glass isn't enough. Take the road to the right. But when you're on leave, remember, if you talk to civilians, the enemy is listening. Heil and good night!"

He went back to lock up the station for the night.

After the plane and the bus, Happy was so tired he could hardly walk, but somehow he managed to make the five miles to Dietmannsried. He had no trouble finding the inn. The moon had risen; it lighted the sign across the shuttered stucco housefront; Zum Ochsen—At the Sign of the Ox—Emil Liebert, Proprietor. Emil Liebert opened the door to his knock after a long wait, in his nightcap with a candle in his hand. Everyone went to bed early nowadays, since there was no light to sit up by. He kept the candle back of the door and shut it as soon as Happy had entered. He read the note from the sergeant. He beckoned Happy to the desk and made him sign the register: Karl Steinberg, Corporal of the Luftwaffe. Happy looked at the names above his own. Only two other guests had signed that day: Gunther and Hubermann, secretary and constable of the Criminal Police.

"It is good you brought the note from the sergeant," Emil Liebert whispered, "otherwise I should not dare take you in after the curfew, with gentlemen of the Kripo upstairs. Do not let them see you."

"Could one ask for a little something to eat?" Happy asked.

"I have only bread and cheese. I suppose you have ration stamps?"

Happy laid the brown stamps for fifty grams of cheese and two hundred of bread on the counter. He unwrapped his remaining slices of sausage and made a sandwich with the crumbly black bread. The innkeeper reached below the counter and brought up a bottle of schnapps and two glasses. One he handed to Happy and the other he lifted to his own lips.

"An den Sieg!" he toasted mournfully. "Now hurry upstairs before the Kripo hear you. Pay my wife in the morning."

"To victory!" Happy repeated, wiping his lips on the back of his hand.

The innkeeper took his candle from the counter and led him up the stairs to a room at the back of the house. He shut the bedroom door behind him.

"This way you won't hear the trucks that rattle along the road all night," he said kindly, "and the bed is comfortable. The cover is made from feathers of our own geese. What time will you start off in the morning?"

"I have been sick for a while. Will you let me sleep till I wake up?"

Unexpectedly the innkeeper patted him on the back. "That's

151

all right, flier. Come down whenever you feel like it. Perhaps the police will be gone. My wife will give you coffee—or what passes for coffee today."

He kindled the candle beside the bed from his own.

"With the shortage of coal these days we do not use much electricity. Schlafen Sie wohl."

"Sleep well," Happy repeated. He hung his damp overcoat on the wooden pegs set in the wall. He lifted his shoulder belt to hang beside the coat, with the helmet and gas mask container still attached. He stripped down to his shirt and shorts. His feet were so swollen that he could hardly pull his boots off. Under the soft down pillow he slid his revolver in its holster, but he kept his money belt around his waist. He looked behind the bed, but there was no microphone. He sank into the yielding feather bed and blew out the candle. In a moment he was asleep, for the third time since he had come home.

Seven

When he awoke there was hardly more light in the room than when he had gone to sleep, for Herr Liebert always closed the shutters of the Ox on the chance of a terror-attack. He looked at the radium dial of his watch. It was just eleven. He had slept the clock around.

He threw open the shutters to the sunshine. Below him was the Bavaria of picture postcards. Across the left horizon paraded the blue spine of the Alps, smaller and paler than yesterday morning. The houses of Dietmannsried huddled like sheep in a storm who keep their tails to the cropland. In Bavarian villages there are no power poles; the wires run from jack to jack on the tile ridges. Frost glittered on the west flanks of the beech trunks in the wood patch and weighted last season's oak leaves, and there was snow in the hollows of the crop strips; but a woman in a white kerchief and black skirt, with a tan apron across her knees, profited by the winter warmth to harrow her flax lane. The Iller gurgled northward, fencing the barnyard of the Ox, and at the back door of the ell Herr Liebert himself was jackknifing at the galvanized pump to siphon

153

liquid manure from the pit into the barrels of his spreader. Under the pear tree below Happy's window a girl sat on a stone bench. She was knitting a pair of socks from a ball of blue-gray Luftwaffe wool. Beside her leaned a long willow switch to keep her geese from straying on the highway. Happy threw on his shirt and leaned out of the casement with his elbows on the stone sill.

"Are you making those for me, Fräulein?" he called down, then ducked back into the room.

Over the edge of the sill he could see her look up at the empty window in surprise. But she turned back to her knitting without an answer, and her silence reminded him he should not have called so loud, for he had forgotten the Kripo. If they were still in the inn they might have heard him; it would not be wise to be noticed by the Kripo. Softly he closed the shutters, leaving a crack open so he could see to dress. He washed his face and hands in the big china basin of cold water on the washstand, then set it on the floor and rinsed his feet in it. They were still swollen, but not as hot as last night. He put on a clean pair of socks from his knapsack. He tied his necktie in front of the mirror; the necktie was part of dress uniform. "Schlipssoldat"—he grinned at the mirror—meaning necktie-soldier. Only the Luftwaffe and civilians in uniform wore ties. He stroked his mustache. He rubbed his fingers over his chin, but it was not yet his day to shave. Over one arm he threw his overcoat, his knapsack, his camouflaged helmet, and his Sam Browne, and lifted the heavy black boots in the other hand, with yesterday's socks inside them. He went downstairs in his stocking feet.

Frau Liebert was busy over the stove in the little enclosure which doubled as kitchen and office, behind the zinc counter. She looked friendly in a spare judicial way, with a topknot of gray in the old-fashioned style on top of her sparse hair.

"Good morning, Herr Corporal," she called. "I hope you slept well."

154

"Perfectly, Frau Hostess."

"Well, there can't be many airmen who sleep till eleven on a beautiful day like this."

"Ah, this is the first day since I enlisted in the Luftwaffe that I have not been wakened by someone else."

She laughed. "Well then, I must get you a good big breakfast."

"Bitte. Give me as much as you can, because I did not have much supper last night. I got in so late, and now it is past breakfast time yet still too early for lunch, so make me enough to count for all three meals. I have to travel a long way today. Maybe I'll get nothing more until supper at some canteen, wherever I happen to be. I know it won't be as good as yours."

She clucked with satisfaction like a hen, a strumming on the roof of the mouth so expressive of sympathy, so unlike the northern way of speech, that he wondered if it wasn't some kind of dialect of the Allgäu. He had heard it somewhere before. Then he remembered; Herr Fidl had clucked just that way.

"I'll do my best," she called gaily. "But the shortages! You in the service can't guess what they are nowadays. Go and listen to the radio while I scrape up some breakfast. We haven't got the paper yet today; the mail gets slower every week. Turn on the Frankfurt station. They have good war news this time of day. If any war news is good."

"Yes, Frau Hostess, but could I ask one thing? May I rinse out this pair of socks which I tramped in so long yesterday?"

"Gewiss, gewiss!" she cried. "There's a pump just outside the door with a basin which I cleaned out myself only a half-hour ago. Run the water on them to rinse, and when they are really clean I will call my daughter. She will darn any holes they may have. If you are anything like my two boys, who are in the Luftwaffe also, you can't wear socks a single day without getting one hole at the big toe and another at the heel."

She chuckled again. Happy padded out to rinse his socks in

155

the spurt of the pump. He left them to soak in the basin and came back to the table pulled up in front of the tile stove. He tuned in to Frankfurt-am-Main. It was the daily communiqué of the high command. The same story as yesterday: in the east containment of advanced enemy spearheads, destruction of a hundred Soviet tanks, successful shortening of a flank to protect Neumarkt. It never stated that Breslau, thirty kilometers east of Neumarkt, had fallen; but any schoolboy who listened would know it must have. In the west we have had to yield Forbach temporarily, after an attack by overwhelming American forces which cost them heavy losses and the town wanton destruction at their hands, but we have regrouped in a favorable position on higher ground beyond; new terror-attacks on Munich and on Mannheim with the toll of forty-six American planes; in England severe reprisals by V-2 bombs on the city of London, which, it could now be confirmed, was three-quarters destroyed.

"Forbach already!" the inner voice exclaimed. "Your friends have started to strike us. And more bombs on Berlin, did you hear?"

Happy switched it off. He could not listen to the Wehrmacht news. Forbach was on the Siegfried Line.

"Is the news good today?" Frau Liebert called.

"It's not that, but I'm on leave. I have four days. I would rather spend them without hearing about the war at all, good or bad."

She sighed, and he knew she meant that she too did not want to listen to the war.

She brought a tray over to the table: a big blue saucer of preserved pears from the orchard behind the house, four slices of bread that were no blacker than the ones he had buried, with plenty of margarine and a whole dish of jam, a quarter of Münster cheese, a two-cup pot of coffee which smelled better than he knew it could taste, even a glass of milk. One had not

156

seen milk in Germany for over a year. And under a china hen two soft-boiled eggs.

"Marshal Göring could not ask for more." He laughed.

They smiled at each other a little guiltily, for the Marshal was supreme commander of the Luftwaffe, and one should not joke about his appetite.

"Well, don't tell anyone that I gave you the milk and eggs and cheese, or they'll arrest me for hoarding, and I should be besieged by others on leave like yourself. I should not dare if the gentlemen of the Kripo were still our guests. Luckily they left at dawn. I do it for you only because my two boys are in the Luftwaffe too. Oh, your poor boots!" she cried, catching sight of the wrinkled leather which Happy had set beside the stove to dry out. "I will have my daughter, Maria, patch the socks, and look after the boots myself while you eat up your good breakfast."

She ran to the back door to call Maria in from the garden. He could hear her whispering advice at the threshold like a stage prompter. Maria curtsied to him when she came into the room. She held his socks, wrung dry, in one hand. He wondered whether Ami girls ever looked as pretty as this, with hair so blond it was almost white, and eyes as blue as the bottom of his saucer, and cheeks as pink as fruit blossoms before they opened, with a dimple on the left side. She had no stockings of her own, but she knitted them for others. She wore a home-made dirndl and bodice of black linen, without ornament, and her shoes were wood.

Out of her workbag she brought a darning egg. Without speaking, she sat down across the table and began darning his socks.

"It is just as I thought," her mother chuckled, "a hole at each end of both."

Frau Liebert produced a tube of Lodix shoe polish from under the counter. She joined them at the table, rubbing away at his boots while he finished his luxurious breakfast. A white cat purred in the window, between the pots of geraniums, thumping her tail on the red tile.

After the war, Happy decided, when he had got his degree from the university, if any university was left, he would like to practice in a village like this, instead of in the city. He pictured himself sitting in the Ox, smoking and drinking Pilsner with the village priest and the lawyer and Herr Liebert, while Maria knitted beside the stove. In the country people were simpler and kindlier than in Berlin, and a doctor need not be a specialist.

"Now," Frau Liebert announced, "I am going to give you something that I keep for my boys. Since you are in the Luftwaffe too, you shall have a little of their foot powder. They never have any when they come home—though God knows it is more than a month now since they have had the shortest leave. I don't know why the Wehrmacht doesn't issue such powder to everyone." She sprinkled the powder inside his soles, from a blue can on the shelf behind the stove.

"Why don't you stay with us a day or two, if you have so much leave? We could give you the best room, now that the gentlemen of the police have left."

"All my thanks, but with only four days to get back to my unit at—"

He checked himself, for she was shaking her finger at him, warning him not to tell her.

"Well, anyway, I can say it is across the Rhine. I don't dare to risk getting back late, for the rules are stricter now than early in the war. Not even we in the Luftwaffe can be sure of getting a ride. If I find I have any time left over, I should spend it at the other end, not here. I have been sick in the hospital"—Maria looked up from her darning—"and they want me to walk as far as I can without getting tired, to bring back the muscles. I will just take it easy, spending the nights in the shelters, wherever the curfew happens to catch me. They will not be as comfortable as the feather bed at the Sign of the Ox. But"—he leaned forward impulsively—"I promise to come on my next leave and spend it all with you, if you still have the room."

Maria looked up again. Frau Liebert shook her head. "Fliers promise much, but that next leave never comes."

"Then after the war, when we all have leave. Perhaps it will not be long now."

He spoke softly. The women looked up, frightened.

"God grant," murmured Maria.

"You won't have any trouble getting a ride on this road," Frau Liebert said briskly, as if she were shaking off the confession that the war might end soon (since one knew from the radio it could end only one way). "It goes straight up through Ulm, and then the trucks which are going to the Rhine turn to the left on the Autobahn. Those are wonderful roads. They are the best thing the Führer has done for us. They say that where the road passes over a valley He has even sometimes built storerooms underneath for the farmers, to hold wheat and potatoes and beets. Someday I hope to see an Autobahn, but we have not been able to drive anywhere since the war started and they took our car. But then, even if we had it, we could not buy gasoline."

"Well, it can't be much fun to hike on an Autobahn," Happy laughed, "even if it were not verboten. I'd rather take the long way, by Aalen and Heilbronn, and down the Neckar. My father hiked that road when he was a student in Heidelberg. He says it is the most beautiful part of Germany."

"Our Gauleiter said in a speech that Germany is the only country which is beautiful and modern at the same time. England and France are beautiful, but they are decayed. America is modern but has no beauty. Russia is merely barbarous."

Maria glanced up at her mother. Happy felt she had heard that sentiment many times before.

Frau Liebert sprang up. "But look, if you go by Heilbronn,

could you not stop to see my boys in the Ninth Flak? I know it is at Crailsheim—oh, I shouldn't have said that, should I?" She clapped her hand over her mouth. "The enemy is listening. But now that I have, could you not at least drop a note to them as you go by? It is hardly out of your way to pass Crailsheim. They are nice boys and you would like them: Hans and Willi. You could tell them you have seen Maria. They are a little older than you, but you could talk about the Luftwaffe together. I write them, but only to a field post number, and I never know whether the officers censor my letters or not. I do not dare to write them direct from the post office here; I should be denounced if anyone found out I knew they were at Crailsheim, but I am sure you would not betray me. They are good boys, but bad letter writers. Perhaps the letters we send them never get through. Anyway, I'll write one now, and if you have a chance, stop to see them, or put the envelope in a mailbox somewhere. You can read it first, to make sure there is nothing I should not say. It is always better to have news of loved ones by the mouth than by the pen, if one cannot have it by the eyes. Do you not think so?"

Happy felt a little sick. Third Flak Training, which his Soldbuch said was his last unit, was a component of 9th Flak Division, and he should have known the division headquarters was at Crailsheim. He would certainly not stop to see her sons, and knew it was verboten to put a town name on military mail. Just as certainly, he would detour by Crailsheim to make sure 9th Flak was there. She took her steel pen and a bottle of nutgall ink from the drawer of the counter. She scratched a few words on the back of a postcard of the barracks at Kempten.

"We have the 91st Training Battalion here, you know. These barracks are so modern; I wish my boys could be here. Such clean showerbaths, I hear. There I go again, with my military secrets. I shall put the card in an envelope. The war will never reach Kempten, though."

Before sealing up the card, she showed it to him. "My dear

sons, this will reach you by the hand of a friend, who will tell how we miss you. We are all well, sad only that you do not write. Hearty greetings from father, mother, and sister."

She stuck two purple six-pfenning stamps of Hitler's head on the envelope and put it in the side pocket of his overcoat, playfully patting down the flap to make sure it did not fall out.

"Now you must leave us your own field post number so that Maria can send you a pair of socks. Would you not like to knit socks for the corporal, Maria?"

Maria blushed and said solemnly, "It would be a great honor."

"Fräulein Maria knits beautifully. I wish I had socks like hers."

"She will make some man a good wife one of these days."

Maria blushed again. She did not ask his size, but held his socks, which she had rinsed, heel to toe with the other pair she had knitted for Hans. She pursed her lips and nodded. Her needle flew a little faster, but she did not look up.

Happy wrote his address on a slip of paper: San. Uffz. Karl Steinberg, FPN 33148. Every Joe had to know the right FPN of his pretended unit. That and his lodging for the night before were the first tests of the Gestapo, before the stripping to look for strap welts. He handed the slip to Maria, who tucked it in her bodice.

"Did you hear about my cousin?" Frau Liebert asked.

Happy shook his head. Maria sighed patiently. "How should the corporal even know your cousins? Everyone in the Allgäu is a cousin."

"It is my mother's cousin, Leopold Fidl," and Happy almost let out that they were friends, as you do to please strangers whom you like. She did not give him time.

"It is he who found the spy," she went on without a pause. "Did you not hear? An American plane dropped some dangerous saboteurs a little this side of the Ammersee. There are said to be a dozen. My cousin Leopold is the air-raid warden. He

161

lives in a village called Böbing. Others saw it as well as he, not only at Böbing but at St. Nikolaus. His wife did not see it, which will make her angry at him. But it was he, my own mother's cousin, who walked all the way from Böbing to tell the Kommandantur at Schongau, since they have no telephone in his village. It is thought they may be a troop trying to kidnap the Führer from Berchtesgaden, if that is where he is; not that I know, of course. Poor Cousin Leopold, he is quite lame, and it is a long walk down that steep mountainside. They always laughed at Leopold a little and thought he was a trifle"—she tapped her forehead—"touched in the head.* In fact," she whispered heavily into Happy's ear, "we always used to think he was not quite serious about the regime. This will clear him of such slanders. Yet, instead of thanking him, there are some now who blame him for not having caught the spies. That is what his wife will say too. By flying in a parachute himself, I suppose! Oh, but it makes me shiver with horror to think they are at large. They cannot escape, though. If they hide, they cannot eat. When they come out of hiding they will be caught, for anyone would recognize the speech of one who is not true German. The Gestapo will throw a net around them. Perhaps our guests of last night are hunting them even now. They are close-mouthed, the police. That is one way of knowing they are of the police, for I believe they do not always wear the badge. If they catch the spy, I should enjoy tearing him to pieces with my own hands."

Happy stood up. "Well, I must start now. Many thanks, Frau and Fräulein Hostess, for the pleasure you have given, but first let me pay my bill and give you my ration stamps. I shall not have many left after such a feast."

Frau Liebert had figured it out ahead. "It will be twelve marks fifty. And you'd better give me your ration stamps to separate. There are so many different kinds of Reisemarken, I have never seen a soldier yet who could understand them. I

* Hirnverletzt

162

shall not take stamps for the eggs and cheese and milk; they are our secret." She winked, and again she resembled her mother's cousin.

He handed her the wad of stamps from the flap of his Soldbuch, and she took them to the counter to separate. Maria rolled his socks in a ball. He pressed her hand as he took them, and was sure that she pressed his.

"Will you really knit me a pair of my own?" he whispered.

"I promise. If you promise . . ."

"For my next leave," he swore, clutching both her hands in his. There was just time to brush her lips before her mother looked back. Maria turned her face, busying herself with his boots. He saw a tear fall on the shiny black leather, and hoped she would not wipe it off.

He would not let either of them help him with the boots. They slid on easily, thanks to the powder and the warmth of the stove. Herr Liebert came in from the garden to join the farewell, taking off his own boots at the door.

"Auf Wiederseh'n! Auf Wiederseh'n!" they all murmured, shaking hands.

"Yes, till my next leave. I have already promised Maria."

They waved from the threshold as Happy started along the highway to Ulm.

It was a beautiful morning for February, almost like spring. A few more days of sun would open the chestnut buds. He touched the lips that had touched Maria's and whistled as he strode along the edge of the blacktop. Yesterday's danger was as unreal as a nightmare, growing more remote with every step. He had not done badly his first day, which was the most dangerous of the five—except maybe the last, his voice corrected him. He was out of reach of Schongau, and had broken his trail at Kempten. For some reason Herr Fidl had not denounced him, and was not likely to give the Gestapo his name after withholding it a whole day, that would put *him* in danger. Even if the Gestapo made him tell, the new Blacklist would not be issued till Tuesday. That was what the Tiger had told the class. In all his service, Happy had never seen a copy. He wondered what color this week's would be. By Tuesday he would be halfway to the Rhine, anyway. No, he thought, he had not done badly. But it was lucky he had not told Frau Liebert that he knew her mother's cousin, just the same; and his uneasiness returned.

Medical Corps of the Flak was too rare a uniform not to be noticed by everyone. As soon as he was out of sight he unpinned the glazed white medical brassard from his sleeve. He folded it carefully and laid it with the two safety pins in one of the leather cases on his belt. It was just inviting trouble to show it, and there would be no suspicion to his taking it off. If he ran into a spot-check, he would say he had taken it off to keep it clean. Without it, he could pass as a combat soldier, even without a rifle. He would not be incriminated by traveling unarmed, because even the veterans were short of sidearms now, to say nothing of rifles.

The traffic along the highway was thick for a part of the country so far from the front. Every few minutes he was overtaken by a truck or an armored car or a Volkswagen, which is like the jeep but with the engine to the rear and the spare mounted on the sloping hood. All were crowded, to save fuel, but they always had room to offer him a ride. He refused each time, for he could not watch so closely from inside a car as from the roadside, and he had plenty of time left before his deadline. There were many soldiers on foot like himself. Coming southward the traffic was mostly ambulances, the sides screened by heavy field-gray canvas, and tall carts drawn by oxen or horses. The soldiers headed north; the civilians and the wounded headed south. Yes, he repeated to himself, so far he had done pretty well. He had thrown off the scent; he had learned where his two divisions were, and now he was going forward to confirm the locations for himself, at Aalen and Crailsheim. He had found Maria, and as soon as the war ended he would come back. Someday, when one could laugh about the regime, he might tell her he was the spy Herr Fidl had almost caught and her mother would have liked to tear apart with her own hands.

"Yes," the gremlin reproached him, "but her brothers are at Crailsheim now. You are going to deliver them to the enemy. When the American bomb has killed them, will you tell her you planned the raid? You have a letter to them in your pocket now."

Cold as it was, Happy's hand sweated as it fingered the paper.

"Won't one division be enough for the little captain?" the voice wheedled. That is the way the Devil starts, by a compromise. "Germany has not many to spare. Let's give him the Twenty-fifth, and be quiet about Ninth Flak."

Happy shook his head to blank his mind about Crailsheim and what he would do when he reached it and after he crossed the Rhine. He trudged along, outwardly one of hundreds of thousands of obscure German soldiers tramping the highways of the Reich back to the defense of her borders. He shook his head again to rid it of the thought of yesterday, when he had been one of the enemy, and of four days hence, when he would become one again, to rid it of the very existence of Maurer, as Frau Liebert had shaken her head to rid it of the war. He must *become* Steinberg. It is not easy to be two men at once.

Germany tilts like a plank from the Alps to the North Sea. The rivers flow north, with the single exception of the Danube, which stretches crosswise, flowing to the east, like a crack one-third down the face of the plank. He had thirty kilometers to Memmingen, and he was sure he could cover them before dark without getting tired enough to ask for a ride. He had thirty more to Ulm, and then he would have reached the Danube.

Thousands of troops like Steinberg were tilting down the slope to the Danube, not only toward Ulm, but toward Donau-wörth and Ingolstadt and Passau, leaving Kesselring to hold

165

the passes of the Alps behind them against the American Fifth Army. Kesselring was a marshal of the Luftwaffe, and its darling. Germany could count on him. Then the troops would fan out from the Danube, east or west, to hold the bulwarks of the Oder and the Rhine. The two-front war was draining Germany of its blood, leeching out its middle-aged and its boys, down to its sick and wounded. They ebbed away at a hundred wounds around the whole periphery, coming back not at all or coming back behind the closed tarpaulins of the wood-burning ambulances. The war drained off even the livestock; the horses plodding up to haul the artillery because no gas was left, and the cows, driven from the farms to feed the troops.

Halfway to Memmingen, at a point where the railroad hugs the highway, he saw a signal train of four boxcars and a locomotive, with aerials strung across the roofs, and on top of the embankment behind, the great bowl of a Würzburg radar. It had no anti-aircraft protection. The only crew seemed to be women, in the same black uniforms that railroad workers wear all over the Continent. Two of them squatted in the swivel seats, earphones at their heads and the traverse wheels in their hands. Another stood by with a telephone, and the fourth fingered the dials of a field radio. Over those wires the announcement of his pursuit might be broadcast from Schongau or Kempten, unless the Americans knocked the train out first. It was just like the Würzburg at Cassino, as he had told the Ami expert, but now the crew were women. He noted the location carefully, so he could spot it for them on the map. He hurried past, pacing the distance to the next kilometer-stone. He wondered if he had not already seen too much to remember. His feet were getting sore again, in spite of Frau Liebert's powder. But he did not accept the lifts he was offered so often, or even fall in with any of the single soldiers trudging in the same direction. He could see more on foot and alone. It was six when he got into Memmingen.

The soldiers' club was on the highway, across from the station, with a big white SOLDATENHEIM sign across what had once been the Hotel Weinsigel. He went through the door in the pink stucco front. The lounge, which must have been the hotel dining room, was filled with troops sitting at round tables. Two crystal chandeliers hung from the molded and cupid-painted ceiling, with half the bulbs screwed out. The great round-topped windows were covered with blackout curtains. Happy dropped into a chair at an empty table. He let all his Klamotten slide to the floor beside him, his knapsack and helmet and gas mask. At a counter in the corner women passed out food and beer under the eye of a fat SA trooper who sat behind the cash register. Happy sat panting for several minutes before he realized he was hungry as well as tired. He still had two slices of cheese left, but he was going to keep them till the Wehrmacht food gave out.

He went to the counter and paid two marks for a plate and a glass of beer. He carried them to his table, ate and drank, and went back for more, hoping the Helferin at the counter would not notice he had been there already. A boy threaded his way among the tables selling newspapers. For twenty pfennigs Happy bought a copy of the *Heidenheimer Zeitung*, the mouthpiece of the regime for the district. He spread it out on the table, eating his potato sandwich while he read the tiny type under the faint light from the ceiling. In a box headed "News from the Allgäu" he saw what he had feared.

From Schongau it was reported that a farmer had found the spy's empty parachute, with his helmet and coverall, hidden in a woodpile on his field. He had notified the Kommandantur. With the help of Air-Raid Warden Leopold Fidl of Böbing they set a brace of dogs on the scent. They tracked the spy along the country road through Böbing and down the Krummengraben ravine, but lost the scent on the highway six kilometers south of Schongau. Continuing into the town, they picked it up again at the bridgehead square. It led them six hundred yards westward toward Kaufbeuren. At the first kilometer-stone the dogs pointed, pawed in the ground, and dug up four slices of gray bread. Five hundred yards to the west the trail stopped dead again. It was suspected that the spy had got a ride from here in an automobile or a cart, as well as across the first stretch where the dogs had lost the scent.

To have been given a ride, he must have worn German uniform, and must have passed along the very path which Herr Fidl himself had followed the day before, when he came down to report the plane. In fact, two sets of footprints were found along this path, one of which Herr Fidl admitted were his own. The other bore the hobnail pattern of the Luftwaffe, steel toes and many large nails on the sole, steel rims with four small nails on the heel. Luftwaffe boots were different from Army. The Kommandantur was making a careful check to determine which pair of boots had passed over the path first—unless, which could not be believed by those who knew Warden Fidl, they had passed over it together. Meanwhile, any citizens or soldiers who might have been at the Schongau bridge early on the morning of the seventeenth were asked to notify the Kommandantur by collect telephone if they had seen any suspicious characters. The driver of the bus from Schongau to Kempten would check the names of passengers on her pad as soon as she returned to Kempten, believing she could identify by name the passenger whom she had picked up at the point where the dogs had lost the trail. The Hitler Youth were helping in the search, and Herr Fidl was being closely questioned to refresh his memory. It was hoped that the name and description of the spy could be broadcast to the police and security troops of the whole Reich in Tuesday's issue of the Blacklist.

It would not do to stare so long at one corner of the page. He turned it over. On the back of the single sheet he read this:

SUCH WOULD BE THE FATE OF THE GERMAN PEOPLE. MILLIONS SHOT. OTHERS DELIVERED TO SLOW BUT SURE STARVATION. PRISONERS OF WAR ENSLAVED TO THE BOLSHEVIK HANGMEN. WOMEN AND GIRLS

DELIVERED TO THE ALLIED SOLDIERY, OF ALL COLORS AND RACES. LET NO ONE BELIEVE THAT THE NORTH AMERICANS ARE BETTER THAN THEIR BOLSHEVIK BROTHERS. ONE IS AS EVIL AS THE OTHER, AND BEHIND BOTH STANDS THE JEW.

An infantry sergeant dropped into the other chair, unshaven and as dirty as Happy himself. He propped his rifle against the counter behind him and laid his knapsack and helmet on the floor beside Happy's.

"You are reading about the spy," he observed. "I wouldn't want to be in his shoes if they catch him, and they will catch him all right."

"Or in Leopold Fidl's shoes." Happy forced himself to laugh.

"That Blacklist is thorough all right. I was in a spot-check near the front once, when the police were looking for a man whose name was on the list. They held everyone up. It took five minutes to check each Soldbuch."

"Did they catch him?"

"Not there anyway. That's what I mean by their being thorough, that they didn't catch him—there. But I bet they caught him somewhere. Tuesday is the big day for spot-checks. They held our column up an hour at the barrier. Well, I'm going to wolf a little supper. Want me to take your plate back for more?"

Happy nodded. The sergeant went away, returned, and munched his sandwiches in silence. When he finished he looked at Happy.

"Back to the front?"

"Yes. Convalescent leave."

"A fine way this is to spend leave! I've been at a class in Friedrichshafen myself for Panzerfaust training. That's the weapon to stop tanks, surer than ditches or dragon's teeth or roadblocks. Replacement companies are getting nine of them from now on. The Yankees have one too, called the bazooka; what a funny language! We had a captured one at the class. But it's not as good as ours. Ours will go through three centimeters of steel at thirty yards, and the flame shoots back three. I can see the farm boys gawping at it already. Only why didn't ordnance invent it sooner? It's like the V-2, good stuff but a little late. I finished the course yesterday. So now I'm going back to HQ to pass it on to the recruits."

"Where is that?" Happy asked. Queer how frightened he was to ask the simple question.

The sergeant pointed to the patch stenciled on his knapsack, a white shield with a flaming sword in red.

"Twenty-fifth Infantry Division, of course, at Aalen. Don't you even know the patches? Oh, well, you're in the Air Force; perhaps they don't know so much. Well, at least I've got my own Volkswagen to drive, so I don't have to walk. It's outside in the parking lot now, but I don't want to drive it in the blackout. There's enough of that up forward. I think I'll spend the night here; they must have bunks somewhere."

"Believe I'll do the same." Happy reflected. "I've been walking most of the day."

"You wait here, then. I'll go see if they have any bunks."

The sergeant walked up to the desk, leaving Happy to look after the gear. When he came back he was carrying two mugs of beer.

"The old Brownshirt says the dormitory here is full, but there are places to sleep in a bunker. He seems proud that Memmingen has a bunker, as if it was really in the war. He told me there's going to be a movie here in ten minutes too."

"Let's wait and see it, what do you say? I'll pay for the next beer."

"I'm broke myself, but if you pay for two more rounds I'll give you a ride in my Volkswagen tomorrow. You must be going at least as far as Ulm; it's the only way to the front from here. I go on to Aalen. Come all the way if you want. Supposed to be there tomorrow, but they didn't say what time. Let's drink up and get the other beers before they turn the lights out. I'd like to watch a while, then turn in. I need to get some sleep."

Happy said, "Prima," and went over to the counter for four more beers.

Surprisingly enough, the movie was American, an old picture they must have saved from before the war, with Harold Lloyd, and German subtitles. Happy did not let on that he understood the English soundtrack. Sometimes it was hard not to laugh between the subtitles, but the sergeant never laughed at all. Halfway through he whispered, "I suppose German pictures aren't good enough for the Brownshirt. What do you say we turn in?"

They stood up, and the other soldiers shouted at them to keep their heads down. They crouched across the aisle to the counter where the Brownshirt watched the movie, his mouth agape.

"I've got to get my papers stamped before I turn in," Happy told the sergeant.

"So do I."

The Brownshirt seemed to be transport officer as well as manager of the club. "Why didn't you have me do this before, while the lights were on?" he grumbled.

He turned his flashlight on the pair of travel orders and muttered, "Soldbücher!" Happy fumbled long enough with his pocket so that the sergeant had his book ready first. The Brownshirt compared the books with their faces, and with the trip tickets, and stamped "Forwarded" on the orders, with the date. The boys threaded their way around to the back of the hall, ducking to keep out of the beam.

They turned left around the streetcorner, as the Brownshirt had directed the sergeant, and through a brick arch into the court of the old city fortress. The bunker steps were marked by a sign planted in the heap of sandbags, with a white arrow and the letters LSR for Luftschutzraum. The shelter was underground, in a kind of natural dungeon, shored up with balks of timber. There must have been a hundred others there already, mostly the jittery civilians who sleep in bunkers before there is any danger, with a few late soldiers like themselves. A curtain separated the women from the men. Beyond the dim light of a single bulb wedged in the rotten rock at the foot of the steps, they heard the coughing and tossing on both sides of the curtain. The floor was gravel. An old woman gave them each a blanket and took ten pfennigs from them. The ventilation was bad, the air was rank with ammonia, and they could hear the water trickling in the latrines.

"Small-town bunker after all, you see?" the sergeant said. "Have you ever seen the ones in Berlin, with air conditioning and tiled washrooms? Better than home, and built above ground, four stories high and so thick you don't even feel the blockbusters."

"I have civilian friends in Berlin," Happy said. "It does not seem that any bunker could be safe in the heavy raids."

"Berlin? It's the safest city for civilians in the Reich, provided they take cover soon enough. By the way, I'm Heinrich Scholz. Headquarters Company, Twenty-fifth Infantry."

He held out his hand. Happy mumbled "Steinberg" into a cigarette, cupping his palms over the lighter to blur his name, but not daring to give a false one in case the sergeant had seen his papers, or might see them tomorrow. "Corporal, from Field Post Number 33148." He smiled, straightening up to shake hands.

"Pretty careful at the front, aren't you?" Scholz laughed. "Well, you're right not to give away your outfit to strangers. For all you know I might be that spy; or no, because his footprints were Luftwaffe. But you might be."

He looked down at Happy's boots. They both laughed. They took off their boots, standing them against the damp wall. Happy placed his so the sergeant could not see the soles. He spread out the blanket and took off his overcoat to put

172

over him. He used his knapsack for a pillow. Sergeant Scholz lay down next to him.

"It was in Paris a year ago tonight." He sighed. "Chauffeur for a colonel at the Hotel Continental. Some difference! Never mind, my wife and I will be going back there soon if you fellows only shoot down enough Ami planes."

"Or you knock out enough Ami tanks."

They chuckled cozily, and Scholz started to snore.

Eight

When they woke up it was only five, but already a few other soldiers were lining up in front of the latrine, or washing their faces under the pump reserved for them, with the hard sandy soap the Wehrmacht issued. Nobody wasted any soap. Happy and Scholz had breakfast back in the club. Afterward they walked out to the guarded parking lot. They climbed into the Volkswagen, dropping their gear in the back, where the bazooka lay in its long oilskin case. Scholz filled his tank at the Aral pump. He gave back his receipt to the guard and started up road nineteen to Ulm. It was colder than yesterday, but just as clear. The Volkswagen rolled gently downhill across the rich Danube valley. The snow flurries of the hills were over. There were no more poles at the roadside to mark the shoulders in a blizzard, and Swabian pine and beech succeeded the cathedral pink-pillared firs of the Allgäu.

Memmingen's little airfield was on a plateau at the edge of town. They saw three Heinkel 5s and a Dornier 17, old-type planes which looked as if they had not flown for months. There was no ground crew in sight. The tires were stripped from the landing wheels. "Decoys for the Amis," Sergeant Scholz explained. As they drew near the Danube, toward noon, they began to pass more carts, drawn by horses or oxen or even by a man and his wife, loaded with family possessions, heading south. That was the only sign they were approaching the action area. Sergeant Scholz looked at the refugees with contempt.

"There are cowards in every country, I guess, even in the Reich. You know, I was over in the Westmark last month. We were driven out of a little town one day by the Amis, but took it back the next. You'd be surprised; in the few hours that we were out the whole town had been filled with sheets and white flags. The Halunken did not dare surrender the place while we were there to watch, but the minute our backs were turned they gave up. Our captain treated that town rough. He caught one man on a roof, lifting the white flag, and he shot him from the ground with his Luger. I can tell you those sheets snapped in the windows after that. The swine!" He spat toward one cart as he passed it. "Our job is hard enough even if the civilians appreciate what we're doing for them, but when you feel they will sell out for their own safety you don't see why we should risk our skins. That was the only bad taste I had in Paris too. The Frenchmen never dared to make trouble, but you could tell from just walking down the street that they hated us. Even the whores, I am told by those who tried them. Well, we had to give up Paris but it was fun while it lasted. We weren't driven out of France, you understand, but it is just part of the high command's policy to withdraw from territory we don't intend to keep after the war is won. So we shortened our lines pretty successfully and, believe me, we caused the Amis a lot of damage in the process. I was in the campaign way back when we took Paris, and I know what that kind of easy advance really costs an army. The farther the Yankees advance the more they pay. Well, now we have a solid line on the Rhine, and I guess we have one in the east too. The Russians have never been any good outside their own country. So I imagine He is going to bleed them all to death. The Americans will never get across the Rhine, you mark my words. Do you believe in prophecy? Read this."

With his left hand he pulled a folded typewritten sheet from his breast pocket. "Someone slipped it under my door at the Continental last April, probably a pacifist."

It was headed "Aus dem Weltgeschehen"—From World History.

Napoleon born	20 April 1760	
Hitler born	20 April 1889	129 years later
French Revolution	1789	
German Revolution	1918	129 years later
Napoleon in power	1804	
Hitler in power	1933	129 years later
Napoleon invades Russia	1812	
Hitler invades Russia	1941	129 years later
Peace in Vienna	1815	
Peace for Germany	1944	129 years later

For 1944: Stalin assassinated; armistice in Moscow; peace without victory in the fall; Japan invades Australia; England and America at war.

"Yes," said Happy, "but this is nineteen forty-five, not nineteen forty-four."

The sergeant shrugged. "Maybe you're a pacifist too. Anyway, it's only February, and what are a couple of months in world history?"

"I've never been in France myself," Happy said, "except just with my old battalion last month into Alsace, before I got pneumonia. Now when I get back across the Rhine I'm not sure where I'll find the new one. I guess they'll tell me when I get to the Mannheim bridge. That's what my orders read, to cross by the Mannheim bridge."

"So you're headed back to the front! Don't worry, they'll see you get there soon enough. And no true German says Alsace is in France. That is just temporary. I can't take you any farther than Aalen. That's thirty kilometers beyond Ulm. Between you and me, our division is being re-formed up there out of what's left of several others. We're taking a new number, the Twenty-fifth, so as to make it sound as if we were adding troops instead of losing them. I guess I shouldn't say that, should I? Where are you from, anyway?"

"Magdeburg," Happy told him. "I bet you're from Berlin."

The sergeant nodded. "That's right. Potsdam, anyway; right outside, you know. Not so far from you. I used to be a gardener in the Sans Souci palace, and look at me now."

He laughed harshly, as sergeants do when they indulge in self-pity. "Well, anyway, take a look at my wife and kids."

He handed his Soldbuch to Happy, to look at the pictures in the back flap. A plain girl, he thought, holding a tiny baby in her arms. A two-year-old clung to her skirts.

"Isn't she sweet?"

"Prima! Some people have all the luck."

The sergeant smiled fatuously. "After the war we're going to start a plant nursery. My wife will do the paper work. There will be a good demand for stock, so much has been cut for firewood or destroyed in the bombings."

He smiled to himself, but kept his eyes on the road to avoid the foot traffic. Even sergeants liked to describe what they would do after the war, when anyone would listen. He shook his head and looked sharply at Happy. "How come you don't pack a rifle? Is even the Luftwaffe short of weapons? Usually they get the best of everything."

"No, it isn't that, but I'm in the Medical Corps and we don't show any. Something in the Geneva Convention."

"Well, the Geneva Convention ought to let anyone shoot

177

the spies and terror-bombers at sight. When you get close to the front they're going to wonder why you don't carry a gun, might even pick you up at a spot-check for being without one. I was going to say, I've brought this bazooka back from school, so I'll sell you my rifle if you want it. I think I could get away with the trade all right. It's a good 98k, with a sling, and only weighs four kilos, the short model, you know; easy to carry and in good shape."

Happy shook his head. "They'd say I stole it, since there isn't any entry in my Soldbuch. If they meant me to have one, they'd issue it."

"Listen, bub, no one gets in the Blacklist for having a gun, not even a chaplain. Think it over for a hundred marks. You won't get another chance close to the front. I haven't got any more right to sell it than you have to buy it, but you know how dizzy everything is these days. This new CP is the dizziest yet. They can't crowd the whole division in the grounds, even though it isn't up to strength. What matter so long as everyone has a gun?"

He sighed. "I guess the Army is always the same. Here I really know something about the Panzerfaust, enough to teach recruits anyway, but after a couple of days I bet they'll ship me out as a truckdriver, and it will be back to the front after all for me too. I miss that school at Friedrichshafen already. Right on the water. You look across the lake and there is Switzerland with the lights blazing all night like before the war. Someday I want to take my wife there to get a closer look. You married? No, you couldn't be."

"No, but I will be, right after the war. I met a girl yesterday—"

"Ach, mein armer Kopf; don't tell me about her."

They eased past a work camp—"for the Eastern peoples," read the sign on the gate—with wire and towers like the cage at Aitrang, and rows of camouflaged shacks. Most of the slaves had marched to work, but three, too weak to walk, gripped at the wire with their claws, staring silent at the Volkswagen. The gray tower of the minster rose ahead of them, across a glimpse of the narrow green Danube winding between stone banks and steep roofs.

They had come to the fringe of the war. Defense began at the Danube, as if the high command knew all was lost once the enemy crossed the river. They had come close already; many houses at the bridge-ends were roofless and gutted.

"That's their phosphorus bomb," Scholz told him. "They dropped them nine days before Christmas. Don't look so funny; you'll see lots worse when you get forward."

Under the direction of a fat Brownshirt with a rifle, a group of prisoners from the camp sweated at building a roadblock across the near side of the streetcar bridge. They dug the foundation pits, barrowed the concrete in, lashed the log uprights with cable, and braced them with seven-inch steel.

"Won't do any good," Scholz decided. "One hit, and the tanks will walk through. Even if we blow the bridge, the Amis will build another. Now if they issued a few Panzerfaust . . ."

On the roof of the slaughterhouse, off to the right, Happy saw a battery of Vierling, but these half-way defenses, he had to agree, would be useless against the American armor.

The bridge itself was mined, but not guarded. When you cross it you cross from Bavaria into Württemberg. The planks rattled under the Volkswagen, and Happy was one province farther from Leopold Fidl. He had come two hundred kilometers from the woodpile and had as many more to go, but he was nearer safety with each kilometer-stone he passed. The city was crowded with military traffic moving north. Hipo cops, with the brassard on their jackets, stood at each corner, draining the stream of wood-burning and horsedrawn vehicles through the series of roadblocks. Scholz's Volkswagen was one of the few that burned gas, ersatz gas from Leuna, which didn't give much mileage or power, but still gas.

"This is HQ for the 151st Field Artillery. For a while anyway." He grinned. "That's their patch you see everywhere, the red T on the white shield. I don't know what the T stands for, but your spy might give something to know they're in Ulm."

In contrast to the struggling and jostling of the troops, the civilians seemed apathetic. They stared into shop windows where there was nothing to buy, or loitered against the sandbags of the air-raid shelters, without looking up as the convoys rumbled across the cobbles.

A Hipo pointed out the way to the canteen. The sergeant looked at his watch when he had parked. It was eleven.

"Ever been in Ulm before?"

Happy shook his head.

"I've got an idea. If this is going to be our last day before we eat army rations again—"

"Not my last day."

"—well, mine then. Let's look around this town for a while and eat late in some good restaurant. Around two. It's about seventy kilometers to Division. We can make it easy in an hour and a half, then you can eat and bunk with us and take a look at that rifle. I've got some extra Reisemarken, even if I have no cash."

"I've got both."

"God knows what we will find, but it couldn't be worse than my division mess at Aalen. When I get there I'll say I had a breakdown. They don't check up the way they used to; that's how I can sell you my rifle. Even the Gestapo is bogging down. Notice our papers weren't checked at the bridge? They'll never catch the spy that way. Red tape is all right while it works, but once it tangles, better to have none. The good old German thoroughness is kaput. The adjutant at Aalen doesn't even know I have a car; for all he knows, I may be hitchhiking like you. Let's stay. And thou mayst call me Heinrich."

Happy reflected. He felt safer now that he was over the Danube, and the new Blacklist was still two days off. Even if it was only to sell him the rifle, the sergeant was calling him "du," like the Joes at the Golden Well. Some of them must be sergeants too. Besides, he couldn't think of any good reason why a soldier on leave should refuse the chance.

"Okay. I have three more days' leave, and I'd like to see the place. But let's not get our papers stamped till we start; otherwise they may forward us now."

"Thou art not so dumb as I thought."

He tucked the receipt for car and weapons in his Soldbuch, and they left their knapsacks at the checkroom in the canteen.

"They've hardly tasted the war here yet," Heinrich said, frowning professionally, "but they're getting ready for it."

"Well, I hope they don't taste any more than they have. They can count on the Luftwaffe anyway. This place is like a history book. It's like Italy. Let's get a map so as to see all the sights without repeating."

They loafed along the river till they came to a stationery store facing the quay. Heinrich bought some lemon candy and a plastic jar of Blendax toothpaste. Happy bought a city map and a pencil. As they wandered through the streets, he marked their route with his pencil, frowning as he checked the street names from the lampposts. But wherever he saw a roadblock or one of the mobile steel pillboxes he put a little dot in the course, which nobody but himself would notice.

(This was only to protect the Americans when they came, he told himself, before the gremlin had a chance to whisper. It was not to betray the city. Steinberg could watch and listen in all innocence; but it would be only Maurer who could betray it, and he was not yet Maurer again.)

They spent two hours like tourists, lounging through the old cathedral and staring aimlessly at the traffic over the bridge.

"The beautiful blue Danube!" Heinrich sneered. "It looks to me like the liquid manure they pump on the fields." He hummed the waltz and spat into the swift green current.

Then they drank beer on the terrace of an almost empty

181

hotel, where they could look up at the lacy gray tower, the tallest church spire in the world. When they grew hungry they found a cellar café near the cathedral, on Adolf-Hitler-strasse. For lunch they had rabbit goulash which wasn't too bad, and some Neckar wine, and a custard pie made of corn-starch. An old phonograph with a morning-glory horn played tangos and the inevitable "Lili Marlene," about three to one. There were three bedraggled girls at a single table who danced with any soldiers who asked them.

"They're on the Wehrmacht payroll just like us," Heinrich whispered with a wink. "They need a boost in their make-up ration. But it would take more than paint and stockings to hook me. No, Junge, Paris spoiled me. Besides, I'm married. Go ahead if you wish, but I'd rather watch the movie."

"Me too." He was thinking of Maria, who was going to knit him a pair of socks. You couldn't think that the Wehrmacht prostitutes were the same species as a girl like Maria, or even the same sex. They did not even disgust him, for he had served time in the pro station—the Sanierstube—next door to the Air Force brothel in Berlin, collecting the dogtags from the cadets before they went upstairs, and injecting perman-ganate (because there was no penicillin), and signing their little white certificates after they came down.

The girls slipped out a back door with three privates of the 151st, but were back at their table in twenty minutes. That was just another function of the body.

The lights dimmed for the matinée, and it was better than the night before insofar as Cristina Soderbaum is better to look at than Harold Lloyd, and German dialogue better to hear than English. It ended at four. Heinrich and Happy hurried back to the club to have their papers stamped for the day, and climbed into the car again. Happy was glad he had stayed over. There was a kind of security to traveling with an old campaigner like Heinrich, instead of alone, like a spy.

North of the Danube Germany rises again, rolling up to the

182

plateau of the Black Forest before tilting downward to the North Sea. Heinrich turned up the cobbled hill. Six kilometers out of Ulm this old road crossed the new Autobahn, part of the great double-lane network which the Labor Service had built and the regime paid for in the war budget. Mostly there is a grass lane between the strips of roadway on the Autobahn, but sometimes the lane is concrete long enough for a plane take-off, and parking space is hacked out of the woods on each side. The Autobahn bypasses all the cities, but there are exits to each over a cloverleaf which leads the traffic out, so there are no grade crossings. At the Ulm junction the old road climbs over the new on a concrete bridge with iron rails, resting on a pylon in the lane. Eastbound traffic to Augsburg turns onto the Autobahn short of the bridge; north- and westbound pass over, the north to go straight and the west to take the cloverleaf. As they approached the Autobahn the traffic grew thicker. Happy put his head out through the side curtain.

"You needn't look," Heinrich groaned. "I know what it is. First spot-check of the war zone. They don't have them in the rear; they don't have them at the front. Just in between."

He had to slow the car down to a crawl behind a horse-drawn 7.5 light infantry howitzer; its stubby muzzle faced them from the rectangular barrel. In the triangle at the foot of the bridge a lieutenant sat at a big table off to the side of the pavement with a shelter-half stretched on poles over his head to keep off the weather. The span of the overpass rose ahead of them. There was a big white Gasthaus on the far side.

"Wish we could stop for a glass of dark." Heinrich laughed.

A far-spaced column of camouflaged tanks was clanking westward on the Autobahn, the crosses on their sides scarred by shell splinters, their crews, standing in the open cupolas, grim-faced under their netted steel helmets, their black tunics open at the neck because of the heat inside. Tigers, Panthers, even one lumbering Ferdinand, heading from some last ordnance reserve to defend the Rhine. Happy could spot the model by counting the bogies, as Heinrich waited his turn in the check. The last tank in the convoy, way off to their right, was towed by oxen, for even the Panzer Corps ran short of Diesel. Between one tank and the next, boys of the Labor Corps shoveled gravel into the potholes cut by enemy strafing.

"I bet you," Heinrich said, "that they're staging this check so nothing can get on the Autobahn to slow up the tanks. I hope that's all, anyway. Now I wish I hadn't cheated the half-day in Ulm."

The 7.5 turned up the bridge and swung down the cloverleaf to join the column of tanks. Heinrich inched his car forward to the sentry, who put his head in the window and said, "Soldbücher."

The two boys handed him their books. The sentry looked at Heinrich's first, since he was a sergeant, compared his face with the picture in the front cover, and returned it. He did the same with Happy's and said harshly, "If you are Medical Corps, why don't you wear your brassard?"

"I took it off to keep it clean," Happy said humbly.

He fished it out of his belt, where it had lain two days, and fastened it around his arm with the safety pins. Heinrich had to snap the pins shut for him.

"Marschbefehle!"

They handed him their trip tickets, both of them stamped for each day since their separate trips began.

"On leave," mocked the sentry. "I wish they would give us leave sometime. Well, enjoy it while you can; you haven't got long. See that you report on time, and from here out all troops wear helmets."

He carried the two orders over to the lieutenant, while the boys sheepishly fitted their steel helmets on and tucked the caps in their knapsacks. The lieutenant, like the sentries, wore blue facings and GFP in white on his shoulder straps. The letters stand for Secret Field Police—they are the field branch of the Gestapo. But the word "geheim" on documents does not quite mean "secret" as the dictionary says; it is more like "confidential." As long as he wore the letters, the lieutenant was just on routine duty. After glancing at the two travel orders he thumbed through an oblong green-bound paper book. Happy saw that he ran his finger down only a single page; that must be because Steinberg and Scholz both began with S.

"That's the Blacklist," Heinrich whispered. "I see it's green this week. Last week it was purple. By the time they issue the new one tomorrow the spy may be out of the country."

But the lieutenant did not find either name. He stamped the orders with the inevitable "Forwarded," and the sentry handed them back. He gave them the German greeting, the Hitler straightarm, and they returned a head-salute.

On the incoming side of the road, to the left, the other sentry stood guard over two civilians handcuffed beside a horsedrawn cart. It was piled with furniture. Their horse sniffed at the withered grass along the cobbles. Perhaps they had been caught smuggling contraband. They seemed to await the lieutenant's leisure to be punished. But military traffic had priority over black marketeers. Heinrich did not wait to see; he drove straight through above the Autobahn as soon as the sentry returned their papers.

This Autobahn would pass Stuttgart. It would veer to the north again at Karlsruhe and cross Happy's own route on the plain just short of Mannheim, and then disappear somewhere down the Rhine. What civilian traffic there was the sentries would shunt straight through the overpass after them; nothing but an old man driving a cow, a girl with a flock of geese, one or two farmers with heavy sacks on their shoulders. The line was still waiting to be checked when the sentry waved the Volkswagen forward. But even civilians had to show the Kennkarte, the little gray identity card with picture and fingerprints which everyone in Germany had to carry, down to those fourteen years old.

Heinrich wiped his forehead, tilting the helmet back. "I don't know why those checks scare me so. I must have been through a hundred, and there is never anything wrong with my papers; but they certainly put the fear of God into me. You never know how much they know about you. Well, I suppose only the guilty can complain, and I'll be at Division before long, where at least they forgive a man's sins, or anyway don't suspect them."

Having passed the crest of the Danube Valley, the road sauntered gently downward through woods and farmland.

"It's funny how little traffic there is," said Happy, "compared with the Autobahn."

"The Army uses the Autobahn as far up as it can, but near the front the Yankees have knocked it out. We're not that far forward yet. Then the tanks have to pull in to side roads like this. You will see them again after Heilbronn. But there's plenty of armor in these hills that we can't see and the Amis can't see either. Take these men on foot we're passing. They may look pretty old to you, and some just like kids, but they're all going up to join the Twenty-fifth. If we have uniforms for them, they'll be wearing shoulder straps like mine within a week. When we get closer you'll see there are barracks along the road too, because we can't get the whole strength of the division into a single camp. Good idea to disperse anyhow, in case of air raids. Well, Junge, we had a good time loafing, but when you come down to it there's nothing like getting back into the Army groove."

Happy chuckled. He was beginning to feel that way himself. "That's right. After a few months it's home, even if you switch to a new outfit like me. I'm getting homesick for it myself. Still and all, I haven't even written a postcard to my family in Berlin—Magdeburg, I mean—since I had this leave. I'll have to do that tonight."

He caught his breath at the slip and wondered whether to explain it. But Heinrich had not noticed.

Happy thought back to his own groove: how Fritz Gruber and he had made plans for after the war, under the vaulted ceiling of the dormitory at Cassino, till the bugle rang the raid alarm and everyone ran out to action stations. He was going to finish medical school, but Fritz was getting married and hoped for leave even before the victory. How they had made up the longest German words they could put together, when neither the present nor the future could be talked about.

Happy had given

HOTTENTOTTENPOTENTATENTANTENTINTENATTENTÄTER

which means "one that libels the aunt of a Hottentot potentate."

On the blackboard Fritz had changed TINTEN, which means ink, to TITTEN, which means in German what it sounds like in English. He had clasped two helmets to his chest and saucered out his lip like a Ubangi and pranced around the stove in his shorts, while the rest of the dormitory rocked with laughter on their cots. Heinrich was right; you got homesick for the Wehrmacht.

Twenty kilometers out of Ulm they began to pass the scattered barracks of the new division, a few temporary huts off the side of the road, camouflaged brown and green like the gun at the Golden Well; sometimes a farmhouse requisitioned for a troop billet; and always in the yard a drill going on, close order drill for the infantry, or a noncom showing recruits how to use the rifle or bipod machine gun. Happy noticed that the recruits themselves had no weapons. In the drill they were using brooms or sticks cut from the boughs of the ash trees. In the classes there was only one rifle to a squad. Heinrich twice showed him a big 8.8 camouflaged in its round emplacement and so located that it controlled the slopes below and on each side, and even when he pointed Happy had to look hard to make out the guns among the netting and branches. These guns were used for anti-tank or anti-aircraft, depending on the ammo and the elevation. They were the deadliest guns in the German Army. And once he saw the five snouts of a Nebel-werfer poking above a hedge of artificial bushes. This was Katyusha, the smoke and rocket thrower which the Germans had copied from the Russians after they had seen her at the siege of Stalingrad. The dogfaces called her "Screaming Mee-mie."

The roadcheck had held them up so long that it was half-past six when they got to Aalen, but Heinrich never stopped talking all the way.

"Now, Junge, you'd better come in with me, because it's so late. I've given you as long a ride as you are likely to get be-tween now and the Rhine. You won't find another tonight. Maybe tomorrow morning someone will be going your way from our HQ."

He chuckled. "I hope to get a promotion out of that course. I passed tops in it. They ought to embroider my Litzenspiegel." He fingered the double bar which every soldier wore on his collar. "If those Halunken we saw by the road can instruct drill and machine gun, I ought to stand pretty high, because I can instruct the bazooka. Something tells me we're going to need them to knock out a few Ami tanks before many weeks are over. The idea of our division being on top of the hill here is that we can cover the whole stretch from the Neckar to the Danube. We can turn up this highway we're on now—it's a good road, though it gets pretty winding along the Neckar—or we can send out detachments back to the Autobahn and spearhead them straight to the Rhine. That's the road the Yankees will try to take if they should get across, because it's so fast. Unless they knock it out completely first so they can't use it themselves. Remember, when we go down to meet them, whichever road they take, they will be fighting uphill and we will be fighting downhill, and we know the terrain and they don't, unless the spy betrays us."

"You haven't much confidence in us over the Rhine." Happy

laughed. "I admit our Vierling won't do much against tanks, but the enemy can't get them across without his planes, and our job is to drop those planes."

"No, I don't have much confidence, I'll be honest with you, because I've seen myself how the Amis forced us back just a little to the north of Mannheim. We withdrew over the bridge at Mainz and, believe me, we got across just in time. We had a raid there. It was only on the third of this month, just before I went to the bazooka class. I had to hand it to the gangsters, they laid the city flat in half an hour. But they didn't harm the cathedral, just blew the windows out. I don't know how they could miss it and still kill eight thousand civilians. Your Luftwaffe didn't do so well against them up there. But here we are in a better position. Just wait and see, they can't do anything with their planes because we are too widely dispersed on the hills. We knock out their tanks with our Panzerfaust, and when everything is ripe our infantry moves in. Man for man, the German infantry is better than theirs."

"Have it your own way," Happy said. "I don't think you'll even be here. I think they'll have you in that Blacklist for having stayed half a day longer on the way than you should."

The sergeant chuckled again. "What a joker! Listen, you have three more days' leave. Come on in and look my place over. I'll show you my rifle at work on the range. You might as well spend the night; I can get permission for you. Otherwise you must start walking as soon as you leave me, and you might not be able to find a Gasthaus before the curfew. They're strict about curfew around here, account of the raids."

"Okay. Your general can only kick me out."

"The general isn't there; he's away at some strategy Klatsch with the Gauleiter. It's only Colonel Forster now. What does that mean, 'okay'? I heard you say it once before."

"Oh, that's Yankee slang. I learned it from the Ami prisoners we took."

"Can you speak American?"

"A little bit. I had it in school at Magdeburg."

They reached the headquarters of the 25th Infantry Division, in a big park enclosed by a low stone wall. There was a sign at the gate with the striped triangle which meant division, and an Arabic 25 below it. A sentry stood at the gate; the same sword-flame patch as on Heinrich's knapsack was stenciled on the gable of his box. Back of him, inside the wall, was a sort of gatehouse converted into the orderly room, with DIENSTSTELLE 25 INF. DIV. on a banner over the arched stone doorway. Through the trees Happy saw a three-story stone institution, with tents and wood barracks spaced around it in the park.

"It used to be a forestry school," Heinrich explained.

The hooked-cross battle flag, with the stripes both ways on the red field, floated in the late afternoon sun from a pole inside the gate. It was still light, for the Reich was on daylight saving all the year round. Heinrich drew up his Volkswagen at the edge of the paving outside, leaving room for other cars to clear.

"Your pass," the sentry demanded woodenly. Then, recognizing Heinrich, "Oh, it's only thou. Scholz, who knows all and steals all. I see thou hast gekriegt a car, even. It's about time thou came back."

"Listen. It is not for the watchdog to bark at his master, nor for a sentry to question one who instructs in the Panzerfaust. I have a comrade with me, a corporal of the Luftwaffe, who will eat with me and sleep here. He is on leave. Wilt thou pass him in?"

The sentry might joke on duty, but he did not unbend. He did not even raise the brim of his helmet to look at Happy, who still sat in the jeep. "Wie heisst er?"

"What *did* he say his name was? Come out, der Karl!"

Happy jumped out of the car. "Corporal Steinberg, to 136th Mountain."

"Well," said the sentry, "I can't let him in without permission from the duty officer. You stay here, Corporal, while Sergeant Scholz takes your papers in for permission."

Happy handed the false papers to Heinrich, who carried them inside. While he waited, a dozen other men and boys straggled up from both directions. They handed their pink induction slips to the sentry, who nodded them in after Heinrich. A charcoal-burning bus loaded with recruits came in from the north. None of these men, except the bus driver, wore uniform; but among the trees inside the park Happy could see figures in Feldgrau moving in squad, and hear Army boots on the gravel paths.

As the sun set a bugle rang out from the base of the flagpole. The tramping ceased, even the clacking of typewriters from inside the orderly room paused. The battle flag was lowered from its mast. The sentry presented arms. Someone inside the park started to sing "Deutschland über Alles," and one by one the whole crowd joined in, even the recruits at the gate, and Happy with them. Beside the Volkswagen he stood at attention till the last words of the old national anthem died away: "Über Alles in der Welt." He turned his back on the sentry to wipe his eyes.

Heinrich came back, striding importantly, sergeantlike, among the recruits.

"The lieutenant says maybe it's okay," he told the sentry. "That's some American I learned from the corporal. You talk to the lieutenant," he said, beckoning to Happy, "while I run the car over to the parking lot. It will be safe to leave our stuff in it till after supper."

Inside the orderly room two girl clerks typed entries on the long muster roll, while the recruits stammered answers to their questions. There was a stack of short wooden signs leaning against one wall of the room, each with an arrow and the symbol of a division unit: line-and-dots for the machine-gun companies, a rhomboid for the tank park, a horseshoe for the corral, a horn for the post office, and a circle for the switchboard. Happy could not see them all. There were twenty or more, freshly painted, ready for setting out as the division organized. A lieutenant sat working at a desk covered with papers. Happy's Soldbuch lay open before him. Happy stood at attention until the lieutenant looked up.

"At ease," the lieutenant ordered. "This request to have you as our guest is most irregular, to introduce into our midst a man from another unit, and even from another arm of the Wehrmacht. However, Sergeant Scholz is a reliable soldier, and if he vouches for you I am willing to make an exception. I do it, however," he went on in a monotone, implying vast duties ahead and vast experience behind, as if he could not waste any emphasis on such a routine problem, "for a consideration. In return for our hospitality"—there seemed to be a sneer in the word—"I request that you exercise for a day or two some of the skill in your branch of the service"—there was surely a sneer in that phrase—"on one of our officers. Our second in command, to be exact. He has greatly hampered the formation of our division by falling ill. He has certain idiosyncrasies about his own care which normally could not be respected in spite of his exalted rank. But in this case we have not yet been assigned a surgeon for the division, and our only medical personnel is a corporal like yourself, whom the colonel executive has seen fit to send to Augsburg for medicine which he insists he needs immediately. If you would be kind enough to attend to Colonel Forster's wants until this corporal returns, we shall be grateful. I shall be glad to see that in case you overstay your leave on this duty a notice to the effect will be sent to your commander from this staff."

"At your command, Herr Leutnant." Happy bowed. He could not have refused this "request," even if he had wanted to. The lieutenant snapped the Soldbuch shut and indicated that Happy could pick it off the desk.

"Sergeant Scholz will take you to his own mess, and after that show you to the colonel's quarters."

Happy saluted and turned outside the door, where Heinrich was already waiting. The clerks looked up at him, but did not stop pounding their typewriters. They knew, if the recruits did not, how conspicuous an Air Force medical uniform was in an infantry division headquarters. The lieutenant went back to the papers on his desk.

Heinrich led Happy toward a portable camouflaged barracks where a line stood with mess kits in their hands, waiting for supper. They unclipped their own as they walked along the path.

"See how many different trees there are." Heinrich waved. "They must have been planted by the forestry school. I expect we'll have to cut most of them down for firewood."

All the trees had labels with Latin names on them.

"The big stone building is the divisional office. The brass* sleep upstairs. It used to be the administration office for the woodchoppers. You should see the officers' lounge. It's all paneled with wood from the Black Forest and the Odenwald, oak and beech and all that; and there are so many stuffed heads on the wall it looks like a real zoo."

Happy could have seen the division was just being organized even if he had not been told. There seemed to be no system to it. A line of KPs brought wood into the cookshed from outside; apparently they just hunted for it on the ground in the fading light. There had been no mess call. The men seemed to straggle in whenever they were hungry or had free time. Supper was potato stew with floating bits of ham, chopped cabbage, black bread, and ersatz coffee. There was no soap in the caldron of water where the mess kits were washed, and the fire underneath it had gone out. They ate in silence, at a long table only half-filled by troops.

"You needn't tell me this isn't like the old Army," Heinrich said irritably. "I know what you're thinking. We've got to telescope a training division into a combat division. It doesn't help

* "Bonzen" was Heinrich's slang.

any that the executive got sick while I was away. Watch out for him; he's a man-eater."

When they went out there was still a little light. Recruits with barracks bags or potato sacks wandered about asking the way to their barracks from others who themselves did not know. At least Heinrich knew his own. It was almost empty, a long shed with a stove in the middle and folding army cots drawn up against each wall. They dropped their gear before the first two bunks and went out again to look for Colonel Forster's quarters.

"Try thirty-eight on the top floor," suggested a captain who was hurrying down the steps of the big stone building. There was not even a guard at the entrance. The corridors were dimly lighted by open bulbs. When they found the right number on a door, Heinrich knocked.

"Come in," a voice called instantly.

"I'll see you at the barracks when you're through," Heinrich whispered. He tiptoed down the corridor, leaving Happy alone.

Happy pushed the door open. The room was almost dark. The blackout curtain was not drawn. He made out the figure of a man sitting upright in the iron bed.

"Pull the curtains, please, and then turn on the light," ordered the harsh voice.

When Happy switched on the ceiling bulb he saw that the patient was a man of about fifty, about his father's age, with jet-black hair and a square unshaven face. A monocle was screwed in his right eye. His cheek was crossed with dueling scars. He sat in his undershirt, with pillows behind him and a blanket over his legs. On his knees he held a plywood tray covered with papers. His uniform hung neatly on a hanger from a nail driven in the plaster wall. The gold pips and silver cording of his shoulder straps were burnished, and the white infantry surround was immaculate.

194

"Who are you?" asked the colonel. "Is there an air raid? I didn't hear the bugle."

Without giving Happy time to answer he muttered to himself, "The Luftwaffe is the only uniform we haven't collected in this division yet. Good idea! I must request a couple of batteries from Ninth Flak at Crailsheim. Imagine trying to form a division without air cover!"

He made a note on the pad in front of him. Then he raised his voice, "Well, answer me, please. Who are you?"

Happy stood at attention. "I am not in the division at all, Herr Oberst. I was traveling on the highway with one of your sergeants. The lieutenant at the gate told us you were ill and directed me to take over the place of your orderly until he returns, to make you comfortable through the night. I am on convalescent leave, reporting from the Luftwaffe to my new unit, which is the 136th Mountain Regiment. My name is Steinberg."

"You may relax, Corporal. This is indeed fortunate for me. It is not often that things happen so well nowadays. I have a recurrence of heart congestion. There is no need, however, to call a surgeon from elsewhere. It is only a question of the drug. I have kept the prescription in my Soldbuch for three years. I require nothing but an injection of digifolin, one cubic centimeter, in the upper arm. Here is all that remains, left in the syringe by my orderly before he left. You will see that I need it only when my chest begins to pain me; hoffentlich, that will not be before he returns in the morning with more. But I never know when the attack may occur. One struck me this afternoon, after many months of relief. We must really attach a surgeon immediately." He made another note on the pad. "The personnel which we recruit nowadays is so old, if not actually wounded or ill, that the Medical Corps must do at the beginning of a battle what formerly they had to do only at the end. They have also subjected me to the humiliation of a bedpan, which you will find underneath my cot. I cannot yet ask a nurse to assist me with this, although ladies are the only recruits still plentiful in the Wehrmacht. So I am doubly grateful if you can help me with such masculine details. There is, however, a private bathroom adjoining these quarters, and so far I have had no trouble reaching it. I should greatly appreciate it if you would sleep in the corridor outside, or better still in this room. I think you can get a blanket roll from one of the other orderlies. Thus I could command your attention at any time in the night if I am in need. I hope it will not be necessary. And it will be a comfort which I did not think an old soldier like myself would ever welcome to have someone beside me, if only to listen to my bear-growls."

"I hope, too, that the Colonel will have a good night's rest," Happy answered. "However, I do not need a blanket roll. If the Colonel permits, I will sleep on the floor. I have left my knapsack at the barracks with my friend. With the Colonel's permission I will fetch it at once. If the Colonel wishes to use the bedpan now, I suggest that I can empty it at the same time that I return with my Klamotten."

"The Colonel would indeed prefer to use it in solitude, when he must use it at all, which is not at present necessary. And please do not salute me each time you enter and leave, for I have too much to do to answer such formalities. And in Gottes Namen do not use the third person, especially when discussing bedpans."

He laid his monocle on the table and smiled at Happy. Happy set the tray of papers on the deep window sill, brought the colonel a glass of water from the bathroom, and put it on the table beside the syringe. The colonel's P38 was also lying on the table, cocked, with the red circle showing above the grip.

He groped his way across the compound to the barracks. The belt flashlight Chuck had given him guided him down the stairs. Heinrich was already curled up asleep, with the Panzerfaust and the rifle both slung from nails above his head. Happy picked up his own knapsack and helmet from the next bunk and carried them back to the colonel's room.

"There is an extra blanket in the locker," the colonel told him. "Use it for your bed."

Happy reached it out and stretched it lengthwise on the floor between the locker and the door. He laid down his knapsack to serve for a pillow. He could cover himself with his Mantel when he turned in.

"Would you like me to get you some dinner, Herr Oberst?"

"I had hoped that someone would suggest the idea. I suppose one has to live, even if he has no appetite. Yes, you may go down to the officers' mess and ask them for a tray for me."

The officers' mess was simply the curtained-off end of the troops' main shack, but that was as far as fraternity went. There were curtains in the windows. The cook set china dishes on a tray for the colonel and picked out the choicest two slices of veal. His bread was whiter than the soldiers', his coffee smelled deliciously of chicory, and there was a whole cone of sugar for his Strudel. The troops standing in line sniffed and glowered as Happy carried it past, but when he got it upstairs, the colonel looked at it distastefully. He ate it without either relish or complaint.

"Also in the locker is a bottle of Niersteiner," said the colonel. "You could perhaps find a glass in the bathroom, for I do not relish drinking good wine from a mess kit. I may enjoy a glass later; for the present I am not in the mood."

Happy set the bottle and glass on the table. He helped the colonel get ready for the night, wondering at what hour he would feel "in the mood." He hung the monocle on the nail over the uniform. He pulled off the colonel's undershirt and helped him into a pair of blue and white striped pajamas.

"This is a folly I permit myself," the colonel laughed, "when I am sure no one will tease me. I fear that even my own orderly gossips about it with his comrades. My wife gave them to me

197

at the beginning of the war, and I have carried them, little used, through all my campaigns since. I tell her they look like the uniforms of the riffraff imprisoned at Dachau, but she is a woman of little humor. She only shakes her head and says that we are all prisoners. It is well that we should turn in early like this; you, so that you may start early in the morning on your interrupted leave when my orderly returns from Augsburg; and I, so that perhaps my heart will behave itself when I am at rest, and I shall not need the drug. But you had better leave it ready on the table anyway. If I need it I shall call you; or if you hear me breathing too hard plunge the needle in my arm anyway, even without the command. Leave the dinner tray in the bathroom; no need to carry it back in the dark through a strange camp. I assume you know a little about the heart. The doctors may not all be quite sound as to the new Germany we have built, but mine little realizes what service he has done to me, and thereby, perhaps, a little to her, by writing out this prescription. We were classmates in Bonn long ago. I should have died often since then were it not for his Latin hen-tracks."

Happy looked at the dog-eared prescription, but did not recognize the signature.

"See, Herr Oberst, I am putting the digifolin, already inserted in the syringe, in a basin of Sepso which I dissolve from my medical kit. With your permission, I shall prepare tourniquets in case of an attack. They are not on the prescription, but I know they are part of the modern treatment. By limiting the area which the blood must supply, they increase its pressure. I have some ready in my kit, also some aspirin. Would you not like to take two tablets with some water? They may help put you to sleep."

The colonel nodded. Happy took two tablets from his kit, counting past the American Benzedrines which looked like aspirin. The colonel swallowed the tablets and drank the water. Happy laid four strips of linen on the table.

198

"And your pistol, sir. Shall I replace it in the belt of your tunic? I can even clean it for you now, if you wish."

"Leave the pistol beside me," said the colonel gruffly. "Do not disturb the papers on my tray under any circumstances. They are all matters for my signature. I ought to attend to them now, but I am too tired. First thing in the morning, perhaps. There is so much for me to do and so little time to do it in! Orders, operation plans, punishments. I must sign the warrant to execute a traitor tomorrow morning, but perhaps he and I shall both sleep better if I postpone it till then."

"A traitor, Herr Oberst?"

"Yes. A civilian from the next village north of us. We have mined all the bridges, of course, between here and the Rhine, ready to blow them if General Patch should cross the river, which God forbid! This miserable farmer was caught cutting the wires of a culvert across his acre, so that if our engineers should prepare to activate the mines they would not explode. He even spliced the wires in such a way that the break could not be seen in advance. If bridges over cattle troughs are not safe from sabotage, what of the bridges over the Rhine? What of Remagen, Mainz, Mannheim, Speyer, Kehl? I dislike to order this shooting. They are messy affairs; even the firing squad is apt to get sick, but there must be an example. There must be a stand made. The death of this one traitor will save the lives of many good German soldiers. If the Wehrmacht cannot maintain discipline in the heart of our own country, where can it do so? And if the execution is to be at all, it should be where soldiers and civilians alike can witness it. The paper is ready for my signature, and tomorrow morning at eight, outside our gate, justice will be done."

The colonel turned over heavily and fell asleep, exhausted by his tirade. Happy stretched out on his blanket, fully dressed. But he could not sleep, thinking of the new Blacklist to be issued next day and of the saboteur who would be shot.

199

He hoped that he could get past the execution post before it happened, or stay inside till it was over. He would have to pass the place directly. Even now, over the noises of the night, he thought he heard the firing squad hammering the stake into the ground. The farmer, he thought, had probably cut the wire with the knowledge of others in the village, to save the village itself from the fire of the Ami tanks. They might even have drawn lots, and the risk had fallen on him. Corporal Steinberg, loyal soldier of the Reich, could not deny the execution might be necessary. Corporal Maurer could plead with the colonel for a reprieve or—it was a crazy idea—inject too much digifolin, or too little, so that the colonel could not sign—the colonel would himself be dead. Karl Maurer, he told himself, does not exist. But the more he repeated the insistence to himself, the more the voice inside him reminded him that the farmer's treachery was less heinous than his own.

He thought of the colonel's prescription. For digifolin to ease the congestion, the colonel should have been saturated with it already, without missing a single day's injection. Even then it would not take effect promptly. The colonel's breath was labored and his lips bluish, and, for a colonel, he was too amiable; but otherwise he seemed all right. That was the trouble with three-year-old prescriptions; they were out of date. He decided to wait for an attack and judge for himself. Maybe the orderly would get back before treatment was needed. But he left his leather kit open on the floor beside his blanket.

Suddenly the colonel turned in his bed. He leaned over the edge. Happy heard him vomit into the bedpan. He gasped, fighting for his breath.

"Hilfe!" he choked between the spasms. "Help!"

Happy jumped up and switched on the light. He lifted the loaded pistol gingerly to the window sill. Now the colonel had fallen back on his pillow, his whole body motionless to save strength for the final struggle locked within his chest. The parted lips began to foam. The eyes did not blink, eyes which stared straight at Happy in the envy, the reproach, with which the dying look upon the live.

"Hilfe!" he gasped again, more faintly. Standing over him, Happy could see that the word was formed only with the black tongue inside his open jaws, as a parrot speaks without moving its beak. The colonel clacked the word, so that the heart might not waste a milligram of its reprieve by a motion of the lips. It was less a human syllable than the groan of an animal in pain.

Happy knew pulmonary edema when he saw it. The colonel was drowning. Even his fingernails were cyanosed. Happy ignored the digifolin in the colonel's syringe. He threw a quarter-grain of morphine from his own kit into the wineglass and poured in a spoonful of the wine to dissolve it. He rolled up a sleeve of the striped pajamas, sucked up the morphine in his own syringe and plunged it into the arm. He laid a tablet of nitroglycerin from his own metal tube under the colonel's tongue. He twisted the four tourniquets, two round the arms above the elbow and two round the thighs as high as he could roll the pajamas. The lips began to move, and though the cry of "Hilfe!" was repeated, it came out of the moving lips now more intelligibly, as a horn sounds more clearly with the lifting of the fog. In ten minutes the spasm had subsided.

It was as his father had often described the relief of acute edema—which occurs when the water in the blood fills the lungs—as he had even seen it once himself on a hospital bed in Berlin; but this time not by his father's hand. In a sense, not even by his own hand, since he denied his own name, but by the hand of a corporal with the false name of Steinberg. By a hand which could a moment before, if it chose, have withheld or multiplied the drug, and so taken the life before him and saved the life to be taken in the morning, and with it many lives—who could tell how many?—in the dissolution of the whole division. And if he, this ghost of soldiery, were to be tied at sunrise to the infamous stake, after the colonel had been found dead from too much or too little of the drug, if he were to be shot (as though one could shoot a ghost) nobody could either rightly praise his sacrifice or gloat over his punishment until a steel safe, four hundred miles away in an enemy country, was opened when the war ended. And Maurer might not even suffer when the bullet struck, since it would be Steinberg who was shot. But the thumb which pressed the syringe had gone just far enough and not too far, with calm and care, to save what might have been better lost. Professionally.

The taut hairy-backed hands on the field-gray blanket unclenched. Happy remembered the mutilated hand of the Tiger on his olive-drab blanket in France. The unmoving eyes no longer stared into death. They drew back into aliveness and hardened into pride, pride that they had not been found afraid. They held no gratitude to the corporal. After the breathing eased they paused a moment longer, still unblinking, to mark their renewed command. The eyelids fell on them, the colonel's head leaned to the wall, his whole body relaxed, and he slept again.

The corporal emptied the pan and went back to his blanket. Maurer had penetrated to the living heart of his target, and Steinberg for the time had spared it. Before he knew he had slept, the colonel roused him.

"Are you awake, Corporal?"

Happy stirred. He looked at the luminous dial on his wrist. It was 0430, before the heavy blackout curtains were even tinted by the sun, before any bugle sang.

"Yes, Herr Oberst."

"I am well again, thanks to your promptness. Do not turn on the light again, but pour a glass of my wine for each of us. You will find another in the cupboard. First give me time to set the safety of my Walther."

"I took the liberty of moving it myself for fear you would jog the trigger by mistake. It is in the window."

The colonel laughed mirthlessly.

In the dark Happy groped for the bottle on the bedside table, for fear he might jolt it off. He found the glasses and poured them with a finger at the edge, so they would not overflow. He held one toward the bed. The colonel's hand met his. The glasses touched.

"To Germany," the colonel breathed heavily.

"To Germany," the corporal repeated.

"Lie down and let me talk, but do not look at me. For what it is worth, you have saved my life, even though you acted against orders. A man who is just reporting from the doorway of death has a right to the second luxury of talking about himself, while he is still as naked as at that moment. Perhaps he reports to himself, or perhaps to God, or perhaps to a visiting casual corporal whom he will never see again and who will now promise on his soldier's oath not to reveal the indignity. Do you promise?"

"Yes, Herr Oberst."

"Say 'On my soldier's oath.'"

"Auf meinen Fahneneid," Happy repeated.

"No, but repeat it in full with me. It will do us good to hear it again." They intoned together the oath of the German soldier.

"I swear before God this holy oath, to offer unquestioning obedience to Adolf Hitler, leader of the German State and People, and to lay down my life as a brave soldier to fulfill this oath."

"Good," pronounced the colonel. "Now I want to record with you who have just seen me at death's gate that I was not afraid of it. I record it with surprise and pride. You have read that Samsonov, the Russian general, shot himself at the defeat of Tannenberg. I will confess that is why my pistol has been on the table tonight.

"I have been in the Army many years and am not afraid to die. It is insane to claim that we can press back the horde of savages from the east and the west. But tomorrow, to my division, I shall claim it. It is folly to think that this division which I am building out of papers on a tray can meet any other fate than the three divisions of which it is the remnant. We call ourselves a combat division! We are not even a good training camp. There is no more time to be thorough now. Think of it, eight 15s and twelve 7.5s to a regiment; one HMG and three lights to a company. And of course only two regiments where there should be three, but one is used to that. These new Panzerfausts of ours will be like pikes in the hands of a rabble, against the armor of the Americans. So far, not even any Flak to protect us. The German Wehrmacht was designed for attack, not for defense."

His sandpaper voice rose, as Hitler's did over the radio. "Until the ruin strikes, we shall be as stern and as brave as we have been to win the greatest victories in history. And I tell you the ruin will not tarnish them. The place of honor is in the heart of the flame, as the safest spot in an earthquake is within the very frame of the door. You will see that when the Führer dies no German officer will want to live. You were not even born at the other defeat. It was not a defeat; it was a betrayal. But your father, if he is living, will remember the shame which Germans bore for twenty years because they had been tricked out of victory. Since ruin must come, let it be complete. Let it be a purification, as our triumph was a purification too. Let the barbarians who reject us fight among themselves over their kill. History will never forget these five years when no German soldier has swerved from the path of honor, in Tunisia or at Stalingrad or on the River Plate, or in Norway or France or Holland, in the air or at sea or on the ground. They quibble about ghettoes and concentration camps. I brush aside their wailing, and history will soon forget it. It is nothing compared to the cleansing, I can even call it the consecration, of a whole great nation. A hero is killed but his heroism lives on. Only a day later the coward dies and is forgotten with his cowardice. I don't know whether you ever read Shakespeare. I am very fond of him, for I feel his soul is German. I cannot read English well enough to understand the original, but must rely on Schlegel's translation. There are two lines which I have repeated to myself in every campaign of the war. One where the king says:

'If we are marked to die, we are enough
To do our country loss . . .'

Do you know it?"

"Yes, Herr Oberst,

' . . . and if to live,
The fewer men, the greater share of honor.'

It is from *Henry the Fifth*. I read it in my English class at school."

"And the other," went on the colonel, "is what he says of Cawdor:

'Nothing in his life
Became him like the leaving it.'

Well, my boy, you have done some small service to your country in saving me, if only for the grand finale, and I apologize for having cut short your leave, if I have done so. It cannot have been so pleasant to nurse an old man as to spend one of your few precious evenings in a cozy tavern, with good food and drink and maybe the innkeeper's daughter in the night; anyway, looking out on a countryside so far untouched by the war, and thinking only of your pleasure and your youth. In half an hour now they will be after me to face the day. Before they come I want you to tell me what reward I can give you for this night. Shall I ask your commander to give you a day or two extra leave?"

"Thank you, no, Herr Oberst. I have a duty at the front also. There is only one thing."

205

"A promotion? You handle yourself as deftly as an expert would have done. That trick of the tourniquets. I must tell our surgeon about it, when we get one."

"No, my Colonel, there is only one thing; perhaps this is foolish of me—but if you would have mercy on the farmer and put him in prison instead."

Happy stood at attention, facing the foot of the bed. His hands were clenched at his sides. He knew that his voice shook a little. The colonel looked up at him sharply from the bed.

"No, no! that request I cannot grant. I know that your profession is to save life, even the unworthy. Remember that mine is to take it, even the worthy. I can give no quarter there, and you have heard me say why. Do not ask me that. Indeed, were it not for the indignity, I should give the coup de grace myself."

Happy unclenched his fists. He felt the color drain from his face. He knew now that the colonel had truly not been afraid of death, if he would send the farmer to it, having himself been so lately spared.

"I feel as well as ever," chuckled the colonel. "Now I am going to get up and shave, even dress. You may need to take my elbow the first few steps, till I make sure. Then I shall treat myself to breakfast in bed before my own orderly gets back with the ampoules of digifolin, and before the adjutant comes in with the roster for the day. It is thinking of all I have to do that makes me dizzy, not my heart, which you have made as good as ever. Go down and get your own breakfast and bring me back a tray like last night, if you will. I shall be shaved by the time you return."

Happy took the colonel's elbow as he stepped out of bed, but the officer shook him off. "You see? I walk as well as ever."

Happy picked up the supper tray. He left the colonel splashing water in the basin and staring into the mirror, and heard him mutter as he lathered his face, "There I can give no quarter."

"And you, Corporal," he called, "get your gear ready so that you can go right after breakfast. My orderly has orders to be back half an hour from now. If he isn't, I'll take the time from him and give you double. Get your gear as soon as you have brought my tray. If I were in your shoes, with two days before me, I should walk down the Neckar to Heidelberg, as I have often done in my youth. Just because you've missed your night there is no reason you should miss your day, and you can get a ride up to Heilbronn in a division car without any trouble. I had to ship a detail to the Rhine yesterday, untrained as they were, to contain an unexpected thrust. I'll see if we haven't got one going your way today."

Nine

But Happy had to get out the gate before the execution, without waiting for breakfast or for a ride in the divisional transport. He fetched the colonel's breakfast without thinking of his own. This early in the morning—it was six o'clock—there were only half a dozen officers in the mess hall, all of them lieutenants, eating at a single table behind the curtain. Among them was the one who had been duty officer the day before. They all looked up at the sight of a Luftwaffe corporal carrying a tray through their mess. They turned stiffly, moving their shoulders and their heads together, and holding the coffee-cake poised for a moment over the bowls of coffee. Happy saw the duty officer whisper an explanation, and they turned back to the silent meal. The duty officer called him over from the counter. Happy stood rigid, with the loaded tray in his hands.

"How is the colonel doing this morning, Corporal?" he asked pleasantly.

"He is in excellent health, Herr Leutnant."

"Prima. I was tired last evening when you came in, as one

gets sometimes; I hope you did not repeat my words to him, for I did not mean to be disrespectful of his rank or even of his illness. Gentlemen, this is Corporal Steinberg"—Happy saw that each officer registered the name in his memory—"who kindly consented to attend Colonel Forster last night, as a way to earn his bread and butter."

"Butter!" one of the lieutenants muttered sourly.

"The colonel's orderly has just returned from Augsburg. I checked him in a few minutes ago when I came off duty, so you may feel free to continue your leave as soon as the colonel releases you. The division is grateful for your kindness. On the way out stop at the orderly room for today's stamp."

"Zu Befehl!" Happy answered. He bowed as well as he could with the zinc tray in his hands. He returned through the curtain and across the troops' mess hall. He hurried across the compound as fast as he could without spilling the bowl of coffee. When he reached Room 38 the colonel was already fully dressed, sitting at his table with the beribboned tunic buttoned on, and gazing at the trayful of papers through his monocle. His peaked cap and service belt, with the Walther back in its holster, hung on the nail. He had already signed some of the papers.

"Ha," he called jovially, "you have moved quickly to get to the mess hall and back in so short a time. I have taken an apéritif of paper work, to fit me for the day." He pointed to two papers in the out basket.

"I thought the Colonel would be hungry, so I postponed my own breakfast until he has the kindness to dismiss me."

The colonel did not seem to notice the lapse into the third person. He did not refer to his confidence of the night. It was as if the monocle were a screen between the officer and the man.

"You have been both kind and competent." He smiled, holding forward a slip with the swastika seal of the division. "I have written this commendation, which may save you some difficulty in the forward zone. It states that you have been of service to this division, and bears my signature with the seal of Twenty-fifth Infantry. Now I suggest that you may pack your Klamotten and get as good a breakfast as our quarter-master can provide. Growing boys must eat. Then start on your way, for it is a long trip, and you may get slowed down by police checks as you approach the Rhine. You are wise to enjoy the scenery on foot. My own orderly has just returned and is eating his breakfast now, but you need not wait for him to relieve you. See, he has brought me enough of the drug to last till the day of victory."

He held up a new carton of digifolin ampoules. He handed the commendation to Happy, who took the slip of paper with a word of thanks, folded it, and put it carefully in the flap of his Soldbuch. He leaned down to pick up his knapsack and refold the colonel's blanket. He buttoned his overcoat, and was ready to salute good-by when there was a knock at the door.

"Come in," the colonel ordered.

It was not the orderly who entered, but a divisional mes-senger with a handful of papers and dispatches, and an oblong book bound in orange paper.

"The officer of the day sends up the new Blacklist, Herr Oberst. Will you kindly initial this receipt and return the book to the orderly room at your convenience."

The colonel rolled his eyes in mock despair at this addition to his day's work. He looked at Happy. "Here's some more Shakespeare for you, Corporal:

> 'When sorrows come, they come not single spies,
> But in battalions.' "

"Yes, Herr Oberst; From *Hamlet*."

The messenger laid the booklet on the table. The colonel did not open it, but signed the receipt.

"In a little while. I'd like to glance it over first. And before you go, Melder," * he said, "here is my signature for the execution."

He held forward the square of white paper which condemned the saboteur. The messenger turned to leave. He had not once looked at Happy.

"Just a moment," the colonel called. "A word with you alone first."

He rose and followed the messenger into the corridor, closing the door behind him. Happy heard them whispering outside. In two soft steps he was at the table. He opened the bright covers of the Blacklist, stamped just like the bulletin at Kempten, "Not to fall into enemy hands." His fingers turned to where the S page should be. He had only time to see the name STEINBERG, KARL before he heard the knob turn behind him. He sprang back and was struggling with the straps of his knapsack when the colonel re-entered the room. Before the door closed he heard the messenger call back, in that tone which with all soldiers is the acknowledgment of a command, "At once, Herr Oberst. Sofort."

Someone had given him away at last. He hoped it was the bus driver, not the old warden. But if it was he, Happy thought, I cannot blame him. It would be hard to be silent under the questioning of the Gestapo. If he has put me in danger, did I not do the same to him? Let us forgive each other.

"Good-by, Corporal," the colonel was saying, "and many thanks."

He held out his hand, letting the monocle fall from his eye to smile. Happy jerked to a salute.

"My thanks to the Colonel, and best wishes for his recovery."

"And best wishes for our victory," growled the colonel.

Happy opened the door and went out. He hurried, but did not dare to run. He strode directly to the barracks. Heinrich

* Messenger.

was just getting out of bed. His rifle still hung on the nail above his bunk.

"Oh, the flier." He yawned. "I bet you didn't sleep as well as I did; the Volkswagen is good exercise, but that colonel is trouble enough even when he isn't sick. Junge, Junge, how sleepy I am! Let's go get some breakfast. Then you can come and watch me train the rookies with the bazooka."

He pulled the boots over his trousers and struggled into his tunic. The other troops in the hut were dressing too, clustered around the stove.

"No, I've had my breakfast," Happy lied. "Besides, I'm on leave, and I don't want to see any more Army till I have to, and I'm in a hurry. Listen, you told me yesterday you would sell me your rifle. I'll give you the hundred marks."

Heinrich was awake at once. He narrowed his eyes, as a seasoned soldier does when he considers a trade. He pretended to be reluctant. "Why, you said yourself that Medical don't carry them."

"Yes, but I'm on the last lap now, and, you see, I can't tell what I might meet between now and the end."

"Well, it's true one shouldn't take that trip without some kind of weapon. This is an excellent rifle. But might they not pick you up for carrying it?"

Happy shook his head. "I'm taking off my medical armband anyway, so I won't be drafted into any more duty like last night."

The sergeant raised his hand to the rifle, teasing Happy to raise the price.

"A hundred and twenty marks," he bargained.

"Okay, only hurry and let me get away."

He fished the money out of his belt. The sergeant sighed. "Lift it down from the nail, then. I'm not supposed to do this, as you well know. They might fine me that much for losing it. This rifle was entered in my Soldbuch nine months ago, but I suppose I can always claim I turned it in to the school when

I got the bazooka, and lost the receipt. It's easy to cross it off the page, anyway, and I don't think there's ever a chance they'd check up on that one, do you?"

"Never," Happy assured him impatiently. "Well, thanks for the ride yesterday and getting me put up for the night. I didn't have such a bad time after all, though it's not the way you want to spend a leave. I'm starting off now, so wish me luck. I'll see you in Berlin after the war."

"Or Magdeburg."

They shook hands. Happy slung the self-loader over his shoulder. He strolled to the barracks door, but quickened his pace as soon as it slammed behind him. It was 0750. He no longer dared wait till after the execution. Even if he had to watch it, he must be through the gate before the colonel found his name in the Blacklist. He headed for the main gate, passing the soldiers who hurried along the path to the mess hall. It was a gamble to try the gate with a rifle, when he had come in without one; but there would be a different sentry and it was worth the chance to pass as Infantry instead of Medical. Yet he dared not take off his medical brassard till he was on the road.

The swastika flag whipped on its mast again in the clear breeze. The soldiers who were not making for the mess hall were making for the gate, like him, and he saw there was already a big formation packed in front of the orderly room. Yet they did not crowd forward; indeed those on the edge seemed to ease backward, away from the opening between the stone piers. He knew why; it was the detail which was ordered to witness the execution. There might still be time for him to get out first, but he knew the sentry would not pass him till the duty officer stamped his orders. He pressed toward the orderly room, trying to edge past the fringes of the silent crowd. He had to step around the roots of the ivy that cloaked the little stone house. He wedged himself up the two steps and through the door.

The same two clerks were pounding at their Erikas, but a new lieutenant, the one who had grumbled about butter at breakfast, sat at the desk. Happy held his trip ticket and the colonel's certificate toward him. Behind him, a soldier came in and lifted out one of the stack of signposts, carrying it back outdoors. Happy heard the Herangetreten signal outside, which was whistled five minutes before a parade. The lieutenant stamped Happy's paper in silence, without looking at him. When he had impressed the cross-and-eagle he glanced up.

"Since you are returning to the front, Corporal Steinberg, the colonel has sent down orders that you halt outside to witness that justice is still done behind the German lines. You can report so at the front."

"No," Happy blurted.

The lieutenant reddened but, because the colonel had recommended the boy, said no more than, "That is a word the German soldier does not use, Corporal."

Happy wanted the lieutenant to look up, but he had already bent his head over the papers on his desk. The typewriters clacked on. Happy could do nothing but open the door to the platform. The crowd had grown so that he could not even step down to the ground, where he might have hidden his eyes among the others.

"Achtung!" a voice called from the compound back of the crowd.

Four men came down the path toward the gate, preceded by yesterday's lieutenant of the guard and followed by a Pfc carrying the cross-shaped wooden signpost. Two others dragged the prisoner between them. He was a short man, sixty perhaps, in the torn faded trousers of a farmer, with a blue shirt, open at the throat. His worn velvet braces crossed the shirt. His horny hands dangled over the arms of his executioners. His stubbly face looked upward. His feet dragged behind him. The angle of his body was like the leaning forward of a plowman pushing at the handles of his plow while his feet lag in the furrow, and the wide expressionless stare was that of one who looks day after day between the heads of oxen for the distant turn. If he was not beyond consciousness, Happy knew, he was at least beyond fear.

The crowd parted before the squad. Happy saw that the sign on the file closer's shoulder read: SO STERBEN DIE VERRÄTER DES VATERLANDES. Thus perish traitors. The words were the ones which Père Nod had seen at Stuttgart, and Happy thought of a picture in his parents' room at Berlin: Simon at Calvary, carrying the cross for Another.

He could not help looking outward, over the heads of the crowd. He saw that traffic had been roped off in both directions on the highway. He saw the four-foot post on the opposite side, where he had heard the hammering in the night. He saw the two privates bind the prisoner to it and knot a blindfold from behind his head; and he saw the signbearer bore the stake of his inscription into the ground at the side. He turned his face away, looking up into the sky above the camp and the hooked-cross banner. They could not punish him for turning his face away.

A horse neighed, but the crowd was silent; the soldiers inside the gate and the civilians to right and left of them outside surrounded the stake like an amphitheater. He heard the feet of the squad shuffle in unison, their rifle butts striking the pavement together, heard the snap of the bolts at "Fertig," and at the lieutenant's "Feuer!" heard the instant roar of the four rifles and the creaking of the cords as the traitor lurched forward, and then a murmur of satisfaction in the crowd, and the sound of someone being sick. The typewriters in the office behind him had not stopped.

The crowd of witnesses parted before the returning white-faced firing squad. No man looked at the others.

Happy made his way out the gate as leisurely as he could pretend. The unaccustomed rifle dangled awkwardly across the back of his long coat, the barrel striking his steel helmet. It

215

was lucky that the sentry who glanced at the stamped paper was not Heinrich's friend of the day before, for he might have noticed the rifle. This sentry looked too sick to notice anything except the heap across the road.

The feet had slid together at one side. Happy saw that the shoes had soles of wood instead of leather. The blood already made a pool about the stake. The head hung forward with the blindfold downward. The arms which had passed Happy so inert a few minutes before now flapped in posthumous spasm; they were more alive in death than in life. Cross-shaped, the black and white verdict of judgment, as neatly lettered as a "Keep off the grass" sign, was driven into the ground beside the post, and it was splattered with red. Red, white, and black, he thought, the colors of the regime, as they had been the Kaiser's.

The ropes across the road were down. The crowd of civilians hastened on to the south; the recruits stepped northward a few paces past the barrier and turned into the division gate. Horses strained at their harness, women pushed at the laden handcarts while the old men grunted and took a whiter grip on the shafts. The procession of the dispossessed moved on. Some looked at the sky and some at the ground, but none at his neighbor and none at the stake.

Happy darted between them to the opposite side of the road. He ran toward the left. They could not punish him for running, either. He ran along the gully till he reached a bend in the road where the stake was hidden from him, and when he was out of sight he let himself cry a little, wiping the grimy tears on the cuff of his Mantel.

"They are all the same," he told his voice. "In spite of their words they are all the same. The colonel's display is as brutish as the garroting at the Plotzensee."

However gently the voice told him that they might have been right as soldiers both times, Happy's last conversion was there on Route Nineteen at Aalen.

He had to put as much ground behind him as he could. At any moment now the Blacklist would go down from the colonel to the orderly room. Any one of the lieutenants who had heard him called at breakfast might see his name in it, even if the colonel did not; indeed, it was their duty to look for it when his papers were stamped, and he had been saved by a freak of timing. He had not been able to read the whole citation in the book, but he had seen the words "medical corporal" after his name, and knew the brassard was his most staring identification, and the first that would betray him. He took it off and folded it away in his belt. He did not dare throw it away. Now, with the infantry rifle on his back, the only way the pursuit could tell he was Medical would be to strip off his overcoat and find the blue oval caduceus patch on the left sleeve of his tunic. He dared still less to rip that off; it was sewed to the uniform. He had no way to sew it back, and would surely be suspected if it were gone. Least of all did he dare throw away his Soldbuch, for there were heavy penalties for traveling without one. The soldier who lost his book had to report at once to the nearest post for a duplicate, and that would have been suicide. He found Frau Liebert's envelope to her sons at Crailsheim. He split the envelope and read the card through again. There was nothing in it which would identify him; she did not give them his name. But he burned it with his lighter, for she had signed her own.

He hoped a truck or bus would overtake him and hurry him along the road; but he feared to hear its motor, lest it be sent to take him back. He dared not lose time waiting. He ran forward as fast as his straggling topcoat and his bumping equipment and his shaking knees would let him. When he got on the straightaway, he could see what vehicles came from each direction. So far he saw nothing but the slow refugee carts; but even in sight of them he dared not run, for fear they would think he was in flight. A truck roared past; he recognized the fanion of 25th Infantry with the red sword-flame on the shield, and had time to duck behind a tree. But the rider in the front seat, though he carried a rifle across his knees, did not seem to be in search of anyone. Happy wiped his face on his sleeve; perhaps the alarm had not been broadcast yet. He ran ahead.

He had gone two kilometers when he heard another car behind him. This time he turned to face it. It was a ton-and-a-half supply truck, camouflaged green and brown like the other, but with a license plate marked WL, for Wehrmacht-Luftwaffe. At least it did not belong to 25th Infantry, and he would be less conspicuous in an Air Force truck than an Army, or alone on the road. He waved both arms; that is the hitch-hiker's signal on the continent, not the cocked thumb and bent elbow. The driver, a quartermaster sergeant, pulled up for him and opened the door. It was good to see another blue-gray uniform like his own.

"Get in, gunner," he called. "I'll take you as far as Heilbronn if you're going that way."

Happy felt safer if even a Luftwaffe sergeant didn't recognize he was Medical. He mounted the high running board. The frayed edge of his coat caught under his heel. The rifle, which he did not know how to handle, jammed across the door. The sergeant laughed.

"Get out and try it all over again. Take it off before you try climbing in these cabs. We're not used to infantry weapons. Throw it in the back with the potatoes."

If the division truck had not been on his trail, still less likely that an Air Force supply truck would be, especially as the Blacklist was issued only to provost units and the Gestapo. The sergeant must have passed by the gate at Aalen just after the execution, but he could not have heard Happy's name.

"I'm Herbert Behrend," he introduced himself, holding out his hand, "from Düsseldorf. Quartermaster to the Ninth Flak. Believe me, I've had a time getting even what you see in the back for the boys to eat. I hope the other trucks have better luck. We're really not Quartermaster Corps any more. They don't have any food to issue. We're Forage. We live off the country, you know, and I carry second class mail besides. Versorgung instead of Nachschub. I pick up and deliver all along my beat. Even the farmers are stingy. When they have any provisions, they hide them. Anyway, I get enough for myself, such as it is."

He did not ask Happy's name. "Where are you headed, Junge? You *are* young to be a corporal."

"I'm assigned to 136th Mountain, at the front. They'll put me on a Vierling, I suppose."

"Oh, you poor devil," the sergeant groaned.

He threw in the clutch and started the truck along the rough road. He could not have helped seeing the body of the old farmer, but did not speak of it. Perhaps, Happy thought, he talked so fast just to avoid speaking of it.

"That's where you're going, Kamerad; where are you coming from?"

"Oh, I'm on leave, coming back from the Alps."

"Worse and worse," grimaced the jovial sergeant, "to leave the corn-fed beauties of the South just to swing around in the saddle of a Vierling, popping at and popped against. Well, that's war. Anyway, I'm glad to have your company; I'm tired of this round. What do I call you?"

"Karl."

That satisfied him. Happy looked longingly at the wide floor of the truck, bedded with potato sacks and bags of flour and packages of mail tied with strings. The tailboard stood about a foot above the level of the cargo. The back curtain was rolled up.

After a while Happy ventured, "Sarge, how about letting me stretch out on your produce? I'm tired and I want to get a little sleep. I won't even nibble at your potatoes."

"All right, Excellency, your bed awaits. When shall I call you for lunch? If the old wagon holds out, we get to Crailsheim about noon. That's where I leave most of my freight. Meanwhile, I've got a little something in my kit, if you want a snack."

"Listen, Sarge, I'll buy you lunch in return for the ride. There's no way to use money where I'm going, and I've got enough left over from my leave. If you know any black-market restaurant on the road, stop and see what we can find. The blacker the better. We ought to get a bottle of wine anyhow. All I have in my own pocket is two slices of cheese two days old, and I missed breakfast this morning."

"All right, Herr Reichsbankpräsident Schacht, I'm not supposed to do it, and they might clip one of the wings off my collar tab if they caught me eating black market, but when a thing is free who can refuse? They don't have many patrols on this road any more—everyone is at the front—and the regulations are kaput anyhow, so let's try eating about eleven, what do you say? I know a little place we'll reach by then. And say, if you're going to feed me later, you might as well help yourself to what I've got in my Beutel." He handed Happy a package wrapped in greasy newspaper.

Happy climbed in the back, stretching out comfortably among the sacks with his face to the rear. He ate the contents of both the packages, piling his slices of cheese inside the sergeant's two ham sandwiches. He ate the few remaining crumbles of his chocolate. He washed his breakfast down with water from his own canteen, which he had filled at the colonel's washstand. He pulled off his topcoat and spread it to ease the knobs in the sacking, but lay on his left side so the sergeant, if he looked back in his mirror, could not see the caduceus patch on his sleeve.

This highway had been the main road from the Danube to the Rhine before the regime, but now it was little used except by the townspeople along it, for the Autobahn was so much straighter and wider. The rubberless tires of the farm carts, the caterpillar treads of tractors and of the division tanks and half-tracks, and a little casual strafing by American planes had pocked the surface with potholes which no one had bothered to repair. The sergeant did not even try to avoid them. The tarpaulin of the back was rolled up; the tailboard was fastened with chains at each side. By stretching out full length, with his elbow braced on top of his Mantel and a sack of flour wedged against his back, Happy could cup his face in his hands and just look over the rounded edge of the tailboard at the road disappearing behind him, through the smoke of the big cylindrical Holzgas boiler.

They met more carts headed south, hauled by horses or oxen or manpower, and loaded with the possessions of the frightened civilians. The only military vehicle going in their direction was a motorcycle driven by a courier, with a fat officer jouncing in the sidecar. Happy ducked when it appeared over the hill behind him, but the courier only waved as he sped past the truck, bumping the officer over the potholes. Happy smiled to himself; if Fred had been there, he would have called the officer "Fatso."

"We may not have any springs, but he's got too many." Sergeant Behrend laughed. "I know that captain. A little shakeup will be good for him. I thought he must be chasing us, he came so fast. You done anything naughty? I have, just last night. The women are another good feature of our racket. Offer them a little food; if that doesn't work, threaten to take away the food they have."

Happy's eyes drooped, his forearm finally slid down, and he fell asleep with his head on a bundle of circulars tied with twine. He woke as the truck braked jerkily to a stop. Instantly his hand slid over to the rifle beside him, and he peered over the tailboard. But there was no one behind him.

"Could you deign to eat a bite now, Field Marshal?" asked the sergeant, leaning back. "Sorry to be late, but I had to stoke up. You never moved. It's twelve o'clock and that's when I have to eat no matter where I am or what field marshal is my guest. Aha, a medical marshal; you made me think you were of the Artillery."

He had seen Happy's caduceus patch. Happy wormed into his coat without rising from the bed of sacks. They were pulled up under a big tree at the side of the road. A kilometer ahead, through the windshield, he could see the spire of a village church.

"Where are we, Sarge? Don't stop on the open road; pull off somewhere where we can eat. That restaurant of yours—"

"The Field Marshal perhaps has indigestion. That is a little place called Stimpfach ahead of us. What's biting you, anyway?" He dropped his banter.

Happy still lay on the floor, clutching the rifle, his eyes peering over the tailboard at the road behind them.

"Anyone would think the Gestapo was on your trail. Sure, I know a restaurant. I just want to make sure you're going to pay for lunch as you promised, before I turn off. I don't have any money myself. They don't pay us messengers much, you know, compared to the value of the stuff we haul."

"I promised, didn't I? So hurry and get off the road."

"All right, flier, take it easy. I was thinking of the widow Bense, right in this town. A little old for us but not bad looking. She plays the black market. She isn't supposed to run an inn, and hasn't got any license. But she's a good friend of a good friend of the party," he winked, "so no one denounces her. I'm not supposed to eat there any more than she's supposed to feed me, but it's off the main road so I'll take the chance again. Look, I'm shaking as much as you."

He turned the truck off the highway to a side street of the hamlet. He parked behind a tall privet hedge and padlocked the wheel. He climbed out and went to the door of a well-kept stucco house. It looked like a widow's house, Happy thought, still crouching in the back; neat and demure. The sergeant looked in through the window and beckoned to him

222

over his shoulder. There was no sign to show it was an inn. The sergeant opened the door without knocking.

Inside, a woman was sewing at a table in the living room. She sprang up when they entered. She had been cutting and sewing some white sheets. She pushed them into her wicker basket, but not fast enough to hide what they were.

"Cutting up your sheets, Frau Bense?" The sergeant smiled politely. "They will be too small for that big double bed if you do. Maybe you are going to sleep alone for a change," he laughed at his own wit, "or maybe you are making some white flags. If so, you should lock your door beforehand."

The woman grew pale. "I'm sorry, Herr Feldwebel," she stammered, "but I haven't anything to give you today. With the shortages, I don't know what our poor country is coming to. Nothing, nothing," she moaned.

She held out her empty hands and shook her head, standing in front of the table with the basket on it.

"Don't worry, Frau Bense. I haven't come to forage for Ninth Flak this time. I just want a little lunch for my comrade and myself. I know you could find us a chicken somewhere."

"Oh, in that case," she laughed, relieved that he was not going to denounce her, "I can scare up something. One sacrifices everything to the gentlemen of the Luftwaffe who defend us poor farmers in Stimpfach from the gangsters." She included Happy in her smile.

"If the gnädige Frau can find one chicken," he put in, dropping into Behrend's satire, "perhaps she can find two. I am on leave, so I could take the second one with me to eat on the road."

"Ach, he should have been in the forage service with me, don't you think, Frau Bense? He requisitions in quantity and thinks of everything beforehand like a good soldier of the Versorgung. Maybe you have a drop of schnapps to start with, and a bottle of white wine to go with the bird."

"Two bottles." Happy laughed.

The woman filled two tiny glasses with schnapps from her cupboard. "I have a brace of Niersteiner which I had been saving for my name day; but for the Luftwaffe," she shrugged unhappily, "one would give all. You will find them on the shelf in the well. Why don't you fetch them in, while I see if there is a chicken left in the cellar."

The boys drained off their schnapps. Frau Bense went through a door to the back of the house. They heard her climbing down the cellar steps. The sergeant put his finger to his lips. "Hark," he whispered. In a moment there was a flutter and a clucking from the cellar below them. They heard her whisper furiously, "Shut up!" at the hens, and slap at them with her apron. Miraculously, the hens did shut up.

Laughing, they went outdoors to the well. Sure enough, on the stone shelf half a yard below the rim of the curb, just above the water, were two bottles of the greenish wine, dewy-cool. The sergeant lifted them out lovingly. A pair of cheeses lay beside them.

"Münster cheese also," he gloated. "We may as well take them, you know. She can get more where they came from and we can't. Sometimes she even has butter here, but I guess she's hidden that. If she had any, she'd never let us find it ourselves. I'll see if I can pry it loose. She's frightened, you see, because we caught her cutting those sheets. You know what that means, don't you? Surrender. She'd be shot if we denounced her, in spite of her friend in the party. She's probably got twenty chickens in that cellar; that's why she's trying to keep them quiet. I shouldn't be surprised if she even had a pig. I could take them all if I were hardhearted, and she couldn't say a word. You get to learn about people in the Versorgung. Frau Bense and I understand each other. I take from her but don't dare denounce her because of her friend. She gives to me but doesn't dare denounce me because of the ration board. Today

I'm one trick up on her, that's all, on account of seeing the white sheets."

Sitting on the well curb, they smoked two of Happy's Neuerburg cigarettes in the sunshine. The sergeant looked curiously at Happy.

"These cost twenty marks around here, but I won't ask you where you got them. Even the Versorgung can't promote Neuerburgs any more. Give me your butt when you're through. I save them for my pipe."

Happy shifted uneasily on the stone ledge. Two cigarettes a little better than Army issue were enough to rouse suspicion.

"A colonel gave them to me, a grateful patient. Where *he* got them I don't know. Maybe colonels always smoke Neuerburgs. Let's go in and eat. Usually all I get is Salems."

He thought back at what he had told the sergeant when he got in the truck. While he had implied he was a gunner, he was certain he had said nothing to deny he was Medical. He lifted his topcoat out of the truck and put it on to hide the caduceus patch.

They walked inside. Frau Bense had plucked the pullets. They were in the oven of the wood-burning stove.

"I could almost eat the smell." The sergeant laughed. "Let's have another schnapps while we wait, Frau Bense, and this time let's really lock the door."

He turned the huge key in the lock. Frau Bense motioned to the schnapps bottle still on the table. Her sewing basket had disappeared. They each poured a drink. In half an hour the chickens were ready. She checked the door herself before bringing one of them to the table, with half a loaf of bread and two pats of margarine. The bread was darker than Chuck's. The sergeant pushed the margarine away in disgust.

"White bread I do not ask for, Frau Bense. Nobody eats it but profiteers or foreign spies, like the one who had so much he could bury it behind the stone down in the Allgäu. But margarine! Why, when I was in Paris, and the French were starving to feed their German conquerors, after their British friends had stripped them first, even a little restaurant like the Ritz was able to scare up one pat of real butter. You would not like to have the Air Force think your restaurant inferior to the Ritz, would you?"

Frau Bense could not keep back her tears. She stared venomously at the sergeant, then went to the back of the house and returned with two squares of real butter. The sergeant uncorked one bottle of the wine with a pocket corkscrew. Without looking at them, Frau Bense wrapped the remaining cheese and chicken in waxed paper, with the rest of the loaf of bread. When they had finished their feast, Happy reached in his money belt.

"The bill, please," he called to her where she sat knitting a pair of socks, with her back to them.

"That will be twenty-eight marks," she said sullenly, without turning around.

"Put your money away, Corporal," the sergeant commanded. "Frau Bense has said she makes every sacrifice for the Luftwaffe, and the sacrifice of money is the greatest she can make. Even greater than the sacrifice of her chickens or her sheets, to say nothing of her virtue. She would be ashamed to take money from a soldier returning to the front."

"Nein, nein," Happy protested. "That is asking too much of Frau Bense's patriotism. I insist on paying."

He laid thirty-five marks on the table. The sergeant whistled.

"You must be an Ami in disguise, to have all that money and Neuerburgs too. Shall I ask her to give us a receipt listing the delicious food she sells? My lieutenant will be glad to know where the Air Force can buy chickens and Münster cheese."

Frau Bense burst into tears. "Take your money, Corporal; for you I really give it free."

But Happy left it on the table, and she unlocked the door

for them. As they climbed into the truck again, they could still hear her sobbing inside.

"Sit in front this time, Junge; you can't sleep all day. Put your knapsack in back, but mind you lay it with the bottle on top, because we've still got some rough driving."

Sergeant Behrend threw the chain and padlock on top of his provisions and backed the old Steyr from behind the hedge.

"I suppose we should have refueled while we were waiting for lunch," he said as he turned into the highway again, "but someone might have seen the ashes in her yard. I like to play fair, and she needs the wood as much as my Imbert.* We've got enough steam to reach Crailsheim, and I can get the Halunken in the motor pool to stoke me up. It isn't right that a corporal or a sergeant should have to do the dirty work. You know, it's just as illegal for me to eat there on a service trip as for her to feed me. With you it's different, because you are on leave. Nowadays everything is so kaput that it isn't much of a chance to take, promoting a real feed once in a while. She's the one that would catch it, selling us chickens and butter. She might even be shot—which makes me think; now that I'm one trick up on her she might give me a tumble. That's one thing that isn't rationed. The Wehrmacht used to have too much organization. Now it hasn't enough."

"You mean she might be shot for that meal like—"

"Yes, like him back there."

They were both thinking of the stake at Aalen and said no more. They drove in silence for half an hour.

"I have a pretty good beat as long as it lasts," Sergeant Behrend said. He could not be silent for long. "I carry second-class mail from the Kommando at Stuttgart, and pick up and leave packages and rustle supplies around my circuit. Aalen, Crailsheim, Heilbronn, and then down to Stuttgart again. It usually takes me a couple of days, and I can bunk with any unit

* A gasogen of Swiss manufacture which burns wood chunks instead of the usual charcoal.

I like along the road. They all know me. Last week I had a real bed in the hospital at Gmünd, with sheets. I like to sleep there or at the Ninth Flak CP in Crailsheim. They're the two safest. The gangsters have enough decency not to bomb a hospital, and I guess they're scared of attacking a Flak division. Either that, or they don't know it's there. Tonight I'll be back in Stuttgart, and that means a night in the bunker. Mind you, I don't carry top secret stuff like the couriers, but there's an awful lot of paper that has to go the round, like those circulars and Blacklists. You might say I carry more paper than food. Well, here's Crailsheim. I'm leaving some of both here. Want to drive in with me to the CP? I won't be long. It's that big castle on the hill," he pointed to the right, "only a kilometer up, and I won't stay longer than to leave my cargo and get stoked up. Then I'll take you to Heilbronn."

Happy saw the turrets of a Schloss through the trees on the hill. The hooked-cross flag floated from one of them. A Junkers 52 was towing a target balloon around the crest of the hill, and he could hear a Vierling rattle in target practice as the plane whined close. It made no hits, he noticed; probably manned by recruits. Driving the towplane was the riskiest job in the Luftwaffe, next to parachuting, especially with rookies pumping lead at the balloon behind your tail. He watched the practice as the truck approached the turnoff.

"You go on up," Happy answered the sergeant. "I don't want to see any more of the outfit till I have to. I want to write my girl a letter anyway, and this may be my last chance. I'll be waiting at this lamppost with the mailbox on it."

Writing your girl a letter was an excuse for anything. The sergeant laughed with that tolerant scorn which sergeants put on when corporals write letters to their girls. Happy climbed out of the truck, slinging his rifle and knapsack on his back, and the sergeant attacked the hill in low grade.

The sidewalks are narrow in Crailsheim; the cobbles run almost to the walls of the houses. Happy walked along a row

228

of shop fronts. At the dead end, where the road divides for Heilbronn or Nürnberg, there was a stationery store. The window was taped with adhesive to keep the glass from blowing out in case of a bomb-burst. A few dusty books lay behind it: *Mein Kampf*, Albert Benary's *Panzer Voran!*, a *History of the Growth of the Reich*, and a little green *Guide to the Neckar Valley*. There was a stack of blue Luftwaffe handbooks, on uniforms, drill, and weapons; and the inevitable portrait of the Führer, framed in the national colors. Happy opened the door, his rifle barrel brushing against the jamb. Three airmen were inside, riffling over the comics on the shelf and turning the rack of postcards over the glass counter. They glanced at him, perhaps wondering whether he was stationed on the hill and why they hadn't seen him before, but they did not speak. The bookseller came from behind a curtain, and Happy caught a glimpse of a cookstove and an open trapdoor to the cellar— left open, he supposed, for a quick descent in case of the siren. Many people in Germany lived that way, beside open cellar doors. Happy wanted to write his parents, but he did not dare, for the mail might be censored.

"Can I have a packet of letter paper, please, and two stamps, and the use of a pen? And how much is the guidebook in the window?"

He had edged to the back of the room. Though the guidebook was on public sale, he did not want the soldiers to hear him ask for it.

The bookseller seemed to understand, or at least Happy imagined he understood. "I cannot let you have a whole packet, Herr Unteroffizier; we are short of paper. For two stamps, will two sheets not be enough?"

He lifted two sheets of thin ruled paper from the top of a box in the showcase, wetting his thumb to make sure of taking only two. He laid them on a table under the rear window, and detached two twelve-pfennig stamps from a strip in his wallet. The pen and a bottle of ink were on the table already.

"This is our writing room." He smiled wanly. "Many from the castle use it when for some reason they wish to avoid the censorship of the Feldpost, where you need no stamps. So I leave the pen and ink available. For the guidebook, it is three marks fifty, if I remember. There are not many hikers along the Neckar in wartime. If you will wait till I attend to these gentlemen, I will bring it from the window."

Happy saw that one of the soldiers, a Flak corporal like himself, with the silver band around the eagle on his red collar tab, bought a book of jokes. Another, after long hesitation, lifted a postcard from the rack. Happy could see it was a picture of soldiers in a dugout, writing by candlelight. The title was "Good Night, Mother," and there was a poem beneath the picture. The soldier looked back, as if hoping to address his card at the table, but seeing Happy with the pen in his hand he shrugged, took out his own fountain pen, and addressed it on top of the glass showcase. The three soldiers went out. The bookseller, who was lame, laboriously opened the inner glass window of the shop front to reach out the guidebook. While his back was turned, Happy wrote his letters, shielding the paper with his arm. He disguised his handwriting by printing them in capitals—not to protect himself, for he would be over the line when they were delivered, but to protect Maria and her brothers. To the Gebrüder Liebert at the Schloss in Crailsheim he wrote:

A COMRADE OF THE LUFTWAFFE WARNS YOU THAT THE AMIS WILL BOMB IN THREE DAYS.

To Maria he wrote:

KNIT SOCKS ONLY FOR THY BROTHERS UNTIL HE WHO LOVES THEE RETURNS.

The envelopes were sealed, face down on the table, by the time the bookseller returned with the guidebook. He presented it to Happy with a bow.

"The Odenwald Klub published it, Herr Corporal. It describes all the points of interest on both sides of the Neckar all the way down to Heidelberg. It is from before the war, but our river and forests do not change, and I have not changed the price. It even shows the inns, and see, there is a fine folding map with all the shelters the Klub maintained for hikers. Though no one hikes now, unless it is refugees or troops on leave. Perhaps the Corporal is on leave; I do not remember seeing him before among our clients from the Schloss."

Happy did not answer; he paid for the book without opening it and slipped his two letters inside it, holding the envelopes so the bookseller could not read the addresses.

"At least it is better to read a guidebook than a jokebook," sighed the bookseller, opening the door.

Happy turned left, back to the red mailbox on the corner where the sergeant had left him. He could just remember that before the regime the mailboxes had been yellow. He did not hear the shop door close, and knew the bookseller was gazing after him. He turned the corner a few steps, then turned again, and when he looked back the bookseller had retreated into his store. No one was in sight; he whipped out the letter to Maria's brothers and dropped it through the flap. Just as the lid fell back, the sergeant rounded the corner to pick him up. He could not have noticed. Happy left the letter to Maria in the guidebook. He did not want it to carry the Crailsheim postmark when it reached her.

The back of the truck was empty now, except for two packages of circulars. The orange Blacklist was tied on top of each package. The other package and all the rations had been left at the command post of 9th Flak.

"Now we shall really bounce," the sergeant laughed as he ground into gear, "without our ballast."

To their left lay the little airfield of the town, carefully terraced up from a flat field, but long ago made useless by a dozen bomb craters. There was no other damage in the town. The sergeant waved at the field. "I suppose the Yankees thought they were knocking out the Luftwaffe when they wasted bombs on that patch of weeds," he scoffed. "The planes they thought they were hitting were dummies. The whole field is a dummy—just a Scheinplatz. If they knew where the real division is, up on the hill, they could do a lot of damage."

"Even that can't be much of a target," said Happy, "if it only has enough men to survive on your few sacks of potatoes."

"Oh, we aren't up to strength, probably only a thousand men; that's the way every division is now. And others besides myself bring them rations. Besides, they farm the Flak platoons out to protect other outfits. I heard at Aalen, for instance, that we are going to detach two batteries there. But on paper it's a full division, and we have three 8.8s, along with plenty of dummies, right around the Schloss."

The road swings around to the left and heads westward through level open country, but before Hall it hairpins down the valley of the Bühler. Farmers had started already to prune the vines. The sergeant left one of his bundles, with the Blacklist on top, at the Rathaus in the square, lifting it out of the tonneau. That left just one more.

It was four o'clock when they reached Weinsberg, where their highway joins the almost finished Autobahn running up from Stuttgart. The roadbed stretched off to their left. Happy half expected to see the same line of tanks that had passed below him at Ulm the day before. It might well take the slow monsters a whole day to move up the eighty miles. Only four or five kilometers beyond him to the west he saw the spires and smokestacks of Heilbronn, where the Neckar flows in from the south and veers northward on its long fall to the Rhine. The big buildings of a sanitarium were on their right; to the left the wooded Reisberg rose a hundred yards in the air.

The sergeant drew up at the junction, crinkling his eyes first toward the city and then leftward along the Autobahn to the south. He hesitated.

"If I didn't have to leave that last Blacklist in Heilbronn," he thought aloud, "I could turn off here and get home to Stuttgart for supper. The surface on the Autobahn isn't poured the full length, and a couple of bridges are missing, so the tanks can't use it. But it's the perfect shortcut for a bus like mine. Otherwise I'll have to take Twenty-seven the other side of town through all the villages. Takes me an hour longer, besides the time I'll lose in Heilbronn. I'm scared to drive blackout with all these carts on the road; they don't carry lights, of course, and they aren't even supposed to be out after dark. But nobody bothers them any more. How would it be if you take my paper work in to Transport for me? You've got to go in town anyway. It's only five kilometers, and you may get a ride. Then I can roll along home to camp on the Autobahn without having to get supper on the way or drive in the dark, and I won't have the death of any civilians or animals on my conscience. How about it, Junge?"

Happy thought fast. He did not want to go into Heilbronn at all. It was a town of sixty thousand, and control point for the whole Wehrmacht in the Neckar valley, right down as far as Heidelberg. But he knew there was no way of bypassing it. If he had to go in, he would rather go on foot than in the truck. You never knew when the Gestapo might spring a spotcheck, and their favorite place was just outside the big towns. If he were in the truck there would be no chance of escaping it without alerting the sergeant. But if he were on foot, he might see the barrier in time and lie low till it was lifted, or take a side street to get past it. Anyway, his forged Soldbuch had passed the check at Ulm, and now he had the colonel's certificate besides, which was almost enough by itself. And then he suddenly thought, Heilbronn hasn't got its Blacklist yet. Here it is, being offered to me.

"Okay, I'll take it, but you'd better give me a slip of paper to prove I haven't stolen it, in case I run into a check."

"Good kid," said the sergeant, scribbling on a leaf from his notebook. He stamped it with the eagle seal in his Beutel and handed it to Happy. "It goes to Corporal Ernst at the counter in the station. That's across the big bridge; you can't miss it. Ernst is the sour-faced one; you'll know him from that. This is like that black-market restaurant; a year ago I wouldn't have dared trust my papers to anyone. But now, if they question me, I'll say I was trying to save the Wehrmacht a little fuel. They'll like that. You'd better sign a receipt for me too, just in case."

He scribbled again, and Happy had to sign "Steinberg, Corporal" on the slip, so the sergeant at last knew his name. He held the paper against the windshield, pretending to cramp his arms, so that he could disguise his handwriting.

"Now you do something for me, Sarge." He pulled his guide-book from his pocket and shook out the letter to Maria. "Mail this for me from Stuttgart, will you?"

The sergeant looked at him round-eyed, turning the en-velope over in his hand. "You want a fake postmark, eh? Writ-ing in capitals, too, so they won't know your handwriting? What's the idea?"

Happy felt himself blush, which wasn't bad cover either. He winked at the sergeant. "Haven't you ever wanted a girl to think you were some other place than where you really were?" —the sergeant smirked—"and the capitals are on account of her old man. He doesn't think I'm good enough."

The sergeant laughed, clapping his hand on his thigh. "You're not so dumb as you look, Junge; all right, I'll do your dirty work, since you're doing mine." He slipped the envelope be-tween the covers of his Soldbuch.

"Now show me the station on the map," Happy asked him, as he unfolded the plan of Heilbronn, but the sergeant did not look at it.

"You can't miss the station, what's left of it. Turn right over the river and follow the big tower. That's the post office, next door to the station. If you think Ulm is kaput, look at what the Amis did on Christmas Eve."

While he reached back for the Blacklist, Happy glanced through the rest of the guidebook. Later, when he was alone, he might not dare to open it. It contained a plan of Heidelberg too, and a long folding chart of the Neckar with the shelter-huts marked by black lozenges.

The sergeant handed him the packet; he buried it with the guidebook at the bottom of his knapsack under the clothing and food. He climbed out of the cab, thanked his superior, and saluted him with the German greeting. The sergeant handed down his rifle, said "Auf Wiederseh'n," and shuttled left down to the track of the Autobahn, leaving Happy alone on the concrete.

Happy slung his rifle across his back and headed toward the city, with the Blacklist and the bundle of circulars in his knapsack. The instant the sergeant left him he regretted having accepted them. If he left them at the transport office, he would certainly have to give his name. Corporal Ernst, "the sourfaced one," might glance through the Blacklist and come across it, even as he handed it to him, face to face. On the other hand, he did not know how to get rid of the book. It was too bulky to tear up or burn, and he did not dare throw it at the roadside, or even open it in sight of the busy traffic. He trudged along, turning the problem over in his mind. Then he decided that, after all, they would have to search him before they found it, and the Gestapo didn't search at a spot-check unless they suspected you already. And there was a sweet and secret justice in stealing what might be the only copy of his own death warrant between here and the end of his mission. Somehow he would find a way to destroy it, after he had studied his own entry more carefully. Meanwhile, the safest place for the Blacklist was on his own back. He shook his head; there was danger in worrying too much, just as there was in not worrying enough. As he trudged through the outskirts of the city, he tried, by an inner concentration, to turn himself into a good soldier of the Reich on his last two days of leave, heading for his regiment at the front in a coat too long for him, with a pack too heavy. If he could think of himself that way, perhaps the passers-by would too.

He had to get transportation at the station, as any combat soldier would. He had only two days left, and fifty miles to go. The last day would be the hardest, when he had to cross the Rhine from Mannheim to Ludwigshafen and on through the line. From this side he could not even tell where the line might be, for the papers no longer printed situation-maps. He did not dare trust a pickup to get him down on time; his luck had been too good already.

Behrend was right. The city was half ruined by the blaze bombs. The Ami planes might have dropped them on the military targets, but the flames had carried with the random wind. The timbers had caught, the roofs had fallen in, all the hollows of the stone shells were black and spalled, as dead as if artillery had pulverized them. Deader, for they would have to be pulled down before they could be rebuilt.

He crossed the four-lane bridge over the Neckar, from the medieval town to the modern. The city was crowded with party members and officials who had fled across the Rhine, on bicycles and in carts, before the American Seventh Army. It was crowded but silent, for the refugees were not welcome where there was so little to eat already. Red pennants two stories high hung on the undamaged buildings, with the swastika on a white circle in the middle. The street names were painted in black letters on white on the faces of the curbs, to guide drivers in the blackout. He had no trouble finding the station. When he drew near it he saw a big banner across the clock tower of the post office: HEILBRONN STEHT. Heilbronn stands firm. The bomb had hit the station first, but the wind had been east on Christmas Eve, so the post office next door was untouched.

Coming or going, troops always gathered in the stations even when there were no trains, as a family groups around the

236

chimney even when there is no fire. This Bahnhof had looked like the one at Kempten, only bigger: a brownstone pediment between brick wings. The roof was down and every window blown out, but the Labor Corps had repaired the tracks. An ersatz station of wood was built inside the carcass of the old.

Happy pushed open the swinging doors of the blackout vestibule. A round counter in the middle of the waiting room encircled two noncoms of the Transportation Corps. They answered questions and stamped travel orders under the FRONTLEITSTELLE sign. Happy spotted Corporal Ernst at a glance—"the sour-faced one" Behrend had said—and smiled to himself.

A hundred soldiers and reservists sat on benches beside a long row of trestle tables, or slept huddled against the walls. He could tell which troops had come from combat by the netting on their helmets and by the vacant stare in the eyes of those who were awake, and the exhaustion of those who had flung themselves down to sleep. He could tell which were going forward. They were the ones who read and reread the tattered papers on the tables, who paced the floor impatiently, who looked up each time the door opened, who crowded the canteen as if they would never eat or drink again, who warmed themselves by stamping on the tile and flapping their arms across their coats. The soldiers wore Kopfschützer under their steel helmets like the one he had worn on his jump. The Volkssturm wore eartabs under their melon-shaped hats, and rustled when they walked, from the newspapers padded under their braces. Across the opposite end of the shack stretched a green curtain, to cut off the groans and the smell of disinfectant behind. Combat troops were in there too. He had worked behind such curtains himself.

The Rhine was fifty miles away, but Happy felt the enemy's distant pressure in the furrowed haste of the Strength through Joy helpers at the canteen, with no time now to be pleasant or joke about the war; in the pitying soft-eyed kindliness of the sergeant at the desk, and even in the sullen impatience of Corporal Ernst beside him. The troops who lined up around the counter asked no questions, as if they dared not hear, or the noncoms utter, what the answers might be. They held out their travel papers; the noncoms stamped them in silence: Weitergeleitet. Forwarded, Heilbronn, 20 Feb., 45.

Hung from the rafters just above their heads in the middle of the shack, and printed on both sides so it could be seen by everyone, floated a huge cloth sign reading THE ENEMY IS LISTENING. Each time the outer door opened and a soldier came through the blackout vestibule it swayed on its ropes a little in the half-light.

Happy had completed his mission already. It had been as simple to find the divisions as walking down to the corner to look for a mailbox. Most of the soldiers in the waiting room knew where the headquarters were; many belonged to 9th Flak or 25th Infantry themselves. Given time enough, he could have found out their whole armament and TO. Any casual in uniform could have found them as easily as he had. Yet the enemy—he called the Americans that, just as Steinberg should—thought his news so important that with great cunning and some risk they had created the very Steinberg who observed it; would even time their attack on the strength of what their fiction reported, hazarding the annihilation of the two divisions, just because one spy had seen them, because under the steel helmet of Corporal Steinberg were the watchful eyes of Corporal Maurer.

Without seeming to watch, Happy waited for a break in the lineup around the booth, for a moment when no one would be near him to listen. When he saw it was empty at last, he strolled across from his bench. He laid down his trip ticket, stamped falsely at Bregenz for four days' leave and endorsed truly at Memmingen and Ulm and Aalen. Corporal Ernst, a stocky man with thin lips and glacier-blue eyes, stamped it once more, automatically. He wore the runic symbol of the SS on his collar, like this: *SS* . Then he looked at the paper more closely, almost incredulously.

"Look, Sergeant," he called to the other noncom, "here's an aviator who is on leave. Do you not suspect an airman who takes leave? I wondered why the Yankee bombers have been getting through lately. It's because Corporal—what's his name? —Corporal Steinberg has been absent all this time. He has been absent from a battery which might have defended the tracks, enjoying himself in the Alps. Now he has decided to return via Mannheim. Perhaps he has been skiing, since he has chosen himself a Mountain regiment, as if the Luftwaffe were not good enough for him. Shall we offer him a special limousine, or attach Marshal Göring's ivory car to the troop train that is taking his comrades to the front?"

He slid the travel order sourly along the linoleum counter, turning back to stamp the papers of a newcomer. Happy stepped along with it. He laid his reference from the colonel beside it, in front of the sergeant.

"Oh, leave the kid alone," and even to Ernst the sergeant's voice was kindly. "He's going back to the front, isn't he? Look, he's even got a kind word from Colonel Forster. Isn't that enough for you?"

He turned back to Happy, gazing myopically at the colonel's signature through rimless spectacles.

"You can go on the train with the others tonight, Corporal, if you want. I'll fix it up. You are in luck, because we haven't got a train through in the last week, and I don't know when we can again. Pay no attention to this Halunke. He's sore because he's going to the front himself. Just give me a minute to think it out."

The sergeant was surrounded by even more papers than Corporal Ernst. He scratched his fuzzy head with a pencil in what appeared to be thought, but which Happy knew was only the delaying of thought. His gaze was kindly but absent, as if he postponed the routing of his troops while considering the

239

larger question of whether there was any use in routing them at all. He does not seem like a sergeant, Happy thought; maybe a ringer from the party. He picked up one of the rubber stamps, frowning at the reversed lettering. He pounded it on the travel order after Ernst's "Forwarded" and slid it back to Happy. The stamp read "By express train to combat station."

"Yes, for the first time in a week we have got together enough rolling stock and fuel on the same night that the line is clear. Even so, the train doesn't go right to the Rhine, but only as far as Heidelberg. But there, with that stamp you can get aboard with the others at eleven.

"Beyond Heidelberg," said the sergeant, shaking his head and speaking low so that Ernst could not hear, "the tracks are kaput. Yankee bombers, you know. No use the Labor Corps repairing them, for the planes come over just as soon as they finish work."

No, Happy thought, that doesn't sound like a party man; more like an old timer impressed by a colonel's signature.

At Heidelberg the cliffs of the Odenwald suddenly drop to the flat river plain which stretches on fifteen kilometers to Mannheim and the Rhine itself. There was no cover whatever on the plain. It would take the train all night to get even as far as Heidelberg, the sergeant confided, because it stopped to pick up recruits from many stations on the way. They would have to get what rest they could in the train, eat breakfast the next morning in the Heidelberg station, where the Red Cross would have a canteen, and cross the plain on foot, for just yesterday a plane had cut the trolley tracks.

"The gangsters haven't hit Heidelberg yet, you know. Maybe they have some conscience after all. The train should get in at four. You can cross the plain in darkness, if it is on time."

Nowadays when there were any trains at all in Germany, they ran only at night, so as to escape the air raids. This train, after unloading its passengers before sunrise, would steam back to spend tomorrow in one of the tunnels under the steep cliffs of the Neckar, out of sight and range of the Yankees.

"So you may as well hop on the same train, Corporal. They'll feed you breakfast in Heidelberg, and you can march into Mannheim with them afterward. There will even be a baggage truck. It's only about three hours from Heidelberg, over good flat ground."

Happy wanted to reach Mannheim as fast as he could, but not by being shanghaied into a strange unit that might not let him go when he got there.

"But look, Sarge," he broke in, "I have two more days' leave. I don't have to report till day after tomorrow. See? It says so on my trip ticket. I'd like to see a little of the country. How about stamping me to stop over in Heidelberg? As far as sleep goes, I don't need much. Then I could take a hike through the woods tomorrow and report in the next day, when I'm supposed to."

The sergeant smiled indulgently. "Well, I don't see why not, but don't turn the war into a Cook's tour. We don't have such things as tickets on this train. You've already got the Tagesstempel for today; get it in Heidelberg for tomorrow, and check in the day after. But be sure you get there on time. It's hard to give anyone special treatment these days, even officers, and I wouldn't do it except for this reference from Colonel Forster. Anyone who can get a kind word out of him deserves the best. Just to make sure, I'll stamp 'on leave' for you."

He pounded one more seal. Corporal Ernst was listening; the three were alone at the counter again.

"In what branch of the Air Force is the Herr Tourist Corporal?" Ernst asked softly.

The sergeant frowned. He would be the first to admit that one must be vigilant, but it was not necessary to be cantankerous. Without being asked for his Soldbuch, Happy laid it on the counter between the two noncoms. Corporal Ernst pounced on it. He studied it page by page.

"Steinberg, Steinberg," he muttered. "What a name for a German soldier! I have heard of Jews named Steinberg. He is in the Medical Corps, and yet he does not wear its armband."

Happy reached in his belt and pulled out the folded brassard with the red cross on it. He pinned it about his left arm; the sergeant snapped the safety pins for him.

"The Tourist Corporal is in the Medical Corps, and yet he appears to be carrying a rifle." Ernst riffled through the book to page fourteen. "But I do not see that this rifle was issued to him by any officer of the Wehrmacht. See, there is no entry on the page."

Laying the Soldbuch face down, he fished in a pigeonhole under the counter and brought out his copy of the Blacklist. It was green, like the one at Ulm. It was last week's. He turned to the S page, but he did not find Steinberg on the list of the hunted. He replaced the book, muttering, "A good soldier does not ask for leave."

The sergeant whispered across, "Wouldst thou make him a better soldier if thou sent him to the front without a rifle, for the sake of the book?"

"It is last week's list. That Behrend, our mail orderly, is he not of the Luftwaffe too? They hang together. He should have brought the new one this afternoon, but nobody is on time any more."

"Except thyself," mocked the sergeant, rolling his eyes at Happy.

Not because this exchange had been overheard, but just because Happy had stood so long at the counter, a small crowd began to gather. A soldier who had been sitting for an hour at a wooden bench opened his eyes and strolled over. Another followed, throwing down the torn copy of Die Wacht he had already read through. (That was the daily of Nineteenth Armee.) Then others, because the first two had moved.

The knot of soldiers looked dully at each of the noncoms in turn as he spoke. Suspicion flickered in their eyes, reflecting

Corporal Ernst's suspicion. One of them felt for the bayonet at his side, but let it go when the sergeant smiled at Happy. Ernst was not convinced, but he did not dare risk a showdown in front of the other troops. He shook his hands over his head in defeat and hunched down over his stack of papers.

"When the new book comes, we shall see," he muttered, but he did not use the word Blacklist in the hearing of the others.

"Nobody is himself at such times, Corporal," the sergeant smiled to excuse his colleague, "not even I. The train comes in at 2215 hours and leaves at 2300."

He closed the Soldbuch and returned it to Happy. The crowd dissolved, returning to the benches. "Twenty-two-fif-teen" was whispered from one man to the next, way down to the end of the shack. They turned away, looking at Happy with respect. He strolled to a bench, unstrapped his rifle, and fell asleep, with his head resting on the knapsack which contained the stolen Blacklist.

When he woke, the blackout curtains were drawn. The train was in. The men, in columns of twos, were marching to the platform. They were marching to defend the Rhine, some of them in mountain hats with feathers in the bands, or in wool scarves instead of hats, in hunting jackets or ski overalls, some bending under lumpy sacks, some holding nothing but a greasy paper package of food. The moon shone through the glassless filigree of the steel trusses over the trainshed, but there was no light on the platform itself except the glare from the locomotive boiler, which a stoker fed with logs of wood, his bare torso glistening in the orange light from the firebox. The eight boxcars, with DEUTSCHE REICHSBAHN stenciled on the sides, waited with gaping doors. The troops did not break rank to enter, but climbed in pair by pair, each man laying his gear on the slats and helping himself up by gripping the doorjambs. Sometimes the young had to help the old. The cars were filled in order, the later ones standing empty till the first were full. The two non-coms ran silently along the platform, sliding the doors shut and ordering the men inside to throw the bolts. For fear of air raids, they did not lock the doors outside. There was none of the peacetime confusion—no shouting, no whistling, no farewells.

There was no light inside the car either. Happy found by touch that three tiers of slat bunks were hinged to the wall, and that straw was spread on the floor for those who found no room on the bunks. He jostled against someone as he reached for a bunk; the other man was reaching for it too, and Happy heard him sigh with fatigue. It was the last empty bunk.

"Bitte," said Happy, releasing it, and lay down in a corner of the straw, straining his eyes toward the square of the still open door. And Corporal Ernst, as he slid the door shut, stared straight at him, and the moonlight came through the trusses full on his face. Then someone dropped the throwbolt. The men settled to sleep in their clothes, just as they were, jostling each other in the dark.

The train started. It crept jerkily along the bank of the Neckar, stopping at the towns on the way, where Happy could hear the reinforcements climbing into the cars behind him. It was passing the castles and terraced vineyards of the ancient river, past Mosbach, and Eberbach, and Hirschhorn.

Someone started to hum "Die Wacht am Rhein"; another took it up, and soon the car was shaking to the roar of forty voices which drowned the swing and pound of the wheels. Happy sang it with the others, shouting it up to the echoing tarred vault of the cattlecar from the clump of straw under his head.

There strikes a call like thunder-clap,	Es braust ein Ruf wie Donner-hall,
Like clash of swords and beat of waves;	Wie Schwertgeklirr und Wogen-prall;
The Rhine, the Rhine, the German Rhine,	Zum Rhein, zum Rhein, zum deutschen Rhein,
Who will guard the sacred stream?	Wer will des Stromes Hüter sein?

When the chorus reached that line someone cut in, "Die Fünf-und-zwanzigste." The 25th Division. Everybody laughed. The chorus ended and the men drifted off into their uncomfortable sleep.

Ten

Happy slept too. Though the train backed and shunted over spur tracks to skip the damage on the main line, though it roared and smoked in the frequent tunnels, and though the recruits who boarded at the river stations shouted and cursed in the dark, he did not waken till the tracks crossed from the right bank of the Neckar to the left on the truss-bridge at Neckargemünd. The creaking of the wheels on the sharp S turn roused the whole carful.

"The bridge is mined," someone whispered. "That is why we have to take it slow."

But they could not see outside, for no one dared slide the door without orders, and the sun had not risen to shine through the chinks in the siding. The men on the bunks clambered down to the floor, stumbling over the men on the straw. The men on the straw groped to their feet like cattle stumbling up in a barn. Even when all were standing there was hardly room to move. They swayed helplessly, like the PWs Happy had seen at the cage. He peered at the luminous dial of his watch; it was half-past four. The train was still ten kilometers short of Hei-

246

delberg, and the sun would be rising soon. That meant the column would have to cross the plain in daylight.

At one end of the car was a primitive wooden box-latrine. One of the Volkssturm drew a farm lantern from his sack and hung it on the wall above. In the center of the opposite wall a Lister-bag of water swayed from a hook in the ceiling. Happy pulled out the flashlight Chuck had given him. He held it to light the men who wanted to drink and flush their faces with the water, but it was still too dark to see his way between the two points of light in the sealed boxcar. He had to stand to avoid being stepped on, and grope for the next man's shoulders to find his place in the lines.

The tracks skirt Heidelberg through a tunnel under the south slope of the town, and emerge to the station through a stone arch at the west end. When the train stopped, they heard Corporal Ernst barking "Aufmachen," so they slid open the doors. The cold half-light of the dawn flooded the car. The reservist blew out his lantern and stowed it in his sack. He pulled out an old-fashioned stem-winder.

"Two hours late," he announced.

From the tightened lips and furtive glances of the others, Happy saw that they knew as well as he that they must cross the plain without cover of darkness. No one spoke. They climbed out in pairs just as they had climbed in. Coughing and cramped, they formed a double line on the platform in the same order as the night before, the first half in uniform and the second in civilians, with the Volkssturm brassard on their arms and packs on their shoulders. Corporal Ernst was already standing opposite the center of the train. He held a pennant with the sword-flame of the 25th. An infantry lieutenant stood behind him on the concrete platform, against the brick wall of the station. Happy fell in at the end like a file closer, the only man there in the blue uniform of the Luftwaffe.

The others did not notice him, thinking he was assigned to the column for first aid. But when the corporal called the roll the two men next to him stared, seeing that his name was not called. The corporal gazed at him too, then wheeled to the lieutenant. His voice was icy.

"All present, Herr Leutnant, and one casual on leave, who has managed to get permission to travel by this train."

The lieutenant returned his salute. The wire gates at the end of the tracks had been closed behind the train, locking the troops inside the station. The corporal ordered them to break ranks and carry their baggage to a truck waiting at the north exit to the courtyard. The lieutenant announced that the trip across the plain to Mannheim would be made on foot, with squads spaced a hundred yards apart, for dispersal in case of air attack. Even as he spoke, Happy heard the distant gunfire begin. The sun had risen.

When the men had piled their baggage in the truck they crowded into the waiting room, where Red Cross aides had set up a canteen for breakfast.

"Red Cross at the front, Strength through Joy at the rear," someone muttered.

The luckiest troops were those who had no baggage, for they reached the counter first. The others stood three deep, with mess kits open waiting their turns. Happy carried nothing but his knapsack and his rifle, yet he waited too. Everybody had as much as he could eat: porridge, ersatz coffee, and black bread with margarine and jam.

But one man, about fifty years old, in a threadbare civilian coat with the brassard on his arm, did not even try to stand in the crowd at the counter. He hobbled to the bench against the wall and sat down. He caught Happy's eye, beckoning to him.

"Herr Corporal, as you are of the Medical Corps, will you look at my right foot, please? It is so blistered that I cannot walk. I came forty kilometers from my farm to Heilbronn yesterday. That would be nothing if I were younger. And we have been trained only on Sundays."

Happy knelt on the floor, standing his rifle against the

248

wall. He unlaced the manure-stained boots. Though the uppers looked sound, the soles were made of pieces of crudely shaped wood with a layer of burlap nailed against the vamps all around. The heel, the ball, the toes of the reservist's foot were three separate blisters which had burst, leaving the raw flesh to press upon the splintered sole. The sock was worn through. What other socks he may have had were in the baggage truck. Happy opened his own knapsack and drew out a pair of his blue Air Force socks, pushing the orange Blacklist to the bottom first. They were the ones Maria had darned. The man stared at the clean pair.

"Will they punish me in the Army for wearing Luftwaffe socks?" he asked. "There was no Luftwaffe that I knew of in the other war."

Happy laughed. "No, and they are certainly more regulation than the ones you have. Change the other sock yourself if you can, and you'd better rinse them both, for the wool will come in handy for darning mine when they give out again."

The reservist smiled shyly down at Happy. "The Army isn't so bad after all, is it?" he said. "No matter how we old timers complain."

His hands were gripping the edge of the bench to keep his foot from the pressure of the floor. He did not wince when Happy covered the skinless patches with Sepso and wrapped them with gauze from his kit. Then he sighed with relief.

"Thank you, my son; that feels better. I could even eat a little breakfast, but I did not think to bring a cup from the farm. In the old days the Army issued mess kits the first day. Perhaps later, in Mannheim, I shall receive one."

"I'm not hungry yet. Look after my rifle for a moment, and I'll bring you something."

He unbuckled his own zinc mess kit and stood in the back row of hungry soldiers. When the sister filled the containers at last, he turned from the crowded counter, elbowing his way back across the room. Through the glass door to the platform he caught the eye of the infantry lieutenant, who beckoned to him. He set his full plate and cup on the bench beside the farmer. He pushed open the door to the platform and stood before the lieutenant.

"Who are you?" The lieutenant looked him up and down, his hands behind his back.

"Corporal Steinberg, Herr Leutnant, from Bregenz Hospital, on convalescent leave, reporting to the 136th Mountain Regiment at the front."

"Leave!" the lieutenant burst out. "When my troops have to walk fifteen kilometers across the unprotected plain, you are on leave from the Air Force. Leave! The very train that brought you here has to hide in a tunnel all day because the Air Force is too weak to defend it. Do you know that no leave has been granted on the whole Rhine front for the last three days? That is how serious things are. Leave! And yet, for all that, you bind an old man's feet."

"Yes, sir, I don't think he can walk as far as Mannheim."

"Very well, Corporal; if you so advise I will order him to ride on the top of the baggage. Tell me, do you always minister to strangers without orders?"

"Well, sir, I didn't see you in the waiting room."

"And even to the enemy, perhaps?"

"We have done so, sir, at Cassino when we shot down American fliers."

"Ah, there were days when our Flak shot down the gangsters," said the lieutenant heavily. "One forgets. You will see that they have spared Heidelberg for some reason. Eat your breakfast and resume your leave. I cannot command you to join us, if your orders give you a stopover; but do not be late to your regiment. In you the Reich has not only one more living soldier, but the many more whom you may save. Get your travel order stamped today. Here, I'll stamp it for you now."

He signed the "Forwarded, Heidelberg" seal. It was the last check Happy would need.

"Allow plenty of time to reach the Rhine bridge, for there will be gunfire. As a single traveler you may perhaps get a ride in a truck if you wait till nightfall, while I must let these poor devils march because I have no transportation for them. I thank you, Corporal. Heil Hitler!"

He turned his back, still holding his shoulders square.

Happy returned to the waiting room. He picked up his mess kit from the bench beside the veteran; he washed it at the pump built into the wall over an iron drain in the floor, and scoured it with his piece of sandy soap. The others had finished breakfast; they waited for the order to fall in. They sat on every available inch of the bench around the hall. The Red Cross aides were cleaning up. Happy was hungry, for he had had no supper the night before, wanting to save the chicken and cheese for his last day. He crossed to the counter. One of the sisters looked at him in surprise.

"We cannot give seconds, Corporal. Did you not have enough before?"

"That was for a comrade, Sister."

She shrugged her shoulders; she did not believe him. But the other women were not looking, so she filled his cup with coffee and ladled porridge into the kidney-shaped plate, with bread and margarine and jam on the side. He ate it standing alone at the counter, his back to the roomful of troops. He heard someone grumble, "The Luftwaffe has all the luck." He finished it standing by himself, the only airman in the crowd of infantry.

Then the grumbling ended abruptly; the rattling of mess kits and shuffling of feet ceased. They heard the wail of an air-raid siren and then the whine of a plane flying low, growing louder as it came in from the west. Happy knew the sound. He had heard it, shivering inside the bomb bay, and dropping through the air, and staring up from the ground beside a woodpile. The plane was an A-26, higher-pitched than a Liberator as a wasp is shriller than a bee. The troops fell silent, though the windows were still locked and curtained. Even the Red Cross sisters, who must have fed many combat details before, froze with the unwashed dishes in their hands. They were silent, thinking the silence could hide them, as a hen lies still in the dust when she sees the shadow of a hawk.

There was no reaction from the German Flak; he felt that the others accused him for its silence. The A-26 is a rooftop plane. Perhaps it flew too low for the Flak trajectory, which can depress only five degrees. Through the curtains he could not tell. Then the whine soared and died away as suddenly as it had come. They heard the belated chatter of their own Flak, so close to them that the windows rattled. The all clear sounded, and the whole roomful sighed out their pent-in breath. Happy did not dare to turn and face them.

He hoped the fall-in would be given before he had to turn, but he could no longer delay sopping up his plate, for the sisters stared at him, waiting for him to finish so they could clean up and escape to the shelters during the lull. They need not stare, he thought; it was only a reconnaissance plane and had dropped no bombs. There would be no harm to Heidelberg till it did drop the bomb, as there was no harm in what Steinberg saw till Maurer told it to the enemy.

He had to turn around and face the silent crowd. He found himself looking straight into the eyes of Corporal Ernst, who sat at the end of the bench beside the platform door—eyes that stared at him without blinking. Happy felt himself redden; he could not shift his own. Just then the lieutenant leaned in and touched the corporal on the shoulder. At once the corporal sprang to his feet and gave the order to fall in.

The covey of recruits rose with a swish of coatskirts and a rattle of tinware. They filed in pairs through the double doors; they formed in the courtyard in the order of the night before. Happy picked up his rifle and followed them, not knowing what else to do. The place of the reservist with the blistered feet was empty; he himself was looking back at the column from the top of the baggage piled in the open-backed truck.

The corporal ordered the left column one step forward to fill the gap.

The older reservists were first in the line, the youngsters next. Corporal Ernst brought up the rear, a rifle on his back and the pennant in his hand. The lieutenant faced the column from the head, a saber over his shoulder, marking time. The column lifted its feet in unison with his "Eins, zwei." Happy marked time with the rest. The lieutenant wheeled. "Abteilung, ohne Tritt, Marsch!" * he commanded. The baggage truck moved forward at the head. The column swung into step behind it. They filed through the pink stone arches of the courtyard, leaving Happy alone on the paving.

He felt deserted, as he had in childhood when the family left him alone in Trebbin if they went to the city for the day, turning the big key in the front door while he watched with his chin on the window sill.

He heard the stationmaster lock the platform door. The three sisters came out in their raincoats, and he locked the waiting-room door behind them with another big key from the bunch hung on his belt.

"Bitte sehr." Happy smiled to them, waving them through the arch. They looked at him sharply, but did not answer. Happy passed out behind them into the square. They disappeared together around the corner of the station, with a last glance over their shoulders. They would run to the Kommandantur, he knew, to report him; a single suspicious airman loose in the city, left behind by the combat troops, and not attached to any formation as far as *they* could see. A sign across the square read: "Hotel Europe Victoria, Radium Sol-Bad." He could do with any kind of bath after his night in the troop train.

He followed the column leftward to the river, but no farther, for he was on leave. He leaned on the stone parapet. The Neckar burst through the dike of cliffs to his right; to his left

* "Column, forward march!"

the impatient stream grew still, softening from the reflection of the beech-carpet to mirror the silver dawn, and broadening between flat sandy banks to wander westward to the Rhine. The city was behind him. He could hear it waken. The sounds of morning came from inside the shuttered houses. Geese cackled to the rumble of the distant gunfire. Somewhere a donkey brayed. The few people who had emerged outdoors, from the cellars or the air-raid shelters, moved close to the walls. Those who walked eastward stared down at the sidewalk, hunching their shoulders as if to ward off a blow from behind. Those who walked westward turned their faces to the sky. They listened; everyone in Germany listened, as one listens in a thunderstorm, counting the seconds between the flash and the clap to judge the distance of the bolt.

The troop slogged straight north across the New Bridge, so he guessed they would hug the shelter of the Odenwald cliff before breaking left across the plain to Mannheim. He turned right toward the Old Bridge, where sightseers always go. He walked through a stone arch between two pink towers, and was on the river. The marble statue of some forgotten elector gestured on the parapet, with two fingers chipped off. Where had he seen a three-fingered hand? He did not stop to remember. Beyond the bridge spread a smaller square, and behind it the great palisade of the Odenwald paraded out of sight to the north. At the top of the first hill, which makes the river's shoulder, he saw a watchtower. He turned to the left along the base of the gorge. From the map he had bought in Crailsheim he knew it was the Bismarck-Turm. A double-hairpin road bucked up the cliff to it. This road, he saw on a sign, was the Philosophenweg: the Philosophers' Walk. Happy clambered up it, his equipment slapping and rattling on his back, between the clumps of fir and leafless beech. They climbed the road with him, clutching their footholds in the brown grass or green moss between their roots. There were iron railings at the side for support, but many of the bars had been wrenched out for their metal. His father had told him Heidelberg was the most beautiful town in Germany, and the Philosophers' Walk its loveliest woodpath.

At least he was alone. If you had to define a soldier, he thought, it would not be as a man who carries a rifle. Many of the Volkssturm had no rifle. It would be as a man who is never alone.

Beyond the first houses the woods on each side of the zigzag path were thick and dark. Crosspaths led off at intervals, but he remembered that the black lozenge of the Odenwald Klub, on the signs at every junction, would lead him to the plateau and the tower at the top. When he reached the summit he was panting from the climb. In spite of the cold, his whole body sweated.

The tower stood in the center of an untended clearing. Seedlings of beech and fir had sprouted from the matted grass around it: The red stone cylinder rose twenty yards among them, pierced by slit windows, to a balcony at the top. It seemed to be empty. There were no wheelmarks on the ground and no wires overhead. He wondered why the Flak had not set up a battery, or at least an observation post, at such a vantage point. Perhaps just because the enemy would expect it. The Bismarck tower was an easy target.

Before he entered the tower he walked carefully around the whole fifty-yard plateau. Though an agent must ever be watching, he must never be seen to watch. It is not easy. He walked softly, but without purpose, stopping to pick a checkerberry or chew a twig of young birchbark, and searching from the corners of his eyes for whatever might lurk in the underbrush. Then round again, close to the base of the tower, as aimless as before.

The studded door in the base sagged loose. He wondered why it had not been salvaged for scrap. The lock had been pried off. The floor inside was stone. A stone staircase angled its way to the platform at the top, the dust thick on the treads.

The light from the slit windows filtered down through cobwebs and drifted leaves. A round millstone on a pedestal served as a picnic table, but if there had been any benches they were gone now, probably stolen for firewood. He creaked the door shut and wedged his rifle into the keeper so that no one could open it from outside.

He laid a few leaves from his guidebook on the floor. He kindled them with his lighter, cupping the blazing paper to be sure there was a draft up the shaft of the tower. He laid his knapsack on the millstone and lifted out the stolen copy of the Blacklist from the bottom. He turned to the S page. He read in full what he had only dared glance at in the colonel's room: STEINBERG, KARL, so-called Medical Corporal of the Luftwaffe. Believed to be an enemy agent, parachuted near Schongau 17 February. May be armed. About nineteen. Deliver alive to nearest station. Height one meter ninety, eyes gray, complexion ruddy, mustache fair.

He ripped out the page and set it afire on the floor, stamping the curled gray ash when it had burned. He had to run the risk that the smoke might be seen outside. The rest of the book he ripped in half, for it was too thick to burn in one piece.

He fed the fragments on top of the S page, throwing them to the fire as fast as they would burn, with the sergeant's circulars for fuel. It took minutes, for the book was thick, with the names of hundreds who were hunted. It charred from the bottom; the orange binding was the last to blacken. The flame caught a cobweb in the corner; the cobweb withered and curled. He shivered; but with the Blacklist burned at least the evidence against him was no longer on his own back. He stamped on the ashes again.

No panic, he warned himself. He unbuckled his knapsack wide and drew out the cheese and the chicken. Spreading Frau Bense's waxed paper on the millstone, he cut the food in half with his bayonet. Each half would make one good meal. He wrapped one to eat tomorrow, for he could not be sure of getting back to the Golden Well in time for the Ami mess. He ate the other with his fingers to avoid dirtying his mess kit—there was no water in the tower—threw the bones in the corner, and licked his fingers clean. He ate the cheese in its rind. The bayonet point pried out the cork of the Niersteiner. He filled his canteen first, then drank the rest and stood the empty under the stairs.

No panic, he repeated, but he climbed the stairs two at a time, steep as they were. At the top he pushed open a door. He was on the little balcony which ran around the peak. Heidelberg clustered far below him to the left, its tile roofs so close together they seemed like a red carpet flung on the opposite hill. Even now there was no smoke from the chimneys, and what sound there might be did not float up. Above the town, and almost on a level with his tower, stood the ruins of the old castle, with the sunlight staring through the sashless windows of the sandstone walls which the French had gutted two centuries ago. But the Schloss seemed no more lifeless than the paralyzed living city lying intact below it. Before him the river plain stretched westward to the Rhine and out of sight to north and south, checkered with fences and hedgerows, pitted with swamps, dotted with toolsheds and barns. This plain is the truck garden of Western Germany. The soil is too fertile to waste on trees, as the forest at the Golden Well was too valuable to cut for crops, and the few farm villages hug close together to leave room for tobacco and strawberries and asparagus. On the left bank of the Neckar he saw the white ribbon of the Autobahn sweep out of a wood, veer west with the river and north again at the Mannheim bypass, to disappear into another wood. He saw where the coupled trolleys had been bombed. The staves and journals of the carriages sprawled on both sides of the track like a neatly split lobster shell. The rails twisted and clawed upward. It had been a bull's-eye hit. There were pits peppered along the Autobahn too, like pictures of the craters on the moon. He could understand why trains no

257

longer moved in the unprotected valley, why tanks and trucks near the front could not use the Autobahn but had to stick to sheltered roads, and why the lieutenant had led the column under the hillside—though Happy could not see the foot—to the shelter of the farmlands, instead of across the long bright target of the highway. He could see no defense, yet an 8.8 emplaced on the crest below his tower, with its range of sixteen kilometers, could have commanded the plain as far as Mannheim and itself been invisible from ground or air.

The Rhine plain was a painted deck where nothing moved: no cattle grazing, for they had been slaughtered; no trees bowing to the wind, for they had been cut for firewood; no sheets flapping in the sunshine, for the farmsteads were deserted or shut tight; no refugees escaping across it, for they dared not travel in daylight. Patches of windblown snow flecked the checkerboard of brown hedges and yellow fields. Then, as his eyes grew used to the distance, he saw his column of troops crawling across it like an inchworm, from the lee of the cliff, the corporal's pennant at the tail, and far ahead of them, almost as far as he could see, the smudge which must be Mannheim. He might not have made out Mannheim at all except for the gunfire which darted toward it at intervals like those neon arrows which urge you into a bar. The smoke-pall which cocooned the site of the city puffed and sprouted, now black, now yellow, now at one end, now at the other, to the same cadence as the flashes. Though he could barely see Mannheim and not hear it at all, he could smell it; for the lazy strata of the upper air freighted across to him the distant sickly scent of decay, out of reach of nostrils on the plain. It came, he knew, from bodies under the rubble, piling higher even while he stared. He had smelled it from the other hilltop at Cassino.

Out of sight on the far horizon, he knew, stretched the left bank of the Rhine, as broad as the right, where the Hardt marches opposite the Odenwald and the Vosges opposite the Black Forest. From the windows of the Golden Well, even now, the other Joes could almost look down to Mannheim and across to him. He was looking at the Rhine as he had looked at it five days before, but from the opposite side, as if he had circumnavigated the earth and returned to where he started. Steinberg looked across the battle to Maurer.

Then out of invisibility came the sharp droning of a plane, the flash of her wings, the whine as she dove, and then the chatter of her guns. The A-26 was back, with eight fifties spitting from her nose and four from her tail. She was dipping to rake the column on the road. They had seen the danger first. The black rods of the inchworm, each of which was a squad, scattered into dots which were men, running to each side and rolling into the gutter under the hedgerows. Even before the first of them melted into the earth he heard the answer of the German Flak, to right and left of him along the cliff below. There was a battery after all! They were the Vierling 2 cms. he had heard so often before, like his own platoon's. The four snouts spit eight hundred rounds a minute. The clatter-back of the quadruple breeching, the creak as the carriage swiveled with the range finder, and the whipping of the belt against the shield as the piece took up—they were sweet to his ears, and he sniffed the cordite and the hot grease. He could not see the guns through the trees, but from the sound one piece seemed sited on the hill across the Neckar, back of the Schloss, and the other on the wooded crest somewhere to his right. A sapling in the forest below him groaned and split, sawn through by a blade of bullets, but he could not tell whether they were German or Ami. The arc of its fall crossed the outskirts of his vision; the tree tottered and crashed among the rest, but he ignored it, trying to keep his eyes on the attacking plane.

She banked and wheeled round after the single volley, unhurt, and in less time than he could have told it she was out of sight again in the west. The miserable dots crept back to the road again as one of them—it must have been the lieutenant—danced left and right to urge them forward. The column reformed, but this time in single file, thinner and longer, hugging the left side and creeping faster—they were really running— toward what shelter they could find in the village of Ladenburg ahead. The sunlight struck a blade; the lieutenant was beating them forward with his sabre. Yet Happy was sure that the big dot of the pack truck was left behind, and that a smaller one —a man—was still lying in the hedgerow.

He had a job to do. He clattered down the stairs. He seized his knapsack from the millstone and wrenched his rifle from the door, swinging them both over his back. He pushed open the sagging door, strapping his steel helmet as he ran across the clearing.

The black-lozenge signs flashing past him led to a ravine that would drop him down to the valley. He skirted some ivied ruins; the guidebook had said they were an ancient basilica. He panted to the last lozenge, at the head of the steep path, as steep as the trail down which he had fled from the warden. The soles of his boots grooved on the pebbles as he slid down it. The tail of his too-long overcoat caught on snags. His hands, blistering even through the mittens, grasped at the saplings as he slithered down, then let them snap back when he found a new footing. A millstream tumbled downhill beside him; there were seven mills on seven terraces, but the wheels were not turning and the water sluiced past them and on down the cliff.

Within a quarter of the time it had taken to climb Philosophers' Walk he was at the foot of the Odenwald, in the village of Schriesheim. It was as smokeless and shuttered as Heidelberg. Through the slits in the tops of the shutters there must have been eyes which had watched the attack and which watched him now, and in the hidden batteries above were the eyes of his own Luftwaffe. Without glancing to the side, he ran across the cobbles between the houses. In a few minutes the village street led him out to the checkerboard of gardens. The road stretched ahead of him between the hedges, as straight as a ruler. In half an hour, running all the way, he could see the place of the dive bombing. Ahead of him, in the gutter to the left, the baggage truck was tilted to its axle. It must have been struck, though from the distance he could see no damage. Perhaps a slug had hit the motor or the tires, he thought, and put the truck out of action without destroying it. The baggage was scattered on the road, and the old man was gone.

The straggling line was fading out of sight toward the pall of smoke that hung over the river city. It had lost all discipline, lost even the form of a column. Some of the stronger ones were still running; the older ones limped behind as best they could, keeping off the center of the road, hobbling in the gullies and along the wire fence, making their way across the plowed fields in the shelter of the hedges. As Happy crossed the millbrook he saw the column pass into the undamaged village of Ladenburg. One terror-stricken soldier was beating at the door of the first farmhouse, but the door did not open; and in a moment the lieutenant, bringing up the rear to force the stragglers ahead, drove him forward with the others. If a soldier stumbled or strayed into the fields to escape, the lieutenant threatened him with his pistol. Twice Happy saw him fire over a coward's head. The lieutenant was merciful not to kill him, yet if it were not for the pistol, Happy knew, the whole mass would have fled backward to the protection of the cliffs.

As he drew nearer to the farmhouse he saw that it was deserted—not only silent like the houses in Schriesheim and Heidelberg, but abandoned. The farmer must have driven his stock before him and fled with what possessions he could, at night, across the no man's land of the plain to the towns which sheltered under the palisade of the Odenwald. A few panes of glass were broken, a few shutters unhinged, a few tiles tilted off the roofs, but otherwise the house was not hurt. Frost coated the old manure in the yard. Some of the slugs from the plane's machine gun scattered across the road, along with the steel splinters of the Vierling shells which had burst on impact and the yellow cases of those which had not. In air attacks, enemy fire and friendly can be equally dangerous to the ground.

The place where the truck had stalled was a kilometer beyond Ladenburg. Happy hurried forward; he saw why the truck had foundered. A shot had ripped the left rear tire. The driver had skidded across the road into a culvert. The truck leaned over to its left axle-ends, resting on the dented cylinder of corrugated steel. Nobody was in sight.

As he paused—and he knew he could not pause for long—a shot cracked behind him and a bullet sang past his ear. He leaped around, his rifle slapping his buttocks. It is not easy to locate a shot instantly, and the nearer it is, the harder to tell the direction. He scanned the hedgerow from left to right, and then he saw the source. A wisp of smoke still hung in the air a hundred yards behind him, curling from under the branches of a dwarf spruce tree. Staring at the truck, he had not noticed when he passed the man. Happy dropped to the ground, rolling instinctively into the gully on the left side. The shot was not repeated. In the opposite ditch, under the smoke, he saw a man.

He edged backward on his stomach to the shelter of the rear wheels of the truck, as he had backed away from the woodpile the morning of his jump. Cautiously he tilted his helmet and looked back. A Luger, still smoking, lay in the powdery snow on the shoulder of the road opposite him.

Happy rabbitskinned the strap of his rifle over the crown of his helmet. He cocked it with the catch at "Feuer." The man was lying with his head to the west. Happy crept on his belly along his own ditch far enough so that if his enemy should try to shoot again he would have to face the sun.

Happy stood up warily, his finger still on the trigger. He crept toward the Luger. Corporal Ernst lay in the snow which had drifted into the gully. His own blood had melted a depression about him and lay as jelly lies in a mold, taking its shape from the hollow of the dish. His field-gray coat had been torn open, and the left leg of his trousers torn down by a projectile from the A-26. Happy saw the end of the splintered femur, protruding through the skin of the thigh. From a wound below the corporal's chest more blood still leached into the puddle. The foreleg, living, beat in spasm like the arms of the dead saboteur at Aalen. The right arm lay angled upward over the edge of the ditch above the pistol it had dropped, already incapable of flexion. The steel helmet had fallen back from Corporal Ernst's face. His lips were closed over the clamped jaws. His breath fluttered shallow through his distended nostrils, sparing his wound the pain of motion.

Happy tossed his own rifle on the ground. It made no noise in the drifted snow. He rolled back the sleeve of the corporal's right arm. He fumbled in his kit for the hypodermic needle. This was his own needle, which he had refilled with morphine after the colonel's shot. It could not save the corporal now, but it would ease his pain. The corporal's eyes rolled slowly to the right, but he could not move his head with them. All he could say was, "Corporal—Steinberg."

His very pause before Happy's alias put it in the quotation marks of falsehood.

Happy put his left arm behind the corporal's head, and the corporal could not resist. With his right hand he unbuttoned the collar of the coat, then of the tunic, then of the shirt, to let the corporal breathe. On a chain around Corporal Ernst's neck, instead of a soldier's zinc oval, hung the oblong silver dogtag of the Gestapo, with his number on one side and the words "Secret State Police" on the other.

Happy pulled the flask from his belt and unscrewed the cap. He held the flask of wine against the clenched teeth. But the corporal, with his last breath, spat the wine back between them, mixed with his own blood. His head, his rigid arm, his shattered leg went limp. His mouth still closed and his eyes still open, Corporal Ernst died in Happy's arms, never to tell what he had guessed, or how.

"Kamerad," Happy breathed.

He stood up, shading his eyes from the glare of the roadside. It was empty in both directions; the sky was empty. He unstrapped the corporal's steel helmet and drew his wool Kopfschützer down to cover the face. He could drag the body to the shelter of the truck, but it was too heavy for him to lift inside. The corporal had no rifle; the others in the column would have been crazy not to take it when they left him. But the sword-flame pennant lay beside him in the snow, trampled by muddy boots. Happy drove the pointed brass tip of the staff into the frozen ground with hammer blows from the dead man's helmet. When it was secure he wound the chin strap of the helmet over the staff for a signal. As soon as the sun faded, the refugees would start out of the city. They would have carts; they could carry him to a soldier's burial. Lastly he pulled out of his knapsack the wooden rosary he had bought in Kaufbeuren for Père Nod. He folded the corporal's hands across his tunic with the rosary between them.

He stumbled ahead toward Mannheim again, trotting as long as he could, then walking to regain his breath. His rifle slapped against his back when he ran. The road passed under the Autobahn. As he had seen from the tower, the paving at the underpass was pocked and heaved by the shelling. If the Amis had dropped the bridge, they would have blocked both roads. Water welled up into the bomb craters through the ruptured earth, and the snow melted down into them. There was an unfinished roadblock at the underpass. He picked his way through the passage left for the carts of the refugees.

At the suburb of Wallstadt the road swung to the left. The half-timbered gables of the farmsteads began to give way to the sandstone and stucco of the city. He was approaching the Neckar bridge into Mannheim itself. Many roads funnel together from the plain at the Neckar bridge. Across the approach lay the carcass of the Brown-Boveri electric factory, and next it a big drill ground and barracks behind a stone arch. The arch was lettered KAISER-WILHELM KASERNE in old-fashioned Gothic carving, but the arrow by the driveway bore a square flag-symbol and the abbreviation "69th Hy. Arty. Repl. Regt." There was no sentry in the box. Through the arch Happy saw that the windows of the barracks were blown out, perhaps by the same blast that had wrecked the factory.

But 69th Heavy Artillery was no longer there, and was not his assignment anyway. He kept on toward the bridge. From all the roads that debouched to it, soldiers were marching toward the city, singly or in pairs. There were never enough together to form a squad. It was four o'clock. A big engineer sergeant, half a head taller than Happy, swung up behind him and fell into step.

"Where are you going, Junge?" he asked jovially. "You look out of place for this action. Still, if the city had seen a little more of the Air Corps *and* of the Medical Corps, it wouldn't be the mess it is today." He slowed down to match Happy's shorter steps, easing his rifle to a more comfortable angle on his back. .

"I'm crossing the Rhine to report at Neustadt," Happy told him. "But I didn't know I'd run into anything like that." He nodded his head toward the clouds and smoke of the bombardment.

The sergeant laughed sourly. "Well, you'll have an exciting trip, but you're safe till you get to the Rhine. At least the gangsters are aiming away from the center of town. This is not what the Tommies call a Baedeker attack."

"My last day of leave." Happy grimaced.

The sergeant whistled. "You've got nerve to keep going forward, but I suppose you have to. If I had orders like that I'd just hide out. You must have had a good long leave, not to know how things have changed in the last week. Have a cigarette? I'll roll one for you. The tobacco is grown right on this plain. Some of us are working on a roadblock out toward Bensheim, where the brass is set up in a cave. A farmer gave us a kilo of his tobacco between us. It isn't so bad at that."

With one hand he rolled the cigarette, holding his pouch in the other and his gloves between his teeth.

"Wait a minute; don't take off your mittens. It's too cold. I've got a lighter."

It was good that Happy did not have to take them off, for his hands were wet with the corporal's blood. There was a little on his cuffs and some on the skirt of his overcoat, but the sergeant did not notice as he set the cigarette between Happy's lips. Bloodstains do not show up on the blue-gray of the Luftwaffe.

"I'm lucky," sighed the sergeant. "I spend the nights in the air-raid shelter just off the Bismarck-platz. Some of the fellows still have orders to cross the Rhine, like you, to the shelters in Ludwigshafen. Ever been here before? No? That's Mannheim's twin city, on the far side of the Rhine bridge if the Yankees haven't captured it today. I don't say there isn't any artillery damage inside Mannheim, because they're pasting Ludwigshafen hard. Some of the overs hit the town the same as shorts hit it when they got the Brown-Boveri. They would claim that was an accident, I suppose. They've knocked out the port pretty well and cut the sewer and water mains. The shelling you hear now is on Ludwigshafen. And of course the fire bombs have been dropping for a year. Well, I'll cross the Neckar with you and walk up Frederick Street till we reach my shelter. The bridge we cross is named Frederick too, and we have to detour for it because one of those 'accidents' hit the Adolf-Hitler Bridge right ahead of us."

"There is something named for Him in every town, isn't there?" Happy said. "Even the smallest. Where they have a river they can name a bridge for Him. Down in the Alps where I've come from they've even named a mountain for Him."

"Well," said the sergeant, "that's no treason. He's done something for every town in the Reich, hasn't He?"

"Jawohl," said Happy hastily.

They slogged along. As they neared the gunfire they had to

raise their voices. They talked more to cover their nervousness than to exchange any thoughts. Strangely enough, the shelling did not sound as loud as it had from the tower; perhaps his ears were getting focused to it.

"Mannheim is a funny town," the sergeant rambled on. "Before the shells hit it, the port was one of the biggest in Germany. It's the farthest upstream that big riverboats can travel. They spent plenty in the last fifty years on building up the quays and straightening the riverbed. You'll see when you get across. It's the transshipment point for downstream traffic on both the rivers. A barge comes down the Neckar once in a while still, but there's nothing moving on the Rhine since we mined it. I saw an old map of the city in a bookstore once. The city was fortified in those days—wish it was now. It looked just like a beetle straddling a blade of grass, with its tail here at the Frederick Bridge, and its head at the old Schloss clear at the opposite side of the peninsula, or the blade, so to speak. Right at the head of where the Rhine bridge now stands. In those days they even had pontoons across both rivers. I suppose the electors were nothing but pirates, charging tribute to everyone going up or down either river. They filled in the fortifications long ago, of course, but you can see the outline in the shape of the boulevard that runs around the center of the town. We call it the Ring. All the old buildings are inside the Ring, so naturally we put the air-raid shelters there too. It's the only part the Yankees don't shell. Historical monument, I suppose—as if *they* had any history."

"What do the numbers on the streetcorners mean?" Happy asked.

The engineer laughed. "I guess Mannheim's the only city in the world where the streets don't have names. The blocks are numbered instead, like A-1 and B-2 and so on, so a stranger can always tell where he is, so long as he doesn't go outside the Ring, where the streets are named like anywhere else. Anyway, the shelters are safe enough. I guess the villages on the plain are too, for the Yankees don't waste ammunition on useless targets. The only trouble with the plain is that they have a nasty habit of buzzing the traffic. The mayor won't let the refugees out till after dark. One was at it this morning. Come to think of it, I don't know why we have any troops in the city at all, because there isn't any artillery there except a little Flak on the Rhine bridge. The heavy stuff is down at Sandhofen. Maybe we're afraid of a spearhead crossing, but believe me, we could blow the bridge any time we feel like it. Maybe afraid of spies trying to set a few charges themselves."

"The time to blow the bridge would be when the first Yankee tanks are in the middle of it," Happy shouted above the din.

The sergeant nodded. They had walked a dozen blocks up Frederick Street from the Neckar. Mannheim was hit as hard as Heilbronn. The whole front of Q-1 had fallen in when the phosphorus burned away the joists. Bathtubs hung head down in the air, anchored by their piping to the black walls. An elevator clung in its guide rails three stories up, but the third story had dropped to the basement like the rest. Yet the Concordia Church across the street was untouched.

"Well, Junge, here's my shelter. You walk straight ahead. That big ruin you see at the head of the street is the Schloss. You turn around it, either way, and you find the Rhine bridge just beyond it on a line with this street. That is, if you still insist on crossing. Otherwise come in with us; no questions asked. Good luck to you and es lebe der Führer." *

Happy waved to him. "Es lebe Deutschland," † he called. He looked at his watch; it was 1620.

"Make it fast," the sergeant ran after him to say. "If you can get across the bridge at all, try to do it before five. That's when they let the refugees move this way out of Ludwigshafen. Once they start, you can hardly get through, there's such a crowd of them."

* Long live the Führer.
† Long live Germany.

He turned between the sandbags into a staircase marked "Wehrmacht only." Happy plodded on up the street. He looked back over his shoulder and saw that most of the soldiers turned into the same bunker, while a few continued like him, apparently on orders to cross the Rhine bridge into Ludwigshafen. He limped along the cobbled street toward the façade of the burned-out Schloss at the end. The city was almost empty. There were long-handled water pumps at some corners, where a few housewives gathered with buckets. An occasional streetcar clattered down the tracks; women and boys on bicycles close to the curb, sometimes an army truck with tarpaulins closed—that was all the traffic. Someone had daubed on a wall "Victory or Siberia," and on another "Better Death than Slavery." There were no red banners of defiance as at Heilbronn, but no white banners of surrender either. The familiar warning sign stretched across the tower between the twin halls of the Bismarck-platz: THE ENEMY IS LISTENING. Mannheim was not defiant; it waited.

He passed other shelters; the iron grills were closed, and the civilians waited in line for them to open, leaning against the sandbags, the women knitting and the old men smoking. Only the Wehrmacht could go below in daylight. Others clustered outside the churches with blankets and pillows, even with cookstoves, knowing that the Americans did not shell churches—at least on purpose. There might be a little more risk in a church, but many preferred to sleep on the stone floors under the high vaults, rather than in the steaming caverns underground.

He overtook a Volkssturm man limping up Frederick Street. He wore a shabby black civilian overcoat with the white brassard on his left arm. When he drew abreast he saw the man was not more than thirty. One of his legs was wood, but he did not use a cane.

"I thought I was out of the Army for good," the reservist laughed, "when I lost this"—he slapped his wooden leg—"but

I can still use this." And he gripped the stock of his rifle. "We'll never let them into Mannheim, nicht?"

He smiled gaily as they pressed toward the growing roar of the guns. He thought that Happy, like himself, was heading for the defense of the factory city across the river. They both wanted company. He walked so slowly that by the time they reached the square in front the Schloss eight more soldiers and reservists had caught up with them. When they rounded the pink stone palace, turning right under the circular alley of chestnuts, a squad had been formed. They all seemed to know the reservist, and they took the pace from him. He had become the Führer of the squad. A German feels better with a leader ahead of him. When he started to sing, they all joined in "Wo die Westmark."

Where the Westland slants down to the Rhine,
Where Ludwigshafen lies in ruins,
Where stone no longer stands on stone,
That is my country, and I am at home.

In Ludwigshafen where the ruins lie,
Where so often we hide in the shelter,
Where bombs crash on so many a house,
That is my country, and I am at home.

Where the bombers swoop nightly from the sky,
Where up and down the city burns,
Where the sirens scream and the lights go out,
That is my country, and I am at home.

Where the cowardly Tommy murders woman and child,
Where so many victims are mourned,
Where the weary eyes are heavy with tears,
That is my home, which I love so dear.

And shouted together, with faces raised in the song:

Where misery cries to the	Wo soviele Nöte auf den Himmel
heavens,	schrei'n,
Where good folks' houses are	Wo in Trümmer liegen vieler
flat,	Bürger Heim,
Where so many lose all they	Wo soviele opfern müssen Heim
own,	und Gut,
Ludwigshafen, my home, fights	Ludwigshafen, Heimat, kämpft
with German courage.	mit deutschem Mut.

The bulk of the Schloss still hid the Rhine and what lay beyond it. When they circled the right wing to the bridgehead park they saw the water lapping the opposite bank, and Ludwigshafen sprawled along it, palled in smoke under the sunset.

"Watch," said the reservist, "the bridge is going to be crowded with refugees when they ring the bell. Since the all-wise Doctor Todt let the Autobahn bridge fall in at Frankenthal, there isn't another bridge that way before Mainz, or upstream before Speyer, and they're both thirty kilometers. Well, what is hard luck for German travelers is hard on the Amis too. No one knows how they got so close, but we'll throw them back."

The cupola of the Schloss had been sheared off like the top of an eggshell, but the battle flag of the regime still flapped from the parapet. At orders from the reservist, the squad swung briskly past the balustrade of the Platz, past the sentry-box at the bridgehead, and under the double arch to the bridge itself. An allegoric statue of Germania reclined across the pylons above them. The left arch carried the railroad, and the double tracks were as rusty as the single one at Peiting. They took the right lane. As the sergeant had said, the bridge was mined; Happy saw the hundred-pound beehive charges of plastic on each side of the pylon, and the detonator wires running to the arches at each end. The top of each arch, on either side of the stone goddess, mounted a Vierling, and two gunners were swiveling in the seats, while a noncom tilted his head to look upward into the range finder. Between the guns stood a sixty-centimeter flashlight for night defense.

A yellow cloud belched up from Ludwigshafen, lighter than the skein of smoke which shrouded the rest of the city, and puffing in spurts as if it were stoked every few seconds from below.

"A hit on the Farben," groaned a soldier behind Happy. "That must be the sulphur vats."

When they were halfway to the center, a whistle blew. A white barrier like a railroad gate was being lowered ahead of them, across the farthest arch. Happy twisted his head to look back; another bar was being lowered behind them by the sentry at the Mannheim end. The two cut off the bridge between them.

"Spot-check!" shouted the reservist over the noise of the explosions. "Papers out, everybody!"

They reached into their pockets, the men in uniform for the Soldbuch, the reservists for the piece of cardboard which was all the Wehrmacht had time to issue nowadays, giving their name and age and the words "Is a member of the German Army," followed by a signature and a seal. Everyone was used to showing papers, even the youngest boy recruit. The squad did not break step, did not even look down from the jagged silhouette of the burning city ahead. As they advanced to the barrier, another shell hit the big chemical plant off to their right. The impact was no louder than a word spoken close to the ear, but at its command a concrete-skeletoned factory unroofed itself and cast down the tile filler of its walls. The red squares were shaken loose in blocks and shattered only when they crashed on the concrete floor of the city, with a burst which drowned the rushing of the stream and the crackle of the flames and the voice of the shell itself. In spite of the new freshet of dust and smoke, the setting sun shone clearer now through the concrete ribs of the skeleton. Still the squad kept time. Happy forced his gaze away from the destruction, down to the floor of the bridge.

Through a crack in the planking underfoot he saw the olive-brown water rushing northward, and the icicles clinging like beards to the under side of the trusses. The Rhine is the mirror of its own banks. Past both abutments of the bridge it flowed tranquilly, tinged on the Ludwigshafen side with the pearl of the smoke and the yellow of the flame, and on the Mannheim side with the reflection of the pink and brown buildings fronting the quays. The blue of the late sky blended the two banks. But when he looked through the cracks of the planking he could see the Rhine for what it was—a rushing, turbid, sullen torrent, without reflection, tossing with pans of melting ice and the flotsam of other bombardments far upstream: splintered pilings, shattered branches, and once the hull of a stove-in ferry skiff, twirling and aimless in the flood of whitecaps. A yard below the surface he saw the black belly and ugly horns of an underwater mine, with the cable ready for detonation from the shore like the charges under the planking of the bridge itself. The steel grillage of the side rails was too close-knit for a man to escape by jumping through; and even if he could have jumped he could not have reached the quay on either bank, for both were faced with steep-sloping stone revetments a good two yards above the water. This double wall stretched downstream as far as he could see in the dusk. Along the top of it on each side ran the freight sidings of the twin cities, straddled by a parade of bombed-out cranes, their twisted fingers clawing wildly at the sky. He was in a cage which contracted with each stride that the squad slogged on, toward the waiting Gestapo at the western span.

The reservist called for halt and left face. They brought their rifles smartly down to the deck of the bridge. Just beyond the barrier, in the Ludwigshafen Square, seethed the crowd of refugees, waiting for the wooden gate to rise. Over the slope

273

of the bridge deck the mass of humanity and animals was dammed back far into the converging streets. It was the same collection he had seen so often already: old men, women and children, heavy sacks of clothing, geese held by the feet with their heads in a bag, goats tethered tight to a leash; the splay-sided farm wagons drawn by an old horse or an ox or a tired man, and piled high with every kind of movable possession; and perhaps the mother and her child perched on top of the mound. There was even an ancient streetcar crowded with anxious passengers, who leaned out the windows to see why they were delayed.

The shells were only a minute apart now. At each impact a groan rose from the crowd and the sea of heads turned back-ward in unison to watch the burst, then quickly away again, and the compaction of humanity pressed even more closely against the bar, as white foam is urged against the shore by the ripples of a tide.

Two soldiers with a tripod HMG stood on a platform strad-dling the steel fence between the railroad tracks and the high-way. The perforated cooling jacket of the gun circled over the crowd; the belt of cartridges coiled down from the maga-zine. Between two such threats, the shelling behind and the machine gun ahead, only a German crowd would have main-tained the discipline to stand without stampeding—not like the hysterical Italian crowd Happy had once seen bracketed on the road below Cassino. In spite of the panic in their faces, there was no sound except the whinnying of the horses and the cackle of the fowl.

Out of the camouflaged sentrybox stepped a stormtrooper and a second lieutenant of the SS, with the double lightning bolt on their helmets and collars, and the black armlet of the Leibstandarte of Adolf Hitler.* They carried sidearms; in the lieutenant's hand was a copy of the orange Blacklist.

* The SS ranks are Sturmmann and Obersturmführer. The Leibstandarte was Hitler's original bodyguard regiment.

274

As the column was faced, Happy was the first man in the rear rank, and thus trapped between the machine gun and the rest of his squad. If he could have dropped his Soldbuch into the river between the cracks of the planking without being seen, he would have done so. Then he could have chosen his own name—neither Steinberg nor Maurer—and claimed he had lost his book in combat. They might jail a man for losing his book, but they could not shoot him here at the very front. But the open planking had given way to solid concrete at the final span. There was not a chink in the surface beneath his feet, and the bridge was too wide to throw the book over the rail, even if he had not known the guards would shoot him as he raised his arm for the toss.

The lieutenant took his station at a high slant-topped desk with a rack of rubber stamps fastened to the back shelf. He laid the Blacklist on the surface, beside his left elbow, with the orange cover on top. The check started at the rear of the line instead of at the front; Happy would be the last. Each soldier held out his book. The storm trooper compared the picture in the front with the face of the soldier himself, nodded, and carried the book, with the travel orders inside, over to the lieutenant's desk. As he wheeled he called out the soldier's name and rank. It was just like the check at Ulm.

The lieutenant was methodical; he had pasted a tab at the page where each letter of the alphabet began. He opened the Blacklist at the tab of each soldier's initial and ran his finger down the page. When he had made sure the soldier was not listed he nodded, closed the book, and stamped the travel orders with the "Forwarded" stamp from the rack. Happy knew, and the Wehrmacht knew, that once on the west side of the Rhine many deserters would try to find their way across the combat to the safety of the American cages. Nobody, he thought, except a fanatic like Forster would toss this helpless troop against the barrage that pounded Ludwigshafen and trust them not to desert. But it might be as heroic to desert as to stand—safer to snipe from a strong wall than to carry a white handkerchief on your bayonet into the field of fire. Whether to surrender or resist, a man's legs cannot carry him into the mouth of armor; and that is not from fear. Crossing the no man's land of Ludwigshafen was a risk Forster had ordered for the others and Happy for himself; for tomorrow was his last day. He stared at the city as a horse stares at his burning stable and strains at his halter to return to the flames.

"Alois Gunther, Gefreiter! Herbert Schaus, Pionier! Hans Bachschmidt, Obergefreiter!"

As the stormtrooper returned them, each man stowed his papers, advanced four paces to the rail of the bridge, and about-faced. So the double line reformed.

A flame burst out of a tile roof in Ludwigshafen—not the Farben factory but a house. An instant later Happy heard the whine of the trajectory and the shock of the fall. Neither the lieutenant nor any of the squad turned his head. In a few seconds a boy climbed out on the roof which had been hit, hanging a white sheet on the chimneypot. Still the squad did not shift its eyes. But the lieutenant saw the sheet, and his face went red with anger. Two children were playing between the hoofs of an old gray horse, just beyond the barrier, while their mother whispered to her neighbor.

"They have blue and white stripes on their shoulders, the Amis," he heard her say. "I saw them creeping down our road."

And he smiled, for that was the 3rd Division patch he had seen on Chuck, and he wondered how they had got so close.

When the reservist in front of Happy received his papers he strode briskly, in spite of his wooden leg, across to the railing with the others. Happy was left alone facing them, as he had faced the roomful at Heidelberg. His hand did not falter when it stretched out Steinberg's false Soldbuch. Alone, he stood a little more stiffly, his heels a little closer together. He gave his automatic jerk of courtesy as he held out his papers. In the interval of the few steps while the stormtrooper carried them across to the lieutenant, his gaze swept around his trap. The Rhine and its bridge were German, but the gunners and mines were Hitler's. The twin cities were German, but the red flag over the Schloss, and the ruin of Ludwigshafen, were Hitler's. The soldiers across from him and the refugees at his left were German, but the uniforms of one and the misery of the other were Hitler's. He was German, but the lie on his papers was Hitler's.

The lieutenant had his left hand on the cover of the orange Blacklist. He held the "Forwarded" stamp in the other.

"Karl Steinberg, Medical Corporal!" called the trooper.

The impact of a shell cracked like a whip at the far end of the square. From the height of the sound, Happy could tell it must have struck the tower of the flourmill at the far left corner, where the refugees were still crowding to escape. The lieutenant did not move, but the sweat broke out on his forehead in spite of the cold wind. The studded leather collar of the draft horse pressed forward, bending the wooden bar. The two children whimpered, and their mother gathered them under her skirt. For a second the crowd held its breath, then let it out in unison. There had been no explosion.

"Dud!" shouted the reservist from the rail. The trooper spun to rebuke him for speaking, but the lieutenant smiled and mopped his forehead.

"Medical, did you say? He's needed at the barracks. Direct the others to the command post in Ludwigshafen. I'll take Corporal Steinberg back with me. He will not need his rifle; give it to the squad leader."

Happy slung the rifle over his head into the hands of the trooper.

The lieutenant's finger had been on the S tab when the shell struck, but he did not open the Blacklist. He slammed it into the desk drawer. He shoved Happy's papers into his breast pocket. He glanced at his wristwatch.

"Not quite five," he said quietly to the trooper, "but today you may open the barrier a little early, without checking those who wish to cross to Mannheim." He exchanged the Deutscher Gruss with the trooper and with the squad.

The barrier was double, with striped planks swung from a counterbalanced iron standard at each side of the roadbed. Between the ends of the two tapered bars there was just enough width for the streetcar. The ancient vehicle stood with its single eye unlighted, abreast of and between the bars. Ducking under them, the lieutenant led Happy to the forward platform, where passengers were forbidden to ride. The rest of the car was too crowded to make room, even for an officer.

Happy saw the trooper bend to crank up the standards. The squad right-faced on the narrow sidewalk. The reservist gave the Gleichtritt, and it quickstepped into Ludwigshafen as stiffly as if it were on parade. Happy's rifle went with it, on the reservist's back.

"I'll get you another somehow," the lieutenant promised. "He will need it more than you."

Eleven

At the same moment, the flood of humanity and animals broke forward to the safety of ruined Mannheim. The motorman stood on the pedal of his gong to clear his path. He turned the lever a full circle to sprint ahead of the stumbling laden refugees. It was almost dark, but he dared not light his headlamp. The cyclops lens rushed blindly toward the home bank. When he had outdistanced the mob he slowed down the car. He squinted into the dusk to see the tracks below him. On the platform to his left was a potato-sack stuffed full of his own belongings. The handle of a saucepan stuck through the twine at the neck.

"That's all I have left." He shrugged. "I live in Ludwigshafen, so I guess this is my last trip. At least I don't have to carry my pack on my shoulder."

The SS lieutenant, standing at his right, stiffened at his impudence. Happy was straddling the edge of the platform, with one foot on the running board and his hands on the stanchions. The lieutenant looked straight over his head.

279

"Medical Corps," he murmured. "What unit did your book say?"

"Assigned to 136th Mountain, Herr Obersturmführer. I am to join them at Neustadt tomorrow."

"We made a strategic withdrawal from Neustadt last night," said the lieutenant heavily. "I cannot tell where you might find them tomorrow. Anyway, you will be more useful in the field hospital than hunting for them. I shall check your papers when we reach the hospital and return them later, if you should be able to join the 136th Mountain."

"But Herr Obersturmführer, tomorrow is my last day."

"Don't worry; I shall be responsible. I will notify your commander that you are necessary here for the defense of the city. If *I* can find him. We may even learn that he is a patient of yours in the hospital. There are many badly wounded now. You will not have cause to regret my order, Corporal Steinberg."

At the end of the bridge the streetcar swung to the left; on the bend Happy clung tighter to the stanchions. Then it curved right again along the Schlossgartendamm, between the two halves of the castle park, with the chestnuts and lindens on each side through which he had marched in the opposite direction only an hour ago. In the twilight he could see the peaks of the city blocks ahead. There were no lights in any windows or on the streets, but the setting sun and the fire of Ludwigshafen reflected from the top windows of the block ahead of him. That was B-5, he remembered, with a tall new apartment house facing the Platz. It was the highest building in Mannheim, except the spires. The reflection on the blacked-out glass of the corner windows and the smaller windows between, where the bathrooms must be, built a ladder of red above the tops of the trees in the park. These trees were the last cover a man would find above ground in the whole peninsula of the city, except the churches.

Happy had watched the route of the car tracks on his march out. When the streetcar cleared the park it would swing around to the front of the Schloss, then turn straight down Frederick Street, past the city hall, past the bunkers, and past the shop where he had fallen in with the reservist. It would cross the Frederick Bridge over the Neckar, on which he had entered, and then the lieutenant would order him out and walk him a few blocks to the right into the hospital gates. Happy had seen them on his way in. Then the lieutenant or an idle clerk or a patriotic nurse would find his name in the Blacklist. Beyond that he would not think.

The lieutenant chose a gold-tipped Régie from his cigarette case. He drew a lighter from his breast pocket. He turned his back to Happy, sheltering the flame against the motorman's shoulder to protect it from the draft of the open door where Happy stood, half in and half out.

At the moment when the lighter, ablaze, touched the tip of the cigarette, Happy took both hands from the stanchions and pushed the lieutenant with all his strength against the right arm of the motorman. He turned and sprang from the running board out into the cover of the park, toward a dark clump of spruce banking the north wing of the gutted castle. He ran as a riderless horse would run, not seeing the ground below him, hampered yet goaded by the useless gear on his back. He veered into the deepest and longest shadows. A shot split the bough of a plane tree above his head. He did not even wonder whether it was the lieutenant's Walther or a stray from the Amis across the river.

His arms pumped at his sides. Behind the verge of the clump he knelt on the ground. His legs were too weak for him to crouch. He peered backward below the tufts of needles, between the mother-trunks of the spruce. He heard a spate of voices, over the stifled cry of children—even the children in Germany had learned not to cry too loudly. Then the angry voice of the lieutenant commanding, and the stubborn voice of the motorman demurring, and then the lieutenant's decision, above the frightened silence.

"Well, he can't get away. We can pick him up any time. He is unarmed."

The streetcar, which had ground to a stop, moved on, but for all the urgency of the search the motorman dared not turn on his headlight in the blackout. He twisted his lever and drove on to clear the range of strays from the enemy guns across the river.

Another slug harrowed the sod ten yards from Happy, and he did not know whether the lieutenant was firing from the platform of the moving car or had jumped off it to prowl the garden.

By now the refugees had reached the pylon of the Rhine bridge. In the light of the flashes Happy saw them rushing toward him, panting, grunting, but without words. He heard the rumble of the farm carts on the planking; soon they would be loud on the cobbles. They would swarm into the garden, turning right or left around the castle. Those in the first rows had seen him on the bridge.

He pulled the steel helmet off his head and threw it in the bush. He swung his knapsack from his shoulder and threw it after, with the chicken and cheese inside, snatching out only his field cap and his guidebook, with the map of Ulm between the covers. He stood up and tore off the heavy overcoat which impeded his running, with the brassard still pinned to it. He ripped the caduceus patch from the left sleeve of his tunic, down to the blue threads, and threw it with the rest of his identity under the thick branches of the spruce, as he had hidden the chute and the striptease in the woodpile. The coat, the armband, the helmet, and the knapsack had been Corporal Maurer's for two years. He had fought in them from Cassino to Lorraine, surrendered in them at Sarrebourg, donned them again to drop through the air, and carried them back almost to France again. If he wore them any longer he might even be hanged in them. Corporal Steinberg threw them on the ground.

The fleeing column would skirt the castle to one side or the other, or both. His only safety was between. It would hurry, for the check at the bridge had cost an hour. Curfew struck at seven; it was six already. It would stream down to the Neckar behind the streetcar, and over to the plain, whence it could make its way in the dark to the shelter of the Odenwald cliffs before dawn brought the danger of the Yankee planes. It would pass Corporal Ernst and the upturned pennant.

Unless the lieutenant still stalked Happy in the park, he would soon, under a hooded light at the hospital or the Kommandantur, find the name of Steinberg in the Blacklist. Already he might be alerting the patrols. No disguise would help Steinberg; he was doomed by the Soldbuch in the lieutenant's hand. His only chance was to be anonymous.

As he edged away from the discarded clues to his treason, he became a nameless corporal, with no sign to indicate his branch. He still wore a single witness to his identity; his dog-tag. It bore no name, nothing but his serial number and his blood type. It was the number in Steinberg's Soldbuch, but the number also in Maurer's. Two identities; that was the danger. Through his collar he fingered the metal disc, debating whether to throw it after the rest. He might need that identification if he crossed the Rhine, and the voice whispered, "Thou wilt likewise need it if thou dost not." He left it on the cord, for wearing it could not add to his risk.

As fast as silence allowed, he crept along the west wall of the castle to the center, a hundred yards from where he had dropped his gear, like stolen goods dropped in flight. He reached into his tunic for the contraband revolver—contraband because, being miniature, it was not standard issue. He cocked it and stood at bay at dead center of the Schloss wall. He listened for the tiptoe of the lieutenant's boots. The shellfire had stopped. He heard the crackle of flames across the Rhine, like mice gnawing in the night, and the footsteps of dead leaves across the park. He could not stay long, for the patrols would search the park first of all; but till the mob of refugees had passed he dared not leave it to cross the Ring. Back of the castle to the east the moon was rising on the heels of the sun's afterglow. It streamed through the sashless windows above him and lighted the twisted trusses of the station across the Ring to his left; like the factory, the station had been precision-gutted by the planes.

Falling back into the shadow that was blacker than an absence of light, he waited. The mob of terror poured from the bridge. The massed treading on the planks gave way to each man's clatter and shuffle on the stones as the column divided—the animals first, jerking the wheels of the carts behind them, then the strong, and last the weak or too laden. He saw them spread, like horses on the stretch. Half swung to his left past the station, and half to his right through the park. On the dark island between he waited (but must not wait too long), his pistol cocked, at bay against the ivied stone walls. The double stream of fear ceased at last, echoing behind him down to refuge.

If the Frankenthal Bridge was down, as the sergeant had said, he would have to try the Rhine bridge again, this time without papers and already hunted. He tried to tell himself that the spot-check had been only an accident of chance, for the Gestapo did not have enough men or time to control every traveler on every bridge; that the sentry would have been relieved by now. He was not convinced, yet if he was to take the chance he must take it before the curfew rang. He hesitated, about to step forward from the protection of the shadow.

Then a bugle rang out from one of the towers of the bridge. It sounded the air-raid warning to which he had drilled at cadet school:

He heard the hum of a plane. The white flare of a Very light burst over the river before him. For a second it lighted the ruins of Ludwigshafen and the span of the bridge and the garden where he stood and himself silhouetted against the wall of the Schloss as clear as sunlight. Even before it began to fade the searchlight on the bridge caught the plane in its beam and clung for the kill. The plane was another A-26. The blue and white star of the AAF twinkled below the wing as he had seen it in France. Happy guessed it had flown out to photograph the result of the day's barrage. A year ago the Junkers 88s would have attacked it. Now there was nothing left of the Luftwaffe but the Flak, and not too much of that. The Vierling on the bridge opened with tracers, and then with a double stream of four-ounce shells. When they struck, the flashlight loosed its prey, for the plane spiraled down too fast to follow, as he had often seen them at Cassino, a torch of fire that needed no light, a roar of black smoke plunging down to be quenched in the furnace of the Farben factories across the Rhine. The flare still burned after the plane that launched it had been destroyed.

The chatter of the Vierling stopped abruptly, and the night was quiet again. But the searchlight swung on its mount to clear the sky, then lowered to rake the Mannheim dockside and the Schloss, as a man glowers about the room after an argument. For an instant it held him in the blinding beam as it had held the plane. His only chance was to stand it out without moving, his eyelids clenched against the impact of the glare. He heard the command "Licht aus," and all at once he stood in darkness again, his eyes still tingling. He leaned against the wall to shake the blindness out, but now he had to run, for the sixty-centimeter light had revealed him. It would be suicide to try the bridge again. Yet he had to cross the Rhine tonight. Tomorrow would be his last day, and daylight would be suicide too. He remembered the horned black mines in the river, and the steep stone bank on each side. He tried to fool himself that the sentry must have changed, and that dropping his coat and helmet and armband would disguise him anyway. It was no use; the alert must be out already. He must either swim the river now, risking the floes and the mines and the bank, or fail his mission. If he hid in the city—and where was there to hide?—he failed. He could reach the near bank in a hundred strides, and could easily slide down the smooth stone facing. If he met the horns, it would not be long to bear. Scaling the Ludwigshafen bank was harder; if he slipped then, the whole mission failed and his divisions would not be delivered.

Before he could choose, the booming of a great bell brought his heart to his mouth. It shook the wall of the Schloss at his back: seven slow bass notes. It was the clock, clinging askew in the skeleton cupola above his head, but miraculously striking the curfew. From now until dawn, whatever civilians were left in the blacked-out smoking city—and he had no idea whether it was the full quarter-million or only a handful of the brave or greedy—must stay where they were, in the bedrooms of their houses or underground in crypt or bunker or cave, like the game of Still Pond No More Moving.

The seventh note ebbed out, and the pistol shook in Happy's hand. He lifted his foot, not knowing in which direction it would lead him. He thought of the bridge at Heidelberg, which had been so easy to cross, and of the three-fingered stone hand of the statue on the rail. And then, before his boot met the earth, the breath caught in his throat, for that hand reminded him of the Tiger. Happy remembered the Tiger for the first time since he had seen him slide into the sky from a hole in the floor of the plane; remembered the address he should not have heard—but, having heard, should not have forgotten. Twenty-seven Wharf Street, Fred had told him.

286

Now, Happy sang to himself, with the curfew, the Tiger must be in that bunker. His knees trembled. Paluka's radio would be there too, or at least within reach. The Tiger could get him across the Rhine bridge. If not by the deadline tomorrow, it still made no difference, for Paluka could flash his message faster than he could pass it himself. So whether he crossed the bridge or not, Fred would know that he had found 25th Infantry at Aalen and 9th Flak at Crailsheim; he had completed his mission and was safe.

He would find no civilians to direct him to Wharf Street, for the order to the patrols was strict: shoot them at sight after curfew. He would not dare ask a patrol; he must find Wharf Street himself. Since it had a name instead of a number, it must be outside the Ring, from the sergeant's description of Mannheim. That saved exploring half the city, and the most dangerous half at that. He guessed that Wharf Street was downstream, along the port, rather than up. As he stood, that was to his right.

The moonlight dappled the park around him with moving tracery as the breeze swayed the boughs of the lindens and chestnuts. He tucked the Olympia in its holster. He darted from the shadow of the wall to the nearest tree, paused, and then on to another, just as they used to play Red Indians in the Tiergarten at Berlin. He knew the creaking of the boughs would muffle the scuff of his boots on the withered grass and drifting leaves, and the lieutenant and his patrols would find it hard to spot a man among the swaying of the black shadows.

He could run faster now, without his heavy coat. He circled away from the pile of clothing he had hidden, like a discarded snakeskin, under the spruce bush; the lieutenant might have found them and be lurking to ambush his return, knowing that one did not waste chickens and Münster cheese. Zigzagging from tree to tree so there would be no continuous motion, he reached the avenue where he had jumped from the car. Before crossing it, he peered along the tracks, left and right, from behind a tree trunk. Nobody was in sight. He ran across it, full in the moonlight for a moment, and made shelter again in the Frederick Garden on the other side. He avoided the gravel paths which wound through the garden. He kept clear of the casino and the little lake which reflected it, for one could never tell when a news kiosk or comfort station might be a pillbox or machine-gun nest in disguise. The Camouflage Corps was wise with plywood and netting.

The north side of the Frederick Garden butted against the first section of the Ring, called the Park Ring. Beyond it stood a single row of houses, which fronted on the Ring and backed on the ship canal connecting the Rhine and the Neckar. The canal was once a branch of the Rhine, and the port beyond it only a triangle of marsh, shelving a kilometer downstream to the tip where the rivers converge. In the days of the electors, their subjects climbed down from the fort to fish and trap on the marsh. Now the triangle was solid with sidings and docks and warehouses down to the city gas tanks at the tip. Between the houses Happy saw the destruction: the shattered parade of cranes, straddling the web of torn spurtracks, the bomb craters on the quays, the skeletons of the warehouses, the burned-out cylinders of the tanks. The Ami bombs had nibbled judiciously around the perimeter of the Ring, sparing the old city inside but blasting the industry around the edge, just as a housewife trims a piecrust. This was the precision bombing of which they boasted.

The Ring was round, following the curve of the old fort. The canal was straight. Happy had to walk a hundred yards without shelter before they began to diverge. He tried not to walk too fast. Then he reached the fork where the Ring swung right, and the canal, with its single row of false-front houses, ran straight ahead. The blackout sign on the curb—he could just make it out in the light of the half moon—said the dockside street was Hafenstrasse: Harbor Street. From its name he hoped that somewhere in the spandrel ahead of him he would find Wharf.

On the Ring a flashlight was moving toward him. It was still half a block ahead. It jogged on and off as the patrol checked the doorways—on at the doorways and off between, to save the battery. There were two guards in the patrol; he heard the click of four boots. Just in time, he ducked into Harbor Street. He crept along the right sidewalk, where the houses fronting on the Ring cast their black shadows. As the street moved down to the Neckar the triangle widened. The backs of houses became the fronts of more factories.

A single figure was approaching him, up the street on the same side. Like him, it was hugging the walls. He stopped to listen, for it showed as no more than a stirring of shadow, and he gripped the butt of the Olympia in his pocket. Standing still again, he was cold without his coat.

He breathed more easily when he heard that the figure wore shoes instead of boots. As it drew nearer, he saw that it ran from doorway to doorway, darting into the shadow at each vestibule as he had hidden behind the trees in the park, padding on soft soles from shelter to shelter along the concrete sidewalk. Then he understood; it was more frightened than he. Its terror gave him the confidence to march down upon it, soldierly again, without hurrying even when he crossed the open intersection of Church Street.

It was a woman. She stiffened rigid when she saw him. He stood against the wall of the warehouse, halfway between two doors, looking down at her.

"Excuse me, Herr Officer," she panted, and he saw that she could hardly speak for fear. "I know I should not be in the street, but my baby was cut with glass in the last terror-attack. I have come out of the bunker for only a moment to run home for some iodine. Don't turn me in; look, I have a little money."

She thought Happy was a patrol himself.

289

He had forgotten there was still one piece of equipment which marked him as in the Medical Corps; the leather first-aid kit hung on his belt. He wrenched it off the japanned clips. He thrust it into her hand, pushing back the bribe she offered him.

"There's iodine in here," he said gruffly. "Go back to the bunker. You have no business on the street after curfew."

She looked from his face to the kit, turning the leather container over in her hand.

"Where is Wharf Street, please?" he whispered close to her ear.

She jerked her thumb down the street toward the Neckar, and held up one hand with four fingers outstretched.

"Four blocks?"

She nodded. Without thanks, without even surprise (for war had dulled surprise) she ran on ahead of him and turned out of sight to the right at the first corner, up toward the bunkers in the Ring. Happy ran too, frightened again as soon as she had disappeared.

Wharf Street runs off from Harbor, but farther down, just before Harbor dead-ends against the arches of the Jungbusch Bridge over the Neckar. There was only one bridge across the Rhine, but three across the Neckar. The whole squalid north-west quadrant of the city was called Jungbusch. But the bridge sprang higher up, from the plateau of the Ring, and spanned the docks and sidings of the quarter for which it was named.

The mouth of Wharf Street opened between a flourmill and the workshops of a shipyard. Happy saw the sign: SCHIFF-UND-MASCHINENBAU A. G. The shops were on the right side of Harbor, and the ways on the left, stretching out into the canal. They were empty except for the carcass of an assault boat which had taken a direct hit. The same bomb which flattened the boat had glanced the shipyard's crane, now crazily strad-dling the street, had ripped the front off the workshop, and torn the flank of the mill silo on the near corner, as lightning claws down the side of a tree.

The cylinder of the silo was empty; cobwebs shimmered in the concrete hollow, and he could see that though the blast was fresh, there had been no grain in the elevator for a long time before.

He turned up Wharf Street between the two ruins. It was the shortest and narrowest alley in Mannheim, dead-ending even before it reached the Ring. Someone had half-heartedly filled the worst craters in the paving with small pieces of brick and tile; there were new footprints in the clay of the potholes. The blocks of concrete and ribbons of corrugated roofing which the blast had dislodged had been pushed aside to the sidewalks of Wharf Street, leaving only a footpath. An electric cable, unmoored by the bomb, swung its sputtering tip idly across the narrow passage in the rubble.

The single block rose steeply. It did not seem possible its few flimsy houses could have escaped the destruction of the shipyard and the mill. Fragmentation of the bomb had gouged out of their stucco walls some pieces as big as Happy's hand, pebbling the sooty yellow surface with pocks of clean white, and a crack zigzagged across the wall of the nearest house. All the shutters were closed, but as the whole city was blacked out he still could not tell whether anyone was left inside.

Number 27 was three doors beyond the silo. The number was stamped on a blue enamel plaque beside the entrance archway. The house was four stories high, with three windows on each floor, the center tier staggering the sides. Those center windows, alone of all in the block, were unshuttered. They must light the staircase, he thought; and because they were un-shuttered he feared he would find the house empty.

The door itself hung ajar, under a round transom. He creaked it open, sliding his feet forward cautiously on the gritty surface of a tile vestibule. He swung it back again, but the bomb had jarred it too loose to latch. He turned his hooded flashlight along the walls. The wainscot was painted in imitation of marble—a poor imitation in graining of red and green. Ahead of him four steps rose to the level of the main floor. To the right hung a directory of tenants who lived, or had lived, in the eight apartments, with their names penciled or printed on greasy cardboard in brass slots above the empty mailboxes. He read them one by one, saving first floor rear till the end. They were unassuming surnames: Bühler, Heurich, Schmidt—except for one card pretentiously engraved SA GRUP-PENFÜHRER KOPPEN. How are the Brownshirts fallen, he thought, since the days when they hounded my father out of Trebbin to Berlin, that a group leader should have to live in an alley like Wharf Street.

He remembered the night the SA squad had tramped into the study at Trebbin, though he had been only nine that year. It was before the Purge. He remembered looking through the door with his arm around Klaus, just as his father stood with his arm around their mother, facing the squad of three. When the Führer of the squad spoke his ultimatum—join the party or leave the town—the doctor had bowed to him without answering. The squad wheeled and marched out, leaving the front door open. His mother had cried—he had never seen her cry before—and his father had kissed her. Next week they had moved to Berlin.

First floor rear read simply OPFER, a word which means sacrifice or victim. A curious name for the Tiger, he thought, who would never knowingly make a sacrifice or become a victim. Then he recalled that the apartment belonged not to the Tiger but to his wife's father. The name seemed more fitting for the Tiger's wife. Herr Opfer: Mr. Victim. Fräulein Opfer: Miss Sacrifice. He chuckled. Strange he did not know the Tiger's own name; it was locked up in the field safe like his own. One might almost picture that the Tiger had no name. Like myself, thought Happy; when you have too many names you have none.

He felt his way gingerly up the long flight. The stairway was not wide; his left hand glided along the wooden rail and his

292

right slid up the scaly plaster of the wall. At the landing, as he had guessed, a window looked out on Wharf Street. The moonlight guided him, shining through the uncurtained sash.

At the first floor he tiptoed to the back. The window threw just enough light to make out the corridor between the two halves of the tenement. Still on tiptoe, he worked back to the door on the right. He listened, with one hand against the jamb. From inside he could hear a slow heavy breathing, a labored recurring sigh rather, like an old man awake in the dark. He was glad to hear the sigh; he had feared to hear nothing. It *was* an old man awake in the dark. The Tiger's good Communist father-in-law, Mr. Victim.

Happy knocked four times as Fred had told him, the last rap a little stronger like the dash in the V-for-Victory. Abruptly the sighing ceased, held midway on the breath. A bed creaked. There was silence.

"Schönen Gruss vom Herrn Tiger." Happy breathed the password through the keyhole. Greetings from the Tiger.

After a full minute the sigh was completed.

"Unten im Bunker." Down in the cellar.

Each man breathed more easily on his side of the door, having feared worse.

Happy had seen no cellar door when he entered, but if he got back to the vestibule he could hunt for it. He stole back to the stairway. Moonlight fingered through the dirty casement on the landing, casting his shadow gigantically down the well.

As he crossed the level the window lit with a moment's flash, as when a lamp is turned up inside a house, but oddly reversed, as if he were outdoors and the watching, listening cityful were within.

An instant later the blast almost loosened his grip on the handrail. The wooden casement shook beside him. The lash of sound, striking from the west (like the gunfire, but sharper and nearer), split and ebbed into the separate sounds of rending metal, hissing steam, tumbling water. It seemed that the whole city shuddered and grew still in that moment. He knew, as if he had watched them from the Schloss, that the Wehrmacht had blown the Rhine bridge to cut the passage of the Americans. And his own.

He clattered down the stairs, his hobnails pounding unheard on the treads. Before he reached the foot, he groped the flashlight out of his belt again. He deflected the hooded beam around the floor of the entry. It found the crack of a secret door under the main flight of stairs, with the marbleized wainscot painted across its flat steel face to match the other walls, and even across the escutcheon of the flush lock. Except for this lock, there was no break in the surface. The hinges were sunk in the jambs to be invisible. He snapped out his light. He rapped with his left knuckles against the smooth metal four times softly—maybe too softly, he thought, to be heard through a shelter door. As soon as they behind it could have translated his call he rapped again more loudly, and then he heard the whispering beyond the door only by hearing that it had ceased.

The sheet of metal swung outward toward him, with darkness on both sides. One invisible arm caught his elbow, another drew the door closed, sweeping him forward in its arc, and the two lifted him down the steps. Someone planted him against a wall and lighted a candle. It was Paluka bulking in front of him.

"C'est toi!" he cried. The two French words bubbled out of a flood of chuckles. Paluka's square leathery face opened in a flash of gold. He set the candle on the floor to free his arms.

"It is thou!" he repeated. He clamped his great hands on Happy's elbows and stared him up and down from arm's length. He seized his fists, pumping them in welcome, and kissed both his cheeks like French generals in pictures. Happy blushed; a German would never have done that.

Paluka wore civilian clothes: white rope-soled sandals and heavy black breeches and an open blue shirt belted outside as

294

Russians wear them, and a holiday coat of green with leather cuffs and collar.

"Thou has come back from thy first mission! It is the reward of our profession, next to one's own adventures, to welcome the comrades home. Especially the beginners. We old ones always come back, eh, Monsieur le Tigre?"

In the glitter of the candle Happy had not seen the Tiger. He was sitting in the dark at the end of the shelter at a table, with his cheek cupped in his hand.

"It is thou," the Tiger echoed in German. He took Happy's hand with a smile.

He was wearing civilians too, with a fleece-lined jacket over his shirt. On the long table in front of him was a heavy pair of three-branched silver candlesticks. Paluka lighted one candle in each and upended a block of wood at the mahogany table. Happy sat down across from the Tiger.

With the added light he saw he was in a wine cellar with a cinder floor and a vaulted stone ceiling. Against one wall were a score of two-hundred-liter casks, two layers high, built up on chocks to keep them from rolling. The casks lay a yard from the wall to clear the curve of the vault. Along the opposite side stretched a shelf and a pole, from which hung a dozen uniforms and civilian suits. The sweat of the stone had glazed to ice.

"Offer our guest some dinner, Paluka, of which we have too little; and some wine, of which we have too much."

Paluka dived behind the casks. He returned with a hambone on a silver platter and half a loaf of black bread. He set them on the mahogany. He filled three silver steins, bunched in one of his big hands, from the bunghole of a cask.

"Welcome to the Venice of Germany," toasted the Tiger. His gesture included the two rivers and all the canals in the port. With a silver knife Paluka flipped one slice of ham between two of bread. He offered the sandwich to Happy, who was suddenly hungrier than he had known.

"Have you completed your mission, Junge?" the Tiger asked.

"It will not be completed till I report what I have seen," Happy answered between swallows. "But I have seen what I was sent for. Twenty-fifth Infantry is indeed at Aalen, in the old forestry school. Colonel Forster is executive to form it. But already he has had to send out detachments without training, just men of the Volkssturm. Some crossed the bridge into Mannheim before me this afternoon."

"What armor?"

"Not much. Write it down, please, before I forget. Eight 15s and twelve 7.5s to a regiment. One HMG and three lights to a company. And a class in the Panzerfaust; there will be nine to a company."

The Tiger pulled a sheet of lined paper toward him and copied Happy's report in script as fast as he poured it out, omitting nothing, for he knew the momentous can hide in a trifle.

"Not enough small arms. Ninth Flak is in the castle at Crailsheim, with only a thousand men, many of whom they detach to man Vierling at the roadblocks and bridges. They have little to eat, and many of their guns are dummies, though I did not let on I noticed. I have two friends there, who I hope may escape before the raid. I have maps where I can mark what I have seen." He opened his guidebook and unfolded the plan of Ulm.

"Mine are better," suggested the Tiger.

He unrolled the gridded maps he had carried on the drop. Happy traced his route with a pencil on the six sheets of U.S. 1:1,000,000, boring dots where he had seen the signal train, the spot-check, the 8.8s, the Heidelberg Flak, the two CPs. The Tiger could read coordinates fast.

"Bavaria we do not care about. The war will end before your roadblocks in Ulm are manned. But you have not done badly."

He nodded judicially, imitating the famous picture where Keitel explains a field map to the Führer and Göring. Then he looked up sharply.

296

"Why have you come here? You are not of my team. One more guest is one more mouth—and one more risk."

"Because I am in the Blacklist, Herr Tiger."

The words echoed back to him from the vault of stone. Paluka looked around; he remembered the word "Fahndungsblatt" from Vati's class.

"And you have come to enroll me in it too? It is not healthy to put me in danger. Who even told you I was here?"

"It was one of the Amis," Happy hedged.

"Then it was the tall Fred, who never gave me justice. He should know that the safety of a team is more important than its reports. The Americans have artillery which is more eloquent than words. By what folly did your name get on the list?"

"It was not my fault—only that I met an old man, and the next day my parachute was found. It was near Schongau."

"That far away? You have come a long way from Schongau; there is little to fear. Burn your Soldbuch in this candle—give it to me—and tell them, if they check, that you lost it in combat. Here at the front that happens, and they do not punish a man as they do at the rear where living soldiers are not so needed. Who can ever know your name?"

"The lieutenant who took my Soldbuch at the spot-check on the bridge knows it. He wanted me to tend the wounded at the hospital, but I jumped off the car and have hidden till now."

"That is indeed bad. Without a Soldbuch, one can at least pretend it has been lost in combat. But if the Gestapo have it and send out patrols, then beware. The patrols would rather hide than walk their beat, but even now no one disobeys the Gestapo. The block leader who patrols the Jungbusch is coming tomorrow to join my brigade. I will sell him a suit from the rack in exchange for his uniform and what money he can bring me. But, coward that he is, if he found you here he would not dare to hide you, even though no one remains on Wharf Street

297

since the bomb but Paluka and myself and the old man upstairs, who cannot be moved. We were not frightened by the
bomb, and in this profession the reward is to the brave." He
fondled the chasing on his stein. "Where are your armband
and helmet and coat?"

"I threw them in the castle park, Herr Tiger, for I feared the
lieutenant would identify me."

"I see the snake-patch is gone from your sleeve, and next you
will say you have thrown away your kit."

"I gave it to a woman, for her baby."

"And your dogtag?"

"I have it on my neck. It is not only the dogtag of Steinberg,
but my own since the war began, given in my true name of—"

"Do not tell me," whispered the Tiger. "It is not right that I
should know your name, or you mine. We can bury the tag, or
sink it in our wine. Did you hear, old Paluka?" he broke out in
French. "An airman walks about Mannheim. His name is in
the Blacklist, and his papers are with the Gestapo who make it.
He throws his insignia, and even his overcoat, in the garden for
them to find, and comes to us for help. So that he may have
companions at the shooting stake, I suppose, like the two
thieves at Calvary. You who are a good Christian of Holy Russia understand me. They are brave men, the Russians."

He switched back to German, turning to Happy. "I have seen
them knock out one of our big Ferdinand tanks. They lay down
in the field before Ferdinand, and when he had passed—for he
could not crush so many, and perhaps his eyeslits did not see
them all—the survivor threw his Molotov cocktail at the crew
from the rear. Before the Yankees are in Mannheim, the Russians will take Berlin. You, who live there—do not lie to me, for
I know the accents of Germany—tell your family to flee before
it is too late. For the columns of the fleeing which you see here
will be nothing to those who scuttle from Berlin. What few
spoils my brigade has seized in Mannheim will be nothing

against the spoils of Berlin. If I could be there on that day . . ."

Paluka filled the steins. The Tiger broke into his wry smile. He leaned forward to pat Happy's arm.

"Nay, I am only teasing to frighten you. I cannot help my game. We shall keep you here with us till the Amis come. We are not so badly off, but what good are silver candlesticks if one does not have food? We ate our iron rations yesterday—pfui! Such as it is, we shall share our food and our danger with you, lest you betray us to the man hunt outside. It will not be for long. The Wehrmacht has wasted our old Rhine bridge in vain, for the Amis have already started to throw pontoons across at Frankenthal, where they can use the Autobahn. I saw their smoke screen this morning."

"I know I cannot cross the Rhine bridge, Herr Tiger; I heard it blow myself. That is why I give you my report, so Paluka can send it on his radio. Tomorrow is my last day."

"Radio!" groaned the Tiger. "Do you think that if we had contact I should be hiding like a rat in the cellar? I should have delivered Mannheim already, with the supplies a radio could have brought me. But he broke the crystals with the impact of his fat body when he landed; even the spares. Why he did not break the neck from which they hung I cannot understand. Where are the three black cats who would so soon devour the dog? I could devour either now. Paluka's radio, indeed! But he has been a good headwaiter, hast thou not, Paluka?"

Paluka heard his name and smiled happily, though he did not understand what the Tiger said. He filled the steins again, while the Tiger rocked with bitter mirth.

"In truth, Junge, you cannot radio your message, and you cannot cross the Rhine with it. Shall I tell you what to do?" He leaned his smiling face across the table. "Stay here with your comrades. In such a case, there is no dishonor."

Happy clenched his hands in his lap, so they should not

strike the smile. "If I cannot cross the Rhine I shall swim through it. I have promised to bring the report tomorrow. I will take the only way that is left."

The very quiet of his voice, and the set of his chin, told the Tiger he could not hold him. He shrugged and leaned back, his smile gone. He beckoned to Paluka.

"Do you understand, Paluka? Here is one who will swim the Rhine through the minefield to make his report to the little black-haired captain. You and I shall stay in our nest. But to see that he does not betray us by falling to the hands of his hunters, I shall guide him through the patrols to the bank."

Paluka grinned down at Happy. He clapped him on the back. "Voilà!" he cried. "That is courage for you, and from a German too. But let it be me who swims, for I am twice as strong."

The Tiger shook his head. "You would be as dangerous outside as he, vieux camarade, and besides I need you here. I would keep him to protect us all. But if he must go, let it be at once, before he needs to eat again."

"Enough," Paluka cried, glaring at the Tiger. "Let the boy sleep. He has walked all day, and it is not easy to walk and remember at the same time. Never, even for Captain Pete, could I remember what he has remembered. You and I will plan his baptism while he sleeps."

He lifted Happy to his feet and began to lead him to the far end of the cellar. "This end is my home," he whispered. "Let the Tiger talk on; here you need not listen. I know the Tiger now."

"From here to the take-off," mused the Tiger aloud behind them, "he can wear any uniform except that of the Luftwaffe. It is lucky for him that I have other clothing, for my brigade. There is a good civilian suit which should fit him. Lay him down, Paluka, while I think. When he wakes I shall have decided how he must be dressed and where he must enter the water."

300

Sleepy as he was, Happy heard. He turned on the gritty floor.

"No civilian clothes for me," he called. "I am a soldier of the Reich. I came to it in uniform. When I go out I must wear uniform too. And my own dogtag."

"When you leave its shore tonight, Landser, you will wear no clothes at all. You will be naked as at your birth. But for the walk to the shore, wherever I decide, no matter how near, you must be clothed. Uniforms? In four days I have found enough to suit all sentiments. With time I could make you a general. But not of the Luftwaffe, which you have betrayed. You may choose between the Army, with 'God With Us' on the belt buckle, and the SS, with 'Honor Is Faith.' Does it matter to you? Or to me?"

Paluka guided Happy to his own corner. From the rack of clothing he lifted down an armful of Army uniforms. He laid two on the ground, beyond the last cask.

"Lie down," he commanded softly. "A man must sleep well and long before the contest. Remember one thing: to swim upstream, diagonally across the current. Then one may land opposite his start, with luck. Otherwise he is carried down and may not reach the other bank at all. It should take no more than fifteen minutes, or twenty at the most, even with the strong current of water. For you? Well, it might be a little bit longer."

He smiled, laying the other two overcoats over the lanky boy, who was asleep already.

"I will wake you when it is time," he whispered. He tiptoed back to the Tiger's council table and nodded as the Tiger explained his plan for the operation. Spread out on the table in front of him was the German General Staff map of Mannheim which he had carried on the drop. The Tiger penciled an X through the Rhine bridge to show it had been blown.

"The shortest way is not always the surest," he pronounced. "The stone bank in Ludwigshafen is too steep for a swimmer to climb, especially in low water as we have now, before the

301

thaw. Even if he could climb that bank, it would not be safe for him to try crossing the tracks, for the Farben doors open right on the rails. Farben is the Americans' real target, and we soldiers are only incidents when wealth attacks wealth. He must take off from our side far enough downstream to land where there are no buildings, and above all no stone bank. That means crossing the Neckar by the Jungbusch Bridge and the Old Rhine by the Diffené, and running across the Friesenheim Island to the new channel. Thus when he swims the Rhine he will land below the Farben; but he must watch for mines in the water—they will be active now, with the Rhine bridge blown—and swim close to the surface. There are bushes at the side of the highway where he lands—how many times have I lain among them with the girls! From them he can watch for the Amis. And he must remember how to approach them: head down, hands up, and shout some Ami slang. Otherwise they may shoot."

"At such times," said Paluka, "I have always called 'Oh, my aching back.' I do not know the meaning, but the sentries laugh and do not shoot. Ah, I could weep to think of my broken radio. If I had my little set, I could send his message back for him, and he would stay safe in the bunker with us till they come to liberate us. I am twice his age—"

"Thrice."

"—but I should not like to swim in this weather with nothing on but a dogtag. This is not like that little creek in France; the Rhine is four hundred yards across."

"And six deep. Do I not know the width of the Rhine?"

With his pencil the Tiger marked on the map the route he had decided: up to the Ring, over the Jungbusch Bridge, past the transformer station on the left and the Lutzenberg gasworks on the right, over the Old Rhine to the island by way of the Diffené drawbridge, work north of the sewage pumphouse and across the filter beds to the river. About four kilometers, or two and a half miles, half of it empty terrain, and not much chance of being challenged late at night. And so across the main stream of the Rhine to the wooded shore downstream from burning Ludwigshafen.

He rinsed his mouth with the dregs of his winecup and spat them on the earth floor. Paluka straightened the hangers on the rack.

"All the same," he said simply, "you envy Happy. You envy him because he is not afraid. You are jealous because he is good."

"No," the Tiger laughed, "I envy him because he is afraid and yet controls his fear. I do not envy one like you who knows not what fear is. All the same, you are not the cretin that I thought. And only a Russian or an Ami could think that one envies goodness."

"Monsieur le Tigre, you are the chief of the mission. Now I may spit in turn." He spat out his wine.

"I am glad that you know it." The Tiger smiled. "Each of your words is more brilliant than the last. Now tell me, what shall we give our guest to wear?"

"Since he may not wear his own uniform of the Air Force, I wish that he may wear mine of the Cossack Legion."

The Tiger cocked his head, considering. Paluka's uniform was too big for Happy but, on the other hand, it had a Soldbuch to fit, which might be useful if they were challenged. He, the Tiger, would wear his own sergeant's uniform and carry his own Soldbuch, and hope that because of his shoulder-pip neither of them would be questioned. The uniform was too small for Paluka. And if it seemed a little too big for Happy, why not? They would not expect a Russian's uniform to fit.

Paluka had another idea. "Let him not carry a rifle, of which we have so few; let him be wounded, with a bandage on his head, and the guards will never stop him nor ask for his book. If they do, is he not Russian by my book? Therefore he need not understand. German guards are kinder to the wounded than Soviet guards are. On my last mission I wore a bandage

303

to get away from my cemetery at Kaiserslautern. When the German officer saw it he even wanted to send me in an ambulance to the hospital. I did not like that, so I told him we Russians cannot fight unless we smell our own blood. He understood Russian, and let me go without even asking for my book."

"Still good," the Tiger nodded thoughtfully, "and even better than you know, for there was a camp for the Eastfolk on the island. It was in the Grün and Bilfinger lumberyard by the Diffené. It was half a prison and half a hospital. That gives us an excuse to cross, if we should need one. The only thing is, even if your uniform should fit, the Soldbuch shows your aged ape-face inside the cover, very different from our guest's. Let me see your book. You can still spare it, having also the worker's passport."

He tore the snapshot of Paluka from the cover; he wrote in ink on a scrap of paper: "The bearer, who speaks no German, may travel without photograph." He signed it with an illegible name and "Leutnant" underneath, and stamped it with the eagle seal they had given him at the Golden Well. He smeared one of the five digits in the field post number just enough to be illegible too.

"If the Gestapo should turn to the second page they would read that the bearer is forty-five years old, with a jaw full of gold teeth. But we need not carry caution too far. At night no guard would ever turn the page, especially with a wounded veteran. Besides, the bandage will make him look older. Find him a cane; I shall have him limp when anyone comes in sight. What a joke if the guard should insist on taking him to the hospital for his wounds! Anyway, for the last precaution, let us shave off the so-called mustache of which he is so proud, against the chance that they might know him from the bridge. I shall put on my uniform now. You must help me with the boots. After that, wake our guest and prepare him for his baptism."

The Tiger slipped into the aisle behind the casks. He kept his own cache of clothing in a narrow locked cupboard which he salvaged from the hit on the shipyard four days before. He was proud that his uniform was always on a hanger, properly well-worn but always clean and darned. That was Paluka's job, as well as polishing his boots with the scraps of wax from the candles. These candles were an unexpected windfall from the same bomb; he supposed they were meant to be placed in the assault boat for emergency. There was no electricity in the cellar and no daylight, and flashlight batteries do not last long. He hoped the candles would not give out before the Americans came.

In the bunker there was one rifle, which he kept locked in the cupboard, and one revolver, which he wore strapped around his waist, whether he was in uniform or civilians. Like his money belt, it had not left his body since the jump. The other weapons of the team he had hidden under his father-in-law's bed, where Paluka could not reach them. Even Paluka's own two pistols, the Walther and the Colt, were upstairs. The Tiger had borrowed them the day they arrived for what he had told Paluka was "an operation against a certain sentry," to be carried out only by himself and another German.

"We lost them in the struggle, mon vieux," he explained sadly that night. "Otherwise the operation was successful. We should not begrudge a Walther and a Colt."

So Paluka was unarmed. While the Tiger was out of sight behind the cask, he cautiously cut two slices of ham, slipping them into the pocket of his own overcoat, which Happy was to wear. In the other pocket he dropped two Benzedrine tablets from the team's medical kit. He filled the canteen with wine, and snapped it to the leather belt. He shook out his own Army tunic and trousers, hoping they would not be too big for the boy. Better that he should wear his own boots than mine, he thought, for his feet are much smaller. It was important for boots to fit. From the shelf over the coatrack he lifted down the package of woman's underwear he had brought on the drop. He chuckled. There had been no chance to offer that bribe, since he could not even leave the cellar to see what women there might be. The rayon stepins he wrapped again in the newspaper; they would not make long enough strips for a plausible bandage. He could bring them back to Giovanna to prove he had been faithful. The slip he ripped into a dozen two-inch strips to wrap around Happy's head. He stroked the smooth rayon; he was sad to waste it thus.

He opened his clasp knife and sterilized the blade in the candle flame. Then, sitting on the bench and bracing himself against the table with his left hand, he cut a gash in his right calf without wincing. The blood welled to the incision and dropped to the thirsty floor. He pressed the strips of rayon against the gash, letting them stanch it long enough to soak a wide stain on each. He spread the bandages on the table to dry. The shortest remnant he clapped against his leg to halt the flow. He filled the basin with water from the hand pump in the corner of the cellar. They were lucky to have this pump; it fed from an old well beneath the very floor of the wine cellar. Too bad not to have hot water to shave in, the first time. The Tiger, he knew without asking, would not let him use one of the alcohol cubes to heat the water in the tommy cooker. He set out his own Rotbart safety razor and shaving soap. They were both Wehrmacht issue.

The Tiger came out from behind the vats, fully dressed in his engineer sergeant's uniform. The black kneeboots he carried in his hands. He sat on the bench with his legs stretched forward. Paluka, leaning sideways, pulled up the boots. The Tiger buttoned his topcoat, buckled the leather belt about his waist and over his shoulder, made sure that his pistol was in the holster and the canteen and gas mask clipped to the belt. He drew on his knitted gloves; he adjusted the wool helmet over his ears and set the steel helmet on his head. He looked at his wristwatch. It was quarter before two. He sat down in his chair behind the council table, where the map was still spread out, weighted by the bases of the candlesticks. He stood his rifle against the stone wall behind him.

"Waken the boy," he ordered. "This is his last day."

But Happy was already awake. He lay in the shoddy at the back of the wine-vault, his closed eyes turned upward to the stone arch. He wondered whether the column from 25th Infantry had got across into Ludwigshafen before the bridge was blown. Perhaps even now some of them were swimming back across the Rhine, through the jostling ice pans. He might even meet the one-legged reservist in the water. He wondered how a man could swim with a wooden leg. He fell asleep again, dreaming that by mastering the Rhine tonight—funny that it was Germany's frontier after so many years—he could somehow erase the destruction of Gérardmer and of Ludwigshafen, of Mannheim, and even of Cassino; could float the crashed American plane in the air again; and set the saboteur of Aalen on his feet behind his plow, and Corporal Ernst behind his counter.

He jumped up as soon as Paluka came to arouse him.

"I will trust the Tiger," Happy whispered, "and I shall not need my pistol on the other side. It is for you."

He took off his blue Luftwaffe tunic, behind the cask, out of sight of the Tiger, and stripped down to his blue shorts. He lifted the strap of the shoulder holster over his head into Paluka's hands. Paluka slid the weapon out of sight under the first cask. The Tiger had not seen it. They winked at each other.

"Your own father will not know you as a Cossack." Paluka laughed aloud. "Let me look once more before the transformation. And don't be afraid of the Gestapo; they will not recognize you either. Now, first, the uniform of your comrade."

Happy slid into the baggy feldgrau trousers and tucked the cuffs into his boots. He slipped on the shirt and tunic, with the eagle shoulder patch which was the symbol of the Cossack

Legion, and the black armlet with Russian letters which he could not read. The uniform was roomy, but not suspiciously outsize. He buckled the belt two holes tighter than Paluka had worn it. The steel helmet was much too big but would fit all the more comfortably over the padding of the bandage.

"Then your mustache." Happy walked over and sat at the table, opposite the Tiger. Paluka leaned his Wehrmacht pocket mirror against the candlestick. Happy's breath clouded the cold glass.

"Your mustache is not that of Stalin, or even of our Führer." The Tiger smiled. "It is more like that of my late mother-in-law. While inconsiderable, it might be remembered for the very reason that it ought not to exist."

Happy flushed. He picked up the razor and dipped it in the basin. It was true that the mustache shaved off too easily to be a serious one.

"Stand up for inspection, Private Rosoff. But remember to speak no German. I was right; the uniform is too big. But it is true that all sorts of scarecrows are loose in the Fatherland these days, and you are no worse than the next. Perhaps it is worth the risk in order to have a matching Soldbuch. But tuck your shirt in at the waist and pin the sleeves shorter under the arms. We will take your own uniform in trade for Paluka's. It will hang on the rack until you lead the Amis into Mannheim; we shall not give it to our brigade. The conqueror should not return to his homeland in the coveralls of the enemy."

"And now the wound of combat," said Paluka. He clumsily tried to wind the blood-soaked strips about Happy's head.

"Give it to me," Happy interrupted in his halting French. "I can turn a better bandage than that."

He wound the strips about his head in such a way that the bloodstains were all on one side, while Paluka held the mirror in front of him. He bound the cloth as deftly as a Hindu winds his turban, and on top of it he planted Paluka's steel helmet.

He bent to look in the mirror. Just enough of the bloody cloth showed beneath the brim.

"On approaching the Americans," Paluka reminded him, "keep your head low and your arms in the air as prisoners do. Do not wait for them to see you, for they might shoot even a naked man. They are as frightened as the Germans, being at the very front. When I came out at Kaiserslautern I shouted 'Oh, my aching back,' as Captain Pete had said, though I did not understand the words and still do not."

"They are like 'Ach, mein armer Kopf,'" Happy translated. "They are a proverb among them."

"It is true," put in the Tiger in German, "that the American is as light-fingered with his rifle when he is sober as the Russian when he is drunk."

"Do not be frightened when they close in with their rifles or Colts," Paluka added, "and be sure to shout 'Soda G-2' when you wade out, even if you do not see them. Voilà; I have shown my two American speeches, though I still do not understand them. And here is a stout cane for the wounded hero, who must not forget to limp even when he does not think he is watched, for this night is full of eyes."

He hung Happy's Luftwaffe uniform on the hanger where his own had hung. He filled the three steins from the cask.

"Do not forget either," commanded the Tiger in German, "that I do not know you and you do not know me. I am helping a wounded ally of the Reich to reach the first aid. But if we have the bad luck to be challenged, and the guard suspects you, I too shall suspect you. And if you run, or worse, if you tell him of me," he patted the holster at his belt, "remember that I am a sergeant and you a Russian conscript. I have shot men before."

He finished his Rhine wine; they all stood up together. The Tiger slung the carbine across his back.

"Well, Junge, tell the little captain that his friend Paluka broke the crystals, but I do not think we need replace them at this late day. We shall meet him with the city corrupted by my brigade. It will not resist—but ask him, if the artillery must fire on Mannheim, to spare 27 Wharf Street. Now let us go."

Paluka blew out the candle. He tiptoed ahead up the nine steps to the steel door. Happy, and the Tiger behind him, leaned against the stone wall till Paluka gave the signal. Softly he drew the slidebolt to the right. The chink widened; he peered into the vestibule. It was empty; he reached back and plucked the Tiger's sleeve. The Tiger plucked Happy's. The two slipped through the doorway into the silent house. As Happy passed through, with the cane in his left hand, Paluka patted his back.

"It will not be long," he whispered as he eased the door shut again and slid back the heavy bolt.

Outside the Tiger took from inside his mitten a key to the flush cylinder lock. He turned it in the barrel, locking Paluka in the bunker.

It was warmer on Wharf Street than in the empty house. Through the half-open door the moonlight shone on the tile floor, and the crisp air of the night eddied into the entry and curled up the stairway like the draft in a chimney. They heard the occasional spit of a rifle off to the west, but the artillery had ceased. Mannheim waited behind her moat of the Rhine, and the enemy on the other side was sated.

"Your arm about my shoulder, thus," whispered the Tiger. He lifted Happy's right wrist across his own shoulder.

"Do not forget to limp. Limp and be silent, that is all you need do."

They walked out into the deserted street and turned to the right up the hill.

"I lock the big bear in the bunker for fear he will talk if I let him outside. The Volksgenossen fear their Russian guests, as I confess I feared you. Tonight it would be more dangerous for you to speak than for him, for you are worse than a real Russian; you are a false one. Even though I have altered you to the eye, I cannot change a good German voice to Russian."

To reach the Jungbusch Bridge over the Neckar the Tiger did not have to expose them to the open space of the Ring. At the end of Wharf Street he guided Happy leftward along Beil to Fraher, which was the ramp of the bridge itself. Happy remembered to limp, though nobody was in sight.

The approach to the bridge began to rise, mounting between the back of the shipyard on the left and an ice factory on the right, with its evaporating pans still intact. The ramp of the Jungbusch Bridge overleaped the freight sidings and revetted quays on each side of the Neckar. On the far side it sloped down again to the suburb of Neckarstadt. It was narrower than the Frederick Bridge by which Happy had entered with the engineer, and still narrower than the Rhine bridge by which he had hoped to escape. These two were monuments; over them the traffic from beyond the two rivers converged into and through the city. But the Jungbusch marked no axis; there was no grandeur to its approach. It had been built long after the others, as the growing dockyards overflowed the peninsula and spread to the east shore of the Neckar. It was a freight bridge. Downstream to the left were the docks and basins of the port, and ahead the overflow of Neckarstadt, and beyond Neckarstadt the Friesenheim Island.

Friesenheim was a man-made island. Once it had been a promontory of the Rhine's west bank, washed by a half-circle coil of the river. Then the dredging of the Rhine ship channel cut it adrift, and now it belongs more to the east, for the Diffené draw joins it to Neckarstadt, spanning the coil of the Old Rhine. The Old Rhine is what they call the original riverbed, winding each side of the new channel as the snakes on Happy's caduceus patch coiled around the staff.

The island which he had to cross spread below them, a two-kilometer disc of sand. It grew one clump of trees, off on the far quadrant. The only two large buildings on it, the electric station and the margarine factory, were bombed hollow. It was checkered by filter beds and irrigation ditches. It was the cesspool of Mannheim.

"Sewage and strawberries," the Tiger said out of the side of his mouth. But Happy did not dare turn his head, lest someone might see that he understood the German words.

"The island is empty," the Tiger went on. "I will take you over the Diffené and guide you to the far side, right to the bank of Father Rhine himself. We shall skirt the sewage station. That is one reason why Mannheim is deserted too, that the Yankees have blown the lid off the settling basin. Follow any of the paths, or walk across the fields, and in twenty minutes you are at the river. Once beyond the shadow of the pumphouse there will be no danger. Even if there should be outposts on the island, who would shoot a wounded soldier?"

Happy squeezed the Tiger's arm. "Cheer up, Landser, and don't mind that you live in Mannheim," he mumbled with a smile. "After the war the Amis will rebuild what they have destroyed, with our German help. Everything will be good after the war, dost thou not think so? What we do now is shameful, but for the good of Germany and the Amis too. One does it for both."

It was the first time he had called the Tiger "thou."

"I do it for neither."

"After the war we shall be brothers again."

"Would you be my brother after the war?" the Tiger asked him curiously.

"Yes; thou hast shared my danger."

"After the war it will be better, I agree; but not as you think. Perhaps the Amis will make me Bürgermeister. I shall have fifteen thousand marks a year and a car of my own. Let us walk faster, now that we have passed the river. No need to limp so slowly. Take your hand from my shoulder, for we shall meet no sentries now, unless it be at the bridge to the island."

312

They swung down into Hirten Street, which ran parallel to the basin of the Old Rhine, but a little in from the edge of the docks, behind the big boiler factory. Happy had trouble keeping up with the Tiger, for his legs ached and his long coat dragged. He had walked twenty miles since Heidelberg. When they came abreast of the ruined gasworks and neared the Diffené the Tiger stopped short. His left hand gripped Happy's arm, for a sentry had suddenly walked out of the dark underpass that led to the draw. With bayonet set, he barred their way.

He was not SS, like the sentries on the Rhine bridge, but a reservist, in a long civilian overcoat and a steel helmet too big for him, and the familiar white Volkssturm brassard on his sleeve.

"Achtung!" he shouted.

"Shut up and duck," whispered the Tiger.

Happy lowered the brim of his Stahlhelm again to throw shadow across his face.

"Soldbuch!" the sentry demanded.

The Tiger disengaged his left arm from Happy, but as he did so he pressed Happy's hand against the holster at his waist, to warn him.

"The Cossack was wounded in Ludwigshafen this evening, sentry. He was crossing the Rhine bridge just before we blew it. A woman tore off her slip to wrap his head. He doesn't seem to understand a word of German. These Russians! They are evil as enemies and useless as friends. I found him at the bridge. Since I am going on to the battery at Sandhofen myself, I have volunteered to leave him at the work camp on the island. You will want to see my Soldbuch, naturally."

He spoke with authority, just like a sergeant. He made himself sound more watchful than the watchman. He reached through his overcoat into his tunic and pulled out his little brown book, holding it open to the sentry for inspection.

313

The reservist studied the picture, then looked up. He nodded and returned the book. "Very good, Herr Sergeant," he said respectfully.

He stood his rifle against the granite wall of the underpass, as no trained sentry would have done, and pulled from his pocket the orange-bound Blacklist.

"Kett, Kett," he muttered, thumbing to the page of K.

He was more like a ticket-taker than a sentry, Happy thought below the helmet. At the beginning of the war a sentry who let go his rifle would have got three days KP. At the beginning of the war, in fact, there would have been two sentries instead of one.

"We have to look up the names," he apologized, wetting his thumb as he turned the leaves. "There is an alert for a Luftwaffe medical corporal, or rather a spy in that uniform. You haven't seen such a uniform since the Rhine bridge, by chance, Herr Sergeant?"

"No; I heard about him over there and have been on the lookout, but I have passed no one till meeting you. I suppose they issue Russians Soldbücher too; do you want to look at my patient's?"

"Yes. If I'm not thorough I won't be following orders. This is an important junction. You see, we have opened the draw from the island so that if parachutists or boats land there they cannot get across the basin to the mainland. Opening the draw is just as good as blowing it. Anyway, even the Russians were shipped out today because of the danger, so the camp is empty. I do not know where they were carted."

"The draw is open?" The Tiger caught his breath. "That is a good precaution. Then I shall walk him to the big bunker at Waldhof, where they will take him off my hands. But what if some of our own should have to get out of Ludwigshafen over the island? It must be almost as bad to swim the Rhine and pick your way across the island, and then have to swim the

314

basin too, as to be captured by the Amis. On a night like this I should not like to cross the island in wet clothes."

The sentry looked at him mournfully, his finger in the Black-list. "There were two squads who came from Ludwigshafen just an hour ago; one Flak and one machine-gun. But they had not swum the Rhine; they had a boat which they have left on the far side of the island. Perhaps they cannot swim. Now they are marooned on the island. They shouted across for me to close the draw, but I do not know how. So I told them to bunk down in the pumphouse till my relief comes on in the morning. Surely the Americans would not bomb the plant again. The settling basin is already kaput. They cannot swim the Old Rhine anyway here, you see, because of the concrete banks. If they want to swim it they must go downstream below the draw. They're over there now, resting up in the pumphouse. It doesn't smell very nice does it?" He laughed. "Yes, I'd better see the Cossack's Soldbuch. I wish I could get the poor fellow a ride, but there's no traffic at this hour, it seems."

He stretched out his hand to Happy, saying, "Buch, buch," as if a Russian could be expected to understand German.

The Tiger whipped his Walther out of the holster and struck the man a blow on the chest with the butt, as hard as he could hit. The sentry crumpled from the knees, falling to the un-tended grass at the side of the granite abutment as if he knelt to pray, then tipping heavily to his right side. The rim of his steel helmet rang on the flinty earth, but Happy knew the leather sweatband would protect him from concussion. The Tiger looked down at him, then at Happy.

"Again?"

Happy caught the Tiger's wrist. "No."

The Tiger picked up the orange book from the sentry's side and whipped it into his own pocket.

"You take his head and I'll take his feet."

The sentry weighed surprisingly little for his height. They

315

swung him around the corner of the underpass, out of the moonlight. The Tiger seized Happy's hand.

"Now you've got to run, Junge. Throw down your cane."

A few steps beyond where they left the sentry, the road curved to pass under the Frankfurt railroad tracks. A freight spur ran left at grade level through the underpass leading to the Diffené. They could see the iron truss of the Diffené draw, pivoted on the stone pier in the center of the basin, and swung open parallel to the estuary. The spur track ran to the open edge.

"Now you must swim two rivers, Junge," the Tiger whispered between his teeth. "Stick close to me and keep out of the moonlight. Throw your cane away, idiot. It's only a hundred yards."

The sprint was a short one. The highway curved to the right, past the wire fence which surrounded the docks. But Happy could not keep up with the Tiger's long strides, and the Tiger did not wait for him. Just beyond the fence, where the dock enclosure ends, there is a clear space between the last houses of Neckarstadt and the first of Waldhof. The road is clear on both sides—no factories or houses on the right, and the currentless stretch of the Old Rhine only fifty yards to the left, over a shoulder of matted grass sloping down to the water, beyond the last slip.

The Tiger hared around the corner of the wire fence with Happy after him, sprinted across the open grass to the edge of the water, and dragged him down under the overhanging sedge where the dredging of the basin had cut the bank away. He laid his hand on Happy's arm.

They listened, but it takes time to be able to listen after a hard run. Happy's tongue lay forward on his lower lip. He stretched it upward, tasting salt sweat where his mustache had been shaved off. He breathed through his mouth, fast and short, to cleanse his hearing for other sounds, or for the silence he hoped for. The night was more silent than sleep. It was as if the whole city, like themselves, strained its eyes and ears across the water. The idle backwater at their feet did not even lap the sand. Across from them lay the island, with the open swing-bridge half blotting out its roofless factories and its single clump of trees.

"Clothes off," the Tiger whispered. "Remember I must risk getting back around the sentry whom you would not let me kill. By now they may have found him."

He did not replace the revolver in his holster, but laid it on a flat stone. Happy pulled off his steel helmet and ripped the blood-spotted bandage from his head. He unclasped the buckle on the belt of his overcoat.

"The meat in the pocket is for you, Herr Tiger; you need it more than I."

The Tiger helped him pull off the boots. His trousers fell to the ground. Before taking off his shirt, he pressed it on his sweating body to cool off.

"Did I hit the old man hard enough?" the Tiger asked. "I must get back over the bridge before he wakes, for he will remember my name and put it in the Blacklist tomorrow. I am too soft-hearted."

"You hit him hard enough. He may remember nothing. Could I not have shown him the book? He was friendly to us."

"Friendly!" repeated the Tiger, spitting on the sand. "You have no friends; in our game there is no friendship. You play it as hard as I—do not excuse yourself—but not as well. What poison in you held my finger from the trigger now, that I did not shoot him? I shall do it on my way back. Before you reach the island your friend will be silent for good, and never can he add my name to the orange book."

He clapped the Blacklist in his pocket. "Yet this list will be the German Hall of Fame when the Americans come. They will give medals, and even money. Perhaps I shall spare your friend after all, so he will add my own name to it. It will not be long before they come. Down where the stream is narrow they are lashing their square-end pontoons and laying the wooden tracks between the ends of the Autobahn where the all-wise Doctor Todt let his own bridge fall in. Your friends? They will forget you as soon as they have heard your news, because you are not one of them. Listen, Junge, you will not dare tell what you have done, even to your father, even in years to come to your wife. I myself am not your friend, though I risk my life to send you to your friends.

"Your friend! I could shoot you in the water if it would save myself, as I may shoot the sentry who endangers me. Lean on my shoulder if you wish, to enter, for the bank is steep. Tell the Americans that the Tiger delivers Mannheim to them. Each of my eight recruits will find eight more of his own, like the cells I spoke of in the prison camp. The cells ripen and spread, and the city falls. Do not shiver. The climate of Mannheim is the mildest in the Reich, under the lee of her two mountain walls. It is the Rhine itself which will be cold, for the sun does not have time to melt the ice from Switzerland as fast as the current swirls it down. Are you not afraid?"

"I am not afraid," Happy answered into his face.

"Then let us meet in Berlin at the dawn of your new Germany."

While he spoke he had scooped out a hollow in the sloping sand with the long nails of his good hand; and as Happy took off his clothes he laid them in the burrow and sprinkled sand to cover them.

"Did you do thus with your parachute? Just a little more carefully, eh, and your name would not be in the Blacklist. And now what have you left? A dogtag for identity. That money belt for riches you will not need among the Americans, who are so rich themselves. Besides, it will impede your swimming. Paluka—yes, perhaps Paluka is your friend—may find us a goose to buy with your useless marks, if I unlock the bunker door for him."

"There are eight hundred and forty-two left, Herr Tiger, from the thousand. Give Paluka enough for a goose to feed the

318

mission till the Amis come. Send the rest for me to Maria Liebert at the Sign of the Ox in Dietmannsried, near Kempten. Inside the envelope just write 'from Karl' in capitals. Do not say Karl Steinberg, for she will understand. You are right; I shall not need the money any more."

"Paluka and his pantalettes! You and your hopechest! His grunts and your sighs! What sort of agents are you? Shall I, who have loved as neither of you could, be pimp for both? But I shall do as you wish, if the Reichspost still empties its mailboxes and I can tip the flap unnoticed. Give me the money quickly."

Happy started to loosen the buckle of his money belt, but his bare arms were covered with gooseflesh and his hands shivered. The Tiger reached up impatiently; he ripped the belt from Happy's waist and stuffed it into his own side pocket. Happy's courage, which was the last injustice, he had not destroyed.

"Quick, into the water now!" Still crouching back of Happy, he threw his arms forward as one launches a skiff.

"I shall wait till you reach the other side."

Naked except for his dogtag, Happy slid down the short bank sideways, like a crab. He dipped his foot in the water. He smiled wryly at the Tiger, shivering, with his arms clasped across his chest. The dogtag glinted as he shook his head.

"Make for the clump of trees," the Tiger whispered into his cupped hands. "There is no current here. Auf Wiederseh'n, Kamerad!"

As he flattened out in the water Happy raised two fingers over his head in a V. His body blended into the dappled water.

The Tiger smiled; every German knew that in English V means Victory, even if he spoke no English.

As Happy waded ashore to the flat bank of the island a private of Task Force Zeisler, left on watch in the water tower of the damaged brick pumphouse while the others slept below, caught, through the shellhole where his carbine rested, a movement of white against the dark clump of trees. It had been another bad day for him—being forced to cross the Rhine with his magazine still full and having to spend the sleepless night in a sewer because an idiot sentry could not close the draw. He was tired and irritable. He did not wait to see what moved; perhaps a sheet of paper blown in the gust. The last thing he expected was a naked swimmer heading west to the hell the squad had left. He pumped the trigger blindly.

At the shots from the island the Tiger wheeled. When he saw the smoke from the shellhole and heard the alarm echo in the hollow pumphouse, when he saw the white figure fall, he dropped his rifle to the ground and fled as fast as he had come.

Twelve

Back at the shelter, Paluka lingered at the head of the steps. Happy might trust the Tiger, but he knew better. A purpose stirred inside him. Though he had failed Pete, he would make sure that Happy did not fail Fred.

The bolt was still drawn back. He pressed his weight against the door, but he knew it was no use. The Tiger had locked him in again. He relit the candle with his lighter, holding the flame close to the door. He studied the sheet of steel. It matched the outside, which he had studied the first day, but it was unpainted and scabby with rust. The core must be wood, for when the door opened behind the Tiger it swung more lightly than the solid metal of the cell in the Sarrebourg cage. It could be locked only from the outside, for the barrel did not run through the core. It could be bolted only from the inside. If the Tiger could keep him in, he could keep the Tiger out, but that was small comfort. The sound of the turning key was still fresh in his ears. He knew exactly the height of the cylinder. He penciled a cross on the inside to mark the point.

No matter how often the Tiger locked him in, the clicking

of the key outraged him anew. He had spent the whole five days in this dark cellar. He had unbolted the door for the Tiger and his recruits, and tonight for Happy, but not once had he gone through it himself. Not so bad if he could have used his radio; he would have been content then, as he had been in the cemetery guardhouse, to send and receive twice a day, and sleep between times. But to sit in the dark with his broken crystals and useless code pads, that was not justice.

Twice a day the Tiger went out that door and upstairs to the old man's room on the second floor, taking the meals which Paluka had cooked over the spirit-stove. Two trips, always in the dark—one just before sunrise, and again just after curfew. Only a few minutes before Happy knocked on their door the Tiger had returned from upstairs, bringing down the plate from the morning for Paluka to wash at the pump. Paluka wondered who had taken care of the old man before the bomb.

On the night sorties the Tiger merely said he had "business"; and each time he came back with a suit of second-hand civilian clothes or some silverware like the candlesticks; but only once with food.

The deserters whom he suborned, two each day since the bomb had dropped, arrived in the uniform of the Army, or even of the SS, when the sun had set or before it rose. After long whispering in the language Paluka did not understand, and poring over maps, they gave the Tiger some money and changed the uniform for one of the civilian suits from the rack. It was part of Paluka's job to fit the suits and make any adjustments with his sewing kit, and to beat the dust out of them with a Wehrmacht issue clothes-beater, so they would look tempting to the buyers. This beater, the Klopfpeitsche, was half a dozen thongs bound in a wooden handle. The Tiger would laugh when Paluka belabored the clothes. "Thou hast the air of a Cossack beating peasants."

Paluka laughed himself; the beater did look like a cat-o'-nine-

322

tails. Then, after it grew dark, but before the curfew, the Tiger would escort the recruits up the steps, unbolt the door, and watch them disappear into the night.

It was no fun to stay all day in the bunker, but there was plenty to do keeping it neat. Paluka could never recruit a deserter, since he spoke no German. He admitted that without his radio he was useless to the mission, and his imprisonment was perhaps a just punishment for breaking his crystals. But it was a needless disgrace to lock in an agent who ever since Algiers had transmitted messages which he knew were valued by the Americans.

There seemed no end of waiting in the bunker, yet he had waited only five days. It was not as if there were a deadline for their return, as there was for Happy's. They must stay in Mannheim till the Americans overran them. Paluka could only guess the course of the battle from the number of recruits who came in to buy civilian clothes, and by the volume of the gunfire he heard when he listened at the ventilator. "They'll cross any day now," the Tiger boasted negligently. He seemed to be in no hurry for the end. But tonight Paluka knew there was no need to boast, for the blowing of the Rhine bridge meant the Germans had given up the west bank. As the end drew near, he grew impatient. Between Giovanna and himself there was nothing left now but a steel door and a few city blocks and a river: the river, perhaps his last adventure of the war.

Late as it was, he would not sleep before the Tiger returned. He carried his candle to the back of the bunker. He lifted Happy's shoulder holster from its hiding place under a cask. He took off his jacket and shirt, fitted the holster over his left shoulder and under the arm by lengthening the strap two holes. The Olympia was beautifully designed to lie flat. The Tiger would never know he had it, and the space between the buttons of his shirt was just wide enough to reach his hand in for a quick draw. He slid the Olympia from its holster and turned it over on his hand. It was no bigger than his palm—a beautiful toy. He chuckled as he pressed out the magazine, slipped the catch to Feuer, and pulled the trigger once for each of the seven cartridges. He wound a last snip of the rayon underwear round a sliver of wood to clear out the barrel. When he sighted through he saw it was clean and still well oiled. He carried it back and up the steps to the steel door. He held it against the cross he had marked; he had heard the key click too often not to be sure of the exact position of the lock on the outside.

Whistling to himself, he walked past the clothes rack to his own end. It was time for his three o'clock QRX, when the direction finders outside were least watchful. Tonight was one more chance. He opened the fiber case behind the cask. He plugged the battery, laced the ground wire to the fins of the ventilator, extended the antenna. He set the dial to nine megacycles, to match the crystal on the transmitter box. He could do all this in the dark, squatting on his hams. Then the dial lit. The square of quartz, no bigger than a stamp, stood on two pins like little legs, and the crack was like a wink across its face. He stood up to close the louvres. Between the fins, from far off to his right, he heard faintly the clatter of an MP-38. He had heard it often enough to be sure. He frowned and flipped the ventilator shut. He cupped the earphones of the TR-1 to his head.

The first four days there had been contact of a sort, a kind of squeak which must have been his own call. He could read Morse as fast as Benny could send it, but there were no da-dits to that jerky squeak. He had tried each of the six crystals in turn, hoping that one band length might get through, and had tapped the QRX to all of them. Neither side dare hold the air more than ten minutes. The squeak had ended abruptly each time.

Tonight there was no sound at all. Benny had given up, and he gave up too.

He had already encoded a message on a sheet of the one-time pad. Now he pretended to send it, though he knew the tapping of the key would reach no farther than the staves in the cask beside him. NR 23 VCFGK IXRYY, it began.

If Benny had received it to decode and translate, it would have read:

KARL'S MISSION SUCCESS RPT SUCCESS HE RETURNS TIGER WAITS PALUKA GREETS YOU.

The game only made him feel worse. He jumped up from the bench. With the shovel he used for digging the daily latrine he scooped out a hole in the gravel, between two casks. The Tiger had found this shovel in the wreck of the flourmill. He smashed his radio with the flat of the shovel and stamped the fragments of metal and fiber and glass into the depression, with the crystals and code pad on top, smoothing the gravel over their grave. He drew a steinful of wine from the cask.

The pad where the Tiger had written Happy's report lay on the table. Paluka looked at it with the respect of incomprehension. He could not understand the German words, and the angular letters all looked alike, for the Tiger wrote in script. But he saw the two numbers nine and twenty-five, which he knew were the numbers of Happy's divisions, and many series of six figures which he guessed must be coordinates. These words which he did not understand were important, and they belonged not to the Tiger but to Happy.

His money belt was lined with oilskin. He ripped out the lining at the seams, folded the sheet, and laid it inside the oilskin. Heating the blade of his knife at the candle, he sealed down the edges of the packet to make it waterproof, leaving a selvage through which he bored a hole with the point of the knife. He strung the packet on the neck-cord with his dogtag.

"And I," he said aloud in Russian, "I, the veteran, like a mushroom in my cellar! To break my crystals! It is as if I did it on purpose. It is as if I had mutilated myself, as the Tiger shot off his own fingers. And though thy old comrade has not the wings of a carrier pigeon, he has arms and legs to swim. Between us, young one, we will bring the message through on time."

Breathing faster with the new excitement, he traced his heavy finger over the path which the Tiger had penciled on the city map: over the two bridges and across the island, and swim the Rhine down where the sloping stone walls of the quayside had ended and a man could wade out of the water instead of dragging against the steep embankment. To make sure he remembered the route, he closed his eyes and repeated the street names aloud: Wharf, Beil, Fraher, Hirten. He could read the Western alphabet, even if he could not pronounce the words. Four hundred yards would not be hard for an athlete in good trim. Adventure was beginning again; he whistled to himself.

He poured himself a cup of the tart wine, to keep himself at the right point of tension that he knew so well.

"Now to my exercise," he grunted, "to limber up for the morning."

He went through his nightly gymnastics, the candle magnifying his shadow on the stone. Twenty times with fingertips to toes; twenty times kicking out his legs from the crouch with arms folded, as in the Czardas dance.

"I am not yet too old," he panted.

But the gravel hurt his bare feet, calloused as they were, and the tension on his calf broke open the gash he had cut in it for Happy. He wrapped himself a new bandage, having tipped the cut with iodine from the first-aid kit. With the candle in his hand he walked back to the far end of the cellar—his end. He blew out the light and reopened the ventilator. The crisp night air filled his lungs; after the staleness inside it was better than the wine. He listened, but no sound came through the fins.

He lay down between the blankets of uniform where Happy had rested, but he would not sleep till the Tiger knocked. He should be here soon, he thought. His bare feet ached from the dancing. His ankle-boots, which alone of his uniform Happy had not worn, stood beside him for the day. He lay on the ground fully clad, still in civilians—he had never undressed since the first day's bomb—his mind swept clear of thought, his body resting but alert as he had trained it. Something Oriental in Paluka inured him to time as a yogi can inure himself to pain. He had no idea how long he waited for the knock. But at the instant of the four raps which were their signal he was on his feet and up the steps, sliding the bolt. The Tiger had not complained about the bolt, for Paluka slid it as fast as he could fit the key outside. The Tiger and he knew each step of their bunker so well that there was no need to light the candle till the door had closed again and the fins of the ventilator had been shut.

"Is he safe?" he asked in the dark.

. "Light the candle."

Paluka lit the candle. The Tiger sagged onto his bench. His jaw dropped, stretching the flanks of his cheeks between the blue stubble and the black mane. His eyes stared ahead. He was too tired tonight for the raking glance with which he had always cased the bunker before he spoke, too tired to see that the sheet of script was gone. He gulped the wine which Paluka set before him.

"You saw him swim safely to the American side, at least?"

"The draw of the Diffené was open; I confess I should have known. He had to swim the Old Rhine first, to the clump of trees on the island. Like this."

The Tiger's long fingernail pointed to the clump of trees on the map, where he had told Happy to aim. Paluka nodded.

"Then," Paluka pondered, "he had only to run the twelve hundred yards across the island; see, it narrows at the end where he swam. He would be cold, and the frozen ground would be hard to the feet, but not for long. Then swim the Rhine. If I could be sure the island was empty, I should have no fear."

327

The Tiger turned on his bench. He dared not tell Paluka that Happy had fallen, almost within sight of the end.

"A dozen soldiers were sleeping in the pumphouse," he admitted irritably, "but see, that was far from the trees."

"Through the ventilator I heard a volley which sounded from beyond the Neckar," Paluka persisted.

The Tiger spread his hands. "I heard it too. Though I was nearer than you, I cannot tell whence it came. But now I must sleep."

When Paluka crossed to the cask, the Tiger pulled the orange Blacklist from his pocket and slid it under the roll of maps.

"Go to sleep also. In two hours I must carry the bread and meat to the old man. Your friend returns this."

He laid the slices of ham on the table. Paluka left them, and the Tiger staggered to his feet.

"I will wake you," Paluka promised.

"Ah," the Tiger groaned, "will he upstairs never die, and must we always be hunted? This breakfast may be our last, unless the recruits should bring some in the morning."

"We are also the hunters, Monsieur le Tigre." Paluka laughed. He turned toward his own pallet.

Before he got there, the rustle of paper caught his ear. Still in his bare feet, he blew out the candle and stole back. He peered between the casks at the Tiger, who stood stripped to the waist before the locker he had salvaged from the shipyard. The second candlestick was on the floor beside him. He had two money belts in his hand, his own of Feldgrau and the other which Paluka recognized as Happy's because it was blue. It took a few moments for Paluka, crouched in the shadow of the cask, to understand that the Tiger had Happy's money. When the bills were folded lengthwise in the Feldgrau, evenly spread, and when the Tiger had laid the empty blue belt in the locker and strapped the fat gray one about his own waist, Paluka

328

knew. He rose to the half-bend stance of a wrestler, his arms swinging and his hands unclenched.

"It is you who shot," he roared.

Through the alley between the casks he lunged toward the Tiger, but his toe stubbed on a wooden chock. The Tiger was too quick for him. Putting one foot on the shoulder of the lower cask, he vaulted to the top of the upper one with his pistol in one hand. With the other he strapped the buckle of the money belt tight, his Walther leveled at Paluka.

Paluka ignored the black muzzle pointed at him from a yard away. He set his shoulder to the lower cask, trying to topple the Tiger from his perch, but there was too much wine in it for his strength to move. He stood back panting. The candle guttering on the floor threw its light full on his left leg. He stood, breathing hard, gathering strength for another assault on the cask.

The Tiger, with careful aim, sent a bullet which barely grazed the skin of his calf and buried itself in the black gravel floor. He had always boasted of being the best shot in his Engineer regiment.

"That will teach you not to roar so loud, great bear," he whispered from his perch. "Also that I am chief of the team, as the Amis appointed me. Do not forget the marksman's badge on my tunic. Now your legs have two wounds, one for yourself and one for your chief. I think you will feel they are at exactly the same height on each leg. Mine will not hurt unless you rebel again. But wrap the last strip of your useless woman-bait about it to make sure. You have twin garters of honor and you smell of woman. It was not I who shot your friend, but the sentry in the pumphouse. Crawl back to your den now, and sleep, but you need not wake me. Do not fear, I shall be watching with the pistol cocked beside my hand, lest you break out to endanger me anew."

He climbed down from the cask. With what courage remained from the bridge, the Tiger struck Paluka's open mouth with the back of his left hand. Paluka lurched forward, ignoring the Walther in the other hand. But he fell back, as the Tiger knew he must, and crept around the cask to his pallet with both hands clutched around his calf. The Tiger blew out the candle and lay down on his own pack of coats at the foot of the steps. Paluka stretched up one hand to open the damper. Neither of them slept. Through the dark they listened to each other, each, though his eyes were closed, turned toward his teammate.

By the luminous dial of the wristwatches it was 0455. The curfew would lift in five minutes. Paluka turned, pretending to toss in his sleep. He touched his mouth. He felt the holster under his armpit better when he lay on his side, but he knew it was not yet the time. Through the barred ventilator, no bigger than a brick, he could see the beginning of the dawn. He dared not risk the street before the great bell struck five, without his uniform.

At the Tiger's end, the hooded flashlight wove back and forth; it shone on the two slices of ham, and Paluka saw him cut a piece of bread for the old man's sandwich and draw a cup of wine, the pistol still in his hand, holding the metal close to the bung so the wine would not splash. Then he cut a slice for himself; Paluka knew it, for he heard the knife scrape the bone. Still Paluka did not move. He heard the Tiger back up the stairs and slide open the bolt with his elbow. The metal door swung to let him through. A dimness of dimness, borrowed from the arch over the street door, grew and was gone. The key clicked in the lock.

Paluka was on his feet before the Tiger had taken the four steps to the ground floor. He pulled the boots over his feet. The boots of the Cossack Legion fastened with a strap. He cuddled the shoulder holster under his armpit. He patted the worker's passport in his pocket. The overcoat on which he had slept he threw over his shoulders like a cape, thrust his arms through the sleeves in a single motion. It was the Tiger's civilian coat with the sheepskin lining. Before buttoning it, he reached through his shirttails to unbuckle his own money belt. The oilskin lining was gone, but the thousand marks of the Americans were still in the canvas. As he tiptoed past the table to the steps he tossed them down.

"Since that is all you love, assassin, take mine," he whispered. "It may console you for your comrade and your coat."

At the foot of the steps he listened. He could hear the Tiger tiptoe up the stairs above. He had bolted this door often enough behind the Tiger to know that after the four steps from the vestibule there was a flight of eighteen, divided by the landing, then twelve steps down the hall to the old man's room. He pressed his ear against the jamb to count. When he heard the Tiger take the last, he tapped his own door lightly four times as the Tiger should be doing at the door upstairs. He reached in his jacket for a nonexistent key, turned it as the Tiger would be turning his. He waited long enough for the old man's door to open and be closed again. He turned his flashlight on the cross he had penciled on the steel. He drew back the slidebolt so it could not jam.

He whipped Happy's Olympia from its holster and wrapped the barrel in his handkerchief. He held the muzzle two inches from the pencil mark and fired.

He had figured it right; the tumblers of the lock fell forward, the pin jarred loose, and the wide strike fell back from the keeper. He pushed the door open; it did not even creak. He stepped into the vestibule.

With one foot he pressed the steel door shut behind him, the white smoke and sharp odor still hanging at the hole he had drilled. With one hand he drew open the outer door; then he was in the street. Either the Tiger had not heard, or he was not quick enough to catch him. Paluka thrust the pistol in his pocket with his finger still on the trigger. He turned sharply to the right, hugging the walls so that if the Tiger should open the staircase window he would have to lean way out for the raking shot. But Paluka did not look back. He hardly hurried as he climbed the half-block to Beil Street.

Even in the easy dawn he had to blink his eyes after five days in the darkness of the bunker. He saturated his lungs with the crisp cold air, as he had often, when pursued in France, drunk water from a spring, drawing as long as his breath would hold. When he turned the corner toward the Neckar, out of sight, he knew he was safe at least from the Tiger. The Tiger would not dare pursue him to the open street; still better, might not miss him till he had crossed the bridge or even till he was swimming the Old Rhine. The Tiger always stayed a good half-hour with the old man, talking Paluka knew not what memories or plots. Or maybe only watching him die.

It was hard to smother the smile on his face and the lilt in his walk as he passed the few troops and civilians who were out so early. They walked without speaking to one another, with eyes staring straight out from their bent heads—all blinking like himself from the darkness of the shelters, and all, even the troops, bound for the hand pumps, with buckets in their hands. They hugged the sides of the shuttered houses as he had done, as if the walls could protect them from the splinters of shellfire.

When he reached the Jungbusch Bridge he looked with the same curiosity as Happy at the damage the Americans had done to the ruined docks below him, at the tanks and warehouses and cranes on the spit, at the gasworks and transformer station at the far end of the bridge. He could see the hits on the island all the way from the bridge rail. In the dawn he saw farther than Happy and the Tiger could have seen by moonlight. By turning his head from the Jungbusch he could look back to the downstream end of the great Farben factory across the Rhine at Ludwigshafen, with the cranes and pipelines twisted crazily above the steep causeway and the spurs, and the great river rushing past below. The shoulder of the city behind him hid the blown Rhine bridge, but he pictured its grilled trusses and cables obstructing the water like a weir, and fretting the surface into eddies and whitecaps which the sun would soon tinge with pink. The daylight grew brighter ahead of him, but one band on the left horizon stayed dark. It was the smoke screen behind which the Americans were floating their bridge, five thousand yards downstream.

He felt happily in his pocket for the little gray booklet he had carried all the way from Marseille two years ago: the passport of a Russian laborer. This civilian cover was better than the military; the Germans were frightened of their Russian slaves, but still more of their Russian conscripts. He hoped he would not be caught in a spot-check, just the same. The questioning and examination of papers would waste time. It was good to be a Russian, for then you could not answer their questions.

Where Hirtenstrasse twists under the bridge trestle, he saw the empty sentrybox. The reservist, still unconscious, lay in the indentation of the granite wall, but Paluka did not stop. Nobody stopped any more for what he saw lying in the road. The Rhine tossed and twinkled clear in the sunrise, for the ice from Switzerland kept it colder than the air. But wisps of vapor hung over the warmer water of the Neckar and the Old Rhine. On the Friesenheim Island, at the far side of the Diffené, he saw the German soldiers shouting and beckoning to be let across. The valve box which controlled the turntable was still locked; the sentry's morning relief had not come on. Paluka waved back at them with a smile, shaking his head and waving his hands to show he did not understand and could not help. He played deaf and dumb to them, as he would have done if they had challenged him on the road. He pointed first back at Mannheim, then at himself, then ahead to Sandhofen. As he strode along their shouts faded out of his hearing. The Tiger might sneer, but sometimes it was wise to be stupid.

Along the fence where Happy and the Tiger had scuttled he

strode easily, whistling softly to himself. The Germans could not expect that a Russian farmhand should be intelligent, or even that he should try to help them. He strode past the Aachen Glassworks, past the bumper on the commercial siding, past the last post of the wire fence. He turned left off the highway to the fifty-yard shoulder that sloped to the Old Rhine, just where the Tiger and Happy had turned. He did not hurry; he did not bother to crouch. At the brink he took off the sleek overcoat—it was too good for a slave laborer, but he cared no longer. He tossed it on the bank, over the very burrow that covered his uniform, left behind by Happy. He saw the rifle on the sedge and wondered for the first time why the Tiger had come home without it. He broke it open; the magazine was full. For once the Tiger had told the truth.

He stripped to his shorts and his ankle-boots. He did not bother to hide the rest of his clothes as the Tiger had hidden Happy's, or even his passport. The boots were a little heavier than he liked for swimming, but better than crossing the island in bare feet. The shorts would not hinder a good swimmer, and he might be able to dry them in the sun.

Without a backward look he flattened into the Old Rhine to swim across to the island, the same course the Tiger had given Happy. He did not swim the crawl, for the soldiers might notice the splash. The breast stroke was quieter. He knew the mist would hide his head from so far away as the drawbridge. It took him fifteen minutes, at a guess, to swim the currentless estuary—the same time he had allowed for Happy. Like Happy, he aimed for the clump of trees, for the air was warming up and soon the sun would burn off the mist. Then he might need concealment, for his head was too big a target to give the soldiers.

Once within the shelter of the poplars, he looked back to the Diffené bridgehead. The draw was closing, turned by a hand which must just before have touched the feet of the sentry to see if he were still alive. The double truss of the draw rotated into its notch. The soldiers formed as carefully as if they had been on a drill ground instead of fleeing for their lives. As he watched they marched across the Diffené in column, and he was alone on the abandoned island, dripping and shivering and almost naked in the morning gusts, but laughing to himself.

The soil of the Friesenheim Island is the silt of centuries' deposit, a checkerboard of truck gardens which grow the best asparagus and strawberries in the Reich. The island is cut by the arms of irrigation ditches from the Rhine, and by the leaching trenches of the sterilized effluent from the city filter beds, both helping the crops to grow. A cart path for the croppers turned from the Diffené bridge and swung northward past the pumphouse. It crossed the downstream third of the island within a few yards of the grove where Paluka stood watching. Now he had only to sprint along the path. He could cross the island in ten minutes' run. Then there would be the main Rhine to battle, where the current would be running strong. He had better hurry too, he told himself, for if there should be an artillery duel between the Americans, now at the very brink of the Rhine, and the Germans, placed somewhere on the high terrain beyond the eastern plain, or even—who could tell?—camouflaged in the houses of Sandhofen, he might be caught in the middle. And though the island was a worthless target, and he worth still less to either side, one never could tell where a short might fall. The gunners would soon have finished their breakfast, and he had not yet eaten his.

He limbered his legs for the sprint. The ·squishing boots would chafe his heels, but it would not be for long. The path curved toward the north tip of the little island, instead of running straight across, but it would be quicker for him to follow it than to scramble across the swampy ditched garden patches. He lumbered out into a trot. The ruts of the cart wheels, unprinted since last fall, were drifted over with the windblown topsoil.

He dogtrotted across sturdily, professionally, not so fast as to waste his strength for the test of the river, yet not so slowly as to endanger him if any soldiers were left, or to gall the kibes of his ankles against the sodden boots. His elbows jogged comfortably at his sides; he found the pace at which his wet skin tempted the cold wind least, and stuck to it.

Halfway across the island, when he was opposite the very tip, a spot of dark and a flash of metal caught the corner of his eye, off to the right. They caught it only because the rest of the soil was a monotone of ochre. The dark was an oblong of earth newly opened in the nutrient loam which lay below the winter cover soil. He would not have halted at a mound of earth any more than he had halted beside the sentry at the Diffené, for the time was growing late now, had it not been for the wink of metal above the dark mound. When he looked closer he saw the crude driftwood cross at one end of the oblong. The sticks of the cross were corded together, not nailed, for nails had grown scarce in the Reich. The two slats were as neutral as the soil itself, only weathered to gray instead of yellow.

It was not until he was a yard from the cross of stakes that he saw the shape of the tag at all, so small it was, hanging by its cord at the joint of the stakes. The pierced zinc oval was no bigger than the ball of his palm. It was one of five million dog-tags. It was the size and shape of the dogtag around his own neck. He lifted it from the stake and held it in the palm of his hand to read it, not daring not to hope. Into the top half was pressed A for the blood type, so that if the owner lost blood anyone else with A could transfuse to him. Paluka had never even thought to look for the type on his own zinc tag which the Americans had made for him three weeks before in Alsace. He lifted it over his neck, with the oilskin packet attached to the cord beside it. His blood type was A also.

The Wehrmacht took care to bury its dead quickly, lest they give the impression of defeat. But the squad in the pumphouse had been too hasty. They had forgotten to break the dogtag. Paluka split it along the perforations with his hands. Only a strong man could have done it in one snap. He wrenched the stake from the hard earth. He set half the tag on the hole. He unstrapped his left boot and pounded the stake, using the heel for a hammer, back into the hard ground over the half-moon of zinc.

He gazed at the other half of Happy's tag. It looked like this:

He put it in his mouth, with the toothed edge at the back, where it could not rasp his tongue.

From the German side of the Rhine, somewhere near Sandhofen, a low shell whined lengthwise down the river toward the smoke screen at Frankenthal. It was a short; Paluka saw the splash in the water where it fell. Another echoed from below; it was an over, and splashed near the first. The Germans were enfilading the pontoon bridge. Even as Paluka hammered the cross, a barrage of mortars broke out of the American side, probing the Viernheim woods east of Sandhofen for the camouflaged German artillery. The morning duel had begun.

Paluka reached the Rhine in five minutes, at a bank exactly like the bank where he had landed. A hundred yards to the left he saw the soldiers' skiff beached against the sedge. He could have crossed in it himself. But he did not want to row; he wanted to swim. He hardly paused to glance at the skiff. He plunged into the swift current, belly-flat, to miss the horns of the contact mines. He headed ten points upstream, knowing the current would bear him down, so with luck he would land opposite his starting point. He saw a clump of willows ahead of him where he could wait for the American patrols. His feet churned into the water, his arms flailed ahead of him, as if he would punish the Rhine for Happy as Xerxes whipped the Euxine for his drowned soldiers.

A second lieutenant and four GIs of 3rd Division, armed with carbines, were reconnoitering the river road on the west bank between Ludwigshafen and Frankenthal. The blowing of the Rhine bridge the night before must mean the Germans had no organized resistance on this side, but they were taking no chances on snipers and booby traps. They were the first Seventh Army troops to pass over this newly won stretch of road. The sergeant drove slowly, with the sawtooth mast of the jeep raised on the hood in case of wire. It was a German trick which had caused a lot of damage, to string an almost invisible wire across the road at neck height. If a motorcyclist or a driver with the windshield down came along too fast and did not see the wire in time, it would behead him. The Lieutenant in the front seat kept his eyes glued to the metaled paving, watching for the wooden covers of schu-mines. The three privates trained their carbines to the sides and rear of the open jeep, on the lookout for snipers in the grass or among the trees. They were passing the suburb of Oppau, where the highway is only twenty yards from the water. It was at 0745 on Thursday, 22 February, 1945 that the right-hand private called "Hold it, Sarge, there's someone in the river."

The jeep slowed to a crawl, but did not stop till it reached the next clump of bushes. The other two privates jumped over the tailboard to cover the bobbing head from both directions.

"First replacement from out of the Rhine," one said. "That must be some kind of record."

"We see this big ape scrambling for a foothold in the mud," the lieutenant told the Team an hour later. "I don't think he caught sight of us yet, but as soon as he makes footing and before he wades in, he puts his hands back of his head and climbs ashore as if he is ducking gunfire. All the time he is repeating,

'Oh, my aching back.' I wouldn't have understood him unless he did repeat, his accent is so funny. When he reaches solid ground he unclasps his hands and stands up to shake himself all over like a dog. He has nothing on but a German dogtag and a pair of quarter-boots, and skivvies just like they wear. That is when we close in on him, though there wasn't a place he could be hiding a weapon. When they bring him up to me, believe it or not, he spits out half another dogtag and says, 'Guard, guard!' Here it is. Then he salutes just like a GI and says, 'Soda G-2.' But I see all his dogtags are oval, not square like ours. Then I knew he must belong to you.

"I have the sergeant back the jeep around. We throw a blanket over him and set him on the hood, where he squats with his hands hanging on to the mast till we get him down here, complaining all the time in some chatter that I don't understand. He keeps pointing back to the island, shouting a name like Happy, till a pothole in the road makes him grab the mast with both hands. It wasn't that we were scared of him, but he was too damn big and wet to fit in the jeep with the rest of us. Besides, for all I can tell he's nothing but a straight Kraut prisoner. Well, now he's yours; I've got to get back to work." He laid the oilskin pouch and the split dogtag on the colonel's desk, saluted, and went back to his jeep.

As Paluka himself had said, the payoff for an operation was the debriefing when the Joes came back, and the lyric instant of it was when they opened the door of Station S for the first time since they had signed the contract. Pete poured half a bottle of his own cognac for Paluka; Vati brought the barracks bag from the attic and helped him into his old fatigues. Before Paluka, crying, laughing, and shivering, had finished his story, Battle Order had transcribed his sheet of paper and sent it on the way to the plastic map in the war room.

Two days later Eighth Air Force knocked out the Schloss at Crailsheim and the forestry school at Aalen. From then on there was no reaction from 9th Flak or 25th Infantry at

Mannheim or farther back. Happy may have saved what was left of the city, for the American artillery ceased fire when it met no resistance. Maybe he saved Maria's brothers too, for they are helping Herr Liebert now on the farm behind the Sign of the Ox. Mannheim withered on the vine.

Remagen, far to the north, was the first Rhine bridge to fall. That was March seventh. But orders to crack the Rhine did not reach Army yet. It was not till March twenty-sixth, with the west bank buildup complete, that they crossed the Frankenthal pontoons. H-hour was 0230. The banks at the bridge were steep. The 8.8s in Sandhofen sank four amphibians, and even after the dogfaces took the town they lost it again. When resistance ceased, the 937th Field Artillery Battalion, wheeling to the right, trundled all the five miles upstream to Mannheim. They passed the Friesenheim Island; the Diffené draw was standing open again. They crossed the Neckar by the Jungbusch and eased into Frederick Street, with the town hall at their left and the Schloss and the Rhine at its far end. Air reconnaissance had reported that the Schloss was a roofless shell and that some of the blocks inside the Ring looked like so many empty beer-racks from aloft. But Mannheim never got an artillery pasting like Mainz, which resisted; and Heidelberg got none at all.

This is the way German cities fall. One afternoon the streets look normal; empty, of course, with the shutters closed on all the houses, but normal for behind the lines in wartime. The next morning every house has a white flag flying or a sheet draped between the buildings—that is, every house where a human could hide. Every house, as if they are afraid the Americans will shoot up any that do not show—the way every store on a block in the United States has to have a neon sign, or people will think it is broke. They must have been cutting and sewing those sheets for months behind the shutters, like Frau Bense in Schimpfach; then suddenly, in a single night, the white breaks out all over the city. Does the Wehrmacht give the order, or does panic break out of a quarter of a million people in a single eruption? Yet, if that is the way, what German would be the first to show his white?

There are still no people outdoors, till the starved towhead kids show up in pairs, braver than their elders, holding each other's hands and looking scared and begging, "Kaugummi," for chewing gum. Then in a while the old people walk out and start about their business, pretending they didn't know there was a war on.

As the column passed through the hanging symbols of surrender, an officer—it happened to be the same second lieutenant who had brought Paluka home—noticed down a side street that one white flag was being shaken from its staff by a hand invisible behind the window. He detailed two privates to reconnoiter. One of them spoke German. That private hoped to get a commission, just because he had been born in Yorkville.

The Tiger, his debonair smile still hanging to his bones, met them at the door of 27 Wharf Street. He clasped his hands behind his neck.

"Oh, my aching back," he began, "Soda G-2."

But that was all the English he knew. One private slapped his pockets for a weapon. The other, covering him with his carbine, said, "Das spielt keine Rolle, Landser; wir können Deutsch." *

"His money belt rustles, that's all," the other reported.

Their search led them down to the cellar. The iron door stood wide now, and the light streamed down the nine steps that had never been lighted before.

"Man, man," said one private when he saw the casks. "Think of liberating this."

To make sure the house was not booby-trapped, they

---

* "No matter, soldier; we speak German."

searched it all the way to the top. In the right rear room upstairs they found an old man dead in his bed. The Tiger waited in the bunker under guard.

"Listen," he told the German-speaking private, "I could give you valuable information. The Twenty-fifth Infantry Division is at Aalen and the Ninth Flak is at Crailsheim." He unrolled a map on his council table and put his fingers on the two towns.

"That's old stuff, Kamerad; Eighth Air Force took care of them a month ago. We wouldn't be here now if they were still in business. Someone else risked his neck to spot them while you were hiding down here with the wine. Let's have one drink to whoever it was."

The Tiger ignored his ingratitude. He filled his three silver mugs with wine and solemnly toasted Happy with a "Pros't." Then he pulled the orange Blacklist from his pocket.

"Here is the list of those who have worked for the victory of Freedom. You should take it to the general for whatever rewards he wishes to make. And the mayor of this city," he went on with dignity, "is hiding at the pumphouse on the Friesenheim Island. If you give me a guard, he will surrender the city to us all."

And so he did.

That evening the two privates looked down from the ruins of the Schloss on the ruins of the Rhine bridge, humping across the river like a school of porpoises.

"Say, this town is laid out like Manhattan, with the two rivers."

"Yeah. Mannheim. Maybe they stole the name."

"The Krauts blew that bridge in one minute, but I bet it takes them five years to rebuild."

"Well, with a demolition that took one minute they held us up one month. At that rate they might have won the war."

"Yeah, might have. But we're here just the same."

Look Ahead

That is the story, pieced together from all we can remember and a little we can presume, of three Joes who took their chance; one for riches and one for risk and one for faith. I wrote it to the doctor, and he has answered me:

Berlin, Easter 1948

Honored Sir:

This is the Resurrection Day. Your letter at the same time takes Karl away from us forever and brings him back to us. We should rather have our son than his medal, but can truly say we should rather have our freedom than our son, as he would wish. We shall accept the medal in his name.

The brotherhood for which he risked and lost his life seems farther away than ever, even than in the time of the regime. This city, the third in the world, is a ruin of souls as well as of stones. But mankind, least of all we Germans, cannot live among the ruins of either.

Klaus is now eighteen, as Karl was when we saw him last. He will take the same risk as his brother, if this hour makes it necessary, for freedom and America are his two ideals as they were Karl's. Can only the young have ideals? My own is the rebuilding of the sick. But the ruin of souls is such that the nations who freed us will not

agree to the starkest necessities of medicine and bandages. I must often use newspapers for dressings, and it depends on the sector where I buy them whether my patient is healed by Russian or by American propaganda. In Berlin, paper survives stone. The hospital requires that patients must bring their own bandages, for the hospital itself has none. They can buy in the black market, but at a cost more than the operation itself. Though linen is scarce for this reason, my wife has embroidered two blouses for your daughters, with our good wishes.

It is not often that an old man survives his son, and not easy to be his disciple.

We are both grateful to you for having seen as deep into our boy's heart as only we had seen. We find comfort and strength in the lines of Goethe which seem written for Karl:

All is given by the gods, the immortal ones,
To those whom they love—
    They withhold nothing:
All joys, unendingly,
All pain, unendingly—
    They withhold nothing.
	Alles geben die Götter, die unendlichen,
	    ihren Lieblingen, ganz;
	Alle Freuden, die unendlichen,
	alle Schmerzen,
	    die unendlichen, ganz.

Respectfully,

Gunther Maurer, M.D.

12 January to 5 June, 1948, at Emergency Hospital, Washington
"That the bones which Thou hast broken may rejoice."

CPSIA information can be obtained
at www.ICGtesting.com
Printed in the USA
BVHW032128121220
595583BV00010B/90

9 781406 756715